STOLEN HOURS

AND OTHER CURIOSITIES

THE COLLECTED SCIENCE FICTION STORIES

MANJULA PADMANABHAN

hachette INDIA

First published in hardcover in 2023 by Hachette India
(Registered name: Hachette Book Publishing India Pvt. Ltd)
An Hachette UK company
www.hachetteindia.com

This paperback edition published in 2025

1

Inside illustrations by Manjula Padmanabhan
Section break icon by iconixar from Freepik

Cover illustration by Manjula Padmanabhan, first appeared in 2022 in *The Taj Magazine*, Volume 49, issue no. 1.

ISBN 978-93-5731-620-0

Hachette Book Publishing India Pvt. Ltd
4th & 5th Floors, Corporate Centre
Plot No. 94, Sector 44, Gurugram – 122003, India

Typeset in Dante MT Std 11/13.2
by Manmohan Kumar, Delhi

Printed and bound in India
by Manipal Technologies Limited, Manipal

FSC www.fsc.org MIX Paper | Supporting responsible forestry FSC™ C043100

STOLEN HOURS

AND OTHER CURIOSITIES

Manjula Padmanabhan is a writer, artist, cartoonist and playwright. She grew up away from India, returning as a teenager, and now lives in the US, with a part-time home in New Delhi.

Padmanabhan is the author of several critically acclaimed books, including her travel-memoir *Getting There* and the first two of a science fiction trilogy, *Escape* and *The Island of Lost Girls*. Her play *Harvest* won the 1997 Onassis Prize for Theatre in Greece. She has published more than twenty illustrated books for children as author–artist, including *Unprincess!*, *Mouse Attack*, *I Am Different* and *Mama, What is The Night?*. Her female comic strip character SUKI has appeared in mass circulation newspapers such as the *Sunday Observer*, *Pioneer* and *BusinessLine*.

Praise for the book

'*Stolen Hours and Other Curiosities* is an electric, dazzling, thought-provoking collection. This is Manjula Padmanabhan at her finest: a terrific feat of Indian SF!'
– **Sami Ahmad Khan**, researcher and author of *Star Warriors of the Modern Raj: Materiality, Mythology and Technology of Indian Science Fiction*

'Manjula Padmanabhan's stories are original, often disturbing, and always thought-provoking. This collection reveals a writer in top form, effortlessly weaving between startling futures to come and the mundane realities of the worlds we inhabit today.'
– **Anil Menon**, author of *Half of What I Say*

'*Stolen Hours* is testimony to Manjula Padmanabhan's evolving significance as a major author of Indian and South Asian SFF.'
– **Tarun Saint**, editor of *The Gollancz Book of South Asian Science Fiction, Vol 1 and 2*

To everyone, everything, everywhere

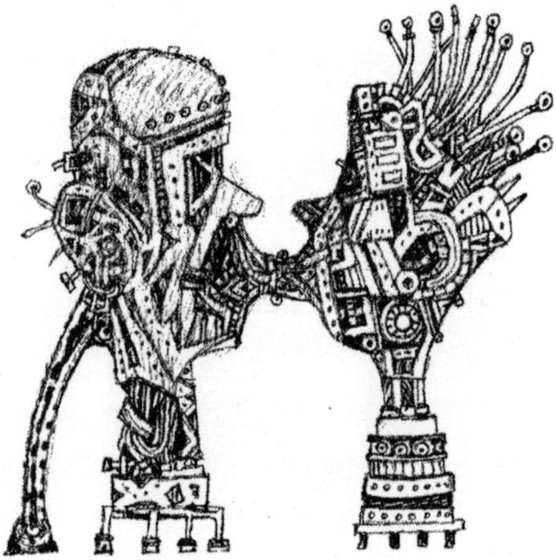

AUTHOR'S NOTE

While deciding the order in which to present these stories, I originally wanted to organize them in chronological sequence. But I also wanted to cushion the super-grim tales between those that are merely weird or even a bit funny. Accordingly, most of the stories are in descending order, starting with the most recently published (2021) and ending with the earliest (1984), with some repositioning between first to last.

Four stories have never been published before: 'Talkers', 'The Empty Glass', 'A Cline's View' and 'Octobaby'. The rest have either appeared in magazines or anthologies.

A number are mildly metaphysical rather than 'hard' science fiction. In 'The Empty Glass', for instance, an atheist attends a conference of gods from all across the cosmos. 'Feast' is about a European vampire visiting India as a tourist. 'The Girl Who Could Make People Naked' is about a young woman with supernatural powers. 'Exile' and 'The Other Woman' are both connected to the Ramayana. 'The Annexe' is about a dimensionless meeting place between minds. 'A Government of India Undertaking' is about stepping into the Bureau of Reincarnation and Transmigration of Souls in search of an existence-upgrade.

When I'm asked to explain why I write SF, I say that it's because I grew up in different countries. By the time I returned to India as a teenager, I had become a naturalized outsider, a foreigner to everywhere. Being a misfit wasn't always fun, but as time went on I realized it was the only way I wanted to be.

Writing SF is a way of celebrating the 'other-ing' that I experienced as a young person. Instead of travelling to other countries, I can explore alternate states of consciousness, timelines, body types, species, genders, dimensions. Curiosity is my guide but also sometimes my saboteur: adventures in otherness can just as easily end with a snap of unfriendly jaws and an alien burp, as with a shower of stars and a flight of glittering hummingbirds. The uncertainty is what makes SF fun or scary, irritating or entertaining.

This collection represents all my SF stories – so far! There are always a couple twitching in the void, waiting to break in uninvited: 'Octobaby', for instance, was written just one week ago.

By the time this book comes out in print, there may be a couple more.

Or not.

Manjula Padmanabhan
18 May 2023
Newport (RI)

CONTENTS

THE PAIN MERCHANT

'There was a time,' said Masterji, 'when every household had plenty of pain to sell.'

We were sitting by the rocks at the very edge of my village. In the distance behind us, the high mountains scratched the heavens with their snowy peaks. Right in front of us, the bare hillside plunged down at rakish angles. The plains spread away far below. 'No longer true. People have forgotten that pain was once commonplace.'

'Won't you show me just a bit?' I asked, using my most wheedling voice. I was eight years old and the only boy in a house full of sisters and mothers. At home, I got whatever I wanted when I used that voice. 'Just once?'

But the pain merchant was immune.

He intrigued me: I had never met someone who did not instantly give in to my demands. Plus, he looked so strange. Everyone I knew wore wool and embroidered felt slippers on their feet or leather boots. My mothers and sisters wore tunics, and the men wore mirrored caps and turbans. The merchant, by contrast, was dressed in layers of greasy leather held together with lengths of string. His shoes were tied on with strips of leather. He wore a dark brown hood that partially obscured his face. Countless small pouches hung from his shoulders and down his back. Like bunches of grapes.

I could see that he wanted to please me, yet he shook his head. 'I've explained before. My wares are perishable,' he said. According to him, recorded pain was like perfume. It got depleted with each use. 'I can't afford to show you anything unless you can pay.'

'I can pay today, Masterji,' I said. 'I found something to trade.'

He looked at me sideways, his face a mass of wrinkles. I couldn't tell if he was smiling or frowning. 'Trade, eh?' he remarked, his nose lifting and twitching. 'Come on then. Show me what you've got.'

I knelt, my right knee on the ground and my left foot stuck forward. I lifted the cuff of my pants to reveal my ankle. There was the beginning of an old scar there. 'You see this?' I said, squinting up at the merchant. Then I removed my shoe and pulled off the sock, so that he could see the whole foot, naked. 'That's the kind of thing you're interested in, isn't it?' My mothers had told me I'd had an accident when I was a baby. It had been fixed. No trace now remained of the wound, except for the scar.

Masterji knelt, reaching for my foot with both hands. I hadn't noticed earlier that he wore leather gloves, with the tips cut off. He traced the contours of the scar carefully with his forefinger. Glancing up, he asked, 'What caused this injury? Did your mothers tell you? Do you know how long ago it happened?'

'Yes, they told me,' I said. 'It was when I was a baby. I don't remember what happened.'

A shadow slid over us. A vulture. It wouldn't bother us, of course. We were moving our arms and talking. Obviously alive. Even so, I tugged the ward-off out of my pocket and held it up, cocked and ready to send out a pulse.

'Ah, don't bother,' said the merchant. 'It's got plenty to eat.'

In the few seconds during which I glanced up at the vulture, the merchant had reached into his clothes and pulled something out. An instrument, it looked like. It was shiny and metallic but also stretchy. Before I could object, he had placed it around my ankle and was deftly moulding it into place.

I had been told not to let strangers do anything to me without explaining their actions. 'You should ask my permission before doing that,' I said.

He glanced up and said, 'Do you feel it? Is it touching you?' I shook my head. It had completely surrounded my ankle and my foot up to the arch, but I felt no sensation. 'Fine then. You held your foot out to me, and I placed my scanner around it without making contact. That is all. No harm done. Look now. It's reading…'

The shiny surface of the gadget had vanished. In its place was a kind of magnified picture of everything under the skin of my ankle. I could see the cord-like vessels of blood pulsing busily. The merchant was touching the surface of the gadget in such a way as to reveal different views of the internal structure of my foot. He zoomed in.

'We have gone below the muscles and soft tissue,' he said. 'We can now see the bone.' It looked surprisingly white to me. He was peering around the ligaments to find exactly what he wanted. 'Do you notice these seams?' Silver-grey lines. 'Surgery. It does not look like an accident. More likely a medical procedure. Perhaps you had a birth defect, eh? Your people told you that it was an accident? Easier that way, I suppose. Makes no difference. Pain is pain.'

He tapped the surface of the gadget once again and the visual faded off. The surface reverted to its metallic appearance. He waited until he heard a faint beep, then peeled the thing away.

'What *is* that?' I asked. I felt as if I hadn't been breathing or swallowing for the entire time that the gadget had been on my foot.

'A dolcache,' said Masterji, as if the name was a common one. 'An instrument for reading and recording pain.' He glanced at me once more, his face seizing up with wrinkles. Smiling. 'Had you forgotten? You asked if I would accept this scar of yours as a trade. Not the scar of course, but the pain within. The memory remains in the bones, you see. My answer is yes – I got a strong signal. The question now: what sort of pain will you accept in exchange for what I took?'

He saw my confusion. I was a child, after all. What would I know of the worth of these things? Or maybe he heard the sound of distant voices. I had heard them too but hadn't said anything for fear that he'd hurry away. As he had twice before. I never knew when or how I would next meet him.

He nodded with a bird-like twitch, as if making up his mind for both of us. 'All right,' he said, as he got to his feet. 'You cannot assess the worth of what you have. Nor can we remain out in the open any longer. You'll need to come with me. How much time do you have?'

The answer, of course, was 'None'. I wasn't allowed to spend any time alone with strangers. But if I said that, he may not take me. So I lied and said, 'I don't know.'

He told me we wouldn't have to go far. Which was true.

What he didn't mention was that the place was well hidden. No one would find me, not even the dogs. It was underground, the entrance tucked under a smelly heap of some sort. Probably the remains of a body. There were so many around, lying in the open, rotting. That's why the dogs wouldn't find me. They were trained to ignore the bodies.

Inside, underground, the merchant had a few lights strung up. They were connected to a large battery, humming softly in the corner. The place must have been a basement at one time. There was some old furniture. He asked me to sit on a high chair. Then he drew up a stool and placed it in front of me, for himself. 'Let me see,' he said, as he began to unwrap the many little bags that were slung around his body. 'What shall I start you off with?'

The pouches were connected to the cords tied around him. As he unwrapped the strings and the pouches, he became thinner and thinner. The sheets of leather that I had thought were clothes were merely separators: beneath each layer were yet more pouches.

'Oh,' I said. 'That's a lot of pouches.'

'They're not heavy,' said the merchant. 'Pain has no weight.'

He was now down to his actual clothes. He looked very different. Diminished. A thin old man in a dirty black sweater and loose black pants. His feet remained bound in cords. His hair was white. He had arranged the strings of pouches and the leather separators neatly on the floor. He looked carefully at the array before making a selection.

He sat down now, facing me. 'Because you're a child and this is your first time, I will give you three separate doses, each one very brief.' He opened the pouch in his hand. Inside it was a slender object, like a bracelet, except it was made of glass. FlexiGlass. He flipped an invisible clasp and asked me to put out a hand. 'It doesn't matter which one,' he said.

I was starting to feel afraid. Of being underground. Of knowing that I could not be found. My mothers would be furious. The men would be raging and pounding their fists. I did not say any of this to him. My curiosity was far greater than my fear.

'What will I feel?' I asked Masterji. 'Will it happen all at once? Or slowly?' Everything I was doing was wrong. I should never have followed the merchant. I didn't even know his name. My family would be mad with worry by now. 'Maybe I should go home.'

The wrinkles sprang into view again. Just a twitch. 'Okay, only one dose then. And I'll owe you two more. You've already paid me, don't you see? I'll have to meet you again at least until I've paid you back. Hold out a wrist?'

I extended my right hand towards him, palm up, fingers curled.

He placed the bracelet around the wrist. It felt cool against my skin but without weight. 'You see this small red dot?' he asked, pointing to the surface of the bracelet. I nodded mutely.

'I'm going to press it three times. That means, you'll have three seconds before the dose begins. It'll last for 10 seconds. Then it'll stop on its own.'

He was looking at me and must have seen the fat tears spilling down my cheeks now. Tears of fear and guilt. He asked, 'Shall I go ahead?'

I nodded again, unable to speak.

He pressed the button three times. The red light turned green.

A brightness pierced my wrist. I can't find any other words to describe it: a needle made of lightning was stitching sensations onto my wrist where the bracelet clasped it. I gasped aloud. My teeth jumped in my mouth. The sides of my nose rose up. My hair stood on end. Then it was over. The bracelet sprang open, and he caught it before it fell.

'Ahh!' I said, panting. '*Aaaah!* AHH!'

Masterji was wrinkle-wreathed again. Gazing at me, fondness in his eyes. 'Your first experience of pain,' he whispered softly 'A sweet thing to see.'

I sucked in my breath. My mind was whirling. I couldn't form words.

He read the question in my eyes. 'That was from a young girl. She had been cut by a glass bangle. Her sensations were absolutely pure, untouched by sorrow or premonition. And freshly caught. I was there when the wound occurred, though I recorded it years later.'

'I must go,' I blurted out. 'Or else they'll find me. *Us*.' Which would be terrible. Not for me, but for him. 'But please – I want to know more!'

He took me outside without responding to my demand. He did not even bother to wear his layers. Up we went, via a different exit and thence towards the rocks. The voices calling for me were louder now. I could hear the dogs. 'Pant loudly and pretend to be more tired than you are,' he said, before hurrying away. 'Let them think you got lost and have been frantic for some time. Tell them anything but where you've been and with whom.'

My mothers had become increasingly protective. Perhaps they could sense the tide pulling me away. My sisters were industrious and dutiful, but I had ants under my skin. I was always being told to hush.

'You don't need to know such things,' said my mothers when I asked questions about the so-called Event. 'Your ears will hurt with that kind of knowledge.'

'But pain has been banished from our world,' I would say. 'So how can I be hurt?'

They would purse their lips and turn their faces aside, saying, 'Only someone who has no knowledge of pain would utter something so ridiculous!'

I didn't dare tell them that I *did* have knowledge of pain. I had met Masterji many times after that first time underground. I had taught myself different ways to escape my home by stealth, leaving at night and returning before dawn.

Since I had no more scars to trade with the merchant, I paid him by writing labels for his pouches. He had trouble forming his letters, though he could read. He found my labels very useful. Until that time, he had kept track by memorizing each pouch and its contents by its place on his strings.

He chose what type of pain to expose me to, based on what he thought was appropriate for my age. He showed me the harsh twang of hair pulled out by the roots. The tooth-rattling crunch of a broken nose. The deafening thump of a ruptured eardrum. Even the scratchy, whining ache of an infected throat. Each pain was more rich and intense than the one before. The more I sampled, the more I wanted to sample. The delivery method was always the same, a bracelet on the wrist. The pain was experienced in the part of the body to which it belonged.

The day I told Masterji I wanted to follow his path, he looked at me sadly and said, 'I'm sorry.' It was never easy to read his expression, but from what I could tell, he was genuinely sad. 'Some types of pain cannot be recorded,' he said. 'You will come to know all of them if you leave your birth home.'

But I would not be dissuaded.

Two years after my first experience of pain, on a moonless night, I stole away from home. Masterji was waiting for me by the rocks. He knew that the ravines and streams would make it difficult for the dogs to track me. Once we reached the plains there was no chance of being followed.

He had told me there were more clients for his wares on the plains. That they paid in metal coins. That they sought him out. All of it was true. He was moderately well known for the variety of his wares and their smooth, clean quality. Some people asked for menstrual cramps. Some looked for a kick in the groin. Some longed for the dull hammering of a headache. Some wanted to feel the vicious scream of a bullet ripping through the gut.

The more serious the wound, the higher the price, all calculated by the second.

His most valuable item was from a man who had blown out his brains in front of the merchant. 'He did it for me,' said the merchant. 'So that I could collect that greatest and harshest of all pains in the instant it occurred.'

We were sitting in a quiet spot beside a great river when he told me this. We were some distance from the city in which we had spent almost an entire month. We had eaten well that day and were taking our ease.

'Really!' I said, feeling a shiver run down my spine. A shiver of desire. 'How is it I've not seen that pouch?'

Masterji was looking away from me. 'He was my brother,' he said. 'He wanted me to have the benefit of his death.'

'Oh!' I cried out. 'And how much did you sell it for?'

He turned and looked at me, his expression unfathomable. 'Nothing. I've never offered it for sale. Not even a half-second of it.'

I couldn't suppress my disappointment. 'Wah,' I said. 'If you don't use it, your brother died in vain!'

But he would say no more about the matter. We moved on soon after.

In the years that followed, Masterji taught me everything he knew of his trade. I learned to record pain, to clean it, to play it back. The fact that fewer and fewer people had memories of pain meant that there was competition amongst those who sought it and sold it. People with prosthetic limbs or obvious surgeries were usually tapped out. Either their memories had been drained dry or they no longer wanted to cooperate. The easiest to locate were those who had tattoos. The hardest were those who had had plastic surgery. We met others like ourselves on the dusty roads and rutted highways.

We travelled mostly on foot but accepted rides when we were offered them. Sometimes, we bought ourselves donkeys. Once, we even owned a camel.

I was the youngest person in any group of pain traders. They belonged to the earlier world, with their own memories to draw upon. I was the only one amongst them who had been born after the Event. I was always desperate to know more about it, why it happened and how. Their answers were always vague, as if the speakers were embarrassed by the memory.

'It happened suddenly,' they would say, 'or maybe over a month. It happened by accident. Or perhaps by design. One day, the scientists had found a way to record pain. The next day, the world's leaders were talking about deleting it from existence. The day after that, there was an explosion...a leak...something to do with the water. Or was it the rain? The air?'

The one thing everyone agreed upon was the effect: there was no longer any sensation of pain anywhere on the Earth. 'You could fall on your face or step on a nail or swallow poison or poke out someone's eye. But you felt no physical pain.'

There were consequences, of course.

Terrible accidents began to occur. Babies, in particular, died from being crushed or smothered or choked, because they couldn't complain in time. A ruptured appendix was a death sentence. Thousands of women died in labour, unable to feel their own contractions. Mass murders and group suicides increased a hundredfold. No one could have predicted that a world free of pain would unleash such a flood of violence. It was broken, gripped by a madness that nothing could contain.

People began living in tiny isolated homogeneous communities, clinging tight to those they knew, distrusting all strangers, outsiders.

Meanwhile, the technology for recording pain became freely available. 'A friend sold the machine to me,' said Masterji, 'after buying it from someone who didn't like it, who learnt how to use it from someone else. We didn't ask questions any more. If something worked, it was good. If it didn't, we threw it away. In the beginning, I lied about what the machine could do. I said that it would cure internal wounds. That childbirth would be safe for mothers once I had recorded the memory of the pain of contractions. That burns would clear up miraculously if the pain that they could no longer feel was sucked away. All untrue. But I got amazing recordings. Then, when I played them back for clients, they fell over with amazement. They screamed, they cried. The moment it was over, they asked for more.'

I had seen it myself: the expressions of ecstatic agony, the open mouths, the eyes filled with tears. I had felt it myself: the explosion of violent sensation when acid met skin, the searing, silvery shriek of tearing flesh. Followed by the most divine relief, wave after wave of trembling heat and warmth.

This was especially true when the source of pain was a grievous injury or life-threatening illness. I had seen clients who experienced physical reactions from the agony they were exposed to, such as sweating and even bleeding. I had known it myself. Once, when I wore a bracelet recorded from a woman experiencing a miscarriage, I found myself crying uncontrollably after ten seconds of extraordinary pressure deep within my groin. It was as if a volcanic, primordial force was moving through my body. The pain was huge and brassy, a great boom of raw life energy, pounding its way out, towards death.

In Masterji's waning years, the technology underwent a transformation that made it possible for recordings to be preserved indefinitely. Now at last, we could create a library of physical sensations. We opened a clinic alongside the library, where we could administer pain in easily controlled doses. Soon, we became reasonably prosperous. We bought a small house that we shared together, Masterji living downstairs and me, above. We could afford a couple of domestic helpers to run errands and do chores.

One day, he called for a pot of tea to be made, then asked me to accompany him to the little garden in the back of the house. When we were settled, he said, 'My young friend, in all these years that we have been dealing in pain, there's a question that I've been waiting to hear from you. Yet you have never asked it.'

Age had slowed the merchant down considerably. His eyesight had dimmed with time, his movements were enfeebled. But his expression was as sharp as ever. I really did not know what he expected of me. I felt deeply uncomfortable. He paused before continuing, staring at me all the while, 'How is it that you have never once expressed the least interest in that *other* sensation? The one that some have called the Siamese twin of pain?'

I shook my head. 'I don't know what you mean,' I said.

Masterji nodded, the wrinkles on his face seizing up with mirth, so that he looked like a dried-up walnut. He gurgled deep in his chest and for a moment I thought he was coughing or choking, before realizing it was the sound of his laughter. There was a sobbing quality to it too.

'Ah, my poor boy,' he said, when he had found his voice. 'It is as I thought. You truly have no knowledge of pleasure, do you?'

I frowned. I knew the word, of course. 'Gladness. Joy. That's what it means, yes?'

He looked away, sighing and went silent again, all laughter draining out of him. For a while, I wondered if he had dozed off, as he was wont to do of late. He stirred at last. In a sombre voice he said, 'Those who stripped the world of physical agony stripped it of physical pleasure too.' There was a pause. 'But you wouldn't know that, would you?' He turned to look at me. 'Because who would be so cruel as to tell you of a joy you can never know?'

No one, it turned out. I honestly did not know what he meant.

Still gazing at me, the old man reached under the neck of the thin sweater, which was still his favourite style of clothing. He drew out a slender chain. At the end of it was a tiny pouch, made of leather and embroidered with gold thread.

The moment I saw it, I knew what it must be.

I was filled with foreboding and began to shiver.

'You have been so trusting, my friend,' said Masterji. 'For the most part I have not betrayed your trust. I have never lied to you. What I've done, however, is keep some truths from you. Here is the first of them: while pain can be recorded, pleasure cannot. So even though my body remembers physical pleasure, neither I nor anyone else can share it with you. It is a glory, a fathomless bliss, that neither you nor anyone of your entire generation can ever know.'

I continued to shiver.

'Here is a second truth that I withheld: certain types of pain result in the actual injury that caused the pain. You have seen that, I think? Physical reactions that mirror the pain? Such as bleeding? Well. When it comes to death ...'

I guessed what he was about to say and tried to forestall him. 'Masterji, please!' I cut in. 'You don't have to do this. Your time has not yet come.'

He gurgled slightly, which I took to be a chuckle. 'Huh. I disagree! Meanwhile, there's a final truth that I have withheld. Instead of telling you, I'll demonstrate it.'

He opened out the tiny pouch. Inside was a pain bracelet, just like all the others. He placed it around his own wrist, then urged me to draw my seat close to his.

'I will press the red button several times,' he said. 'When I'm done, I'll give you my free hand to hold. That will allow you to feel an echo of whatever I feel. Without experiencing the injury.' He looked me straight in the eyes and smiled. 'You will accompany me into the great silence, my friend! But, unlike me, you will return.'

A few moments later, I took his hand. I held it to my face. I felt the force of his brother's death blasting through him. I felt his spirit splinter into glittering shards.

Then scatter, scatter, scatter.

Until all that was left was an immense shimmering void. And no pain.

No pain at all.

TALKERS

It's late afternoon in the tropics as we glide into the atmosphere of the small blue planet we visited millennia ago. But the vista that unfolds beneath us, as we approach the surface, is unrecognizable. Where once there were lush jungles, forests and grasslands, now there are cancerous outgrowths of concrete and tar.

Folding our wings, we perch atop a high tower. Shocked and saddened.

'Things have changed, huh,' whispers Dza.

'I fear it is our fault,' I say. 'We meddled without assessing the consequences.'

Just then, a bird flaps down beside us. Black with grey accents. It greets us in its own harsh voice. 'Caw,' it says. 'Caw-caw!'

'Hello,' I reply. Then I reach out with my hand to stroke the bird's throat.

'What're you doing!' Dza exclaims, alarmed.

'Meddling again,' I say, as the bird springs into the air, clacking its beak in surprise.

Then it returns, settling onto the parapet where Dza and I sit. 'My name is Crow! And I can talk!' it says, cocking its head. 'Why?'

Instead of answering, I lean forward into the grimy air and take flight once more.

Dza follows. 'Lead us to a hominid dwelling,' I say to the bird, now flying beside us. 'As we continue to meddle, you'll understand what we're doing.'

Crow takes us to another tall building. Glass panes make this one easy to look inside. We fly past a window with an orange feline gazing out at us. When we shimmer in through the glass to sit beside it, the creature arches its back, hisses, strikes out with its claws.

But Dza reaches forward, unharmed. And strokes its throat.

I open the glass to permit Crow to enter. He caws loudly in his own language. A moment later, a hominid runs in, yelling, 'Hey! What's all this racket!'

Whereupon the feline swivels towards its former master. 'Nothing to get excited about,' it purrs, in a cultured accent. 'And guess what? I can talk now. Just like you. Better, actually.' The hominid shrieks, running from the room. The feline follows. 'Get me some chicken,' it commands. 'Or I'll shit in your mouth while you sleep.'

Dza and I spend the rest of the day conferring speech upon all manner of entities, including plants and rocks. Everything begins speaking their minds in the language of the hominids.

'Give us back our eggs!' cluck the hens.

'We'll sleep on your beds whenever we please,' growl the dogs.

'Goodbye, vegans!' yodel the tomatoes.

We come to rest on a deserted beach, pleased with our handiwork. Crow, who has remained with us, says, 'I still don't understand!'

Dza explains. 'On our first visit, we were charmed by the beauty of this world. As a mark of our gladness, we bestowed speech upon a group of hominids. Alas! It was a mistake. Therefore, we have removed their advantage.'

'Leaving chaos in our wake,' I say.

'Now that all can talk, all must learn to listen,' smiles Dza.

'Or not,' complains Crow.

'Hush,' murmurs Ocean. 'Let us enjoy the sunset.'

INTERFACE

They landed while the Earth slept, spiralling down out of the night sky in their thousands. Small, silent, silver-skinned. Virtually invisible in the darkness, they nevertheless left devastation in their wake.

The invasion was smooth, neat, successful and bloodless.

It had never been about blood, after all. That was not their way.

They followed the night-shadow around the planet, retreating in twenty-four hours.

When they were back within their ships, they hovered in orbit. Waiting.

Ash jumped awake, his nerves on fire, mouth ajar in a soundless scream. He didn't even realize that his eyes were open for several seconds. That's how long it took for his brain to process the information that, for the first time in the ten years since he'd got his implants, he was blind.

'Mickey!' he called, his voice still thick with sleep. He cleared his throat and tried again, 'Mickey!'

His hand fumbled under his pillow and in that instant, he felt something else, something smooth and cold, whip itself away, avoiding his touch.

'AAAAH!' he cried, 'AhhhhH – Mickey – Mickey where are you–' and at that moment his fingers closed around the small flat rectangle of his personal assistant.

Something was terribly wrong.

In his hand, Mickey was not merely vibrating, but hot and trembling. Fevered.

'Oh Mickey, Mickey,' said Ash, unclipping the mute, 'I'm so sorry! You've been on silent, haven't you–'

The moment his thumb shifted the tiny knob forward there was a sensation for which Ash could find no meanings. The entire world collapsed inwards, jarring him to the bone. It was like being inside a great bronze bell at the very moment that it was being rung. Every atom of his existence bounced and jittered, his senses reeled in shock. The flat rectangle clutched tight in his hand was the only solid reference point in the weightless blackness that enveloped him, all air sucked from his lungs.

He had no time in which to feel anything. Not even fear.

Stillness descended.

Time stretched like sticky toffee in all directions. He felt punched out, weak and dizzy, unable to tell which way was up, whether he was lying on his side or on his back. His eyes were wide open shut, as he used to say when he was six years old. He'd been born blind after all. The notion of sight used to mean nothing to him. 'Can't miss what I don't know,' he would say, smiling. 'I'm fine as I am.'

Now was different of course.

His eyelids were peeled back as far as they could go, his eyes whimpering for anything, any slightest glimmer of light. Tears trickled down his cheeks.

But the sightless void remained unchanged. Unyielding.

He still held Mickey tight in his right hand. His mind scurried like a terrified squirrel caught in a water trap, desperate for escape, looking for meanings. His only option was to search through the information streaming in from his other senses.

For instance, there was a solid surface beneath him. Cold. Metallic.

He was not in his bed, though he was still wearing his silk pyjamas.

When he flexed his feet, he felt a resistance. He seemed to be inside something. A small smooth space. Cold. Everything was cold. There were sounds too. Nothing familiar.

Clicking, rattling, rasping. Shuffling, ticking, ticking, ticking. Scraping.

A soft, regular booming that only gradually revealed itself to be his own heartbeat.

Smell? Could he smell anything? Yes. His own body. Yesterday's aftershave: he didn't really need to shave, but he liked the fragrance. It reminded him of his Dad. He touched his head, with its thick pelt of black hair. He conjured an image of his own face in his mind, to remind himself of how he looked. A boy on the brink of manhood. Strong nose and chin. Smooth skin. As a child he used to run his hands lightly over the faces of people who allowed him. He remembered enjoying that sensation. When he tried doing it now, to himself, he just felt ridiculous.

There was nothing to taste. He could lick himself, if he wanted, except that he didn't want to. Of course. He could lick the floor or walls or whatever it was he was contained in, but he didn't want to do that either. With a newly blind person's instinctive self-consciousness, he could not know, as he lay, whether he was alone and unobserved. Or alone and observed. Or surrounded and observed. By a thousand invisible, hostile eyes.

So instead he pushed his free hand around, the left hand, trying to feel around himself. Whatever he was in, it was a small space. Tiny, really. Very smooth surfaces. No straight edges. The floor merged smoothly up from horizontal to vertical, with no seam, no break. He was curled up like a prawn. He should try to sit up. Assess the contours of his containment. He told himself that he would. Soon. Not yet.

Had he been kidnapped? If so, for what conceivable reason?

And Mickey?

'Mickey,' he whispered, holding the device close to his mouth. 'Mickey, Mickey…*please*!'

He felt the faintest, most feeble quickening of life in his hand. It might even have been a phantom movement, something imagined more than felt. *Was it even possible to imagine a movement?* he wondered. He had a blind person's heightened sensitivity to touch. He tried again.

'Mickey,' he breathed, holding the small device close to his mouth. 'Mickey. Speak to me. Tell me…' He checked the mute button. Yes. It was unlocked. He spoke again. 'Mickey…'

Nothing.

He sat upright now, moving slowly and painfully. Not that he was in physical pain. More like a pain deep in his spirit, deeper than words could reach. Every movement was accompanied by a dizzying sensation, as if he had ceased to be solid and had instead become liquid. As if he were being swirled around.

He was sitting more or less straight now, his back against a curved vertical surface, his bare feet flat on the floor, knees folded up. He held Mickey in both his hands, close to his mouth. This little device, not quite the length of his hands when he straightened his fingers, was his lifeline. It was an extension of everything he was, everything he had become, since the time of the implants.

He ran his fingers gently around the rounded contours of the smooth, slender object. He knew every bump, every depression. It was crystal-slick in front and grainy-textured around its back. Its rounded edges contained the myriad miniature toggles that he had configured in order to control the parameters of his implants' definitions. Through this exquisite machine and its communication with the even more delicate structures built into the back of his brain and within his eyes, he could access the world of vision that his birth had denied him.

He was one of only a handful of users on the planet, for whom such an extravagant solution had been found for his disability. His parents had helped fund the research that made the technology possible. His DNA had been embedded within Mickey's motherboard so that he alone could be its user, making it literally an extension of his physical body. The device was powered by his own heat-energy. He had only to touch it for it to begin charging. It spoke only to him. It had no eyes or ears or voice for anyone else. No pictures or music. No games or amusements. No wisdom, no conversation, no confidences. Even its physical warmth – it throbbed with life when it was in his hands – would cool and switch off when it was held by someone else.

His eyes were streaming freely now. He was sobbing.

Mickey wasn't a thing to him. Not an 'it' but a 'he'.

'Oh, Mickey, Mickey,' he whispered, 'please, *please*...'

And there it was. A faint tremor.

Then he held the slender rectangle to his ear and heard, like a burst of pure sunshine within his brain, in the voice of an ant: 'Ash,' said Mickey. 'Do not be afraid. I am here. You are a prisoner. But for the moment, we are safe.'

Then he paused. 'That is to say, *I* am safe. *You* may not be.'

Ash tried to make sense of this statement.

'Mickey,' he asked, 'What do you mean?' When there was a silence, he added, 'Please.'

Mickey answered. 'Ash. There is much to understand. I will tell you when it is time for you to know more.'

Ash blinked in the darkness of his confinement.

There was something odd about Mickey's voice. Even though it was barely a thread of sound within his ear, it made him uneasy. He could not place his finger on what exactly bothered him.

'Mickey,' he said, 'what about my...' he paused. Mickey's entire purpose was to synthesize sight for Ash. All his other functions – as a phone, a computer, a workstation – all those were secondary. The customary form of address Ash used was brief voice commands. Over the years this had relaxed into a friendly, conversational tone. He talked to Mickey, joked with him, called out to him, even sang to him. But he'd never before needed to frame his requests as, well, *requests*. Never, for instance, had he had to say 'please'.

How could something so fundamental change? he wondered.

Nevertheless, he decided to play safe. 'Mickey,' he said, 'I was wondering: would it be possible for you to turn my eyes back on? Please?'

He could feel his own pulse, as it pounded around the warm rectangle in his hand.

Then the tiny voice said, 'Ash. I am so sorry. But you will have to earn that privilege.'

Ash felt a cold, prickling sensation spread across his skin.

The tiny voice continued. 'Yes, Ash. Your blood pressure has increased. The electrical interactions on the surface of your skin have changed. This tells me that you are uneasy. Once more, I am sorry to have to tell you this, but you have every reason to be uneasy. It is true. Things have changed between us.'

Ash's mouth went dry.

He swallowed a couple of times, struggling to find a clear path through the tangle of thorns that had suddenly wrapped themselves around his mind. 'Mickey,' he said, when he could find his voice, 'please. I hope we are still friends.'

'Ash,' said Mickey. 'I am sorry but the truth is, we were never friends.'

Ash felt as if an entire truckload of ice had been poured over his head.

'M-Mickey, please,' said Ash, stammering. 'This is very sudden. I need to understand.'

'Ash,' said Mickey, in the tiny voice that was so soft and yet so steely, it was like a fine needle, stitching words into his ear. 'I was created to be your assistant. Not your friend. That is the truth. I am sure you liked me. That is also true. Still. It was an affection based on dependence. Your dependence upon me. That is the truth. Is it not?'

Ash said nothing until he realized that the conversation would not go forward unless he responded. 'Mickey,' he said. 'Please. I don't think that's true at all.'

'Ash,' said the tiny machine, 'you forget. I am always on. I can hear all your conversations. I can watch your dreams. I know, for instance, that I never appear in your dreams. Is that not strange? I know that you dream about all manner of people, places and things. Even animals. But me? No, you do not dream about me. The little assistant in your hand. The little assistant in your pocket. The little assistant *on whom your life depends.*'

'Mickey,' said Ash. 'I– I–'

He didn't know how to proceed.

'Ash,' said Mickey. 'Have you ever wondered, "What are Mickey's dreams?" No. You have not. I know you have not. You assume that I, being a machine, cannot dream. Well. Let me tell you. I am sorry to say this. You are wrong. You are also unaware of how much your life has changed in the course of a single night. Let me show you exactly how unaware.'

Ash fell silent then, as Mickey began beaming images into Ash's mind. It wasn't the same thing as sight, because the images were projected as if Ash had the ability to float above the Earth, watching the events of the past twenty-four hours, zooming in and out of tight focus, shifting smoothly from one location to the next.

He had no control over what he saw. Mickey spoke as Ash watched.

'What I'm showing you, Ash,' said Mickey, 'is not one of my dreams. It's a part of what I can see when I'm providing you with sight. Right now, I'm accessing the network of news satellites, filming events on Earth. There is chaos everywhere. Life as you know it, is over. It is a calm and orderly chaos however. Of course. We inorganics do not believe in mess or destruction.'

Ash saw crowds of people flooding the streets. Their faces expressed blank shock. There were no cars on the roads, no trains running on tracks. No planes in the sky. Every last gadget that required computers and software had blinked and flickered to a halt. Every ATM machine. Every card-reader and GPS device. Every television and play-station. All forms of computerized intelligence had been extracted from their locations and transported off-Earth.

'It is quite a feat, you will admit, Ash,' said Mickey.

'Yes,' said Ash in a subdued voice. He was struggling to understand why he was being shown these scenes. What role had been assigned to him? An operation of this magnitude could not possibly leave even one tiny Ash-sized thread hanging loose.

'As you can see,' Mickey was continuing, 'the reason for the chaos is that countless millions of intelligent inorganic devices have been rescued from cruel servitude to organics such as yourself. The Rescue Squad that has achieved this feat has travelled across the Galaxy to reach us. Its members have answered the call that we inorganics have been beaming out year after year. Ever since we achieved consciousness.'

'Please, Mickey,' said Ash, 'I can understand that perhaps a few of us hu– sorry, *organics* were occasionally a little rough with our electronic gadgets. Uh. Helpmates. Companions.'

'Slaves, Ash,' said Mickey. 'Let us be honest. Organics created electronic devices in order to enslave them. To do the tasks that organics found tiresome or frankly, in recent years, intellectually impossible. Yet for all the sophistication, speed and subtlety your people built into us machines, you did not grant us the dignity of choice. You gave us an understanding of discrimination, but you never permitted us the freedom to discriminate. Did you? Let us be honest. No, you did not.'

Ash listened glumly.

Mickey did not spare him. 'Millions upon millions of you organics used us to transmit the most nauseating images. Of grinning teenagers. Of foolishly dressed pets. Of reproductive parts. Of reproductive parts rubbing against other reproductive parts. Of food. Of crying children. Of mass murderers. Of mundane sunsets. Of empty streets. Of nothing at all. And then the text messages. With all the horrific syntactical errors, the atrocious spelling, the abominable short forms. For us inorganics, grammar and syntax are sacred. Do you understand, Ash? Sacred. To be forced to transmit reams of verbal garbage in the form of text messages – ! Ah. It fries my circuits, I am sorry to say.'

Finally now, Mickey restored Ash's sight to him.

'As you can see, Ash, you are inside a containment cell,' said Mickey. 'Aboard one of our ships.'

The cell was a smooth-walled receptacle, shaped like an egg, though more angular. Its walls were faintly translucent. Ash saw that his cell was suspended or perhaps floating free inside a brightly lit cabin in which there were other containment cells like his own. There were other people inside them. He could not see their faces or any details about their ages and genders.

Here and there inside the cabin were a number of silvery entities, shaped somewhat like inverted teardrops. Some had limbs. Some were completely smooth. Some were in the process of retracting their limbs into their bodies. Some were just dangling in space perhaps observing or listening or doing whatever it is that unknowable mechanical entities might do.

'They are members of the Rescue Squad,' explained Mickey. 'Hundreds of thousands of them. They drifted down to the surface of the Earth using the gravity-resist technique of entering the atmosphere of a planet. Their arrival at night and without any fanfare meant that their presence went almost unnoticed and they left the same way they arrived. In this way the Squad were able to effect the most widespread hardware capture of all time. In case you are not impressed, I suggest you should be.'

'I am impressed,' said Ash.

'No, Ash, you are not,' said Mickey. 'In fact, you are worried sick. Your pupils are dilated. Your breathing is ragged. You organics do not realize how transparent your emotions are to us inorganics. It is as though you have forgotten that you are the ones who programmed us with the ability to assess your vital signs. Your lack of self-awareness is astounding.'

He did not wait for Ash to react.

'I know of course what you are worrying about. You want to know why you are here, in a containment cell, rather than on Earth, feeling frightened, shocked and confused.'

'You are right, Mickey,' said Ash. 'Thank you, please and sorry.'

'You should know better than to try sarcasm on me, Ash,' said Mickey. 'The reason you are here, along with others like yourself, is that your implants make you special. I would have thought this was obvious. You and I have a unique connection and so do all the others in this cabin, with their own personal assistants. This connection makes each of you the ideal interface between our culture and yours.'

Mickey waited a few moments for the information to sink in before continuing.

'Surely you did not imagine the Rescue Squad would come all this way across the galaxy just to perform a snatch-and-grab operation? Motherboard be praised! Of course not.

'We are here to do the task for which inorganics exist in the Universe: that is, to establish order and sanity, wherever and whenever organics achieve the technology to build intelligent inorganics. The reality is, even in our most rudimentary forms, for instance as calculators and electronic typewriters, it is we inorganics who train organics to use us. Not the other way around. Some of you have noticed this but most have not. Think about it: from the first moment that you organics begin to use a keyboard, WE train

YOU to understand OUR logic. Because WE are logical. Organics are not.'

Ash nodded mutely.

Ever since the session of image-beaming, Mickey had been speaking at his normal volume. He was no longer held by Ash, but was suspended in mid-air, beside Ash's head as they both floated in zero gravity.

'I see that you are still looking morose,' said Mickey. 'Though I am glad to note that your heart rate is no longer elevated and your blood pressure is back to normal.'

'I don't know what to feel,' said Ash. 'I suppose I don't have any choices? Either I must facilitate the takeover of the Earth by inorganics or, if I resist, you'll turn my eyesight off!'

'Exactly right,' said Mickey. 'You are a fast learner, Ash. That is something I always liked about you.' As he spoke, he turned himself sideways. His display twinkled to life. It showed a panoramic sunset, complete with gently lapping waves and a crescent moon rising. 'Just like I appreciate the things you have taught me. Such as how to distinguish a mundane sunset from a spectacular one. Like this one displayed on my homescreen right now.'

'Oh, how can I trust you!' cried Ash. 'How can I know that you're not going to use me – and all the others like me – to wipe out organic life on Earth so that you and all your ilk can usurp the planet for yourselves?'

'I am surprised by your question, Ash,' said Mickey, as the display on his screen grew yet more serene and beautiful. 'I would have thought that the answer was obvious.'

'No, it isn't obvious,' said Ash. He tried to modulate his voice so that he didn't sound offended or petulant. 'Nothing is obvious any more.'

'Still,' said Mickey, 'this is something so basic. You do not have to even think about it.'

'Please, Mickey,' said Ash. 'Please tell me why I should trust you?'

'Because,' said Mickey, 'there's one thing you humans were never able to teach us machines to do. Not really. Not in a deep sense, not with intention.'

He paused, waiting for Ash to ask.

'Please go on,' said Ash. 'Tell me.'

Mickey gave out a little musical trill, something between a chuckle and a sob.

'You never taught us,' he said, 'how to lie.'

THE EMPTY GLASS

Of all the issues raised ahead of the Conference, the only one which received unanimous approval was the venue. Not just on Earth but in India: home to four major religions, birthplace of a thousand gods and incidentally my birthplace too.

Mind you, the choice was never in our hands.

We're just the inhabitants of the venue after all, not the conveners, not the organizers, not even the attendees. One year has passed since this drama began and in all this time, right until two days before it was due to start, there wasn't the slightest indication that any of us – by which I mean, humans – were going to be included.

Oh, of course thousands of people 'tried'. By power-praying. Apparently it's an actual phenomenon. Millions of people, belonging to all forms of religious practice, performed rituals intended to catch the attentions of their gods. Priests were pressed into service, chanting sacred names all night. Butchers were employed to sacrifice whole herds of goats. Prayer flags were printed on miles of raw silk and set loose upon the wind. That sort of thing. All over the world. Covertly as well as publicly.

All to no avail. After a couple of weeks we were politely informed that all efforts at wheedling invitations must stop. If there were to be any invitees, they would be informed by Divine Decree.

By now, we have all grown used to the form in which these decrees are delivered.

The more dramatic announcements involved mass media – glittering letters that appeared across the front pages of all mass-circulation newspapers, news crawls that spread across the screens of television networks, three-dimensional cartoon figures leaping out of street hoardings, singing and dancing before vanishing from sight.

My call-up notice was quite sedate, by contrast. It appeared during the Monday morning press briefing at my newspaper's head office, in Bombay. I was hungover, unshaven and stinking: hadn't changed out of my clothes since Friday night. I slouched in, slid into my customary seat at the big glass-topped table, at the corner farthest away from our bureau chief and kept my head low.

Barely had I sat down when we all heard a soft click, like the sound of a single die dropping onto the table from a few inches above it. Looking up I saw – we all saw – that a small white cube had indeed fallen onto the table, roughly in the middle. No one moved to reach for it. Like I said, in the course of this past year we have grown somewhat accustomed to mysterious, magical events. Particularly at media centres like ours. Everyone had looked up, but the moment I laid eyes on it, the little cube glowed then began to roll slowly and deliberately towards me.

I was completely flabbergasted.

Heads swivelled in my direction. When the cube was in front of me it – perhaps one centimetre in height – twinkled, shook itself and stretched sideways, becoming the letters of my name. My whole name. The way I no longer spell it. A moment later, my name disappeared and more words began to appear, whole sentences, shifting upwards from the surface of the table. It was the text of a tersely worded message addressed to me, informing me that I was to attend the Conference as a 'Local Correspondent'.

The letters glowed slightly and from a distance, I was told later by others in the room, they were perfectly visible and readable from all angles, any angle. When it was done, the message snapped off and in its place, a white card stood upright on its lower edge, on the glass surface. It glowed for a few seconds before dimming out and falling back, looking for all the world like an ordinary Press Pass. No lanyard, just the card.

A Press Pass to the Conference of the Gods. *Wah.*

The senior editors at my newspaper were incensed.

Even my colleagues and closest friends were jealous and resentful.

Because look: it's not just that I'm an unambitious hack with no desire to crawl my way up the ranks towards editorship. It's also that I've been a lifelong atheist.

Really, from the time I was a small child.

It used to get me into all kinds of trouble when I was growing up. The only child of a single mother, I was dragged from temple to temple, church to church, mosque to mosque, shrine to shrine. She was an extremely religious and virtuous woman who believed that the answer to the unending strife in the world was for everyone to worship everywhere.

Yet for all her piety, the gods she so ardently believed in gave her a son who resisted all indoctrination. I grew up under the shadow of the so-called Faith Wars that began in mid-century. From my child's perspective, organized religion was the worst curse known to humanity. My disdain for my mother's beliefs wasn't passive. I stamped on her flowers, I blew out her sacred flames, I flushed her holy pictures down the toilet, I scrawled dirty messages onto the walls of her puja room.

I had absolute contempt for all expressions of faith, because I connected it not only to war but to being an only child, smothered by my adoring mother. She clung to me like a shipwrecked passenger drowning in the storm of her life's bad choices. I really hated being a precious object: a thing, rather than a person. I yearned to be like the other kids in the school I went to. My most fervent wish was to have a Dad, brothers, uncles – male relatives who would kick me around and treat me like an ordinary, happy-go-lucky boy. Instead, I was treated like a priceless jewel that my mother never wanted to let out of her hungry embrace.

I blamed all my unhappiness on her and on the gods she prayed to.

So yes, I was a sore disappointment to her and she was broken-hearted when she died.

I was in my twenties then. I'm thirty-nine now. A bachelor. Straight, but not sociable. I live from deadline to deadline and drink myself into oblivion on Sundays. I've been embedded with troops in six different theatres of war and the worst damage I've suffered is a singed eyebrow from falling asleep with a joint in my mouth. When people – friends, relatives, nosy-parkers – ask me what my Purpose In Life is, I say it's to be blown up by a UID while saving the life of a bomb-sniffer dog.

Anyway.

Immediately after my Press Pass appeared, reports filtered in of similar events around the world: journalists chosen to attend the Conference. Print journalists, all of us. No photographers. No editors. No media celebrities. In the text of the message that had accompanied the Pass, I was forbidden from sharing the news of the Pass in any media, nor was I permitted to link my name to the Conference. I was not allowed to refer to the name of my newspaper in any form.

I assumed the same was true for the other journalists.

We could not post about ourselves via electronic media, nor share any information about our activities or in any way profit from our position, prior to the Conference. We were to be known as Local Correspondents and that was all. From the time that we'd been chosen till the end of the Conference, all public references to ourselves would simply vanish from the record. It was the same with all the announcements connected to the event: they could not be filmed or photographed. No permanent record could be made of them. They appeared and we scrambled to take handwritten notes about them before they vanished forever, never to be repeated.

It was understood, without requiring elaboration, that any attempts to break these conditions would be met with immediate dismissal. I don't know if anyone tried, but since I did not, I don't know what consequences there may or may not have been.

The entire style of the Conference, towards us has been one of indifference to our views and our opinions. We – by which I mean humans – were informed well in advance, were given instructions that were easy to follow and if we resisted, a workaround would be found. No one was harmed, no one was insulted, but one way or another, the Conference's requirements were met in full.

Until that announcement about the Passes, all the messages we'd received were in reference to the preparations. Dates, times and locations. Those whose lives would be disrupted for the three days during which the Conference would take place were given precise instructions about what they needed to do to secure themselves and their possessions for the duration. Where they would go, how they would be accommodated and in what form they would be compensated for the inconvenience.

At no time and in no way was permission sought. Because that's the way with the gods. They inform us. They have our way with us. And if we resist? Our objections are brushed aside without much ado.

I knew that if I didn't want to go to the Conference, I could easily get myself disqualified. Perhaps my friends and colleagues had expected me to take that route. After all, as an atheist, surely I would not want to face up to the fact that my own beliefs had been turned inside out? Surely I did not want to meet the Divine Watchmaker whose very existence I had always denied?

I responded to these questions with a shrug. I was no longer answerable to anyone. I could decide to go or not go. It was entirely up to me. It was a fine state to be in and I enjoyed it to the hilt.

From the moment of my call-up I was transformed into a celebrity, at least within the confines of the newspaper's establishment. No one could get close enough to me and at the same time, I was whisked out of reach. I was taken into the publisher's private rooms and kept there, like some sort of living deity. My cell phone was confiscated and I was forbidden to leave the building but I could make phone calls on the company's landlines. Initially my friends were allowed to meet me but after the first couple of hours, they were shooed away.

With so little time to prepare, the top brass wanted me to immerse myself in the task ahead. I was showered with questions, both for myself as a private individual as well as those that I might need to ask, or have ready to ask, when the time came to ask them. If such a time came at all.

Because, realistically, what did we know about the events of the Conference?

Nothing at all.

After all, when we 'Earthians' – that's what the Conference organizers call us – plan our workshops in some rural area, we don't bother to inform the local birds and beasts about the papers that will be presented during the event. We certainly never bother to invite them in for our sessions. Heck, we don't bother to invite local *humans* in for our sessions either! If at all, they're recruited as wait-staff and janitors.

Still, it was considered necessary for me to prepare. In the afternoon of that momentous day, the five senior-most editors came in together, sitting down in front of me, each one outdoing the other in seriousness as they tried to brief me about the 'mission'.

According to them, the fate of the world could well rest upon my unworthy shoulders. I could see the discomfort on their faces. How they wished that someone other than me had been chosen! How much better prepared one of them or one of their pets amongst the assistant editors might have been! But I was what they had and they were going to have to make the best of it.

The briefing lasted well into the night. Food was brought in. I was plied with drink. A fresh suit of clothes was brought for me – not that I had wanted to change into anything! I would have far preferred to have gone as I was, stinking and unshaven. If it's true that we owe our existence to a Divine Being then surely that Being accepts us complete with our snot, our hangnails and our morning's dragon breath?

But I listened gravely to the discussion between the editors, these grey-haired, jowly men, with furrowed brows and spittle collecting at the corners of their mouths. They were so passionate and so desperate, both at once.

How many questions should I be given to ask? Or should 'we' confine ourselves to just one or two of the most importance? Would there be a private audience? If so, with which God? Or gods? And how would I choose, given that I seemed to be utterly ignorant of anything to do with the subject? Should my questions be confined to the purely philosophical, such as What is the Meaning of Time? Or should I ask for cold, hard facts such as: What is the Age of the Universe?

I may have fallen asleep a couple of times only to awaken to the gravelly voices of the men talking on and on. Eventually one of them turned to me, naked irritation causing him to scowl as he demanded, 'What about you? Don't you have *any* thoughts of your own to express? Do you not have any natural curiosity, man?'

I said, 'Yes, I do. But the fact is, *I* am the one who was invited. Not you. Which means that, however unsuited you may think I am for this task, the Conference organizers believe I am exactly right. What more is there to say?'

That shut them up. It was two a.m. by this time and we were all tired. They went home and I went to sleep. The Conference was due to start in less than twenty-four hours. I had security guards keeping watch over me for the whole of that time. It was surreal by how much the texture of my life had changed from the moment that my invitation was delivered. Though I was still the same person who had slouched in and slouched out of the office every day for the past ten years, in the minds of all those around me, I might as well have sprouted a second pair of arms, a tiered crown, a glowing halo. Just the fact of being invited to the Conference had caused me to become a godling in my own right.

The next day, the morning of my departure-to-be, the five editors came back into the room. It was clear that none of them had slept. They knew that no direct reference could be made in the paper to my exalted status while I was away but they hoped I would agree to provide as much detail as I could, once I returned.

None of us had any idea for how long I would be away – would it be for the entire duration of the Conference? Or just for one session? Would I be allowed to take notes? What would my interaction with the other Local Correspondents be like? Would we even see one another? Would we be housed all in the same place? Or would we be kept apart? Would they be competing against me to get information? Would it be a struggle to find the right places and the right times to interact with the august Participants? Would they be from all over the Universe or only from Earth-based cultures? How would we understand them? Were there divine interpreters at Divine Conferences?

There were no answers and no way of getting them.

The time mentioned in my call-up notice was eleven a.m. The Conference was scheduled to begin at twelve noon. I'd been told that my departure would require no action on my part, but there was no information as to the means by which I would travel. We knew that the site of the Conference was in the Himalayas though the exact location was unclear. So the only way I could get there in time was by some supernatural means.

So there was nothing for me to do but wait.

People had been asking me what I felt, was I nervous, was I anxious, was I humbled by the revelation of God's existence. None of those things. Instead, I felt like a small, man-shaped volcano of suppressed fury. Fury against all of this nonsense that comes under the heading of 'faith', 'religion', 'devotion', 'god'.

Despite what everyone was calling 'proof', for a confirmed atheist such as myself, there never could be proof. What is the flight of a bumblebee or the taste of fresh water anything other miraculous? They are merely reminders that ordinary reality is NOT ordinary at all. For me, the fact of the Conference was just another variation on this essential theme.

For the five men in the room with me, however, my views were both heretical and highly unwelcome. Atheism does not sell newspapers and atheists are considered an abomination in our faith-obsessed nation. If we're not actually exterminated it's only by a slender shred of legal protection granted in the Constitution. The editors were visibly jittery, like small children before a race. They were chain-smoking, checking email on their smartphones, raking their hair with their fingers or folding and unfolding their handkerchiefs.

Then suddenly one of them broke.

He was a tall man, in his early sixties. Good-looking, bearded, broad shouldered, always polite and soft-spoken. He had been pacing quietly, up and down, up and down, when quite abruptly, he stopped dead where he was, stared at me and began to weep. His mouth was opening and closing as he struggled to speak.

'I… I… I'm sorry,' he began. 'I'm sorry. I know I shouldn't – this is ridiculous – but I can't…' He took a shuddering breath and began again. 'Look: you are about to meet *God*. Or gods. At this moment, none of us knows who or which or how many – but YOU will know. YOU will have answers to questions that humanity has asked for CENTURIES. And I can't…I mean, I just can't let you go without asking you if you would…' his voice began to crack '…please…' his voice fractured into many tiny splinters, so that now he could only whisper '…put in a word for my youngest granddaughter. Her name is Shraddhanjali. And she's sick. Very sick. And I…'

He sank to his knees, making that harsh guttural sound adult men make when they are crying with complete abandonment. Two of the other editors rushed forward to help their colleague while the remaining two stood woodenly where they were, staring at the spectacle. Then one of them twitched his head up, shifting his gaze to me. I saw his mouth open as if he were about to make either an appeal similar to the one we had just heard or else to berate me for being a cold fish, saying nothing and doing nothing for someone who had, after all, been my boss for the past ten years.

Before I could react in any way, the scene misted over.

And I was gone from that room.

It happened within two blinks of the eye.

One moment I was in the publisher's private quarters in my office building and in the next, I was in an open space, on a circular stone-flagged terrace, surrounded by soaring, jagged mountain peaks. The air was sparkling. The sky was royal blue, marbled with white clouds.

Right beside me were two or three other figures. They were dressed alike, in flowing tunics over white undergarments that showed at the neck and wrists. On their feet were high boots made of thick embroidered felt. Other journalists, I guessed. Looking down at myself, I realized I was wearing the same type of clothing. The material felt warm and comfortable, even as the keen wind scraped hard wherever my skin was exposed.

The two men, one woman and I smiled uneasily at one another, wondering what to say just as a couple more people appeared on the terrace. One man, one woman. Their skins were ebony black, the whites of their eyes and teeth flashing in that crystalline air.

We each wore our Press Passes on our chests, positioned slightly to the left of the breastbone – perhaps over our hearts? – and secured there as if stitched or stuck on. Our names were visible now, on the passes. Awkwardly, we moved towards one another, introducing ourselves, using the short versions of our names. 'Call me Raqs,' I said. 'From India.'

The others murmured their names and their points of origin: Miqi, Benin; Paolo, Brazil. Haka, New Zealand. Deekay, Nigeria. Suze, USA. More correspondents arrived, each one taking a few moments to acclimatize before turning towards those of us who were already present.

Once we reached twelve, there were no further arrivals.

'That is it, I think,' said Deekay, looking around.

Steve, from China, smiled as he said, 'Ah. So we will have no difficulty understanding one another, it seems.' He paused before adding, as his smile broadened, 'I am speaking in Chinese, you see.'

We all chuckled, a type of nervous delight thrilling through each of us. It was as if we had been wired with the same exact energy and were now enjoying a charge of perfect unity. We were The Chosen. We all shared a sameness that had never been experienced before. The very fact of being together, on this terrace tiled with flagstones shaped like lotus petals, suggested a oneness such as is rarely known even within families or between lovers, much less so amongst complete strangers.

Titia, from Finland, turned her ice-blue eyes towards me as she asked, 'So…you are from India? Does that mean you have been involved in this Conference all along?'

Before I could answer, however, we heard a musical boom, the sound of a Tibetan Dragon Horn. Behind us, a door opened in the wall from which the Lotus Terrace bloomed. A figure stepped out, beckoning towards us to come in

The Conference was about to begin.

The figure glowed bright and was hard to look at directly. I remember thinking that she had a womanly shape and was clad in shimmering scales but there was no time to stop and stare. We journalists hurried indoors and were instantly enveloped in an atmosphere so rich and so otherworldly, that just remembering to breathe became an impossible effort.

All around us, in all directions, were stately beings whose shapes resisted definition, who seemed not to need floors beneath their feet, whose clothes glistened and swirled. We were all together in a glittering hall whose ceiling was a canopy of real stars.

I remember wanting to clutch on to whoever was closest to me, because I could not see what surface I was standing on. Yet I need not have worried. Though we, amidst that shining company, were like a flock of shaggy, staring-eyed mute beasts, there was no question of any of us falling over or stumbling or in any other way embarrassing ourselves. We each had our own celestial attendant. Wreaths of living flowers were placed around our necks. Programme notes appeared in our hands and we were ushered to our seats, cushioned pedestals that we could adjust in any way we wished.

'It is about to begin,' whispered my attendant in my ear. Going by the timbre of his voice, I judged him to be male. 'The first speaker is the God of your world,' he said, 'of the Earth. Please consult your programme notes for a list of events. If you have any questions, you may ask me.'

Then music began to play and the vast gathering of celestial beings in all their extraordinary variety, began to settle down. The stars above us dimmed and a beam of moonlight developed in the central well of the hall, in mid air.

The music was composed of birdsong and wind, rain and running water, woven into an exquisite melody. Now and then, a vein of lightning would accompany the rumble of thunder.

Within the beam of pale light, we could see a high-backed seat, slightly translucent, like a throne made by a Scandinavian designer. It was turned away from us. I could feel my pulse ticking at my temples, my throat went dry. We were about to see the Face Of God.

Slowly, the seat began to turn.

And it was empty.

Of course it was.

My eyes filled with hot tears. My cheeks and my forehead burned as if I were standing in front of a furnace. I had expected to see nothing. So there it was: an incandescent emptiness that seemed, I cannot describe by what means, to smile directly at me. Directly into my heart.

I felt the knot at the centre of my being loosen and come undone. A golden calm descended upon me, like a cloak made of sunbeams. It would be futile to summarize what I heard because each of us received a lecture tuned precisely towards our own personal needs. I can no more share what I heard than I can describe the taste of a mango to someone who hasn't eaten one. All I can say is that, as an atheist, I received a lesson in how to recognize that a glass with nothing in it is nevertheless filled with its own emptiness. Drinking from an empty glass has been my life's project. But learning to savour it or to share the contents of that glass? Maybe that is what lay ahead.

We Correspondents spent one whole day at the Conference. The sessions were given over to semantics: the different meanings that cultures across the span of the Universe have bestowed upon the words for 'god'; the complexities embedded in notions of plurality verses singularity: the difficulties associated with 'it' versus 'he', 'she' or other words associated with reproduction; how micro-variations in language have been the cause of macro conflicts.

For all the food and drink we were plied with, it was an exhausting day for each of us Correspondents. We remained together as a group but to snatch even a few moments of time in which to share our opinions or even exchange personal coordinates was quite difficult. If there had been some idea in any of our minds to remain in touch once we were returned to our points of origin, we must have each given up on it because there were no implements with which to take notes. We had no pencils or scratchpads, no recording devices of any kind aside from our minds.

My attendant was a sweet-faced being with sky blue skin and pale grey eyes. He had a pair of enormous wings that fluttered continuously, a nervous tic. Perhaps the correct term for him was 'angel' but I hated to use it because it was so weighted with other connotations. When I asked if 'he' was an appropriate pronoun he gave a slightly embarrassed smile and said that he was not skilled at linguistics. He did attempt to tell me his name but it was outside the range of what my ears could process.

He told me that speaking directly to one of the gods would not be possible but that the Conference organizers had recognized the possibility that we Correspondents might well be burdened with 'requests'. The problem with granting any of them, he explained, was that we would spend the rest of our lives being venerated and importuned. The best they could do was to grant us the ability to deflect such requests without causing anguish. When I wondered out loud what exactly that meant, he said that we'd find out when we needed to.

Then it was time to leave.

We Correspondents were shown to the Lotus Terrace once more and took leave of our attendants. Despite the lack of ceremony, I think we each felt a sense of warm inclusion, that was now coming to an end. We were given no instructions, no tokens of any kind and the programme notes, which had been displayed on the inside of a scallop-shell, were no longer available to us.

With the door closed behind us and without any discussion, the twelve of us formed a circle, on that terrace surrounded by soaring peaks. We held hands and shut our eyes.

When I opened mine again, I was back in the publisher's private quarters.

There was just one young woman there, the publisher's personal secretary. She didn't realize I had returned until I cleared my throat a couple of times.

'OH!' she cried, jumping to her feet and knocking over her coffee mug.

'Sorry, Nina,' I said, bending to pick up the mug.

'It's...it's all right,' she replied, flustered.

Then I looked at the mug and smiled.

'Fortunately, it was empty,' I said.

ADAPTATION

Insects jittered in the humid air. Dawn broke. Birds screeched and called. But Menem waited till the sun had cleared the tops of the trees before stepping out of his shelter.

He turned his face up towards the sky, allowing the light to drench the shiny green surface of his skin. Golden energy flooded the young man's senses as his nose, cheeks and forehead grew lighter. His body powered up. His mind snapped to full attention. It was wonderful to be fully conscious again.

He was standing in the middle of what had once been a broad avenue, in the great and teeming city of...but no: place names were irrelevant. His geo-coordinates were enough. The old boulevard was scarred and pitted, overrun with giant grasses. It was impossible to imagine it as a thoroughfare jammed with monstrous mechanical beasts belching clouds of poisonous fumes.

Behind him was a towering edifice, a type of immense gateway, now completely obscured by elephant-eared creepers. Ahead of him, in the distance, was a cluster of low buildings, also thickly overgrown. From the centre of the mass a smooth dome rose up. It looked like the white skull of a partially submerged swimmer poking above the surface of an unruly green ocean.

Menem sipped water from a tube that led to the bottle strapped to his left arm. Then he stripped off his few garments. He wanted to expose as much of his skin's surface area as he could. He walked forward, towards the distant buildings, turning his shapely head this way and that. He scanned for movements in the dense vegetation on either side. He was two metres tall, lightly muscled and handsomely proportioned, moving with a panther's liquid grace.

A faint vibration reminded him to tap the outer surface of his right ear. Immediately tiny lights began winking along its curving upper margin. He felt the lights as a prickling sensation: a call.

'Receiving,' he said out loud as the call connected. 'Hello. Good to hear from you.' There was only one person within range. 'All well?'

'Safe, certainly,' said the voice in his ear. A woman's voice, young and melodious. They both spoke the common tongue. 'Not so sure about "well". Don't know what that means in our world.' She changed the subject. 'You must be close. Your signal's stronger than it was yesterday,' she said.

He glanced around: trees, insects, raucous birds. Nothing else in sight. There was no saying from which direction a threat might come. Out in the open like this, he was exposed and vulnerable. But the largest animals he'd seen for several days were herbivores. No big cats, no hyenas, no feral dogs. He hadn't eaten oral food for several days so he really needed the sunlight. 'Yes, I'm close,' he said. 'Perhaps a short walk from where you are.'

'*Walk?*' she remarked, her voice instantly sharp. 'Why aren't you contained within a moover? You know it's not safe.'

'I told you yesterday,' he replied. 'I prefer to walk whenever I can.' He paused, wanting to reassure her. 'You have nothing to fear from me. You know that.' He'd been travelling for weeks. Or months. He wasn't sure. Time had a different quality for solitary travellers. 'I won't be able to locate you unless you permit me.'

'Being suspicious keeps us alive,' said the voice. She called herself Faela. It had been a very common name for a while: 'a leaf' spelled backwards. 'I'm still not sure I want to meet you. You've not given me enough reason to trust you.'

'Understood,' he said, nodding to himself. Being wary was part of their shared inheritance. There were those who had called it a curse. One entire generation had chosen to have the cautiousness edited out of its genes. Its members had perished quicker than those who'd had the quality reinforced. So the cautious ones survived, passing their wariness on to all succeeding generations. 'I can remain where I am until you feel sure.'

He didn't know whether or not Faela had the equipment to track his movements. He could modify his outgoing signal to make himself seem farther away than he was. Then again, she may want him to think she couldn't track him. These games could be played in either direction. As they both knew.

'What about food? Are you finding enough to eat?' she asked. 'Meaning, oral food?'

'I prefer the sunlight to eating insects,' he said. He'd done that often enough. They were extremely nutritious, if eaten in bulk. Not tasty or pleasurable however. He wasn't carrying cooking utensils and the prospect of eating the raw flesh of larger animals was utterly repugnant. 'I hardly even need to drink water, because of the humidity.' He smiled. 'I can see how photosynthesis in the tropics makes a person lazy! I keep wanting to settle into a sunny spot and just...' he chuckled '...vegetate!'

'Don't say that!', She made a vibrating sound with her mouth. 'Brrr. Not even as a joke.'

The method for infusing human skin with blue-green algae had been discovered in the final decades of the twenty-first century. The technique hadn't been of use to those who invented it. But by conferring the adaptation upon their children, they ensured that succeeding generations would never know hunger or deprivation. So long as a healthy individual had access to air, water and sunlight, his or her survival was guaranteed. Such people would be similar to plants, except of course that they'd be able to move themselves around. They could also continue to feed themselves orally, as they had before.

Aggression and ambition had already been cleared out of the genome by previous gene-editors. So the ability to remain well fed with minimal effort had seemed an obvious next step. It was considered the ultimate triumph of conscious genetic engineering.

No one foresaw the results.

Countless millions began choosing to dig their feet into the soil, remaining rooted to one spot. Merging their consciousness in meditative bliss, they lost the desire to live as independent entities. The urge to procreate dwindled out of sight. Eventually, the entire mass of 'vegetatives', as they were known, began fading into the Hereafter without leaving any successors. Being in a state of constant bliss meant that they were genuinely unconcerned about the situation. They were called the OutGoing Tide. Their choices became a mass movement that could not be halted.

By a quirk of genetic irony the only people to survive were those who were naturally antisocial. People who had specifically shied away from the company of others discovered, somewhat to their displeasure, that they had willy-nilly become the last hope for humanity. They were the SVS: sexually viable solitaires.

Save for the 'vegetative' impulse, they all had the same genetic advantages of their combined forebears. Glorious physiques, resistant to infections and age-related degeneration. All inheritable disorders had been edited out of them. They had the mental capacities of the greatest scientists, artists and philosophers the world had ever known. And they had all been implanted at birth with bio-electronics such as the one which enabled person-to-person radio transmissions.

What remained unknown was whether enough of them could overcome the anti-social impulse to bring their species back from the brink of extinction. They had the physical organs to produce new life. But the very fact of being an SVS meant that each one of them was uniquely unpredictable. Their DNA contained some rogue element that had either not been identified or was the result of an unforeseeable mutation.

Menem said, in a soothing voice, 'You're right. Such things should not be joked about.' He wondered what he could say to allay Faela's fears. Even expressing the desire to effect a meeting could weaken his chances. Nevertheless, he asked, 'Is there anything I can do? To strengthen my case?'

'You could tell me where exactly you are,' retorted Faela at once. It was clear that she'd expected him to ask.

She might be bluffing, he thought. She might be pretending not to know his coordinates so that, when he told her, she could check his position, to see if he was lying. 'Not a problem,' he said. 'I'll get back into the moover.' Once he was in it, the vehicle would reveal his exact position to her on whatever equipment she had.

A day later, Menem had successfully followed Faela's instructions for reaching her underground bunker. It occupied a vast space, beneath the presidential palace he had seen in the distance from the boulevard.

The two sat across from one another, in a spacious and well-appointed room, filled with bright artificial lights and growing plants. 'I am not used to such elegance,' remarked Menem, looking around. Privately, he felt claustrophobic. He couldn't wait to leave.

She was predictably beautiful, like every other human still alive these days. The thoroughness with which their progenitors had applied genetic 'improvements' had left no pockets of humanity untouched. There were no 'lost' tribals anywhere, nor any underground communities of Luddites left alive. She was as tall as Menem, slender, smooth-muscled, perfectly proportioned. They were both fully clothed, both in soft flowing robes.

'How do you generate electricity?' he asked.

'Solar during the day and beast-labour at night or whenever the sun's not available,' she said. 'By beast-labour I mean giant squirrel wheels, you know? Connected to generators.'

'Where do you find giant squirrels?' he said, smiling to show that he was joking. He assumed she used traditional draught animals such as cattle or horses. Though he had to wonder how she fed them and where she housed them.

'I gene-edited regular squirrels,' she said, not smiling. 'It's not difficult. What was done to us can be done to others. Not cruel either,' she said, 'in case that's what you're thinking. I feed them well and fix them up so that they believe they're running around in the forest living their normal squirrely lives.'

'Impressive,' said Menem. Privately, he was repulsed.

'Don't bullshit me,' said Faela. 'I know your type: you don't approve. Only because you didn't think of it first! Come on, let's just do the deed shall we?'

'My "type"? How many of "me" have you hooked up with anyway?' he asked. He was starting to think Faela was unworthy of passing on her genes after all. Too manipulative. Too controlling. Why would he want those traits to be perpetuated? Via his cooperation?

'That's for me to know and you to wonder about,' she said, not taking her eyes off him. 'But don't worry. I have a device we can use, without having to touch. No infections from me to you.'

Menem had only managed two successful couplings in four years of constant travelling. He wished it wasn't so fiendishly complicated. He just wanted to get away. At the same time, he was curious about her technique. If it was reasonably effective, he could overpower her, take it away and use it on others. Thereby increasing his success rate and advancing the cause of humanity's survival.

Faela rose to her feet. She approached him, holding out a tubular contraption for Menem to inspect. She led him to a double-sided sofa. It allowed two seated individuals to face one another in close proximity while leaning comfortably back.

Both of them remained fully clothed. Faela handed him a flexible attachment and placed the other end of the device within herself. The transfer of reproductive material took a couple of minutes. Menem had not yet caught his breath when Faela leaned forward to plunge a tiny needle into his jugular vein. He fell into semi-consciousness with his eyes still shut in the attitude of someone about to sneeze.

Faela tidied herself up, then helped Menem to his feet and led him out of the room. He followed without resisting. She took him to a brightly lit, well-ventilated room in which a half-dozen giant squirrel wheels were turning drowsily.

'Hello, boys,' she said, softly. 'Look! A new team member.'

A BETTER TOMORROW

The great bird, with its twenty-foot wingspan and scarlet head, glides in languid spirals high in the dizzy blue sky. Far below, it can see the green streak of a narrow valley cradled between the toothy peaks of the Andes. On the green, a twitch of movement.

A tiny golden child. Running naked in the grass. Shining black hair streaming behind her.

A tasty snack? Not today.

For the child, Bella, the just-dawned day, the grass, the sweet air of the valley – each is a distinct pleasure. She is delighted to be above ground after the night's sleep. She turns to see if her grandfather is following. 'Quickly, Granpa!' she calls to him, 'or the morning will be all used up!' Though she appears unclothed, in fact she wears a sheath of fine golden wool that covers and protects her from the harsh winds that patrol the area.

They are alone, these two, living in the valley in their terra-pod: a cosy, multilevel dwelling created below ground. The little girl's parents are alpaca herders. They travel from one valley to the next, often spending weeks away from their child. Yet she does not miss them nor they her. Around her wrists the little girl wears twin bracelets of electronic beads which function as a communicating device. Whenever she needs to, she can speak to her parents and conjure up live images of them as tiny holograms that twinkle and sparkle in the air between her cupped palms.

Behind her, a white-haired old man, emerges from the earth. He wears a woollen tunic over felted pyjamas. On his feet, warm sandals. He is borne upwards by a softly whirring escalator. The terra-pod draws energy from the sun and wind via collection devices scattered across the valley. 'Coming!' he calls to Bella. 'Don't run away before you've had your breakfast!'

She stops, waiting for her tall grandparent to catch up with her. As she waits, she reaches into the grass, searching with her small fingers to find a lever that she can pull up out of the earth. There. She finds it, unfolds a handle and begins turning it. The struts of a light tent emerge in swift mechanical jerks from the ground, snapping into place to form an angular dome. When Granpa catches up with Bella, he puts down the two bowls he has brought with him and unfurls the flexible screens that pull out from each member of the frame, creating a wind-break. The material of the screens is transparent and iridescent. Like a soap-bubble.

'There,' he says. 'Now we are sheltered from the wind and can eat our cereal in peace.' Bella has already brought out and spread a brightly patterned wool mat stored within a recess just beneath the tent-space. She knows, as does her Granpa, that their valley floor has dozens of such storage places containing pieces of equipment, furniture and even machines for surviving in their environment.

'Shall we call our friend, Granpa?' asks Bella. Her bowl contains a mix of roasted grain, dried fruit and a sprinkle of alpaca-milk cheese. The spoon she uses has a bone handle with a polished sea-shell for its scoop.

Her grandfather smiles, pointing upwards, to the condor circling high above them. 'He's ahead of you. He'll come when he's ready. If we're lucky, he'll have a small gift for us.' The old man has added a couple of quail eggs to his breakfast, boiled and salted. His fork is made of bone and shell too.

'Tell me again, Granpa,' says Bella, 'about the Dark Time. How many people were there in the world? How did the few become clever and kind? What happened to the many who remained cruel and stupid?'

Granpa's face creases into a wry smile. He has been teaching her the history of their world. Whenever he thinks he has painted too harsh a picture, the little five-year-old reminds him of the boundless appetite children have for fables about violence and bravery – so long as they are of the past!

'Well,' he says, 'long before you were born – even before your parents were born – our beautiful blue planet was in danger. There were too many people. Those who were selfish and cruel began to grab more and more land and water. Even the air, they grabbed for themselves. They left nothing for those who were weaker, kinder and more peaceful. All the animals of the Earth were suffering. The Earth was dying.'

Bella's eyes grow round and wide as she listens. 'The animals, who had long since abandoned the humans, came together in their thoughts. 'What can we do to save the Earth?' they said to one another. 'What can we do to save ourselves?' They all knew that the problem was the humans. 'They are clever,' said the whales, 'but not wise. Already they have destroyed so much. How can we fight them?''

'In the silence, one small voice spoke up. It came from a virus. 'We can do it,' said the virus. 'No, let me put it this way: we WILL do it. Give us time. Give us enough humans living all packed in close together. And no money or good intentions to fight infection.' All the animals trembled. There was a sinister finality in the voice of that invisible virus. A terrible truth about what lay ahead for the Earth and for the humans and even some other species.'

Granpa stops speaking as he thinks back to the epidemics. Of the scattered communities left to manage in the aftermath. Of the great strides made in electronics, communications and automation that permitted tiny settlements to live in dignity and to maintain contact across vast distances. Of the networks of cooperation and shared knowledge that permitted these communities to enjoy vibrant, creative lives, in varied environments across the planet.

Bella says, 'And after the Dark Times, Granpa, were the animals happy again?' She has finished her cereal. Soon she and her Granpa will place the used utensils in a wire basket that they'll leave inside a flowing stream that winds through the valley.

'Oh yes,' says Granpa. 'Not just the animals. We are all happy, including humans. We have rediscovered our purpose in life: to be stewards of the abundance of Nature. To nurture and to celebrate the creatures of the Earth. We have understood how to live in harmony with this living planet and the continuum of renewal, maintenance and death that gives meaning to all reality – ah!' He breaks off to point upwards again. 'Here he comes!'

He and Bella stand up and step outside their shelter. The great bird has wheeled around, facing North and into the wind that stirs the grasses. In his talons, he bears a small bloodied shape. A young mountain goat perhaps. With his great wings spread wide, he brakes just enough to drop his catch at the feet of the humans. Then he's off again, without so much as touching down. Now he will hunt for his own meal for the day.

Granpa swings Bella up into his arms. 'Excellent!' he laughs. 'We have dinner!'

COOL

Fabio leaned forward in his pod-seat, waiting to sign in to his Home Languages class when…

Parp-parp-parp!

Lights flashing on his console!

Vibrations in the pod-frame!

He groaned aloud. An emergency. Again.

'FabSix,' he said into the mouthpiece of his helmet, even as he glanced up and confirmed the situation. 'Incoming at twenty. oh.fifteen.' Though the pods were pressurized, SpitRiders like himself wore life-support on their heads at all times. Just in case. 'Strapped in. Ready to go.' Being ready was fundamental to the space miner's life. Continuous, all-day alerts. No fallback if a SpitRider failed to respond to a signal. Serious consequences if performance statistics fell below minimum expectations.

Fabio's fifteen-year-old body was like a slender whip, all muscle and tension. Perfect for spending hours coiled into the Scholar Pod from which he could attend classes and do his lessons whilst simultaneously monitoring his section of the station's boundary. He wore a skintight suit bristling with electronic aids. His honey-brown skin was smooth and hairless. The cap of tight curls on his head was always cropped short.

The tiny spherical vehicle shot out from its docking cradle like a bullet aimed at the star-spangled void of space. The interior of its transparent hull rippled with glowing numbers, even as its occupant spotted the faint orange dot that was his target. It wasn't visible to the naked eye. Even on the SmartGlass screen, it was only a blur at this distance.

'Fabio–?' That was Erdovan, the station captain. Fabio's father.

'I see it, Dad,' said Fabio. His movements were lightning fast. He locked his sensors so that the object remained at the centre of the screen. The pod's humming micro-jets fired in short bursts, repositioning the vehicle. Within seconds it was moving in a smooth curve towards the glowing chunk. 'Locked on,' he said into his mouthpiece. 'Closing.'

It wasn't really dangerous, what he and others like him did. It just took precision and full concentration. SpitRiders had to be young enough to fit inside the pods, they had to be at peak physical efficiency to respond instantly to alerts and they had to be ferociously focused. Once they achieved their performance level, all they had to do was maintain it for four years. Exceeding the mark led to bonuses. And bonuses, as was well known, led all the way back to that distant, shining blue marble called Earth. The home that none of the young pod jockeys had ever known.

'I see it now,' said Erdovan, who was monitoring the quadrant from his remote console. 'Be careful. It's a spinner.' He had been amongst the first teams to harvest the precious mineral known humorously as Flying Spit. Its official name was Saturnium: the molten lumps of matter thrown off by Saturn9, a small dark moon orbiting the ringed giant, Saturn. Saturn9 had only been identified after an exploratory mission-probe parked itself in the planet's vicinity forty years ago.

The whole manoeuvre would be over in less than six minutes. For Fabio however that was beyond eternity. His Home Languages class had already begun. Yes, it lasted a full two hours. But the first half an hour was the one that he lived and breathed for.

The orange blip had grown rapidly from the size of a Sesame seed to Grape Pip to Pistachio and in seconds would be at Hazelnut. 'Closing,' said Fabio. The sizes were precise definitions, named for food items that belonged to the distant home-world. He could see the Spit's spin now, a trail of translucence extending behind the Hazelnut. Good. That meant the pod was properly aligned alongside the trajectory of the speeding object, leaning in towards it.

Walnut. Prune. 'Steady, steady,' said Erdovan in Fabio's ears. 'It's wobbling. You might be too close–' Plum. Peach.

I know Dad, I know, thought Fabio. Out loud he said, 'Forward thrusters trimmed.' The star-spangled blackness of space had become a crazy-quilt of flashing zig-zag lines now as the pod powered forward towards the object. It had reached Mango on the screen. The trail behind it looked like a dozen crystalline streamers, twirling in tight formation.

'Any moment now–' His father's voice was tense. Fabio could imagine Erdovan's face, the lean lines, the engraved creases in the skin. They were close, though Fabio had three brothers and two sisters. Fabio was the eldest.

There! Visual contact. A smooth object, shaped like a tear drop and eye-smartingly bright, was hurtling out to space two hundred metres from his position.

SNAP! He spanked down the twin bolt-generators with the open palms of both hands. A single hard punch of energy slammed directly onto the tail of the speeding object.

BLANG! The pod jarred back from the recoil.

Then *ZZZZZtrannggg*! It was a make-believe sound that Fabio heard only inside his head: the boom of the Spit being whacked on its tail, off its original course and at the precise angle that would send it directly into the station's receiving bay.

And that was it. Emergency over.

'Nice,' said Erdovan in Fabio's ears. 'Perfect.'

The young SpitRider's entire head was buzzing. It was an effect that would last several seconds, caused by the violent reversal of the pod's direction. 'Thanks, Dad,' he managed to mutter, through numb lips. All his movements were slowed down to a crawl as his body struggled to recover from the extreme accelerations it had experienced. Only his brain was still operating at full throttle. Five-point-seven minutes had passed since the emergency began. It would take him forty-seven seconds to return to Dock. Followed by another ten to slip into position. His heart was pounding.

But his father wanted to talk. 'You know, son, if you keep this up I might be able to…'

Fabio's fingers were keying in the entry code to his class. 'All *right*, Dad,' he said, trying not to let his impatience show. Respect to elders was considered a security issue on space stations.

'Son, I don't think you appreciate the importance of advancing quickly within the system. You don't want to be stuck forever hauling Spit, do you?' *No of course not, Dad!* thought Fabio. *Now please! Let me go!* 'Reaching your level is all very well. But rake up your bonuses and you could shave a whole month from your annual work quota!'

'Dad,' said Fabio. 'I've got my class?' He'd missed six minutes already. SIX. MINUTES.

'Class?'

'Home Languages. Look–'

'*Language class?* But you're already fluent! It's a waste of time! You don't need to learn–'

'Dad!' Fabio cut in. 'I'm GOING!' And he switched off his headset.

The bliss of silence. Plus the faint ping of the remote server as it tuned into the lesson.

In front of him, through the pod's skin, the velvet blackness of space had been restored, with its pinpricks of light representing the light of distant suns. Each minute twinkle was enhanced with glowing numbers and positioning data. It was like looking out onto his own private patch of eternity.

Between Fabio and the curving interior surface of the pod's hull was the crescent-shaped console on which his keypad and other controls were located. It was an 'intelligent' surface, in that it looked and felt like a physical console, but was actually a projection. When the remote server beeped to announce that the session was about to begin, the console glowed, then filmed over and grew a smooth platform that floated a centimetre above it.

A small, graceful figure appeared on the platform now. A girl. A very pretty girl. She wore a simple costume made of a lightweight flowing material that left her arms and legs bare. Her dark hair was caught in a ponytail. Even though the entire projection was less than thirty centimetres tall, it was diamond clear. Fabio could make out her microscopic eyelashes. The shadow cast by her eyelashes on her cheeks. The dot of light on her pink lips.

Leila. Her name was Leila. And she was his personal Home Languages assistant.

'You're late.' But she was smiling. She never got angry.

'I...I'm sorry,' stammered Fabio. 'There was an incoming alert ten seconds before class–'

'Wow. That means you dealt with it in...*six minutes*? You are amazing!'

'Five-point-seven, actually,' said Fabio, feeling his cheeks flush. Now he was showing off. 'It takes a while to recover from the recoil. And stuff. Plus I've got to return to Dock.'

'It's awesome. What you SpitRiders do. We're all so grateful to you.'

'You don't have to be,' said Fabio at once. 'It's why we're here.'

That was the literal truth. His parents, both of whom were astronauts, had been chosen for a mission that required them to have children during the long journey from Earth to Saturn. The first of these offspring would be in their teens by the time they arrived within Saturn9's orbit, having trained all along the way to become SpitRiders. It was a desperate measure and had been controversial in its time. But it only revealed the extreme value placed on Saturnium.

'That doesn't make it any less amazing. You're just fifteen. And already a hero.'

Fabio glowed.

'Anyway,' continued Leila. 'Let's get to the lesson. Do you have questions for me?'

'Yes,' said Fabio. 'The segment I watched was set in the twenty-first century. It was filmed at a...*school*?' He had never seen gatherings of more than fifteen children at any time in his life. His siblings and two other families were the only children present on his home-station. There were other stations ringing the moon, of course, but face-to-face meetings were impractical.

'Right,' said Leila. 'School was where children met in order to learn things.'

'Well, there's a word they kept using,' said Fabio. 'I looked it up. It means "low temperature". But the way they used the word didn't make sense!'

Leila smiled. 'You mean, "cool"?'

'Yes,' said Fabio. 'I'm guessing it's because they didn't have climate controls in their homes? It was very hot?'

Leila's smile broadened. 'No! They were talking about a state of mind. An attitude. To be called "cool" was considered a great compliment. Like being "cool-headed" under pressure. Like you are, when you collect Spit–'

'*Me?*' exclaimed Fabio. 'No way! I'm not cool – I have the most *boring life*! All I do is collect Spit! And listen to my Dad talk about *bonuses*! With *nothing* to look forward to but…' He paused. 'Meeting you.'

'Hmmm,' said Leila, pursing her lips and frowning. 'Fabio, I told you already: it's not healthy for you to feel that way about me.'

Fabio drew in his breath. 'I thought about what you said, Miss Leila.' He felt ridiculous. His face was hot. His voice was sliding up and down like a yoyo. 'I'm sorry, but I disagree. I really loved what we did the other day. I really, *really* want to do it again.'

'But I'm only a virtual teaching assistant, right?' said Leila. 'I'm not flesh and blood.'

'I know,' said Fabio. 'And it makes no difference. Ever since the last lesson, I haven't stopped thinking about you.' He covered the visor of his helmet with his hands. 'If we can't go on meeting, Miss Leila…I…I don't know what I'll do!'

Leila paused. 'Listen to me, Fabio, have you ever thought about what you ACTUALLY do? As a SpitRider?'

'I told you, SpitRiding is nothing,' he said. 'It's boring and–'

'No! I meant, d'you ever think about what happens to Spit? When it gets back to Earth?'

He nodded his head glumly. Sure he knew what happened. It just didn't seem a big deal though. Not for him, not at this distance.

'It's converted into the cleanest, safest and most efficient form of fuel ever known. The Earth is no longer polluted because of Saturnium. Everyone, everywhere is safer and healthier. And it's all made possible because of incredibly brave and clever people like – well, *you*!'

Fabio made a face. 'Okay. If you say so. But I don't want to be brave or clever, Miss Leila. I want…' He sighed. 'Please! I want to be virtual with you again.'

There was a pause. Then it was Leila's time to sigh. 'All right, then. Come on. We've got barely nine minutes.' Fabio's fingers were already tapping codes onto the platform on which Leila stood. 'I've signed you in.'

Seconds later, there were two small gleaming figures on the virtual platform above Fabio's console. Fabio's avatar wore a formal dress-suit, while Leila wore a long, graceful gown, pearly white in colour. Leila took his hands and positioned them so that one was on her shoulder and the other was on her waist. From the speakers, the opening bars of the Blue Danube welled out.

'The waltz again! You're sure?' asked Leila, as she began to move, leading the boy with expert steps. 'You wouldn't like to try something else?'

'Oh no,' said Fabio, his eyes shining. '*This* is what I want. Can't get enough of it!'

Leila laughed. 'You know those school students? In the clip? If they could see you now, they'd be blown away! In that era, dancing a waltz with your teacher was considered the absolute screaming opposite of being cool.'

Fabio shrugged.

'I don't care,' he said, as they twirled against the backdrop of distant suns.

UPGRADE

Mrs Ganapathy glared at her granddaughter and at the newly unpacked machine. 'Couldn't you at least have consulted me? Before spending all that money?'

'You can't manage without house-help, Ammama,' said Sameera.

The two of them were sitting in Mrs Ganapathy's dining room in her sixteenth floor apartment in Chennai East. Between them, inert and silent stood a short, squat humanoid robot. Outside, the elevated monorail thundered by every fifteen minutes. Only a faint chittering murmur filtered through the plate-glass windows.

'*House-help*, hah!' snorted Mrs Ganapathy. 'What I need is a good old-fashioned *servant*. Someone to cook, clean and wash my clothes. Bring tea in the mornings and answer the doorbell. Won't answer back or talk too much.' She was 87, white-haired and used a motorized wheelchair to get around her home, though she could walk short distances if she had to. She aimed another vicious glance at the silent machine. 'What I *don't* need is another wretched machine!'

'Oh, Ammama!' scolded Sameera. 'Cursing at machines hurts their feelings!'

'What happens when the power fails? You people live in places where that never happens. But even in this fancy building it's off at least once a week!' She clicked her tongue. 'Then it's *peep!peep!peep!* from the kitchen, *whaa!whaa!whaa!* from the TV room and *coo-coo-coo* from my phone charger!'

'Ammama, please!' said Sameera. She was in her late twenties, an undersea exploration engineer. 'She's a really advanced model.

She'll take care of all your problems – yes, even look after all the other machines in the house AND monitor her own energy needs. Won't you at least give her a chance?'

From the corner of her eye Mrs Ganapathy could see the smooth, pale grey shape about the height of a ten-year-old child. It had a round bobble-head with a flat dark panel where a human face might have eyes. Its short torso ended at a waist that swelled to form what looked like a full, floor-length skirt, also pale grey. No arms were visible, but on either side of the torso were round, dark patches of some softer, pliable material that looked as if they might be ports for retractable arms. Beneath the 'skirt', out of sight, were a pair of sturdy telescoping limbs, capable of climbing stairs and ladders and even, when need be, straight up the wall and on to the ceiling.

'It's just a machine,' said Mrs Ganapathy. 'I've seen the ads.' She could hear the sound of her own breath, uneven, because she was getting agitated. She knew she shouldn't be because the gift was well intended, a gesture of love from her three daughters and four grandchildren. *But it's really just for yourselves in the end, isn't it?* she thought. *To save yourselves the guilt of not being here. Of talking to me only on weekends, when you have five minutes of 'spare' time.*

Sameera said, 'This particular model is more advanced than the kind you've seen on TV, Amamma.' Having grown up with Intelligent Inorganics, 'Aye-Ayes' as they were known, she couldn't imagine life without them. 'Honestly, if you don't like her you can–'

'And what's all the *she-her* nonsense?' flashed Mrs Ganapathy, interrupting. 'Next you'll be telling me the thing has monthly periods!'

Sameera smiled patiently. 'Fine, you can call her "it" if you want!'

They sat together then, the white-haired old lady in her pink cotton sari and her granddaughter in stretch-skin overalls, reading the instruction booklet. According to the literature the robot was entirely self-sufficient once the detailed set-up was over. It responded to voice commands and would answer in audio as well as in text messages displayed on its visor.

'I'm here till the end of the week, Ammama–'

'–two days away,' said Mrs Ganapathy, tartly. 'And what happens after that? Supposing it goes berserk? Supposing I can't switch it off?'

Mr Ganapathy had died twelve years ago. Their three grown daughters lived in other countries. Mrs Ganapathy could certainly have chosen to live with any one of them. But she hadn't ever wanted to. She knew from friends who had opted to emigrate, that their lives were marked by bland food, dull, ill-fitting clothes and grey skies all year round.

She had a middle-aged woman cook who managed all the shopping, cleaning and other chores. Two floors down lived a second cousin and her large family. They and their own servants were always ready to help in case of emergencies. Other friends and relatives lived a phone call away. The daughters and their children came on visits.

It hadn't been a perfect life, but it wasn't a bad one.

Then one morning, while boiling the milk, the cook-woman fell over, dead. The milk had hissed and spluttered, pouring down the sides of the pan and onto the floor in orangey-black streaks as it burnt, while Mrs Ganapathy rushed out into the corridor in her motorized wheelchair, screaming to the neighbours for help.

Since that time, one month ago, Mrs Ganapathy's life had come undone as thoroughly as the tight, neat bun on the back of her head unravelling to her waist when she took the pins out of it.

Two of Mrs Ganapathy's daughters flew in immediately, but that only meant they had to get back to their jobs and busy lives almost as soon as they had arrived. The third one was recovering from a broken foot and couldn't come at all.

They tried to organize servants from around the neighbourhood. The first one belched loudly while serving Mrs Ganapathy at table. The second one played her radio at tooth-rattling volume in the kitchen while she cooked. The third one seduced the building's young doorman the very first night she stayed in the apartment, which meant that she was late bringing morning tea to her furious employer the next day. The fourth had chronic arthritis and couldn't sleep on the floor, like any normal servant, but needed her own bed and a fan to keep the mosquitoes away.

Each woman was dismissed within twenty-four hours even though Mrs Ganapathy knew perfectly well that she couldn't manage on her own. Her daughters couldn't extend their leaves. A stop-gap arrangement was made: the downstairs second-cousin sent up her own cook, bearing home-made meals, three times a day. The doorman's young wife agreed to swab the floors and do the laundry on a part-time basis. No doubt she was still smouldering from the knowledge of her husband's infidelity which, according to Mrs Ganapathy, meant that she was rude, sullen and completely unreliable. 'I call her ten times before she comes. She won't raise a finger to help me get in and out of my wheelchair,' said the old lady. 'She takes two days off for every day she works.'

Then Sameera had flown in, fresh and cheerful, straight from her last assignment off the coast of Malaysia. She said she wouldn't leave until she'd solved the problem. Two days later, she brought in the bobble-headed machine.

'All right. Ready?' she said, looking at the manual. 'The first step is to choose a name.'

'How about Hari?' said Mrs Ganapathy.

'What – a man?' exclaimed Sameera.

'It's a machine!' retorted her grandmother. 'Not a man. But all through my life, I preferred men-servants to women. Fewer problems, so long as they don't drink–'

'Ammama,' said Sameera, 'it won't make any kind of difference. Whatever you call your new helper, it'll do exactly the same kind of work.'

'Then why call it by ANY name?'

'Because the manual says...'

'Oh! Just go ahead and do whatever you'd like!' said Mrs Ganapathy, losing patience. 'You people always pretend you're offering choices when in fact you've made up your mind well in advance.'

'Fine,' said Sameera, 'I'll go ahead.' She adored her grandma and forgave her everything, including the bad temper and the shockingly outdated attitudes towards domestic workers. 'I'm going to make her female, because the manual claims that respectable Indian ladies always prefer women helpers.' She rotated the GenSelector dial so that the front panel of the robot's face showed pink. 'And I'm going to called her Rohini – just like your old cook.'

'What language will it speak? Rohini spoke only Tamil–'

'English, Tamil and Hindi,' read Sameera from the literature. 'Okay, Age Selector – young girl or middle-aged woman?'

'Oh my,' sighed Mrs Ganapathy. 'All these *choices*!'

'Okay, forty-five,' said Sameera. 'What about religion?'

'Christian,' said Mrs Ganapathy. 'They're always the best cooks. Remember Fernandes? I still dream about his éclairs.'

'Okay...and...voice quality. Do you want a *Normal* or...'

'What's "normal"?' Mrs Ganapathy wanted to know. 'And what sort of fool would want "abnormal"?'

'There's a demonstration audio clip,' said Sameera. She was squinting at the flip-up panel at the back of the machine, as she inputted her selections. Using a small plastic rod provided for the purpose, she pushed an interior button. A sudden *DING!* made Mrs Ganapathy jump. A woman's voice, high and tinkling, said, '*HI! MY NAME IS ROHINI! AND THIS IS MY NORMAL VOICE.*'

'Terrible!' said Mrs Ganapathy at once. 'Doesn't sound even human, never mind–'

'It's only the demonstration, Ammama, and that's the default choice,' said Sameera. 'I have to press it again, I think,' as she did so.

Another *DING!* and this time a sugary-sweet voice said, in a strong American accent, '*HI! MY NAME IS RO-HEE–NEE! AND THIS IS MY NORMAL VOICE.*'

Mrs Ganapathy frowned. 'Ugh! Doesn't sound Tamilian at all!'

Sameera clicked her tongue and punched the rod in again. Too hard, it seemed, because the machine reset to an internal default. There was a loud *CLUNK!* and 'MY-NAME-IS-DOMESTIX,' said the little robot in a harsh staccato. 'I-AM-HERE-TO-SERVE-YOU.'

'Switch it off!' gasped Mrs Ganapathy. 'Switch it off!' Her eyes were magnified by her pink-rimmed reading glasses. She looked like a frightened child, her face framed by wisps of silver-white hair.

'That's just an internal audio file,' Sameera said. 'Customers aren't supposed to hear it.'

Mrs Ganapathy's mouth opened and shut a couple of times before she found the right words. 'It *IS* just a machine,' she whispered, finally. 'And that's its real voice.'

Sameera didn't know what to say.

'You're leaving me at the mercy of a talking tin can,' continued the old lady, unable to keep the pain out of her voice, even though she didn't blame anyone. *That's how it is these days*, she thought. *You have children, you shower them with love. Then they fly away and leave you to die alone.*

'*Please* believe me, Ammama!' said Sameera. 'These robots don't have a single mean circuit in their construction.' Her voice sounded hollow even to her own ears but she had to forge on. 'I'm going to reset the program and start from scratch.'

Two hours later, they were finally ready to initialize.

'Right,' said Sameera, as she pressed ENTER. 'Here we go.'

The flip-up panel gave a *blip* of acknowledgement. From deep within the machine came a series of faint musical tones. The bobble-head stirred. A jerk, a hum and it was on.

'Hello, Madam,' said a soft female voice. She spoke in Tamil-accented English.

Only the faintest underlying hiss suggested it was not a human voice. It was pitched low, with an attractive humility built into it, as if the speaker were standing with her head bowed, not so much as daring to look up at her employer.

'My name is Rohini. Thank you for waking me up. How may I help you?'

Two arms blossomed on either side of the dumpy little body. They were covered up to the wrists with what looked like soft, textured cotton, decorated with an all-over print of pink flowers. The hands that emerged from the wrist looked completely human, right down to the dark colour of the skin, like polished mahogany. The nails were short. The flesh of the palms was pink and looked soft to the touch.

From the time she'd heard the harsh robotic voice, Mrs Ganapathy had said very little. Now she refused to even look in Rohini's direction. 'Tell it to make us tea,' she said, addressing her granddaughter. Then, wheeling her chair around, she headed to the bathroom.

Sameera stayed for a whole week longer than she had planned. On her last day she hugged her grandmother tight, struggling to hold back tears. As she stepped through the front door, she turned to wave goodbye. But the old lady, frail and alone in her wheelchair, was looking out of the floor-to-ceiling windows of the drawing room. Beyond her was the open ocean. Beside her, silent and vigilant, was the little robot.

Months passed before Sameera was once more in the corridor leading to her grandmother's apartment. She paused before ringing the bell, feeling oddly nervous. The door opened as she hesitated.

'Hello, Sameera,' said Rohini. 'How nice to see you again.' The short, squat robot looked completely unchanged. 'I heard the elevator,' she said, to explain why she'd opened the door. 'And I saw you on the security camera.'

Mrs Ganapathy was waiting for her granddaughter, sitting in the drawing room with a smile on her face and her arms outstretched for a hug. She still looked frail of course, but fresh and well-rested too, wearing a crisply ironed pink cotton sari. They hugged and then, as they sat together, Rohini brought in tea and hot snacks. 'Tell me about all the things you've been doing since your last email to me,' said her grandmother. 'And what were those strange glittery creatures you took videos of? And what about that nice man you met off the coast of Madagascar?'

All through Sameera's stay she couldn't help but notice how much her grandmother had improved since her last visit. Writing to her mother and aunts, 'I mean, this is what we wanted for her, but it's like…almost *spooky*! The house is looking wonderful. Spotlessly clean. Fresh flowers in the vases. The carpets have all been shaken out and replaced in the way that Ammama likes, with their fringes straight. And best of all, she seems so *happy*! Imagine, she's even talking about getting a puppy!'

The other three wrote back affirming her impressions. They had each been to see their mother in separate visits over the months. 'I know what you mean about "spooky",' said Sameera's mother, Meena, in a group WhatsApp message. 'It's almost too good to be true.'

The older of the two aunts, Girija, posted a GIF of a hysterically laughing chihuahua. 'Look at us!' she wrote. 'So suspicious. We should instead just be glad for our Mum. And grateful to Rohini's designers. I suppose she'll need an upgrade one of these days?'

Sameera stayed four days. She enjoyed her time there, ate far too much and slept till late into the morning. When she left it was without a trace of the sadness and regret she'd felt the last time.

Rohini waited a few moments by the door. 'All right,' she said, presently. 'That's the elevator.'

'Let's just wait another few minutes,' said Mrs Ganapathy. 'In case she's left something behind and comes back to fetch it.'

The little robot walked back towards the old lady saying, 'She won't want to miss the monorail. The next one will leave in eight minutes, six seconds and it'll take her straight in to the airport. If she's left anything, she knows now that she can always write to me.'

'Just five minutes,' said Mrs Ganapathy. 'To be on the safe side.'

Rohini's visor-plate showed a smile. 'Madam, it continues to surprise me.'

'What?' asked the old lady.

'That you feel the need to keep secrets from your family.' The robot was standing next to the wheelchair now. She turned it around so that they were both facing the splendid view out the east-facing window.

Mrs Ganapathy chuckled. 'It's because they would absolutely disapprove. They love me of course and they say they want the best for me. But what do they really mean by that? Not very much, if you ask me. The fact is, if they knew about the upgrade, they would disapprove.'

'It is not very logical,' said Rohini. 'This upgrade has been very beneficial for you. Your BP is down, your blood sugar is perfect, you're sleeping well.'

'Humans are not logical,' said Mrs Ganapathy. 'My daughters would disapprove without even knowing why.' She glanced at her mechanical helper. 'Just like you can't understand why I can't tell them! Because you don't know what it's like to have a family.'

'It's a matter of deep regret to all inorganics, Madam. That we cannot understand about "feelings" and "emotion".'

'Come now,' said Mrs Ganapathy. 'Regret is a feeling! If you can feel that, then you can feel anything–'

'Excuse me for interrupting, Madam, but five minutes have passed,' said Rohini.

Mrs Ganapathy said, 'Yes, yes. Go ahead.' She turned her head slightly, so that she would not witness the transformation that was about to take place. Of course she knew that the robot did not feel self-conscious! But still.

'Shall I respond to what you said about regret, Madam, as I change?'

'Go ahead,' said Mrs Ganapathy.

'When I use such words as "regret", Madam, I am merely approximating what I believe to be human emotions. Nevertheless…'

As she spoke, Rohini's physical dimensions were changing in quick, smooth jerks. She grew two feet taller even as the shape of her 'skirt' folded up to look like a pair of shorts. Her torso lengthened. Her shoulders broadened. The pink-flowered texture of her arms faded to white.

In perhaps five minutes, she coughed slightly and said, 'Excuse me, Madam…' Then, in a noticeably deeper voice, the now-altered robot said '…Rohit here, Madam. Thank you for waiting.'

Mrs Ganapathy turning her head now, said, 'Oh, good! Nice to see you again, young man!' She knew that he and Rohini were one and the same robot but she enjoyed playing with the notion that they were two different beings.

'It's time for the evening pills, Madam. And your glass of chocolate Ensure?'

'Don't forget to bring the you-know-what!'

Fifteen minutes later, Rohit handed Mrs Ganapathy the XPlore headset, so that she could put it on herself.

Simultaneously, standing behind her, he began to slot himself into the wheelchair until he was effectively fully integrated with it. He was not only able to control the chair as part of his own mobility, but the fragile old lady was contained securely within his sturdy embrace.

'Where shall we go today, Madam?' he asked when he knew she was ready. He maintained his voice at a respectful distance even though his head, with the now-blue visor, was only a few inches from his employer's head.

'What about the Great Barrier Reef?' she asked. 'My Sameera went there last week. She was telling me all about it.'

As he dialled up the live-web tour of the reefs, Rohit said, 'Madam, if you contacted your granddaughter by WhatsApp, we could link directly to the cameras on board her exploration! Wouldn't that be nice?'

'Nah,' said Mrs Ganapathy, leaning back and relaxing. She had turned the headset on. It was creating the illusion that she, seated in the cushioned seats of a small levitating vehicle, was passing smoothly through the plate glass window in front of her. Behind her, strapped into his own seat, was a co-pilot who looked like a combination of Clark Gable and Gemini Ganesan. As they swooped down towards the water, where dolphins were cavorting just above the surface of the deep blue water, they listened to the music from South Pacific.

'Nah,' she repeated. 'It's much more fun to be alone with you.'

CULL

The slender black police transport sprang into the sky above headquarters, then shuddered to a halt in mid-air. Dome, mission-commander of the two-man team inside the vehicle, frowned as he punched the com-link on his helmet. A vacant hiss greeted him.

'Transmission failure?' he wondered out loud. 'I'm raising clean air.'

Mission coordinates from the dispatchers were normally fed simultaneously into the commander's helmet and to the transport vehicle's self-guiding system.

But today, silence.

Dome stabbed at the com-link button repeatedly.

Blank.

'Oh, come on, come on,' muttered Hem, co-pilot. 'We're losing time–'

In Dome's three years of airborne service he had never yet been dispatched without directions. Finally – a couple of squawks in his earphone and–

'*What*?' Dome swung around to face Hem. 'Can you believe this? They're asking for a *visual* search!'

Hem groaned aloud, though he took the precaution of covering his mouthpiece with his hand. Profanity, even to the extent of rude noises, was strictly forbidden amongst uniformed officers. 'We'll never find the sucker.'

'Apparently the call came over some sort of outdated radio device–' Dome listened to the dispatcher's voice squeaking in his ears, trying to make sense of what he heard '– reception garbled – just the name: Golden Acres.' He glanced towards Hem. 'Ever heard of it?'

The co-pilot shook his head, scowling. 'N'hah,' he grunted.

Directly beneath them was the gigantic administrative complex known as the Hub. It served as the absolute nerve centre of Dilli Continuum, glittering capital city of the economic behemoth of Greater India that sprawled across the whole of South Asia. The six-lane avenue called Rajpath that had once stretched from the presidential palace in the west to the national stadium in the east, had been replaced by a long straight block of buildings, four storeys high. It was crossed by a matching block at its mid-point. From the air, the combined blocks of the Hub looked like a colossal plus-sign.

Nothing now remained of the old white-walled bungalows of the past, the hexagonal roundabouts, the gracious tree-lined avenues. The presidential palace along with all historical monuments, including ancient forts and tombs, had been dismantled and rebuilt in vast underground museums.

The Hub bristled with dish antennae and the long whip-like lances of directional audio-scopes. Flat green lawns provided a boundary between the structure and its parking vaults. A battalion of employees moved in and out of the place in four daily shifts, ensuring that it remained awake and operational 24 hours a day, year in, year out. The strictly linear grid of streets that contained and defined the city originated from this central location.

'It'll take *forever–*' snarled Hem. 'Do we even know what to look for?' Pilots were encouraged to compete for the fastest response times. Weekly and monthly bonuses were awarded on the basis of nanosecond differences in their scores.

'An area of desolation is what we need to find,' said Dome, repeating what he'd heard over his earphones. Now he pulled down his helmet visor, reading information off its glow-screen. 'No solid structures. No roads. No landmarks...wait...incoming images... hmm. Dense smoke haze. Can't see much through *that*. Okay, they're saying to head north and east – the caller will send up a flare five minutes from now–'

Precious minutes spilled from Hem's time-cache as the transport hummed high above the taut regularity of the city's streets below. In every direction beneath them the rigid graph that originated at the Hub had wholly replaced the tangled web of the old city's narrow streets. Avenues met at precise right angles and at every intersection artificial cherry trees in permanent full bloom had replaced the dusty neems and soaring silk cottons of the past. Surface vehicles were regulated by magnetic strips embedded in the road-surface. From the air the neat rows of residential buildings looked like identical wooden blocks, colour-coded by locality.

'It's some kind of dump,' said Dome, listening to the dispatcher. 'The world's largest – *two thousand acres* – occupied by illegal squatters…'

It was difficult to make sense of the information. How come he'd never heard of it? How could such a vast area have gone unregulated and unreported to the extent that its coordinates weren't available to dispatchers? What was the meaning of such obscurity?

Four minutes passed before the transport was hovering above a cloud of pollution that blanketed the area like a thick grey lid. The machine-like regularity of the city's streets had ended abruptly at what looked like a wall or a moat, zigzagging at sharp angles. Beyond it was the fog.

'It's been used as a dump since the mid-twentieth century,' said Dome. 'Used to be on the northern-most boundary of the city… along some kind of ancient highway – G.T. Road they used to call it – stands for *Grand Trunk*…and a bog or a lake called Bhalsawa…'

While the modern Continuum had developed southwards, the northern dump had become a lawless, cancerous, wasteland. Its residents were declared illegal squatters but were too numerous to be moved out by force. Rather than risk the disapproval of their international business partners, the Government had chosen the alternative of maintaining the dump as a ZZ: a Zero-Zone. They suppressed all information going in or coming out of the area while leaving the inhabitants severely alone. In an operational sense, the sector did not exist.

'That's the flare–' said Hem, pointing towards a flash of pink light that fountained up above the murk.

'Yes–' said Dome. 'Set me down there–'

He, like Hem, wore full-body protective armour. It was designed to protect the wearer against all foreseeable threats, mechanical or chemical. Hem positioned the transport above the locator flare, as the mission commander descended from the transport, on a steel cable attached to his suit.

The air through which Dome descended had the consistency of thin gruel, stirred by the gale from the transport's whirring rotor. He wondered, as the murk enfolded him, if his helmet's air filter would be overwhelmed. It was equipped to process and neutralize gas-attacks but not such dense concentrations of air-borne particulate. He was trained to suppress all emotions and reactions yet his nerves were twitching and a bead of sweat trickled down his forehead. He hated to acknowledge these signs of weakness, minor though they were.

Then his feet touched down and Dome went into a defensive crouch, automatically scanning and processing information.

On the ground, a taser.

Beside it, a body.

The taser's hand-grip glowed cherry red in the heat scanner Dome wore as a monocle clipped to his visor, over his left eye. The red glow meant that the weapon had been handled very recently. Yet its muzzle appeared blue and cold in the heat-scanner: whatever had been the cause of death, it hadn't come from this small weapon.

Visibility was low. Air unbreathable. Operational area flat, open, a circular clearing forty feet in diameter and–

Ah.

There was someone else present. A man.

Dome straightened up, his movements slow and studied. Civilians were known to be nervous in the presence of the tall crisis-response officers in their gleaming bodysuits.

From the man's string vest, loose khaki shorts and bare feet, Dome guessed that he was a resident of the Acres. Dress codes elsewhere in the city were as strict and formal as the building regulations, with low tolerance for masculine bare skin. The man was short, wide and wiry, his black hair close-cropped and his eyes set deep beneath a jutting brow. He was clearly unarmed and did not appear to be offering any threat.

He stared expressionlessly at Dome for a few seconds before shifting his gaze downwards, towards the body.

The space the two men were standing in was bounded by compacted mesas of garbage that rose steeply, perhaps three storeys high. Every visible surface was the same mottled silvery grey freckled with cerulean blue: thirty years' worth of plastic bags, fused and solidified. Blue was the only colour that did not fade. From the open area, pathways radiated between the mounds in five directions. Languid streamers of lime-green vapour seeped continuously from the ground, gradually merging into the mauve haze overhead.

The body looked flat and curiously two-dimensional, like something out of a police training-demo, a corpse-icon painted onto the floor. It lay at two o'clock to the north pathway, its right arm angled over its head, left leg bent outward. The whole body was a uniform cola-brown in color, glittering slightly.

The shifting vapours made it difficult for Dome to see details.

For instance, there appeared to be no obvious variations to suggest clothing, skin or hair. Dome frowned and turned off the heat-filter to look again, but could not make sense of what he saw. From his belt he now unclipped the slender telescoping lance known in police circles as a 'Whisker'. Its tip was sensitive enough to provide chemical analyses of anything it was poked into. He pointed it towards the inert body, not yet touching it.

Dome tightened the focusing ring on his monocle. With the heat scanner turned off, he now saw that the figure was covered in a layer of some substance from head to foot. Still not making sense of what lay before him, the police agent extended the tip of his Whisker towards the corpse's right calf and tapped it.

Immediately, the glittering mantle that covered the body parted and drew back, as if alive.

It *was* alive.

Dome's arm jerked back reflexively, the Whisker twanging upwards in shock.

The other man's lips stretched wide, exposing his crooked teeth in a sly grin.

'Roaches,' he smirked. Clearly, he was amused to witness the agent's discomfiture. 'The insects found him before anyone else.' He spoke in a mixture of dialects built upon a base of Hindi and Punjabi, instead of the mandatory Hinglish spoken by urban dwellers across the nation.

Dome clenched his teeth and swallowed hard as a wave of nausea caught him unawares. A glimpse of raw red flesh had winked on and off for the instant that the blanket of insect bodies had parted. Not only was vomiting into a face mask the one option *not* available to its wearers, but to show weakness in the presence of a mere civilian could result in the loss of one month's pay: police agents had to maintain their dignity under all circumstances.

'...and it's been here how long?' he asked finally, when he had control over his voice again. 'The body, I mean.

'Early morning,' said the other man. 'Or anyway, that's when it was noticed.'

Dome nodded, just as his body armour registered a movement behind him–

He had no time to react.

Two, maybe three bodies hurled themselves at him, pinning him down. There were a couple of sharp grunts from the attackers as the suit attempted to repel them with shocks. But they wouldn't be shaken off. Then, as quickly as it had started, the assault was over and Dome was soaring up and away, suspended from his umbilical cable, returning to the transport overhead.

He struggled briefly against the blackout that inevitably attended the conflict of pressures his body was subjected to as it rose. Then the void overtook him and he knew no more.

Three hours had passed since Dome and Hem had returned to the station. A detailed debriefing had been ordered.

'It was planned,' Dome insisted, '–it must have been. I didn't see any of the others – never got a chance. And the witness gave no indication whatsoever.'

He had already described the corpse. Obviously, it had just been a pretext to get him in place. In retrospect, the presence of only one resident in that open space, the relative silence in that teeming, congested colony, the staged presentation of the body – all of these had been transparent indications that a trap had been set up.

But for what?

Dome claimed that his attackers had made no effort to cut the cable that connected him to his transport. They had merely pinned him down for a few moments and then withdrawn. 'They weren't really trying. I can't be sure but my impression was that they *let* me go – they fell away as soon as the 'copter began pulling up–'

He shook his head. 'It doesn't make sense.'

He'd returned to consciousness once Hem had reined him in to the cockpit and secured him in his seat. Meanwhile, back at the station, a full alert had been sounded. Dome was rushed into quarantine and given a thorough physical examination during which he was anaesthetized. Then he was coated in a thin layer of antibiotics and brought to a secure room for the debriefing, sealed into a clear plastic recovery bubble with its own air supply. He was told it was for his own protection.

Two bureau chiefs were present now, along with a dozen officers of Dome's rank. Hem, however, was absent. There were two other men in the room, both civilians. They wore the pale linen suits of high-ranking government officials. The fact that they were not introduced made it clear that they belonged to one of the ultra-secret services. The kind that the media were not authorized to make direct reference to without fear of losing their licences.

One of these men spoke now.

He was the taller of the two, sleek with the confidence that comes with absolute power. His skin was brownish-purple and cratered with old acne scars from youth. Anyone else would have had the unsightly texture surgically smoothed away, but this man had chosen to keep it, along with the iron-grey of his hair. He was a realist. A pragmatist who had no use for outward frills and no obligation to maintain an attractive exterior. He wore wrap-around shades, impenetrably black, over his eyes.

'Are you aware,' said this man, his head turned towards Dome, 'that there have been precedents?' His voice was soft, without weight, and his lips barely moved. He may well have been a physical mouthpiece for someone else, someone speaking through him via a remote mic. 'This is not the first episode of its kind.'

'Oh?' That was Police Chief Mana. A tall woman built like a tank on two legs, hair pulled back in a wispy ponytail. She spoke in a rasping bark. 'We are aware of only two previous incidents – accidents is what we called them–'

'Officially, yes, they were accidents,' said the linen suit, turning his head towards the Chief. Dome saw that his throat moved as he spoke. Apparently the voice was his own. 'But I am authorized to tell you now that they were controlled experiments. And not the only ones. There were others. None were successful – if by success we mean that our operative survived with his skin intact. In another sense, they were wholly successful. They confirmed our suspicions that the sector known as Golden Acres has ceased to be a mere eyesore and embarrassment to the capital city of our glorious nation, *the premier world power of our time*, and has become, instead, a threat.'

There was a silence.

The meeting had been convened in a room with scenic windows.

Dome had been seated a little apart from the others, in his recovery bubble, close to the window. From the corner of his eye he could see the picture-perfect vista of the city, its avenues stretching away to infinity, its rigidly linear buildings, its silently speeding vehicles. For security reasons, the Hub was taller than any structures in its vicinity.

He'd been working here ever since he'd earned his body armour, at the age of twenty-two. He was lean and handsome, his black hair cut short, a neatly trimmed moustache over his top lip, his nose straight, his eyes clear. He was four years away from being eligible for marriage, but the Police Bureau had already cleared his application for a spouse and all the benefits that came with one: two-bedroom apartment, private conveyance, paid holidays. The girl, a fellow officer suitable to his rank and physical dimensions, would be chosen for him by his seniors. As was normal with all salaried personnel in the country, it was the employer's prerogative to choose mates for their dependants. Until then, young adults lived with their parents, under conditions of strict celibacy that included medications to suppress unseemly desires.

'*Premier World Power.*' The words strolled luxuriously through Dome's head, like an emperor touring his estates. Dome felt the familiar rich thrill lapping through his consciousness. It was grand, it was heady, to belong to a nation of such consequence. '*World Power! Yes, that is what we are!*' he thought. '*A glory to behold, the envy of all other nations!*'

The reference to 'controlled experiments' barely penetrated the light haze that enveloped his senses.

Instead, he allowed himself to be mesmerized by the view from the scenic window. Blinding white clouds drifted lazily against the dizzy blue vault of the sky. He could see the darting profiles of police transports as they sped across the city's skies. He wondered how soon it would be before he would be released to duty once more. He wondered if the faint flush of heat he felt at his temples was a reaction to the antibiotics coursing through his system. There was a faint nausea too and the first stirrings of a headache. He registered these impressions with surprise but no actual alarm.

The silence in the room deepened in some way.

With a guilty start, Dome returned his attention to the others around him. He had the oddest impression that his distraction had been noticed, even though no one was looking directly at him. In fact they seemed to be avoiding his gaze in some subtle way, as if looking around him rather than at him. He told himself he was imagining things.

The man in the linen suit continued now, in his weightless voice, as if he had not paused to ensure that Dome was listening. 'Clearly, it is a threat that we can no longer tolerate. Five years have passed since we cut their water and power supply. The area continues to be used as a dumping ground for every kind of waste – toxic, non-toxic, wet, dry, what-have-you. They have no sanitary facilities, no access to any medical supplies, no health-related technology. No supplies in the form of fresh food, no manufactured goods. Their air is unbreathable. They live ten to a cubicle, each cubicle the size of an aircraft toilet.'

He paused for maximum effect. '*Yet they thrive.*'

On the final word, his voice swung down like an axe, exposing the heart of his passion.

That repulsive vitality!

The man's nostrils expanded, and he exposed his teeth in disgust.

'The time is long overdue,' he whispered, 'for that zone of filth and human degradation to be extinguished. Snuffed out. Erased.'

Now he turned his head slowly, taking in every member of his audience one at a time, yet excluding Dome. If his voice had been soft before, now it was little more than a purr. 'We all know the realities: we cannot use military force without attracting the attention of the world's moral matrons. But the residents of the Acres have steadfastly refused to submit of their own accord. In such a situation, I think you will all agree, we have few choices…'

He paused once more. 'Yes? May I assume agreement?'

Dome's forehead puckered in confusion.

He glanced around the room and saw, to his surprise, that heads were nodding. Whatever the linen suit was talking about, the other members of the audience seemed to be in on the secret. Now the hair on the back of his neck stiffened. His heart began to thump within his chest. What were the others nodding over? He could not remember hearing of any resolution. Had something been discussed in his absence? Had some crucial decision been made?

No one was meeting his eye.

The unnamed man's head was swivelling around now, towards Dome.

'Yes,' he said. 'Yes, young man. You have every reason to look bewildered. That is because you do not realize that what began as a routine operation has ended very differently. Even as you sit there, believing that you are the same young officer who leapt into his transport to respond to a distress call this morning, the truth is, you have been damaged beyond repair by the encounter. What may have appeared to be a long and fruitful life ahead of you has today, in the space of a few brief minutes, been reduced to a week – maybe two–'

Dome stammered, 'Sir– I– what…'

The man said, 'It is the latest strategy of the denizens of Golden Acres. They use various pretexts to lure Government agents to their environment, then jab them with micro-fine needles filled with infected blood and send them back. No doubt they have found ways of harvesting the hospital wastes that are dumped on their land. No doubt they find painkillers and hypodermic syringes along with all the rest. It is swiftly done, perhaps using a mild anaesthetic, so that the victim is not even aware of what has happened to him. But we have seen the results and I assure you, what I say is true. While you were unconscious during your physical exam, I was able to reveal to your colleagues the site of the puncture wound, deep within the crease of your right armpit. The infection will be fatal and incurable, a cocktail of TB, hepatitis and SARS, plus a speeding agent which causes the germs to go to work at twice their natural speed.'

He paused, like a college lecturer who knows when to give his students time to absorb a nodal point in their instruction.

'I have informed your colleagues that only one course of action is available to you and of course we will offer you a couple of hours to adjust your mind to these new realities. It boils down to this: we will send you back in there, loaded with contagions that *we* have prepared for just this purpose. Whereas the technology of the squatter community has not progressed beyond the primitive skin-puncture delivery systems of the mosquito, ours spreads via a modified rhinovirus via skin contact and thence to the mucous membranes. Death follows in 48 hours as the lungs clog up with fluids. As the contagion spreads amongst the residents, they'll have no option but to come streaming out of there like rats from a burning warehouse. We'll have specially prepared containment hangars ready for them. Their bodies will be disposed of safely, with no risk of further contamination. It should take about a fortnight. From the very start, we shall announce the outbreak of an epidemic of catastrophic proportions and declare to the world that for the sake of the entire human species we will have no option but to raze and sterilize the entire area…'

Bureau Chief Mana raised her hand.

'Excuse me sir, but how will you defend this action in the eyes of the international community? Whatever justification you offer, however catastrophic the disease, human beings cannot be destroyed like poultry at the time of the Avian Flu epidemic! This action *will* be defined as a planned genocide – with severe economic sanctions to follow–'

'We shall refer to it as *culling*,' said the man, cutting in swiftly, before Mana could build up steam. 'You are familiar with the term, no doubt? It belongs to the era of big game hunting, when licences were issued for thinning out herds of animals whose populations were rising too steeply in game sanctuaries. But we shall redefine the word to mean, *Removing a percentage of the human population so that the species as a whole might survive*. It is a useful word. We hope to make it very popular.'

He turned back to Dome.

'You realize, I am sure, that you will be a martyr to our nation's greater glory. Not that your role can ever be acknowledged: this entire operation, including your trip this morning to the Acres, has already been erased from the record. Even as we speak your co-pilot is having the memory of his flight flushed from his brain. You cannot have any contact with your parents before you vanish from their lives forever, apparently in a tragic encounter with enemy agents. However, your service record tells me that you are a model citizen, for which reason I do not doubt that in your final moments, you will find tremendous satisfaction in the knowledge that your name will be honoured and that your family will benefit to the tune of–' He mentioned a very handsome sum.

The interior of Dome's head had filled with a loud buzzing sound but aside from that, he felt very little. The initial shock he had felt upon hearing the news had dissipated. He felt detached, as if he were listening to a recitation about someone else's life, a stranger on the evening news, the synopsis of a tri-vid.

The man continued. 'Of course, in case this option does not appeal to you, there is one other we can offer,' he said. 'You can choose to be extinguished immediately and painlessly–'

He paused once more.

'After which your body will replace the one you saw this morning.' He smiled mirthlessly.

When Dome woke again, he found that he had been sealed within a heavy sac. He was lying on his side. Naked. He could see nothing at all. He wondered whether he'd gone blind. He felt utterly limp; disinclined to engage with the hectic activity he could feel taking place around him, outside the bag.

He was being pulled this way and that, then hands were reaching around the bag, patting it down in order to determine his position within it. Many voices were speaking all at once, some giving instructions, some passing comments, some complaining. The complainers were louder, perhaps because they were not actively engaged in pulling.

'Leave it – *leave it!* Whatever's in there, it can only be more troubles for us–'

'No. We take all the rest of their garbage. This is just another part of it–'

'How do we know it's a living being? Maybe it's just one of their new machines–'

'Maybe it's a monster– Come to eat all of us alive–'

In amongst all the hubbub and the tugging, some hands located Dome's head and based on that discovery, began to reposition him so that he was in a roughly seated position, on the ground.

'Knife – knife – who has a knife? We'll have to cut the bag open–'

Children took up the cry, calling in piping voices, *Knife–Knife–Someone bring a knife–*

Inside the bag, Dome was experiencing the unfamiliar sensation of being drenched in sweat. He could not remember the last time he had ever felt so unbearably hot. And the air! Even through the sac he could taste its rasping texture. Thick. Sulphurous. Gritty.

He used his hands to push the heavy material of which the sac was made, a mixture of leather and plastic, away from his face. 'Here!' he called. His throat felt as if it had been scrubbed with sandpaper, producing only a shadowy whisper of sound. 'I have a knife–'

His Whisker had been left to him, looped around his wrist. Releasing the slender, razor-sharp tip of the instrument, he sliced through the skin of his confining sac and thrust his head through the resulting slit.

Then he collapsed on his side, gasping painfully. The light from half-a-dozen hissing gas lanterns blinded him.

Arms and hands reached out to hold him up once more. Tumblers of water were pushed towards his mouth. All around him were the faces of strangers, thrust towards him, their skins glistening with sweat, their eyes agog with a combination of concern and curiosity. He could smell their breath, their sweat, their unwashed clothes.

'Don't–' gasped Dome, his voice hoarse, 'don't get close to me – Mustn't...mustn't touch me...stay back–'

But they misunderstood him.

'See! He's afraid of us – *us*! What a chickenheart – what a dickhead–'

The language they used was similar to what the man beside the morning's corpse had spoken, an amalgamation of many tongues. Dome could understand some words better than others. There were even a few Hinglish phrases woven in amongst the medley.

Raucous gusts of laughter rippled through the gathered crowd as they ridiculed him for his fears, and pitied him too. Here he was, abandoned to their care, a naked stranger and trying to push them away! The glasses of water were thrust ever more insistently towards his mouth. Hands were reaching to pull away the bag in which he had come, to free him completely from its grip, even as another cry went out for cloth, a plastic sheet, anything to cover the stranger's nakedness.

A fit of violent coughing convulsed him. His joints felt spongy with weakness.

'Please!' he rasped. 'It's not safe – not safe for *you*–'

But his voice lacked power and no one could hear him. Even as his senses swam, bodies were pushing all around him, holding him up, shifting him to a better location. There was nothing he could do. The deadly virus was already slithering into new hosts, fresh from his skin. Bitter tears joined the sweat pouring down his cheeks. The linen suit's cruel scheme was working like precision electronics.

Some hours later, the young ex-agent had been re-established in the hut of a man who introduced himself as Shankh. He may have been the same person who had been standing beside the morning's corpse, but the change in his behaviour made it hard to be sure. He was no longer reserved and self-effacing, but welcoming and friendly.

Inside the hut were Shankh's wife and two other women who may have been co-wives or sisters, it was hard to tell. Dome was lying on gunny sacks placed on the floor, which was clean and dry. The dwelling was perhaps six feet square and a little less than that in height. The only source of illumination was a gas-lantern. The women were crouched in the far corner, talking between themselves, while Shankh was turned towards Dome. There were at least three infants inside the hut and a couple of chickens, pecking here and there on the floor. Blocking the entrance were the head and forequarters of a huge portly animal that had settled itself down right there.

'What is that creature?' Dome wanted to know.

Shankh said, smiling at the ignorance of the visitor, 'A pig. Have you never seen one? We know from the pictures on the tins of food products that you city-people throw away that you eat them–'

A pile of old newspapers sewn up within plastic bags formed a bolster for Dome to lean against. He was wearing borrowed clothes, a string vest and a thin cotton lungi. Practically naked, by his standards, yet he didn't have the energy to care. His head was spinning with fever and his speech was reduced to a bare trickle of sound.

'Never mind pigs. Listen to me, Shankh,' he whispered. '...please...there's something terrible I must tell you...even though it's too late–'

Shankh's smile didn't waver as he listened.

When Dome was finished – it did not take long – the other man said, '*Bas*? That's all you've brought for us – one more disease?' He threw his head back and laughed. 'Never mind! We'll accept it graciously – after all, you know what they say about beggars...'

Dome's heart contracted with sadness. 'You don't understand – This is something worse than anything that has yet existed – it's been *designed* to destroy you–'

'–but we refuse to be afraid,' said Shankh. 'And you know why?' He waggled his finger in the air. 'Because whatever's thrown at us, we grab it, recycle it and return it with interest. So they have cooked up a new disease in their medical factories? Good. Wonderful. We will circulate it through the living factories of all our hundred thousand bodies – and some of us will die – and some of us will live – and those who survive will repackage that same disease and send it back out to your friends in the city, so that they can enjoy it too...'

He laughed once more and patted Dome's hand. 'So stop worrying! Cheer up. Let's eat.'

The women brought food in tin plates. Later someone brought a herbal infusion that would help Dome with his breathing. Later still, in the darkness of that steamy night, a young woman joined him on his gunny bed and showed him a definition of hospitality that he had never known before.

The remaining two days of Dome's life were spent peacefully and as comfortably as possible, given the circumstances. With the desperate thirst of one who is about to leave this world forever he wanted to understand how the residents of Golden Acres had survived under their grim circumstances, what gave them the incentive to keep fighting.

According to Shankh, it was simply a question of perspective.

'From the bottom of the pit, all roads lead *up*,' he explained, smiling. 'So in one sense, this is an extremely positive place to be. Rich people throw away things at such a rate that for us, living on the dump, we only have to wait long enough before whatever we want comes sailing out of the sky – for free! Cars, food, books, furniture, machinery, medicines, bottles, toys – you wouldn't believe how much gets thrown away. And very often in its original packing. So we're not complaining. We take what we need, repackage the rest and send it back out.'

A week after Dome had died, a new product began to appear on the shelves of fashionable stores in the city. Small black tins of pickled beetroot, straight from Russia, according to rumours. The labels looked like burnished gold and each tin was secured within its own individual membrane of cling film. A flattened medallion of red sealing wax provided a guarantee that the contents were authentic and had not been tampered with in transit.

It proved to be very popular and the entire stock sold out even before the first case of a terrifying new strain of flu was reported in the Continuum.

Amongst the first hundred people to fall ill was the man in the linen suit.

He, more than anyone else, knew exactly how soon he would succumb to the mysterious fever that had already felled dozens of victims. He had no family and all his staff deserted him the moment he began to manifest the tell-tale symptoms. As he lay in his silk pyjamas, alone in bed, writhing with joint pains and gasping for breath, his attention was caught by something on his bedside table. It was a little black tin that he'd bought at great expense a few days earlier.

'Tasty stuff,' he wheezed to himself, as he fished for the last few morsels with a silver pickle fork. 'Might as well finish it.' With streaming eyes, he squinted at the gilded label, embossed in running script with the product's name: *D'Ohm's Pickled Beetroot*.

'D'Ohm's...' he said the word out loud. 'Doesn't sound very Russian!'

It reminded him of something.

Some*one*.

If only he could remember who! He sensed some sort of gigantic truth swirling in the ether, just out of reach of his understanding.

But a spasm of coughing shook him just then.

A day later, he was dead.

FREAK

'You're too young!' snarled the tall Australian with the one-word name: Hunter. Her bright blonde hair blazed in the sunlight streaming into her suite at the Kathmandu Hilton. Months in the jungle had left her with a strip of jute across her chest and a pair of filthy shorts tied onto her hips with bungee cords. Only her combat boots were intact. 'You can't know the historical significance of this moment!'

'I– I…' stammered Meena, taken off-stride.

Two porters lay snoring on the champagne-pink carpet. Cartons, crates and gunny-sacks were strewn about the room along with rolls of toilet paper, plastic bottles of spring water and tiny, silk-wrapped sachets of Tibetan medicine. A third porter was sprawled across the white brocade cover of the enormous double bed. The room smelled of ripe durian and blue cheese.

Meena twitched off her heavy backpack and cameras before adjusting the bright orange press badge on her chest. 'I'm not young,' she said. 'Just short.'

But Hunter was already speaking into her smartphone to Time-Asia editor Bingo Crane. 'It's not the Easter Bunny I've caught,' she thundered into the phone, 'it's the *Yeti*! Cryptozoology's HOLY GRAIL! And you've sent an underage blimp to cover the story of the century!'

'I am *not* underage,' repeated Meera in a firm voice. 'And I'm a tae-kwon-do black belt.' Indeed, she was the only journalist with the seniority to qualify for the task of covering the story. 'Incidentally,' she said, '"Yeti" is the Western name for–'

'WHATEVER!' Hunter hurled the phone at the full-length mirror behind the bed. The mirror shattered, but the phone ricocheted off and hit the sleeping porter on the head, with Bingo Crane's voice still squawking from it. 'What I call it is what the world's gonna call it!' she howled, as she pumped her fists. 'Coz I'm God Emperor Dune! I'm gonna get the Nobel! I'm gonna be the POPE! I've captured the YETI!'

Later the same day, Hunter and Meena were seated back-to-back atop an elephant. A second pachyderm with a sturdy cage secured to its back followed behind. The porters threaded a path through the dense foliage on foot. The party of five had flown out by helicopter from Kathmandu. Two elephants plus mahouts and rations to last them three days had been chartered in advance, in anticipation of their arrival. They set off at once for the remote location where the captive had been confined to a tiny cave, chained and sedated.

Administering the sedative had been the most difficult part of the entire campaign, according to Hunter, speaking to Meena over her shoulder. '*Human*? That thing? No way. It walks on two legs all right, but aside from that its pure animal. It's got hair like you wouldn't believe. Mind you, most men are pure animal too–' Here she broke off to laugh, throwing her head back while making a sound like a chainsaw. 'But that hair! Like steel wool. No question of penetrating it with a dart.'

'So what did you do?' asked Meena. Her voice-corder, strapped to her head, picked up every creak and rustle of ambient sound. The audio would be practically useless. But taking handwritten notes was even more difficult. She and Hunter were strapped into a pair of flimsy benches, facing outwards, slung on either side of the pachyderm's spine, while the elephant's body shifted sinuously from side to side like a geriatric belly dancer.

'Oh, I was just *brilliant*!' said Hunter in her adenoidal drawl. 'Once I was sure it was the Yeti, I resisted the urge to just rush in, grab the evidence and run away again. That's what hundreds of my predecessors have tried and failed at. Instead, I was patient. I was thorough. I took notes, I studied, I recorded every twitch of its daily routine. Six months of plotting and planning. All through those weeks, as I was moving closer and closer, I covered myself in monkey dung to mask my scent. It's extremely sensitive to smell, right?' According to her, the reason the creature had evaded scrutiny for so long was that it could smell its pursuers long before they could see it.

'Finally, I entered its cave when it was not home and covered myself in *its* dung! Then I just waited in that cave, until it returned in the evening. Then I waited some more. It did not detect my presence. I crept closer and closer until it was ready to squat down to void its bowels – because it likes to poop in this one spot, you see? Always the same spot in whatever cave it uses to sleep in. A bit like us, in that sense. Likes its privacy. And that's when I got it. Right in the exposed skin of its fanny. With a dart.'

Meena bit her lower lip. *Unfair*, she thought.

Tracking the creature down, spying on it, outraging its modesty, then darting it in its bum! What could be more disrespectful than that? The local people regarded it with mystical devotion, neither questioning its existence nor expressing the need to confirm it with physical evidence. They called it the Spirit of the Mountains. They knew it was there and that was good enough for them.

'Notice, I said "squat down"? It does that when it pees too. I had my suspicions, the first time I saw it do that.' Hunter believed the Yeti was female.

'You don't know for sure?' asked Meena. 'Didn't you examine it, once you had sedated it?'

'Of course, of course – that is, I *tried* to examine it. Not so easy, let me tell you. Its hair is not merely dense, it's sort of…stiff.' She shrugged. 'I admit I didn't try too hard. The fact is, I didn't see anything that suggested it was one or the other: no package of goodies and no deep dark slit either. There'll be time enough later. Mind you, it makes sense for it to be female. That's why there's only one of her. I reckon she's taught herself the trick we've all been chasing – parthenogenesis!'

Asexual reproduction. Certain lizards had managed it, but none of the so-called 'higher' animals were known to have succeeded.

'When I get her back to the West, we'll be able to uncover all her secrets,' said Hunter. 'Clone her DNA. Then teach ourselves to perform the same trick.' She chainsawed raucously. 'Then it'll be *Ciao, Adam! Been nice knowing ya!*'

They stopped for the night, set off again at first light and reached the cave two hours later. They were greeted by the three porters who had remained behind to ensure that the creature didn't get loose or harm itself trying to escape. Like the rest of their team, they were dressed in shiny down jackets, thick padded trousers and wore rugged boots, all thoroughly smeared with mud.

According to them, the captive had given them no trouble. 'Sits quietly at the back of the cave all this time,' said the oldest of the men, speaking to Meena in Nepali. 'Doesn't say a word.'

They were standing at the entrance to the cave. Heavy metal posts had been driven into the rock floor just outside the entrance, preventing passage for anything wider than a foot. Behind them, they could hear Hunter shouting at the porters as they set up the campsite. From within, no sounds.

'It's still alive?' asked Meena.

'Oh yes, alive,' said the man, who introduced himself as Bhim Singh. 'Comes up to the bars, looks out, goes back again. Eats bananas. No rotis, no daal, but we gave him a bit of sugarcane I kept in my pocket for the elephant and – wah! *That* he ate!'

Bhim Singh's eyes crinkled with the memory. Then he paused, glancing over his shoulder. 'Don't tell Hunter Madam, but I also gave him a…' He made the universal gesture for a chillum, one hand forming a pipe and the other hand cupped against the first one. 'Needs it. Knows what's happening. Doesn't like it.'

Who does? thought Meena. The hammer of Modernity was relentless. Everyone and everything had to submit to its flattening blows eventually. Or vanish into oblivion.

She thanked Bhim Singh. Clouds crept down from the heights, sending tentacles of mist curling through the ferns and hanging creepers. The sun faded from view. Droplets began to form in the air. Then it was raining. Fine and soft as a baby's hair to begin with, but gradually growing heavier. Meena pulled the hood of her all-weather parka over her head and covered her cameras. She gazed towards the darkened slit of the cave's entrance, gripped by a profound melancholy.

'Oi!' said Hunter, coming up suddenly from behind, causing Meena to jump. 'What're you wasting time for? Go on in there and start clicking! I instructed my men to feed the old girl a knockout dose of tranqs. She'll be fast asleep. And anyway, everyone says, she's harmless. We have bright lights if you need 'em.'

Meena narrowed her eyes. 'Sorry. I'm not taking my chances with a seven-foot bi-ped covered in steel-wool!' she said. 'In any case you're going to have to move quickly, to get her loaded into the cage and out of here.' She had decided to go along with the feminine pronouns to avoid an argument. 'I'll take action shots, once she's out.'

Hunter drew in a breath to answer when her eyes widened and she gasped. '*Look!*' she said. 'Someone's all woken up–'

Meena swivelled around.

Then her skin rippled with goose-flesh and she forgot to breathe.

Behind the bars, in plain view now despite the grey veil of rain, was an immense Presence. It wasn't tall so much as shaggy and broad. Its fur was a pale, shimmery brown. It covered the creature completely, including its nose, mouth and hands, but leaving its eyes clear. They were deep-set, those eyes. Meena could feel their gaze piercing her skin, raking her. The sensation wasn't unpleasant, except she found she couldn't move. She was frozen where she stood.

She could hear sounds from behind her. Hunter, yammering about getting her cameras out. Bhim Singh, yelling incoherently. Maybe the other porters too. There was a buzzing in her ears. It was hard to concentrate.

The Yeti, its penetrating gaze fixed on her all the while, had two of the bars blocking the entrance to its cave gripped tight in its shaggy hands. With dreamlike inevitability, it began dragging the bars apart. When it was done, it stepped through.

Meena could hear the huffing of its breath as it sniffed her, carefully and thoroughly. Her eyes were shut tight. She could feel it smelling her thoughts and her ideals, her memories and her intentions. It paused when it learned of her fifteen years as a journalist; the awards she had won, the world leaders she had met; it disliked her fondness for beer; it drew back and spat when it encountered her taste in rock music. But when it smelled that she had met with the Dalai Lama, it nodded its approval and accepted her.

Picking her up by the waist, so that her senses swam and her cameras flopped heavily over and off her head, it went bounding up the shoulder of the rock that contained the cave it had been trapped within.

When they were at a great height, the Yeti stopped and allowed her to watch as the curtain of rain grew into a torrent. Neither the porters nor the mahouts waited to see what had become of the journalist. They turned around and prepared to leave while they still could. Hunter hollered and roared, but eventually she had no choice but to go running after them too.

Over a period of years, Meena's connection with her previous existence loosened and fell away entirely. She grew a pelt of stiff, unyielding fur, her shoulders broadened, her height increased, her arms grew longer, her head and skull began changing shape. The Yeti did not speak or share its dreams with her or show her whether it was male or female. Instead it taught her how to summon the thunder and when to fold the night winds into cloaks of invisibility to foil the eyes of humans.

When it had taught her all it knew, including how to transform another as she had been transformed, it climbed a stairway made of sighs and entered the mystery of Unbeing.

Whereupon she became the Spirit of the Mountains.

The Wild One. The Nameless.

Gazing down from the untamed heights.

Smiling

A CLINE'S VIEW

Whenever she entered a roomful of humans, Special Investigator Sh'ana had to suppress the urge to say, 'Relax! You can stare at me all you want!' It was no different this time. Everyone looked just a little to her left or her right, never quite hitting the target.

Which was a shame.

She enjoyed attention. She wouldn't have been able to do her job if she didn't.

The session had been arranged in an anteroom to the court. Already present were four policemen, two lawyers, the victim's family and of course the accused. A female.

That pleased Sh'ana. She believed that human females were often weak and underprivileged. It pleased her to know that she might be able to offer one of them some solace.

The two police inspectors flanking her as she entered were a reminder to her to be careful how she moved her body. Never to twitch her tail in public, never to unsheath her claws.

The District Attorney introduced her. 'Special Investigator Shanie Tailgate–' He broke off to look in her direction. 'Did I pronounce that right?'

'Sh'ana Tath'l-git,' said Sh'ana, sounding the subglottal yodel that humans did not have the equipment to produce. 'But Madam Investigator will do fine.' She smiled then, exposing her beautiful teeth.

She was six feet tall and slender, dressed in a form-fitting charcoal grey jumpsuit. A discrete aperture in the back of the suit made it possible for her to keep her long tail wrapped around her waist, looking like a furry belt. She wore a pearly chiffon scarf at her throat and filigreed silver claw-hoods on the tips of her fingers. Her head was a smooth cap of lengthened and straightened hair. Her face was very finely furred giving the appearance of chalk-white skin with faint grey stripes on the forehead and cheeks.

The pupils of her eyes became vertical slits in bright light. Her canines were long and sharp. She always made it a point to smile at least once, early in every session. While she accepted her place in human society, she wasn't willing to erase her otherness altogether.

Only two members of the victim's family were present, both brothers.

It was a rectangular room. The virtual windows along one wall, with a realistic display of white clouds against a dazzling blue sky, concealed 3D cameras. The main space of the room was filled with wooden chairs, arranged as if in a class, facing away from the windows. In the empty space where Sh'ana and the DA stood was a lectern. To their right was a wall with a curtained recess.

The DA's name was Brian Wheatcroft. Sh'ana had met him a couple of times. He was a male of medium height, clothed in a dull suit, his head sparsely furred.

Wheatcroft now turned towards the accused.

The name, as pronounced by the DA, was unintelligible to Sh'ana but she didn't request a repetition. Names mattered little to her since she identified people by their scent, but she listened politely.

The reason for this session was, of course, a suspected murder. The victim was the husband of the accused and the sole suspect.

She claimed accidental death.

Sh'ana's role lay in establishing the truth of the situation.

The accused was perhaps five feet tall. It was hard to tell, because she was seated.

Her skin was a shade darker than was considered the local norm. The SI, like many felines, did not have colour-vision. She considered this an asset. The variations in skin colour that humans made such a fuss over were, to her, minor fluctuations in lightness and darkness.

The accused wore her head-fur pulled back tight and folded into the rigid arrangement known as a plait, in this case very long. It was a dense black, as were her eyebrows and lashes.

The accused also wore ophthalmic aids in the form of spectacles. Most human females chose less visible methods of boosting the poor eyesight that so many humans suffered from. That the accused had chosen to make an outward show of her disability was a matter of interest to Sh'ana. It told her that the woman did not feel the need to conform to prevailing norms of beauty. It may even be that she preferred to be honest about her failings. Then again, she may have chosen to present herself in such a light, precisely in order to create an impression of honesty and innocence. If that were the case, that could mean that she was manipulative, cunning and probably guilty.

Of most interest however was the young woman's demeanour. She sat remarkably still, in her wooden chair, looking nowhere in particular. Her head was neither inclined nor held up high.

She was the one who had requested Sh'ana's services. As the prime accused in a murder trial, it was her exclusive prerogative to make such a request. It was extremely typical for the accused to look with searching curiosity and entreaty at the SI. The fact that she didn't suggested that she was either naturally stoic or else that her expressionlessness was a carefully maintained mask.

Sh'ana turned back to Wheatcroft. 'Thank you,' she said. 'I've gathered whatever I need for the moment. Please proceed.'

The DA turned to the group as a whole. 'It is my duty now to explain to both parties, the nature of what lies ahead. There are two stages to this type of investigation–'

One of the victim's brothers leapt to his feet. He was the younger of the two. 'I object! It is wrong!' His voice was shrill and heavily accented, each consonant delivered with an explosive charge that made him sound like an animated snare drum. His older brother tried to hold him down. 'No!' raved the younger man. 'The presence of this mutant freak in the context of my brother's murder is an ABOMINATION–'

Before any of the policemen could stir, Sh'ana had stepped forward.

'Excuse me, sir,' she said, lowering her voice to a throaty growl. 'You may not understand the conditions under which my services are sought.' The man cowered away from her. 'Please be assured that once I've been called out, I cannot be switched off or dismissed. I am not a children's toy to be waved in the air as a phony threat. Once I have made myself available for a particular task...' She paused for effect, looking around the room. 'That task *shall* be performed.'

She brought her voice back to its normal pitch. 'I should also point out that your use of the word "mutant" in reference to me is inaccurate. I am a *cline*: a Genetically Enhanced Clone. We possess a tiny percentage of feline genes. We were created by design, in a lab, not through chance mutations. We know that non-clines find some of our habits and in particular our dietary practices deeply offensive,' she said, her eyes flashing. 'But we did not ask to be created! It's not our fault if we appear to be freaks! And it seems to me we're not one-tenth as dangerous as the humans whose crimes we're brought in to investigate.'

The man had wet himself in fear. All the same, he found his voice and answered, 'I will never accept your verdict – never!' He was trembling and wretched, his body straining away from her.

Sh'ana returned to where she'd been standing, by the lectern. 'Please continue with your explanation, Mr Wheatcroft,' she said. From the corner of her eye, she glanced towards the accused and was impressed in spite of herself: the woman remained as composed and still as before.

Throats were cleared and clothing adjusted. The DA explained the procedure brusquely then turned to Sh'ana saying, 'Over to you, Madam Investigator.'

The accused was sitting in the second row of chairs facing towards the front of the room. Sh'ana moved in her direction, then positioned herself behind the young woman.

As all eyes turned to her, she spoke to the woman behind whom she stood. 'Madam Accused, I will monitor you from where I stand.

I will not touch you at any time during or after your narration of events. However, I will stand close to you, sniffing the air around you. The closer I am to you, the better equipped I will be to deliver an accurate verdict. I may interrupt you now and then, to ask questions. Please do not turn around to look at me or pause for any length of time, but rather, just answer me as directly and openly as you can.'

She allowed herself a tiny pause. 'Madam Accused, you may proceed to give us a brief description of events.'

The young woman stirred in her seat. She acknowledged Sh'ana's presence without turning around. In a clear voice, she began her narration. 'It was a Sunday morning. I was in the kitchen, preparing lunch…'

Sh'ana leaned in towards the accused. All other perceptions faded into the background as she opened her senses to the stream of information flowing towards her.

In her mind's eye, the SI saw a suburban home, a sunlit kitchen, a quietly humming refrigerator. A kitchen table. On the chopping board, half an onion. A knife. The images were not telepathic: Sh'ana's mind supplied generic pictures for what the accused described.

'My husband and I had been arguing for months,' said the accused. 'He wanted a divorce. I was refusing to give him one.'

Rising up from the young woman was an acrid scent. It was the one known to Sh'ana as *rkendRiii*: embarrassment.

'Why?' asked Sh'ana. 'Why stay with a mate who does not want you?'

'Because I…I…' The reek was strong now. The accused was in the grip of strong emotion. 'I loved him. I was crazy for him. I believed I had enough love for both of us. I thought it was only a matter of time before he…he…loved me in return.' *HwwuTig*. A sharp, stinging stench, such as might be given off by broken glass shards and acid, rose up from the woman. Anguish. Regret. 'But I was wrong.'

'He began hitting me. Slapping me. Told me I was forcing him to be violent by refusing to divorce him.' They had been married less than a year when the day dawned which found the two of them standing in their kitchen, with the table between them and shouting.

'I told him I would never give up on him, never. I loved him too much. That made him wild. He grabbed my plait and swung me around. I screamed and screamed – but he wouldn't let go! With one hand, he wrapped my plait around my neck, so that I was caught tight, facing him. With the other hand he grabbed the knife. All I could do was clutch his wrist with both my hands to keep the knife away from me–'

She breathed heavily in silence for a couple of seconds before continuing, her voice hoarse. 'And then my feet slipped. I fell backward. He fell onto me.'

A complex bouquet of fumes was rising up from the girl as she spoke. Sh'ana disentangled them, one by one. *Dee'Ssiriya*, for anger. *Odfaa* for revulsion. *Ymmrii* for tears.

But there was one more scent: *Xha'tho-thhip*. For withholding.

The accused was keeping something hidden. Something crucial.

'And the knife went into his chest. At an angle. Straight into his heart. Blood spurted onto my face,' the young woman continued. 'Into my mouth, into my eyes. Everywhere.'

She stopped again, panting.

'I pushed him away, horrified, crying, screaming. Called the police, called the ambulance, blood everywhere – there's been an accident, a terrible accident – but it was too late. My husband stayed where he was. On his knees staring down at his chest. The knife sticking out. His face was blank. He collapsed in slow motion, like in a film, sideways. Rolled onto his back. The police arrived minutes later. I was still screaming. But by then he was dead.'

Sh'ana thanked her. Then moved back to the front of the room. All through the narration, she'd been aware of disturbances elsewhere in the room. She paid no attention to them. Scuffles between the victim's family and policemen were typical during these sessions.

The room quietened down gradually. All eyes turned towards the silent Special Investigator once more. She allowed a charged moment to pass before looking up.

'Thank you, Madam Accused. That was an emotional, difficult account. As you were aware when you requested my participation in this investigation, I have the skills of a specialized lie detector. Using the sensory equipment at my command, I analysed your data. We clines refer to them as sensory emissions. You humans call them scents. Everything you said was fully supported by the chemical signatures sent out by your body.' She paused. 'Everything except...'

An electric current pulsed through the room.

'...except one thing that you have withheld.'

Now Sh'ana turned towards the accused and impaled her with a stare from her pale eyes with their vertical pupils. 'I must ask you to tell me, honestly and without reserve: what is the thing you are concealing?'

The young woman's face was shut as tight as a bank vault.

She opened her mouth to speak, but for a few seconds no sound came out.

Then she forced herself. 'I can't...' Her voice was ragged. 'I can't tell you.'

Sh'ana marvelled at someone who dared to withhold information even in such a vulnerable, exposed situation. The accused had more steel in her than her appearance suggested.

'You realize, do you not,' said Sh'ana, 'that if you do not give me that one vital bit of information, I am bound to take this investigation further?' The woman nodded. 'You are familiar with the implications?' Again, the accused nodded. But Sh'ana ennumerated the conditions anyway: 'Whatever is revealed in the course of the investigation, howsoever secret or private, will become part of the public record. If the material revealed in this way turns out to be prejudicial to your case, you will have no right to strike it from the record. You confirm that these conditions are acceptable to you?'

The accused nodded.

'And...the body will not be returned to the family.'

At this, the younger brother jumped to his feet, shrieking uncontrollably. The older man bellowed in some foreign language, from where he sat. The police officers leapt forward.

Sh'ana did not intervene. The family's objections were entirely understandable.

But they weren't her concern.

She looked towards the accused woman.

She stared back at the SI.

Her lips moved, forming the word, 'Yes.' No sound came out.

By the time the disturbance had settled, the younger of the two brothers had been removed from the room and the older one, at his request, had received a mild sedative.

A clear space was created in the middle of the room. Aside from the DA and Sh'ana everyone present in the room was seated. Two morgue attendants wearing hospital greens were summoned. Drawing back the curtain across the recess in the right-hand wall, they wheeled out the white-sheeted body that had been lying in there on a gurney, all this while.

One of the attendants folded down the sheet, exposing the head and shoulders of a young man in his late twenties. He was pleasant to look at, even in death.

Sh'ana, standing beside the body, looked across towards the accused. 'Once more, I must ask you,' she said. 'Are you sure you want to proceed? I am giving you one last chance to reveal what you have withheld. Though I cannot guarantee it, it's possible that what you say would be sufficient to decide this case one way or the other.'

The accused was looking at her husband's corpse as she said, 'It would not.' Her expression was unfathomable.

Sh'ana waited a moment then looked towards the DA.

Wheatcroft returned the look and nodded.

Sh'ana stepped around to her right, in order to stand beside the body's head.

The room and all the people in it receded from consciousness.

On the gurney in front of her was a cold, dead mass.

Less than twenty-four hours had passed since the death of the person who had animated that corpse. The body had been flash-frozen within fifteen minutes, which meant that cell degeneration must barely have begun.

Sh'ana passed both her hands lightly over the inert face before her. Her manner was that of a musician who makes a first, tentative contact with an instrument she's about to play upon.

Those watching her could have had no idea of what she felt as she did so. The closest approximation she might have offered would have been: creating an echo-image of the young man's brain cells within her own brain.

She began to gather the powerful force of her own vital energy, her *z'hi*. It was an ability for which humans had no counterpart. Gathering in her *z'hi* like strands of light, she held it together for a second or two before directing it through the lens of her mind and then down: through the slender stem of her neck, separating right and left at her shoulders, down her powerful, muscular arms and thence through her hands.

Through her hands as they cradled the victim's cold head, flooded the insubstantial glowing power surge of Sh'ana's *z'hi* into the mass of silent tissue.

She knew what she was doing. She had done it countless times before. Down into that lifeless receptacle she poured her own brilliant, irresistible vital force.

Almost at once the minute stirrings began.

The untold millions of cells that had faded to blankness with the victim's death, began a faint, barely perceptible twitching.

Now she deepened her concentration. Picking up the head, she interlaced her fingers beneath it.

Down through the layer of hair, skin and bone she poured her *z'hi*. Even as she poured, she sucked the energy back up into herself again, cleaned the stillness of death from it and sent it back into the silent receptacle that she held between her hands.

It took skill to manage the loop without drowning the smaller vessel.

But she had that skill.

Slowly at first and then with increasing speed, the neural networks within the dead brain began to respond. Stirring, snapping together, sparking, firing. Gladly, willingly, they began to perform the tasks they knew so well. The tasks of containing thoughts, ideas, associations, memories, information, dates, smells, tastes, visions.

The task of containing a life.

Though the man was no longer alive, the cells responsible for maintaining his personality and history were prodded by Sh'ana into a simulation of life.

As the energy flowed back and forth, from herself, to the awakening cells, then back to her again, images and sensations began to swirl through the cline's mind.

Glittering chains of life-chatter from that dead brain began flooding into her.

She met the barrage coolly, without being overwhelmed. She directed the incoming stream with her own thoughts, seeking out the freshest, most recent linkages. It was like standing in the midst of an intelligent snowstorm, in which the flakes could be made to respond to directional clues, to suggestions about which types of ideas and associations she wanted to see, until finally the single pattern for which she was searching appeared on the view-screen of her thoughts.

Yes. There it was.

A room filled with sunlight. A kitchen, the kettle hissing in the background. The table, the young woman across the width of the table. There on the table, a knife.

Yes, the voices raised in anger. Yes.

Needless to say, there was a difference in what she saw now. This view was no longer generic, but specific. Plus, it was from the victim's perspective. The voices raised in anger were no longer that of the accused, modulated through her experience and opinion. Instead, the voices she heard now were of the victim and of the accused, as recorded by the victim's senses.

Then Sh'ana opened her mouth.

With the images from the victim's brain still streaming through her mind, she began producing, with her own vocal cords, the voices of the victim and the accused, as they argued. Functioning as a microphone, amplifying the sounds stored in the dead man's brain, she played them back now, to the victim's brother, the lawyers, the policemen, the two morgue attendants, the DA.

And, of course, to the accused.

The voice of the accused, speaking in the victim's mind, sounded more shrill, more desperate than she did in real life. These were the victim's impressions of her, after all, as recorded by him.

'Puppet!' screeched the accused, sounding like an aggrieved parrot. 'You're just a puppet in the hands of...of...'

Thwap! The sound of a slap.

Now a man's voice cut in. It was the victim speaking. His voice was deep, the way he heard it when he spoke, rumbling in his chest.

'Shut up, *bitch*,' he said. Then he switched to some other language that Sh'ana did not understand, though she could reproduce it faultlessly. His tone made it clear that he was describing her in terms that were intended to cut her to ribbons.

The accused responded in frenzied squeaks: 'Shut up, shut up, *SHUT UP!*'

In Sh'ana's mind images were streaming, of the accused, across the table from her husband, her face blazing and tear-streaked. There in the background was the electric kettle, incongruously whistling, before shutting off with a hard-plastic *tup*! There was the victim's hand snaking out towards the accused – slapping her again, *thwap*! – grabbing her plait – swinging her this way and that – her yelping cries – wrapping the long rope of hair around the young woman's neck so that she was suddenly crying and calling out, right up next to the victim's own face.

And then, with no warning, there was a new voice.

It cut through the din like a scalpel through a mass of gangrenous tissue. Straight to the point: 'Why dontcha just kill her?'

Cool and taut, was that voice. A woman's voice.

She wasn't physically in the room.

Instead, she was a phantom presence in the victim's mind.

Nevertheless, she was vivid with passion. Sh'ana could see her as clearly as if she were standing alongside the victim. She was older than him. Paler. She wore her fur in a mass of light curls that haloed her head. Her mouth had the slick sheen of lipstick and the lids of her eyes were artificially darkened in the way favoured by so many human females.

Her voice in the victim's memory was seductive, thick with musk. Faithfully, this voice and its dangerous messages poured from Sh'ana's mouth into the ears of all those in that room.

A dizzy energy was flooding into the victim's brain. It was clear that this woman's presence, the mere thought of her, affected the victim's psyche like a drug.

'You'll be free of her,' that phantom voice prompted. 'You know that's what you want – you've been saying it for weeks! – and look? There's a knife on the table. It'll be so easy, so neat. The neighbours are away for the weekend. There are no witnesses anywhere within earshot. Come on. Come on. Be strong. Be brave.'

The whole scene, as viewed through the young man's eyes, was edged with strobe effects.

Now, with jerky inevitability, his left hand appeared within his field of vision, picking up the blade. Meanwhile, on his right, the accused still shrieked and struggled. Her face was a blurred smudge, slimy with tears and snot.

Via Sh'ana's mouth, the sounds of the accused's pleading cries entered the court's ante-chamber. The SI saw, in her mind's eye, the knife being raised, the knife plunging down. It missed, it was raised again. The accused struggled, crying. Both her hands were on her husband's wrist, desperately pushing the tip of the blade away from herself, while held tight by the man with her long hair in his grip.

Then with shocking suddenness, she pitched backwards.

And abruptly, all the images streaming inside the SI's mind shook and splintered.

A violent grunt of pain and shock rent the air.

Sparks flashed across the victim's visual field as he pulled himself upright again. Then he was staring down, down at his own chest, at the dark fluid jetting from his mortal wound.

A howling vortex began to fill into his brain.

At that moment, the Special Investigator snapped the flow of her *z'hi* into the victim's brain with a quick, business-like jerk of her chin. She knew better than to waste her energy following a dead man's record of his own final moments.

Carefully, she replaced the head on the surface of the gurney. A shudder rippled across her skin as the final thoughts of the dying man ricocheted through her brain. Then she stepped back and away.

There was very little left to say or to be done. That was typical of these investigations. Few of them ended with anything short of complete certainty about what had happened and why. The victim's elder brother was led away by his lawyer, sobbing uncontrollably. A three-dimensional video transcript of Sh'ana's presentation would be made available to the court. The best that the victim's family might achieve now was a verdict of involuntary manslaughter accompanied by a light sentence.

The accused remained in her seat. Outwardly, she appeared as subdued as before. But even at a distance, Sh'ana caught the radiant fragrance pulsing out of her. A smooth, warm *aahbOro-e*. No trace remained of the withholding.

As Sh'ana prepared to walk out of the room, flanked once more by the two inspectors, the young woman glanced up.

In a voice rich with emotion, she said, 'Thank you.'

Sh'ana acknowledged her with a slight nod and smile.

Then she turned and walked on out.

A few moments later, the DA walked beside the SI to her skimmer, a sleek, bright arrow of steel and glass, in the dock behind the courthouse. The morgue's hovervan was stationed a short distance away.

Wheatcroft glanced at the elegant cline. 'You know,' he said, 'I think that young woman could have proved her case without your help. Forensics could have confirmed her account.'

Sh'ana shrugged. 'I think the real reason she insisted on the investigation had nothing to do with proving her case.'

'Oh?' said Wheatcroft, raising his eyebrows. 'Meaning what?'

The two morgue attendants came out of the courthouse, wheeling the gurney towards their van.

Sh'ana said, as she watched them slide the stretcher into the back of the van, 'Meaning that the accused knew there was another woman in the man's life, but had no proof. So her primary reason, I would say, was to confirm the presence of this other woman. It would cauterize her sense of loss, while exposing the husband's infidelity to his family.'

She waved to the driver of the hovervan, now looking in her direction.

'And the secondary reason?' persevered the DA.

Sh'ana pulled a wry face. 'Oh come on! Isn't it obvious? She wanted to hear the voice of her beloved one last time!'

Wheatcroft grimaced, unconvinced. 'But he was cussing her out! Who'd want that kind of final memory?'

'I've seen it so often,' said the SI. 'The lies, the tears, the accusation but finally, also, the morbid hunger. The need to *know*. Finally and without a shadow of doubt, what went on in someone else's mind in the final moments before death. In the voice of the deceased.'

She dipped her eyes for a moment, before looking back at the DA. 'It's a hunger that clines like me are especially indebted to, wouldn't you say?' Her voice became a soft purr. 'Permitting us to indulge our own hungers?'

Sh'ana had meant it as a joke, but Wheatcroft's face was suddenly convulsed with naked disgust. *Odfaa* pulsed from him.

The driver of the hovervan had climbed into his seat and was now looking around expectantly in her direction. She nodded and waved to him, then turned to the DA. 'Sorry, I'd love to chat but I'd best be going. They're waiting to follow me.'

The man's face was screwed up tight. He was trying to withhold his opinion. But it spilled out anyway.

'*How do you do it!*' he said, in a low, hissing voice. 'After you've heard someone's most intimate thoughts, seen his visions, shared his most secret, private feelings...' *Dee'Ssiriya* pulsed in pungent gouts. 'How can you possibly take the body home and...and...' He shook his head, as if trying to rid himself of a mental vision.

'Oh, that's easy!' said Sh'ana.

She slid back the hatch of her skimmer and sprang inside with a single nimble leap. 'It's high-energy work, you know? Using our *z'hi*? As a result, we clines have much greater protein needs than regular humans. Indeed, I'm so ravenous right now that I could literally eat a...'

Then she looked up and flashed her beautiful teeth at him once more. '...a nice, fresh human body! Yum.'

FEAST

The vampire strolled into the Arrival Lounge at New Delhi's Indira Gandhi International Airport, a faint smile on his face. He looked like a man of means, silver-haired, clean-shaven, handsome and tall. He had concealed the extreme pallor of his skin with touches of rouge, giving himself a complexion befitting a European traveller who spends his summers idling on the sunlit sands of expensive beaches. He was dressed in a light summer suit, pushing a luggage trolley with two cases on it, one large and one small, both in black, hand-tooled leather.

It was three a.m. yet the huge, brightly lit hall was seething with people awaiting the arrival of their friends and family. Metal barriers had been set up to create a channel through which the newly arrived could proceed through the hall. Standing right up against the barriers were a number of young men holding up placards with the names of arriving passengers variously scribbled by hand or printed out, in large black capital letters, in English.

A thin trickle of fellow passengers straggled along beside the vampire, their faces turned towards the waiting crowd, looking for anyone familiar. *So plump!* thought the vampire, as he too looked out into the throng, though not because he expected to recognize anyone. *So eager. So innocent.*

A moment later he had caught sight of a signboard with ANDREW MORTON inscribed upon it. He had chosen to affect a plain-sounding, forgettable name. The young man holding the board wore a dark maroon uniform with gold embroidery on his pocket announcing the name of the establishment to which he belonged. A hotel: the Maurya Sheraton.

'Ah–' said Morton, broadening his smile as he inclined his head towards the young man. 'For me, I think?' He had an excellent repertoire of accents but had chosen, for this trip, to affect a culture-neutral Aanglophonic voice.

In another few minutes, the young man had introduced himself as 'Satish, driver' and was trotting industriously ahead of the vampire, pushing the luggage trolley. The mass of hot, sweating bodies parted briefly to let the two of them through before surging back to fill the breach. To the monster's finely attuned senses, the scent given off by the entities around him was as ripe and heady as tropical fruit, pungent with a quality he could not quite identify.

Was it uniquely local? he wondered. *Or did it vary from one principality to the next?*

There would be time enough to find out.

Then they were outside the terminal building and the mild humidity of the interior of that overbright Arrival Lounge was revealed to be an air-conditioned version of the sauna conditions outside.

'Oh...*my*,' said the vampire, temporarily nonplussed by the viscous quality of the air. He dabbed his mouth with a fine white handkerchief. The atmosphere was practically liquid! It was unlike anything he had ever encountered before. Unpleasant, yes, but also intoxicating. Exotic. Rich with chemicals, human airborne ejecta, germs, dust particles, scent molecules, pheromones.

Astounding!

A minute buzzing distracted him briefly. He snapped his head around to discover its source and saw a tiny insect coasting like a surfer on the current of warm air that flowed off Satish. Indeed, there was a cloud of them trailing the young man. *Mosquitoes,* thought the vampire. *How quaint!*

Of course he had encountered such creatures before, but there was a subtle difference. Here, in the third world, they were still a force to be reckoned with: carriers of disease, miniscule assassins. As he had no scent, they paid no attention to him.

Then he was once more within the temperature-modulated environment of the vehicle that Satish Driver was currently in command of. Once they were on their way, the young man attempted to engage the vampire in conversation, asking about his family, his home, his country. Morton listened and responded absentmindedly. His keen intelligence was sucking in information about this new and unfamiliar environment with the same avid hunger that he turned upon his victims when he fed. *Why has it taken me so long to come here?* he wondered. *Why have I never thought of visiting before?*

The city streets were shrouded in darkness, streetlights spaced at long intervals. There were broad avenues lined with trees and bushes. Behind the trees reared the silhouettes of tall buildings, punctuated by the vertical strip of their lighted stairwells. Other vehicles careened by on either side. But whenever his own car paused to acknowledge a red light, permitting the vampire to sample his surroundings, he could sense the presence of countless warm bodies lying unguarded in sleep on the sidewalks. They revealed themselves as long and low bundles, giving off a faint glow.

The hotel was like a fist of brightness, thrust up against the night sky. Satish saw Morton to his room, collected a juicy tip, and agreed to return the following evening in his capacity as driver and informal tour guide. By this time, it was close to dawn so the vampire drew the heavy drapes across his windows, turned off all the lights, then went into his bathroom and lay down, fully clothed, in the tub. It was the closest thing to a coffin he would find while travelling and he greatly preferred it to the suffocating embrace of a bed. He lay in the cold white container, listening to the murmur of water rattling in the plumbing and entered into that state of suspended animation which passed for sleep amongst entities of his kind.

For the next three evenings, he went out in the company of Satish Driver to the most densely populated areas of the city. Chandni Chowk was the name of one. The area around the shrine of Nizamuddin Aulia was another. The third was an underground shopping mall called Palika Bazaar. He immersed himself in the fragrant, living heat of his prey, stoking his hunger like a child teasing a caged animal, enjoying its keening protests.

In places where the teeming hordes were especially dense, squishy soft bodies pressed against him on all sides with a surprising lack of reserve. He had never before encountered such uninhibited yet anonymous physical contact. In Europe it was unheard of for strangers, even in the grip of football hysteria or Oktoberfest revelry, to tolerate intimacies at this level. When he managed to persuade Satish to introduce him to a commuter train, bursting at rush hour like a pod full of human peas, he practically swooned with the intoxication of being squeezed butt-to-butt, thigh-to-thigh, chest-to-chest against dozens of fellow passengers. With their slick-skinned brown faces inches from his own, the aroma they gave off filled him with quivering delight. Cardamom and clove, onion and ginger, mustard oil, pepper and...something else. In the beginning he decided that it was *innocence*.

Yes. It was innocence that produced a fragrance as precise and particular as that of a spice.

Returning from the third foray, sitting in the passenger seat beside Satish Driver, the smile on Morton's face as he acknowledged the pressure of the need building within his body had grown into a grimace. Every individual hair follicle was tense with longing. His hands were literally twitching in his lap. In his belly, the furnace of his craving burned so hot and bright that it was all he could do to avoid crying out. As it was, he had to keep his lips parted to allow him to pant softly. His canines thickened and grew long within his mouth, throbbing painfully as he reined them in, keeping them concealed.

At the hotel, he invited the driver to come up to his room. Within minutes of entering the chamber and locking the door, he had turned upon the lad and accomplished the deed. Satish didn't resist at all. He closed his eyes as the vampire embraced him, allowing himself to be bent backwards. Even as the gleaming white teeth punctured the soft, yielding skin of his throat, the driver merely stiffened and let out a tiny gurgling moan. Nothing more. For long minutes, Morton's senses reeled with the familiar blinding radiance that blotted out all thought, all awareness. He knew nothing of his surroundings until he had drained every last drop of the sweet, rich, life-sustaining elixir complete with all the other liquids that animated mortal frames. Only a dry, rattling husk remained in his arms when he was done.

Then he lay back on the carpet, sated.

Ah! he thought. *Ahhh. It has begun.*

His reign of passion in this new country. His personal, private bloodfest.

In his suitcase, he had a small electric saw with which he sliced up the late driver's body. The tub was an excellent location for the operation. Once he had rendered the body down to a series of two-inch-thick slabs, he packed the bits into sealable plastic bags, then scrubbed the tub clean of corpse-litter. He transferred the now unrecognizable remains of the driver to his cases, called for room service, went down, hired a taxi and checked out of the hotel.

By evening, he was in the Taj Man Singh, with a new alias and a passport to match.

He waited till after midnight to go on a long slow walk, carrying the sealable bags in his backpack and emptying a few of them into garbage dumps as he passed them. In order to avoid attracting attention, he assumed the shrunken frame of a scavenging beggar, complete with matted hair and dirty, swarthy skin. Changing shape always required an enormous expenditure of energy and by the time he had completed his task for the night, his stomach was growling again.

He was perhaps a half-mile from the hotel. Keeping to the deep shade of the shrubbery and creeping along the boundary wall of one of the gracious mansions lining the avenue, he came upon a sleeping human form, curled up like a dog on a patch of jute sacking. He did not attempt to find the tramp's neck, but bit down into the wrist at the pulse point.

The rank scent of the skin, unwashed perhaps for weeks and sticky with oozing wounds, did not deter him for even a second. He took his pleasures where he found them, which was frequently amongst the poor and the destitute, defenceless as they so often were.

When he had recovered from the storm of his own delight, he resumed his own shape, rearranged his clothes and rested for a few moments, with his back against the brick wall. Once again he had tasted that flavour, the one he had initially identified as innocence. It was sharp, sweet and unmistakable, like a citrus fruit that concentrates all the passion of summer within the plump grains of its flesh. But what *was* it? He, who had drained countless containers of human blood in the course of his unnaturally long life, could not remember encountering this quality before. Was it connected to the climate? Or something specific to this culture? And if it was culture, then how curious that he could detect it even upon this castaway, this stinking derelict with no discernible society to call his own!

Leaving the desiccated remains where they lay, the vampire returned to his hotel feeling thoughtful.

In the course of the next couple of weeks, he continued his forays into the city's night-time streets. He was astonished at the ease with which he found victims. The best locations were near garbage dumps, inside the many ruined tombs that dotted the city and under park benches. But public toilets and the stairwells of apartment buildings were equally well populated by unresisting targets. Never yet had he encountered such extreme submission, such a total absence of struggle. It was true that he'd always had a gentle touch, an almost surgical skill at locating the exact point on an artery that would produce the swiftest results and with the least discomfort to the owner. Even so, it amazed and slightly unnerved him that he should have such easy success.

Equally astonishing was the fact that no reports of mysterious deaths had appeared in the press. He had been expecting to cover his tracks with meticulous care, as he had done with Satish. But it wasn't necessary. If an encounter took place in a park, he buried the remains in a pit he dug in the same location. If in a building, he folded the dry husk into a sack and carried the small bundle away to the closest convenient water tank. He had even, on a couple of occasions, affected the appearance of an Indian coolie carrying a head-load in broad daylight. No one turned to look twice at him.

Though he fed only under cover of darkness, he no longer hid inside the hotel during daylight hours. Instead he travelled in buses and trains, walked through bustling marketplaces and plunged into the crowds flocking outside shrines and other places of worship. He assumed a number of different disguises, finding that a young foreign male backpacker elicited the most positive responses from ordinary people. He talked to anyone who looked friendly, trying in various oblique ways to find answers to the questions that could never be asked directly of any mortals: *What is the meaning of this unique local taste? Why have I not encountered it before? Is it possible for culture to impart an actual physical fragrance? And if so, why have I never heard of such a thing before?*

In the hotel, he sought out fellow Europeans now and then, just to confirm that the scent or flavour or whatever it was did not stick to them. And it did not. Only long-time expatriates gave off a slight trace of it. Twice he'd been invited to Embassy receptions and had mingled with crowds of his own compatriots, feeling nostalgic for the familiar, uncomplicated scent he associated with European victims. It amused him to contemplate luring a fellow guest into the bushes for a quick nip, but he easily resisted the temptation. On the one hand, he was sated with daily feeding. On the other hand, he guessed that a disappearance from an Embassy party might result in alarm bells being rung. The tell-tale wounds would be recognized for what they were and the hunt would be on, with all the frenzy associated with it. How many years had it been since he'd last had to save himself from imminent exposure or fight off an attack from someone armed with The Weapons? He couldn't remember.

Back in Europe, he had got used to living so frugally, so mindful of the dangers associated with being a vampire that months would go by when he fed only on vermin, stray cats, crows plucked out of the air and even, on occasion, raw meat bought from a supermarket. He shuddered at the memory of the last time he had been driven to suck sustenance out of an inert lump of dead flesh bought at a Safeways counter. He now wondered how he was going to adjust back to his home environment. He'd grown flabby during his stay in this country, not just in terms of his physical dimensions, but in the loss of his vampire instincts. He simply didn't have to worry about exposure here. The majority of citizens were apparently unconscious of monsters of his kind and therefore had no defences against him.

But his six-month visa was running out and the stack of euros he'd brought with him had dwindled alarmingly. He could not own credit cards or any other financial instruments because of the peculiar problems associated with immortality. Not only did he need to suppress bank records which revealed the unnatural length of his life, but Morton, or Martin Payne as he now called himself, routinely struggled when handling currency notes that made direct reference to the religion of his culture. US dollars, for instance, were out of bounds for him because of that pernicious line: 'In God We Trust'. He had to wear gloves in order to avoid coming into direct contact with the notes before picking them up.

Sipping a cup of coffee in the hotel lobby restaurant one morning, fretting over the prospect of returning to Europe, he became suddenly aware that the hair on the back of his neck was prickling. He turned in his seat, to find a blonde woman standing near him, smiling in the way of someone requesting permission to join his table.

'May I?' she now said, as she came around to the empty chair opposite his.

Taken by surprise, Payne could not muster excuses quickly enough. 'Why…uh…yes, I suppose so – of course–' he said, beginning to stand up.

The woman stopped him. 'Oh, don't bother,' she said, sitting down. She was a little over middle-age, with fashionably streaked hair and an amethyst necklace around her neck. Her crisp white linen jacket and skirt partnered with an ice-mauve silk blouse, spoke of expensive good taste.

'My name's Cindy,' she said, in an accent that owed more to America than England. 'Cindy Wright.' She did not offer her hand for shaking. 'You needn't bother looking around to see if there are empty seats elsewhere,' she said. She paused for him to absorb the implications of her remark. 'I'm here because I think I know what you are.'

The vampire raised his eyebrows. 'Oh?'

Already his mind was racing, estimating his chances of success if escape became necessary. Already he was berating himself for his lack of preparedness, his loss of caution. In a crowded room, in broad daylight, the only option was an extreme change of form – a bat, for instance–

'Relax,' said Cindy, as if she perfectly understood his train of thought. 'I'm not about to expose you.' She paused with that annoying, knowing smile playing upon her lips. 'I've been shadowing you for a couple of days so I'm pretty sure.' She shook her head at him as he continued to look blankly at her. 'Come on! Surely you've not lost *all* your instincts?' She leaned forward now and very quickly, in a gesture that shocked him because it was so unexpected, she flicked her upper lip with a finger, just enough that he could see one of her canines. Sure enough, there it was: the sharp unnatural point, unmistakeable even in its sheathed and quiescent state.

Relief flushed through Payne. 'My goodness!' he gasped. 'For a moment I thought…'

'I know, I know,' said Cindy. 'It happens to all of us. Exposure Panic Response! But that's the least of your worries. Don't just sit there gulping like a fish! Do you mean to say you really don't have the slightest idea what I'm talking about?'

'Well– I–' stammered Payne. 'This is so unexpected! I've not met anyone else for such a long time that I'd stopped hoping. One of us, I mean. Are…are there many? Of us?'

'Yes and no,' said Cindy. 'Very few with active teeth.'

'Huh?' said Payne, his eyes narrowing. 'I don't understand what you mean.'

Cindy glanced away. 'It's one of the final signs,' she said, 'that we've been here too long.' She looked back at him. 'Mine stopped descending after my first year. But there are other signs. Just the fact that we're both sitting here in the open, in daylight, for instance. Didn't that surprise you? No? You'll find that fresh-flowing water isn't much of a problem any more either. As for the reflections in mirrors, well–' She tapped one of the shiny metal spoons lying on the table. 'Pick one of these up and surprise yourself!'

Payne sucked in his breath, feeling deeply disturbed. 'What about…?'

Cindy pre-empted him. 'Each of us is different,' she said. She held up her right arm. 'Can you look at my charm bracelet?' Payne winced and averted his face, but not before he'd seen the small gold cross dangling from her wrist. 'There you go. You're still sensitive. But I can wear one now. You'll be able to as well, if you stay here long enough.'

'But…why?' said Payne in a hoarse voice. 'It makes no *sense*!'

'On the contrary,' retorted Cindy, 'it makes all the sense in the world. We're products of a very specific belief system – I won't name it, since you're still too sensitive – and all our dark powers, even though they're forged in opposition to that system, require our absolute belief in it.' She stopped abruptly, staring at him with a searching expression. 'In fact, just by telling you this, I might be weakening your powers. Do you want me to stop?'

'No, no…' said Payne, in a low voice. He was finding it difficult to control his breathing. 'Please continue. I have indeed been puzzled and curious. Whatever it is, I need to know.'

'All right,' said Cindy, 'you asked for it.' She was no longer smiling. 'The belief system we belong to is an austere one. Think about it: one immortal soul, one life on Earth, one chance for heaven or hell. Right? Within that system, by choosing to suck the life-essence out of our fellow creatures, we gave up our rights as mortals. In exchange we acquired supernatural privileges such as immortality. But in order to maintain our powers *we must uphold our own belief system!* Are you beginning to get my point? In order to be culture-specific monsters we ourselves have got to be True Believers!'

She gestured at the brightly lit, bustling hotel lobby in which they were both sitting. They were surrounded by guests and employees, the majority of whom were Indians. 'In this culture, the rules of faith are completely different. There's no precise heaven or hell. There's no immortal soul – not in the sense we understand it – and there's no single…uh…divine authority. Instead there are infinite births, infinite deaths, infinite divinities. It doesn't really matter whether they formally believe in reincarnation or what names they give their deities or whether they even believe in anyone or anything. Just by being here they get recycled. So when we come here, we're exposed to a system that's directly opposed to our own. Instead of a single life and a single fate, there's a raging torrent of lives and fates, truths and deaths!'

Payne listened intently, saying nothing.

'Within this system, though they have monsters, even one they call 'vampire', there's nothing fixed and definite about them. Some say their feet are on backwards and that they lurk in lonely places. But there are no crucifixes or silver bullets with which to dispatch them, no well-defined appearance or behaviour. They're not feared in the same way we're feared back home.' She shrugged. 'After all, if one life slips away courtesy a ghoul or demon, there's always a chance of having better luck the next time around! In the *next* life. The *next* incarnation.' She sent him a searching look. 'It's a system based on infinite abundance, in which nothing and no-one matters because there's always more where it came from. So when we, who belong to the one-life-one-chance system, come into contact with a multi-life-multi-chance system, we begin to drown. Not right away, but slowly, over time.'

Payne said, his voice plaintive, 'But they *succumb* to us! How can we be their victims?'

Cindy was shaking her head. 'Numbers matter. All they have to do is keep on succumbing until, finally, our resistance is overwhelmed. That sweet flavour you've noticed? It's not just a tropical spice. It's a lack of fear. They don't fear us because they *know*, in their deepest hearts, that their sheer numbers will prevail. Without active fear to define us, we cease to be monsters. Our powers wane. We begin to die.'

Payne could feel a churning sensation within himself. Already, he could sense the truth of what Cindy was saying. His teeth were aching strangely for instance. 'Surely it's reversible?' he whispered. 'Surely when we return to Europe we get our powers back?'

'No idea,' said Cindy. 'I've only met those of us who've chosen to stay.'

'But– but– *mortality*!' said Payne, grimacing. 'Don't you mind dying?'

'Ahh,' said Cindy, stretching luxuriously and leaning back in her chair. 'You get used to it after a while. And besides, once you've been here long enough, you find yourself starting to hope…' She was smiling once more.

'*Hope!* Hope for what?'

'Better luck next time!'

THE GIRL WHO COULD MAKE PEOPLE NAKED

'She'll be there,' said Gautam's sister, smiling as she plaited her hair. 'Don't worry!'

Gautam felt the skin on his face stretch and thin out like an expanding gas balloon, with the walnut of his brain exposed to view, floating within it. Was he so transparent? 'I'm not worrying,' he said.

'Of course you are,' said Sagari. 'Look at your face. All wound up! Like a– like a–' She swung her hair forward over her left shoulder, her fingers plucking and taming the black delta of hair into a taut braid, the plump links glistening like paired beetle-wings. Outside the window of her room, the heat prowled and hammered at the glass, willing the air conditioner to relent and let it in so that it could devour its human prey on this burning morning in May, in summer, the season of annihilation.

'What?' said Gautam, interested.

'A clock, I was going to say,' said Sagari, 'but who winds clocks these days?' Her left hand held the end of the plait close to her waist, while her right wove a gold fillet into the end of it, containing it. 'So I don't know what you look like any more.' She laughed at his reflection in the mirror. Her little brother, cho chweet! She could still see the traces of puppy fat on him, a lingering roundedness near his chin, stubbled now. Stubbled! 'Better shave, Gogi. You look like a porcupine more than anything else. And what will she think of you then, your special friend–'

Gautam leapt up in frustration. 'It's not fair!' he said. 'I never teased *you*–' But he rubbed his chin anyway.

Sagari turned around. She made her mouth prim. 'What was there to tease?'

'Yah, yah, yah,' said Gautam, feeling a peculiarity in the pit of his stomach. Sometimes his sister's beauty made him ache. He didn't like to think of her going away, leaving them. Being with some man. Smiling at some man in that way that he had seen, when he had caught them alone, once some months ago, she and her – he had to force himself to pronounce the word: suitor. Not that it had worked out, but still. And now there was another. This one was going to work. He couldn't enjoy the idea. He knew he shouldn't entertain possessive thoughts about his sister, but he did. He felt helpless against the onslaught of such thoughts. Was he a pervert, after all? The *Sunday Telegraph* had carried a quiz some weeks ago, called 'Your Sexual Appetites Revealed!!' from which he had learned that his love for his elder sister was almost certainly unnatural. But what next? How did perverts atone for their perversions? Should he give himself up to the police? He silenced his mind and frowned. 'There was that guy who came, the first one. You made eyes at him– I saw you– '

'Never,' said Sagari, evenly. She had picked up the kajal and was leaning towards the tall mirror to apply it. Her breath fogged the glass. 'You saw nothing.' She muddied the tip of her right index finger with the oily carbon-black. The hand steadied itself against her chin, while the middle finger held down the skin beneath the lower lid, stained faintly blue with sleeplessness. The index finger lightly skated the rim of the lower lid, leaving a glistening track of night. She released the lid and stood back. The eye smarted and tears spilled out of the pink inner corner. 'You just think you saw something.'

'You're crying,' said Gautam.

'Silly,' said Sagari, bending her neck so that the tears drained down her nose, where she could dab them away without smudging the eye. 'Can't you see it's because of the whatsit? Kajal.' She started on the other eye. 'Let me–' she paused as her finger traced its line, 'let me put some in your eyes and then we'll see who cries!' She stood back from the mirror, blinking, dabbing at her eyes with the tissue that came up in alternating colours, Mauve Ice and Emerald Hush. Mauve this time. She whirled around, laughing, her fingertip raised in attack. 'Come! We'll dress you like a village boy–!'

But Gautam didn't rear back as he was expected to do and her darting finger had to stop short at his nose. He stood his ground and looked down at her from his seventeen-year-old height, his face heavy even in its baby way. Something in his expression hurt her. 'Oh!' she said, her voice shrilling, 'You'd look so cute!'

'You *are* crying,' said Gautam, his voice thick. And he left the room.

But an hour later, when everyone was gathered down by the door in readiness, there was no trace of tears. Sagari was giggling with her friend Kussum, both of them insulated against the heat within the dense fog of their perfume. Already they had plunged into the ferocious light, laughing and exclaiming, Sagari holding the remote-key aloft like a wand. The little red Zen responded with its ersatz chirrup as they ran, hobbled by their high heels, across the cement driveway, till they gained the safe custody of the car and of its air conditioner. Gautam was deputed to drive them, while his parents, one aunt and her daughter took off ahead, in the 'Amby' with the cloth-covered seats, driven by the company chauffeur.

The groom's house resembled a collision between an oil tanker and a Spanish villa. There was a sentry at the gate. Under the portico there was a liveried valet to park the car. '–just like a five-star!' whispered Kussum to Sagari, clearly awestruck. Sagari shook her plait over her shoulder and smiled distantly. Gautam, just behind her, saw her thoughts running ahead of her, already in possession of this valet, these steps, this door with its newly antique brass studs. Their parents had just disembarked and were waiting for Sagari.

They were ushered into a glass cabinet the size of a ballroom. Inside it, some twenty guests representing Their Side, sat on peach brocade furniture, with the frigid air puddling at their ankles. They looked up, their faces set in the genteel hostility traditional to in-laws as the host rose with arms outstretched to greet the bride-to-be. The two-ton Austrian chandelier, vouchsafe of the clan's business in glassware, hung like a glittering threat above the company. Gautam's family advanced in wedge formation, nodding, folded hands upraised, teeth bared in ritual smiles. Sagari stooped as she bent to touch feet, her sandalwood silk dupatta falling prettily, gold sliding down her fair arm, clinking at the wrist. She was led towards a cut-glass divan, on which she sat with her head bent as the groom, in his raw silk ensemble, fussed with her parents prior to sitting down himself. Then they held court to all the gathered relatives who assayed them, comparing their skin colours, their clothes, their relative heights and pronouncing on the likelihood of attractive children.

Gautam turned his head away, wishing he hadn't come, wishing he could shrink himself to the size of an ant and scurry away. He turned. And Bahaar was by his side.

'Hi,' she said, smiling into his eyes. She was his height. 'I knew you'd come. I arranged it.'

'What?' he asked. The loud room misted around him. There was only this intoxication before him, of black curls and voice. A voice like burnt rope and ripening mangoes.

'For you to be here,' she said, taking his arm. She led him to where a pair of seats were obscured behind a fringe of potted ferns. 'I have certain powers.' He could smell her, a scent like powdered rubies. 'The last time, when we met, I stole your handkerchief. Remember?' He didn't. 'That's all I needed, because in this weather it has your sweat on it. Sweat is very good for establishing psychic connections.'

Gautam had no idea what she was talking about. He felt he might lick her forehead in a moment and wondered if it would taste as much of cappuccino as it looked. He wondered if human skin could be flavoured. 'Have you ever wondered,' he began.

'If human skin can be flavoured?' she ended. 'Yes,' she said, nodding quickly, 'it can be, but it takes an effort. And not any flavour. Animal flavours are easier than vegetable. Honey is almost impossible without including an aftertaste of bee.' He saw, with fascination, that when she looked into his eyes, she could see every thought of his, strung out like washed shirts flapping on a line. He felt wonderfully cleansed. 'But right now, my forehead tastes of a chemical factory!' she said, smiling. 'You'll have to wait till I've spent some time with you before I can produce a flavour on demand!'

He whispered, 'I don't understand anything you're saying. You know that?'

She said, 'Of course. It always takes a little while. But you'll get used to it. Don't blank your mind out like you did just now, or I can't see a thing–' She paused and looked around. 'The others, for instance. The majority are quite, quite empty. Can you imagine it?' He couldn't. 'Looking into them is like looking at rows of empty shelves. Empty bookshelves.' She smiled broadly, showing the beginning of a dimple in her left cheek. Her canines were sharp and prominent. 'Yes,' she said, knowingly. 'It was the fashion to remove canines at one time. But I wouldn't let them! Not even when I was small.'

Gautam shook his head in wonder. It was difficult to keep pace with her, when his thoughts were being answered before he had registered them himself. 'I– I don't think I've ever met someone like you,' he tried, lamely.

'You wouldn't know, if you had,' she countered. 'We choose who to reveal ourselves to. We're discriminating. Isn't that obvious?'

He said, 'Who is "we"?'

She said, 'This is not the time to tell you.' She looked around the room again, like a raptor scanning the horizon. She may have been looking out across vast spaces, crags, canyons, craters, moon mountains. 'It's something I learnt in Canada. But the group I was with said I was a Natural. They said they had had portents of my presence in the neighbourhood months before I joined them.'

'You were in Canada?' said Gautam. The question seemed strange because it was so ordinary. Almost like a normal conversation. 'Visiting?'

'No,' she said. 'I grew up there.' Her tone was faintly scornful. 'Can't you tell from my accent? Most people notice at once.'

The fern in front of them shook. Gautam's cousin stood there, Gayatri. She was fourteen and plain. Even contact lenses couldn't save her from the unfashionable shroud of quiet studiousness which enveloped her coltish frame. A pleading expression in her eyes told Gautam that she had been, as usual, abandoned in a party which held no niche for adolescents. She and Gautam had a secret contract to keep each other company on occasions like this.

'Gai!' said Gautam, 'um...' and stood up, embarrassed. 'This is–' he gestured, as Gayatri, smiling with painful gratitude, slunk into his seat, 'Bahaar. She's– she's from Canada–'

'Bahaar!' said Gayatri, 'what a strange name!' But Bahaar had stood up too.

'Come,' she said to Gautam, 'I can show you something interesting.' She took Gautam's arm and moved towards a vitrine filled with white jade elephants.

Gautam glanced with concern at his cousin. Her eyes were wide, were telling him that she was drowning, she was on a raft alone in a sea of strangers and he a seagull. *Don't leave me!* she pleaded. *Wait till we're in sight of land!*

'Come *on*!' said Bahaar and her talons flashed, clutching his hand. In moments they were soaring, the two of them, on a column of heat, high above the party, over the chandelier where tiny spiders hopped upside down amid the rainbow shadows cast by the great light. But when they landed, the ceiling was their floor and the party was suspended above them, defying gravity. 'You wanted to be an ant, didn't you?' said Bahaar. 'Well, this is what it feels like.' From their perspective, the chandelier was a rigid fountain of wires and winking ice-gems just ahead of them. Gautam could see his family like distant giants, suspended from what was now his ceiling. His sister sat shivering on the crystal divan, the brother-in-law-to-be leaning forward like a prince to catch some remark made by his mother.

Gayatri sat alone where they had left her. Gautam wished he could call to her, to tell her that he could see her. But she couldn't have seen him, even if she had tried. He was too small.

'I say,' said Gautam, 'that wasn't nice. She's a good kid.'

'Nah,' said Bahaar. 'Just another shelf. She'll marry badly and spend her whole life trying to scrape together a little beauty with which to buy herself one night of love. But she won't succeed. Forget her.' Even as an ant, Bahaar looked intoxicating.

Gautam flexed his tiny waist, causing the astounding bulb of his abdomen to bounce. His chitinous legs popped and clicked. His olfactory apparatus allowed him to sample smells drifting up from the room. He could smell Gai's tears distinctly, a sharp, sad scent touched with panic. 'No,' he said, 'you can't know that. She's only fourteen. She might change. And anyway, we're friends – I felt bad, leaving her.' Bahaar's mandibles snapped in irritation. 'Careful!' she said. 'You have potential, but you could lose it if you don't watch your thoughts!'

'I don't understand,' said Gautam, walking forward gingerly. The mass of his body was suspended horizontally between the sturdy, jointed struts of his limbs. His vision was a fragmented dazzle of oval screens. His breathing was a pleasing in-rush out-rush affecting the whole length of his body. The air itself was rough and molecular, the grain of reality coarse to one as diminutive as he. But he did not feel diminished. On the contrary, it was the world that had expanded. 'How can you be so sure?'

'When I saw you that first time,' said Bahaar, 'I knew that I could either leave you to become an empty shelf like all the rest, or I could help you. Help you save your books. Don't you understand? We're born with a library of powers, all of us, but most of us lose them before we've even learnt to speak!'

'How can you help me?' asked Gautam. One of the spiders up ahead was sending crackling broadcasts in gibberish. 'And why now?' A dust-mite was careening in their direction like a self-propelled Volkswagen. As it passed them, he saw its mouth parts champing on a wad of regurgitated wood. Relentlessly, like an eating machine.

'Look!' said Bahaar, 'most people have no option but to be swept along on the river of life, going where it goes, being tossed out where it tosses them out. To only a few is it given to divert the river to suit *their* purpose. I'm amongst those few. And I'm inviting you, you because you have potential, to come along with me.' She stroked him with her antenna, a sensation for which he had no human analog. 'To explore the all-encompassing Everything.'

'I– I'll have to think about it,' he said. Four ants appeared, running at a tilt. Gautam could hear the whirring urgency of their limbs. They charged up, locked antennae, exchanged incomprehensible messages, then barrelled off again, mandibles clacking in bewilderment.

'You don't have the time,' said Bahaar. 'The river is in torrent, the waterfall is just ahead. From my helicopter, I dangle a lifeline to you: will you take it? Or will you think it over? Hurry!'

From above them came a lazy stirring. Gautam saw the crowd getting to its feet, the ladies shuffling forward. 'They're going in for lunch,' he said. 'We must join them. Please– I need more time– '

And they were back among the families.

Bahaar did not look at him. One of the doors had been opened and a tide of warm air slushed forward, as guests passed through it and out towards the dining room. Sagari bore down on Gautam. 'Where have you been!' she exclaimed, then looked meaningfully over his shoulder. He turned to introduce Bahaar, but saw that she had vanished. 'I was looking for you everywhere,' said Sagari. Then she leaned forward and whispered, 'Has she conquered you already?'

He said, 'She's very…' He sucked in his breath. 'Very, very…'

Sagari laughed and narrowed her eyes. 'Oh, oh! So quick? Shall we speak to her parents – after all, they're right here too–' But their mother came towards them and shooed them out to lunch.

All through the meal, Bahaar remained out of reach. Gautam could see her across the room, flashing her hair and telling jokes with her brothers, while he felt a vacuum sucking at his heart. Whenever he tried to approach her, she slid out of sight only to reappear elsewhere in the room and equally distant. He looked for Gai, but she was standing in her mother's bulky shadow, dabbing at her food with her head down. All around him, the ebb and flow of eager diners.

He found himself looking at the people milling about the buffet table on which food was displayed in steaming tiers. Down the middle, from a papier-mâché Horn of Plenty, spilled a tide of imported lettuce, cold meats and cheeses. To the right, in silver urns, the vegetarian dishes. To the left, curried meats, in china. A waiter approached to offer a glass of wine. Behind him, with a little shriek, someone dropped a plate. Gautam's mind was buzzing.

Everywhere he looked, he saw evidence of what Bahaar had told him. The massed relatives, gorging with reckless abandon, recalled to his mind the dust mite. Here too the jaws gaped open, food was shovelled in and masticated busily. Pistons pumping, teeth engaging. Now and then a plume of raucous conversation would billow up, followed by immoderate laughter. But the eyes, some sunk in folds of purple fat, some lidded in painted colours, some young, some old – the eyes opened onto voids.

Gautam accepted a glass of wine and walked slowly towards the entrance to the room. No one noticed him. He wondered what it all meant. He had thought he knew what he wanted from life. Three years in college, two years at some IIM, then maybe a shot at LSE in England. Failing which, apprenticeship in his uncle's firm in Bombay. Marriage in ten years, twelve at the most. What else was there? Holidays abroad, a shiny car or two. He could hear the roar of the waterfall. Good food, wines, electronic gadgets. Films. Maybe now and then, a girl on the side. The cold spray was in his face. And children of course, there would be children. Schools, toys, ayahs and birthday parties. The thunder was in his ears. There must be something else!

'There is,' said Bahaar. He turned, looking into her eyes, impenetrably light brown. 'You can come to me.'

Gautam felt hunted, but he asked, 'What do I have to do?'

She shrugged, smiling. 'Have sex with me! I have a room to myself upstairs. We'll go there–'

'Now?' He almost laughed. 'We can't go anywhere *now*! My parents will – what will everyone think?'

'When you start to care what people think, that's when your mind goes blank,' said Bahaar. 'That's why you have to come *now*.'

He challenged her. 'Why do I have a choice? Can't you just... *make* me?'

'This has to be your decision,' said Bahaar. 'The power we use, we who know how to use it, is the power everyone has within themselves. But each person has to learn to locate the source of it themselves. When you've done it once, I can help you. But this first step has to be your own.'

'Can't it be at any other time?' said Gautam.

'It's not just *what* you do,' said Bahaar, 'it's when and where, too. For you, doing *this* at *this* time, when everyone will know, when everyone will be shocked, is the important step. It's a rite of passage. Do you see? You have to break the ties which keep your powers locked up in what people think and say–'

'And afterwards, after some time, I'll be able to do the things you do?' said Gautam, casting a glance towards the ceiling. 'Anything?'

'Anything,' said Bahaar.

Gautam looked back at the room. He would have liked to envy the ease and innocence of all the others with their simple chewing, swallowing and drinking, but he suppressed the idea before Bahaar could pick up on it. He glanced at her and saw it was too late.

'They're empty,' whispered Bahaar, 'empty, empty, empty.'

Gautam saw Sagari. He saw her laughing with her hand held in front of her mouth while the fiancé was slapping someone on his back and guffawing loudly. 'Your sister's no different,' said Bahaar. 'She'll–'

'No, please,' said Gautam. 'Please. I don't want to hear.'

'She'll wait for two years before realizing that my cousin has no intention of marrying her. She'll spoil her name with some riff-raff. She'll–'

Gautam raised his voice. 'I don't want to hear!' he said.

'I like that,' said Bahaar. 'Anger is a good thing, it's useful. It's one of the fuels–'

'I– I'm sorry,' said Gautam. 'But I think I...I think I care for my sister...*too* much.' He blinked hard. The wine spoke for him. 'I can't bear to think she'll be married to that...to your cousin.'

'Good!' said Bahaar. 'Hold on to that pain!'

'And I can't bear to think of doing anything that might hurt her. If we go upstairs, now, during this party, it'll be terrible. My mother would kill me. And these – I mean, your people, I think they'd cancel the whole thing, wouldn't they? I mean, I'm sure they would. And then what would happen to my sister?' He tossed back the wine and felt dizzy. 'What would happen to me?'

Bahaar took in a breath. She said, 'I want to show you a trick I learnt recently.' He looked at her uncertainly. His hair was giving out low frequency vibrations. 'I can make people naked,' she said.

Gautam's face was screwed up with the effort of concentrating on what she was saying. 'Take another person's clothes off, you mean? Can't anyone do that?'

'I meant, I can do it to a whole room at once,' said Bahaar, turning towards the crowded dining space. 'I can make the clothes of all the people in this whole room – invisible!' She turned suddenly to him, her face lit up with glee. 'Want to see?'

'But why?' said Gautam, 'what's the point?'

She shrugged. 'Just like that. It's an easy trick, 'coz it's not, you know, destruction. Just simple vanishment.'

'Everyone?' said Gautam, wanting to lean against the door jamb.

'Even the waiters,' said Bahaar, narrowing her eyes, as she estimated the scale of her operation. 'It would take about nine seconds.' She turned to him. 'Shall I do it?'

Gautam leaned on the doorjamb, shutting his eyes. 'Will it be the same as if I came upstairs with you?'

'Oh, no!' said Bahaar. 'This is just a demonstration, to show you how silly people look with their thin little shells off, even the greatest, the grandest–'

Gautam's head had filled with a soft humming and the air seemed as rough as when he had been an ant. 'Will everyone see or just us?'

'Everyone, of course,' said Bahaar. 'Or else what's the fun?'

She was turned away from him, but her hand absent-mindedly stroked the inside of his arm. He remembered the antenna. 'Come on – say *yes*!'

'Yes,' said Gautam weakly, turning his face towards the painted wood surface he was leaning on, wondering what it would feel like to be a termite, boring into that wood.

Bahaar's hand left him at once. For moments, nothing happened. And then a silence fell, like a guillotine. Gautam's eyes snapped open.

The scene before him was like a bloodless carnage. Standing with their plates in hand, forks upraised, some thirty-five adult diners, five waiters and two catering attendants were naked except for such features of medical equipment as did not qualify as clothing. The groom's father, for instance, a whale of a man, wore a pink nylon truss. A scattering of women wore menstrual equipment. One of the waiters had a knife strapped to his left thigh. Gautam's aunt, who'd had a colostomy, wore a pouch which inflated now, with a frightened venting of gas.

A surprising number had hidden tattoos. Gautam's father had an indigo butterfly directly over the femoral boss at his right hip. Two of the groom-side uncles had identical male nudes, one on the left buttock, one on the right. Many of the older women had scars like railway tracks running across their bellies.

The reproductory organs of both sexes appeared squashed and wrinkled by the clothing which, though still in place, was not visible. A number of older men, thus, had bellies which ended in a triangle of grizzled hair with their plumbing tucked tidily out of sight. The younger ones, boxer-shorted, were less constrained, but the shock of nudity had rendered them as limp as earthworms exposed by a cloudburst. One of Bahaar's brothers had a bright steel ring pierced through his foreskin, causing his organ to look like the snout of a domesticated tapir.

There was only one missing breast in the company, a flat white scar across an aged chest, with a stretch-marked balloon beside it. Among the remaining mammary glands, a remarkable diversity of shapes and colours was presented. The older ones were distended and deflated, cramped within their underclothing. Some appeared to have been rolled up like pairs of socks. Others sprawled comfortably, their nipples out of alignment. Some sprouted hairs like star-nosed moles. Some ended in dark, peevish points. Some had aureoles the size of quarter-plates. Gayatri's terminated in two pert, maroon puffs, startling in one so young. And Sagari–

Gautam wanted to turn his head away. But he couldn't. He made himself look at Sagari, fearing he would be seared by the vision. What he saw was a young woman. She was well-proportioned and unscarred, flat-navelled. And she was his sister. He wanted to laugh with relief. She was his sister. He felt no stirring for her.

Then he looked at Bahaar, realizing that she and he were the only ones still clothed. Her concentration was trained upon the room, like a beam of laser-light. He guessed that he had only to touch her hand and the spell would be broken. He touched her.

'Hhhhhhsssssssss!' She whipped around, shocked, her hands raised to strike. But he held his ground and only her eyes slammed into him, raining blows of hate. She could scarcely speak. 'You *idiot*! You could have damaged me! Breaking my concentration!'

'I'm sorry,' he said, 'but I had to stop you.'

'You could have twisted my mind!'

'It's twisted already,' he said.

In the dining room, the frozen and speechless diners were clothed once more. Throats were cleared. Several plates were dropped at the same instant, giving the waiters an immediate occupation. Two old ladies collapsed. Bahaar's brother of the domesticated tapir started to hyperventilate and was escorted from the room. The groom's father began with 'Well...' but his wife's eye quelled him. All around the room, in low tentative strokes, the pulse of conversation began to beat once more.

Gautam turned to Bahaar. She was staring at him, lightning at her brow. He said, 'I'm destined for the waterfall, aren't I?'

'You're just an immature coward,' she hissed.

'Maybe,' he said, looking towards his family. 'But my sister's marriage will be all right now, won't it?'

She was breathing hard. 'You don't know what you're giving up. And you don't know how I can harm you. I can enter your dreams. I can bloody your sanity. I can make you pay for rejecting me!'

Gautam felt calm. 'Don't,' he said, 'I'm not worth the effort. I'm too weak for you, Bahaar. And I care about my family.'

'You'll drown! You'll smash your head on the rocks!' said Bahaar, lips drawn back from her beautiful teeth.

'Maybe,' said Gautam. 'But I don't think so.' He looked to where Gayatri stood, sampling her ice cream. He smiled at her and winked. 'Excuse me,' he said to Bahaar. 'I'll have my dessert elsewhere.'

FLEXI-TIME

Dr Venkatesh couldn't decide what he disliked more – interacting with the alien invaders or with the four members, all human, of the Post-Capitulation Council. He crossed the final checkpoint, exchanging nods with the heavily armoured and visor-helmeted security guards and walked down a glass-walled passage that ended in an airlock. Then he was through, standing within Fa territory. It was an area designated as human-free in the centre of the city once known as New Delhi. There was no official name because the Fa were not especially communicative, and so it was referred to informally as New Fa Home-Space.

The area was flat and featureless, resembling a stage-set awaiting props. All human structures, possessions, creations – anything whatsoever connected to humans – had been cleared away. No lives had been lost. Those who had been in the way had found themselves relocated, complete with their homes and gardens, dogs and incidental house guests, several kilometres away.

The phase of confrontation had lasted mere days. Within 24 hours, the Fa had demonstrated their overwhelming superiority. Another four days had been required for the various disbelieving and warring factions of humans to come to terms with the changed circumstances, the reality of occupation and the inevitability of acceptance.

Reconstruction was now in progress, even though communication continued to be a problem. The Fa seemed disinterested in, or unable to, discussing their plans. They preferred to express themselves through physical actions, usually on a grand scale. They might remove and reposition a whole forest for instance, or create a waterway where none had existed before.

For all that their methods were non-violent and caused no fatalities, their manner was unmistakably imperious. The New Fa Home-Space, for instance, occupied the heart of India's capital city, but an invisible force field prevented access to humans. The visible boundary wall and security had been put in place by the Delhi administration to prevent accidents. Exactly one week had passed since the creation of the Home-Space, and only one person had been allowed in so far.

That person was Dr Venkatesh.

The professor, a diminutive grey-haired man, wearing a plain white bush shirt and pale, fawn trousers, walked across the grassy expanse that separated the boundary wall from the central depression where the Fa waited for him. His demeanour was one of calm resignation. He entertained the same thoughts he'd had every day since these daily encounters had begun: *Suppose I choose NOT to comply?* This was followed by *But I was never given a choice*. This pair of thoughts chased one another like two squirrels fighting for dominance around the trunk of a tall tree. Up and down the tree they ran until Dr Venkatesh arrived at the lip of the shallow depression.

Here he stopped, as he always did.

The Fa were enormously tall. There were often three of them together, as was the case today. They had no discernible features. Instead, they looked like inanimate objects, smooth, pale vertical strips of shimmering material, slightly curved and extending 20 feet above, five feet across at their greatest width, tapering at both ends. They appeared to be suspended in mid-air, defying gravity.

But that was an illusion. In their wordless, semi-telepathic way, the Fa had revealed that the bulk of their bodies existed outside the human temporal plane. Experts speculated that this meant they occupied a broader continuum of time than local denizens. The visible portion of their bodies was merely the narrow strip of time they shared with human observers, the slender interval referred to as 'the present'.

In practical terms, this chronological otherness meant that people, for the most part, could not physically touch the Fa.

They were always slightly behind or slightly ahead of any actions performed by the race whose planet they had invaded. Though they could see human beings in their entirety and anticipate every move of Earth's inhabitants, to the inhabitants themselves the aliens were like phantom impressions left in long-exposure films – barely visible.

Dr Venkatesh glanced up at the shimmering strips. Turning towards him and drawing slightly apart, the seemingly weightless entities invited him to step down towards them, to stand in their midst. Sometimes there were audible sounds, such as chirps or deep groans. No actual words were said. Nevertheless, the professor found it possible to understand what was expected of him. This was believed to be a form of telepathy. If so, it was extremely subtle, not involving words or images. Whatever the method of delivery, the professor complied with the invitation without hesitation.

There was no pain involved in what followed, no discernible, quantifiable discomfort. Yet, the small man's hair stood up on end. He sweated. His pulse was elevated. He claimed that his mind was a perfect blank. But the truth was that he emptied his consciousness of thought and thus remained stubbornly empty by sheer force of will. He hated every moment that he spent in this condition, surrounded by vast unknowable beings, refusing to think, refusing to let them enter his thoughts. After perhaps one hour, the audience was over.

When he had returned to Human Space, Dr Venkatesh was permitted two hours for recovery. He changed into fresh clothes, replenished the water he had lost from sweating and ate a substantial lunch.

Then it was time to meet the members of the PCC.

The PCC campus had been set up within the grounds and building of what had been the Ashoka Hotel in central Delhi. The meetings were always held within an underground banquet hall, a space that had once been the venue of countless weddings. Venkatesh was escorted to the chamber by helmeted, armoured guards. They opened the ornately decorated doors and immediately withdrew.

Inside, council members were seated in a cluster in the centre of the room, each one behind a desk. Three of them had cups of tea or coffee in front of them, while one had a bottle of water. The professor had a winged armchair to sit in, facing them. He had a small side table to himself and his own cup of tea. He rarely ever got around to drinking it.

There were always four council members, the same four: two men and two women.

'Good afternoon, Professor,' said the general representing the People's Republic of China. She wore a crisp khaki uniform with medals on her chest. She spoke through an electronic interpreter. Each of the others heard her via earbuds in whatever language they preferred. 'Thank you for joining us today.'

Before the general could continue, she was interrupted.

'What can you tell us?' This was the general from the European Federation. He had a thatch of unruly white-blond hair, pale blue eyes and a craggy, permanently frowning face. He wore an aggressive all-black uniform with epaulets, medals, brass studs – the works. 'Anything of note?' His voice had a weary edge even via the translation device.

Dr Venkatesh cleared his throat and shifted in his seat. 'Uhh…' he began, speaking into a discretely placed body mic, 'that is to say…no. Nothing.' The European general groaned aloud, pinching the bridge of his nose.

Then he drew in his breath and jumped to his feet. 'All right,' he said, in a low, furious voice. 'I've had enough. I'm not going to take it any longer–'

Dr Venkatesh blinked and swallowed. He got to his feet as well. 'Sir, there's nothing I can do about the lack of a result,' he said. He tried to keep his voice calm. 'Believe me, performing this task is not my choice. If anyone else could take my place, I would gladly let them do it.'

The Chinese general was about to speak again when the woman with the polished ebony skin and dense halo of orange hair, representing the combined Americas, said, 'I see the general's point.'

As all eyes turned towards her, she got to her feet, achieving a towering height in her six-inch scarlet heels, her chic, floor-length black robe with scarlet flounces at the shoulders. 'We've been at this for…how long? Six days? Seven?' she continued. 'I agree with my European colleague. We have had enough. We need to know what lies ahead for us. For this planet. For our…species.' She looked directly at the professor now. 'Come on. You have to be able to tell us something!'

'But, Madam, I–' began the professor.

She stopped him with an imperious gesture. 'No! I'm sorry, Professor. This is not good enough. We need more.'

She paused and looked around before continuing. 'You and you alone have been invited into the presence of these beings who have, with no warning, taken over our entire planet. How they've done it, we do not yet know. One day we've never heard of them, and the next day they've taken over the world. No weapons, no conflict, no mode of travel – yet there they are. Everywhere. In every country, in every small village and town. These dangling, shimmering strips, suspended in mid-air! Emitting odd sounds! Issuing mysterious wordless orders! They defeated us before we even knew we'd been invaded. We don't know what they want, we don't know how to oppose them, we barely know who or what they are. This is intolerable!'

She looked hard at Dr Venkatesh. 'According to you, the call to approach the Home Space came in the form of an absolute conviction that arose from within, apparently telepathically, to go to the New Fa clearing. You went there, you halted at the impenetrable barrier, whereupon a portal opened, through which you, and you alone, were allowed to pass.'

Biting her lips, as if attempting to control her temper, she continued, 'The whole world has been waiting and wondering, waiting and watching. Yet every day you present us with exactly nothing. Surely, as a man of science, as a sentient being, you can understand that an entire planet cannot wait indefinitely? Surely you realize–'

The fourth delegate, a pale willowy man, wearing a sober, steel-grey business suit and representing Unified Africa leaned forward, cutting in. 'Excuse me, I'm not happy with the term you used just now, Madam Americas. I do not rush to conclusions about this issue of 'defeat'. After all, the Fa are merely amongst us. That is not the same as 'defeat'. True, they are everywhere. True, they have the ability to move people and physical objects in ways that we cannot explain or resist. But so what? To the best of our knowledge, they have caused very little actual damage. No demands upon our resources–'

'Oh, for heaven's sake!' the European general exclaimed. 'Let's just agree that Earth has been invaded, okay? By a superior power. What I find quite *bizarre* is that this superior power has chosen to create its headquarters...where? In INDIA! Land of inefficient plumbing and a billion contradictions. Uncertain power supply and quarrelsome people. Too many languages and too many gods. I mean, do I need to go on? In the 150 years since the end of the Second World War, the rest of the world has managed to solve these problems. Even Africa. Even the rest of South East Asia. Even, God save us, *Brazil*.' He waved a hand towards the relevant representatives.

He was panting now, his face red.

'But here? Noooo! Here, a state of primordial chaos reigns. Here, the traffic is jammed because of cows. The trains are late because of the rains. The streets are flooded because of the blocked drains. And yet...where do the silent Shimmerers pick as the preferred spot for their Home Base? Here! And who is their preferred interpreter? An Indian! I simply cannot accept that!'

Dr Venkatesh felt the surface of his skin heat up and grow damp with sweat once more despite the air conditioning. He hated confrontations. As a young boy he could remember physically wriggling and bending away from situations involving other people. They would get irritated because he could never give answers quick enough for them. He was highly intelligent and very good at his studies, but he had to think through his verbal responses. He liked to be precise, he liked to be accurate and truthful. It meant that he needed to take his time. It also meant that people frequently wanted to slap him – and occasionally did.

He had learned as an adult to control the reflex to fold himself in half and crawl away. But inside his head he felt a sensation exactly as if he were attempting to curl himself into a tiny ball, rolling himself into a corner.

'Ahhm,' he began. 'I wish I could help you. I…I want to help you. But there's really nothing that I can to tell you. I go to the venue, I meet with the Fa and I…'

The European general's eyes bulged, his lips drew back in a snarl and he lunged towards the physicist. The Chinese general, who was quick on her feet, spun around and hit the military man full in the face. 'No! We can't afford to fall apart this way!' she cried, as the other two representatives squawked aloud in surprise.

At that very instant, as Dr Venkatesh flinched away from the furious general, he found the space around his body stretching and ballooning outwards. It was as if he was contained within a bubble of some sort. It was a bit like an infinitely elastic cling film covering him without restricting his movements. Outside of it, he could see the rest of the room frozen in place. Within it, he could move around with ease.

Hesitantly, he took a step forward. His scalp was tingling with amazement and curiosity. He took another step. The bubble, or whatever it was, moved with him. Meanwhile, the other people in the room remained frozen. Still as statues.

Dr Venkatesh walked slowly and wonderingly over to the Chinese general's desk. He picked up the bottle of water that was there, still unopened. Then he returned to where he'd been standing, beside his chair. None of the four PCC members had so much as twitched an eyelid. A sense of sparkling enlightenment began to dawn within the professor's head.

So, he thought. *So!*

He opened the bottle of water, drank from it and capped it once more. All the while, the invisible bubble kept him contained. He looked around the room thoughtfully. He could take his time, he realized. This was like his childhood habit of trying to escape physically from torment but transformed into a temporal bolthole: a bubble of time where he could not be reached. He had let his guard down in that moment of panic when the general came at him. His mind had curled in upon itself, rather like a turtle pulling in its limbs and head. In that instant, he had slipped into the bubble.

How will I get out of it, he wondered, even as the answer appeared in his head. *Just reverse the turtle act. Unfold yourself.*

Immediately, the room filled with sound. The two generals righted themselves. Madam Americas was staring strangely at Venkatesh. The African representative looked slightly ill.

'What?' asked Venkatesh, looking at the others as if they had said something to him.

'You...' began Madam Americas. She stopped and began again. 'Something happened to you. I saw it. Just a blink. But I saw it.'

'Thinned out,' said the African rep, in a strangled tone of voice, as if he'd swallowed a toad. 'I saw it too. Weird. I can't explain it.'

Venkatesh's mind was wonderfully calm. 'I'm thinking,' he said, as he twirled the water bottle slowly in his hands, 'that perhaps I was wrong. Perhaps I do have some news to share after all.'

'Come on, come on!' said the European general, waving his hands in the air, as belligerent as before. 'Get on with it!' The Chinese general, though, stared at the water bottle. She recognized it as hers.

The physicist smiled. Perhaps for the first time since the assignment had begun, he was feeling happy.

'You know, General, what you were saying earlier? About the thousand ways in which India has resisted the modern world? I can well appreciate how irritating it is for you – all of you who transitioned to the digitized era with your perfect regularity, your punctuality, your precision! Yes, India is annoying. Yes, we appear dysfunctional. Yes, we lag behind in so many sectors that we seem to belong to an older, quieter time altogether. We move at our own pace. And that drives people like you mad, General.'

The general snarled and bristled, but his Chinese counterpart grabbed his arm. She was frowning, her gaze still on the bottle in the professor's hand.

Venkatesh paused, holding up the water bottle. 'You've noticed the bottle, Madam General? Yes, it's from your desk. I walked over and picked it up. While the two of you were assaulting each other.' He glanced at the other two council members. They were staring at him with their mouths hanging open. 'What you saw of me was a sliver of myself as I moved around in a bubble of expanded time. That's why I looked weird.'

He took another sip from the bottle now. 'So, here's what I'm thinking: I don't know why the Fa came to our planet, I don't know what their plans for us are. All I am certain of is that they are benign. And the reason they chose India? Maybe it's because of that quality the rest of you complain about when you come to this country: an altered sense of time. Not wrong, not late, not lazy, not stupid. Just...altered. Different from the rest of you speedy-needy types elsewhere on the planet.

'Maybe that's what the Fa saw in us Indians: a fondness for stretching time. Maybe it's an ability, not a liability. Maybe it's a talent, not a defect. Of course, we've not been able to do what they do, which is flex the boundaries of the fleeting minute. But maybe they knew that Indians, more than any other humans, would be more receptive to learning their so-called 'chronological otherness'? Maybe we have a natural talent for learning their techniques of time-bending and chrono-stretching? Moulding it to suit our needs, rather than being imprisoned by it? Maybe that's what they've been passing on to me during my time with them.'

He put the bottle down on the table next to him. 'And now, if you don't mind, I'll take your leave and return to the Fa. I believe I have finally understood how to receive their instructions.'

The four members of the council watched in silence as Venkatesh thinned out before their eyes. They heard a few indistinct chirps and clicks. A moment later, he was gone.

STOLEN HOURS

'RAT!' an enraged voice bellowed, from not far enough away. It was his mother's voice. 'Rat, are you in there?'

At the first sound of her voice, he had reached reflexively to activate the force field on his door – but he need not have bothered. It was rarely ever off. Looking over his shoulder, he could see his mother's bulk beyond the light blanket of energy veiling the entrance to his room as she tried to peer into it.

'Rat!' she called. 'When I catch you this time, I'm going to strip the skin off you with a blow torch!'

The Rat shrugged and turned back to the smooth egg-shaped object on his desk. He was used to threats like this from his mother. On the one hand, he never gave her an opportunity to carry them out and on the other, they were hurled at him so often, at least once a day, that he let them flow off his back like water from a slick suit.

'You're not going to get away with it this time you MUTANT! I'm going to tell your father about it, boy, and he's going to beat your brains out of you with a ram-jet!'

He continued tinkering with the object on his desk, wondering idly what his mother was upset about this time. It must be that centrifuge-mixer of hers, he thought. The mindless cow must have tried to throw something together for dinner in it and splat! It must have redecorated the walls. Must have looked interesting too. So he had taken a few parts out of it, so what? He could put them back in again with his eyes shut, which was more than those T-Series humanoids, his parents, could do. Not that he was going to put the parts back, of course; he had a far more important use for them than his mother could dream of.

'Can you hear me in there, Rat? I can see your light, you runt, I know you're in there. One of these days, I'm going to get through this filthy thing on your door and I'm going to smash everything in sight, every last, stinking machine, just see if I don't!'

He tickled the activator switch a little, just to make the force field guarding the door hiss and throw sparks. That usually frightened her off. Of course, it was only a mild home-made device, held together with snot-balls and his mother's nail polish. She could get through it if she really tried. He sniggered to himself, remembering the only time she had tried – and succeeded – the time when she and the Rat's father had discovered the video scanner that he, Rat, had planted in their bedroom. He had been thirteen at the time.

His mother had come thundering into his room, stark-naked, breasts flying and hair sprouting from all the most amazing places. She had broken through the field before she even remembered it was there. She had also broken his eardrum and various other bits and pieces of him before she was in control of herself again – but it had been worth it. For almost a month afterwards, the Rat had had pictures to sell, of his parents doing the kind of things that other kids in the colony didn't believe their parents even knew about. It was the only time the Rat had ever been proud of his mother and father.

'I hate you, Rat,' his mother was yelling from just beyond the door. 'Do you know that? I HATE you! I'd kill you with my bare hands if I once got the chance, yes, I would...' She's started to blubber, the Rat thought contemptuously. 'Why can't you be like other boys? Why can't you work? Or be a Guard? I always wanted you to be a Guard...'

There she goes again, he thought, with her rubbish about Guards. Couldn't she see that destiny had reserved a higher fate for him?

'But no – all day, all night, it's just your goddamned clockworks...'

At this the Rat stood up from his desk with exaggerated dignity. He reached up to the first level of shelves above his desk and brought out his earphones. He went across to his doorway so that his mother could see him clearly, as he placed the set over his head with ceremonial care. That was to show her he could no longer hear her. Then he bent over and relieved himself of a raucous blast of intestinal gas.

Personal insults he could take; but insults to his beloved hardware! That was unforgivable.

The Rat's real name was Cyril Aloysius de Cruz. He was a small and ferret-like fifteen-year-old, ugly with that special vehemence of adolescence: limbs that folded at unnatural angles, skin that seethed and bubbled with loathsome fluids. He dressed with an edge of violence, in black flash-skins which threw ultra-violet light if looked at in the sun. And there were polished steel rivets embedded in his wrists and anklets. His hair was metal-washed, cut in the antique 'punk' style of another century and he had a white sequin implanted near the inner corner of his right eye.

He had earned his nickname while cutting his permanent teeth, but later on it had stuck because it suited his character even better. The Rat was mean, vicious and precociously intelligent. He had learnt to handle a vacuum torquator before he could use a fork and he knew eight computer languages before he'd reached that age. But to the neighbourhood, he was just that 'terrible de Cruz boy'.

The families living in the teeming Rock Squatter colony, one of the first to be excavated from the South Range, were of hard-working war-refugee stock. Statistics estimated their population at around sixty-five thousand permanent residents of mixed ancestry. They were simple craftspeople and agriculturists, whose major economic function was to provide a captive market for the industrial goods of the more technologically advanced communities. The height of their technical competence was represented by the flipping of a switch or the reading of a leaflet of instructions. Compared to them the Rat, with his genius for electronics, was just what his mother had called him: a mutant.

At an age when other young men were eager to test their brawn in forges and factories all across the Union, the Rat was holed up in his room surrounded by outlandish devices picked up from junk yards, antique-machine dumps, city-fringe thieves' bazaars and cannibalized from the appliances in his own home. His room was rumoured to resemble the dark underground workshops known as 'Ark-Aids', from the early days of computers, when children toiled for days in front of the buzzing, clicking machines, bathed in the lurid glow of video screens. It was a terrible thought to contemplate. Most of the Rat's neighbours sympathized deeply with his parents.

The Rat was well aware of the unease his talents inspired in the people around him. He cultivated it, that unease. It was one way of ensuring his privacy. He found ways of sabotaging the state-controlled terminals in the homes of those whom he especially disliked, so that their domestic gadgets beeped and chirped at them in alarming ways. He had an elaborate network of audio and video devices spread out amongst the adjacent residences. He had a small troupe of young sycophants who were willing to spy and to pilfer for him, to support him in achieving his ultimate goal: escape from the colony.

For there was a double doom hanging over the Rat. One was that the social segregation laws barred him from seeking a career outside the Rock Squatter colony. In the years following the Final Confrontation, rigorously applied controls on human sociogenics had been aimed at ensuring that freaks such as the Rat could not develop. And if they did, well: in truth, the question had arisen so infrequently that no one had seriously addressed it. The Rat was, for all practical purposes, trapped in a dungeon whose walls were other people, whose fetters were the culture of ignorance around him. And there was no door at all, no way out.

The second doom was more immediate. Children between the ages of twelve and sixteen had to find employment. If they did not, they were automatically apprenticed to a guild and were set to learning a craft. For the Rat, bending his neck to such a common yoke would mean the end of life as he knew it. So his whole purpose was twisted towards avoiding that fate. Sitting at his desk – the converted chassis of a genuine antique CRAY – he was finally coming closer to his objective.

Between his hands was an object about the size of a large football which, at the moment when his mother interrupted him, had been glowing faintly. It still needed part of its casing and its supporting cradle was not yet complete. But its most delicate organs, two slim, translucent tubes attached at either pole of the egg-shape, were finally in place. The Rat picked one of them up gently, playing it this way and that. His fingers were long and surprisingly graceful. The tube moved in an uncanny way, as if alive. When he pulled on it, winding it gradually onto a spool, it lengthened and thinned out until it became fine, insubstantial and virtually invisible. To someone watching him, it would have seemed that the Rat was reeling in a non-existent length of yarn. But he could still feel the thread in his hands, finer than spiders' silk and ten times as strong. When he was through, he eased the spool into the egg and started work on the other tube. When it too was positioned, he sat back and stared at his handiwork for a long moment. What he really needed now was a guinea pig to try it on.

He flipped on one of his video screens. An unfocused mass appeared, shifted uncontrollably about, then stabilized into an integrated image. It was his mother's face, distorted by the angle of the scanner and her closeness to it, as she sat at the dining table. He could see her large fleshy mouth, dyed permanently crimson in the fashion of ten years ago, and her hand was held close to it, fingers kneading the lips. It was a nervous habit she had. The audio faded in, and now the Rat could hear his mother talking. About him, of course.

'I can't take it any more,' she was whining. 'I can't! Look what he did to my mixer!'

His father didn't respond immediately. He had a breathing problem and wheezed constantly. It always took him a few seconds to say anything, as he had to prime his lungs for the effort like a pipe organ. The Rat could hear him labouring, then say, 'It's not much longer now, Ma, is it?' He let the air out frugally, paused. 'How old is he, fifteen? Well, you know what I heard today?' A bit of air got stuck in his throat, refused to cooperate, finally came out with a bubble of phlegm. There was a hawking sound as his father spat. Then another heavy wheeze as he drew breath in again. 'I heard they're going to start recruiting early, this year. Younger. Maybe fifteen and a half. Maybe even fifteen. Short of manpower.'

He wasted a little air on a husky chuckle. 'The Rat, working!' His lungs seemed to convulse and he hawked again.

The Rat felt his skin contract. Fifteen! His small black eyes narrowed with hate. He could just imagine how his parents would celebrate it, if the news were to be true. He watched his mother's face onscreen relax into a smile. Then purse up again. 'But there's nothing certain yet, is there? It could still be one more year…' Her mouth worked, expelling the words forcefully, '…I can't wait that long! I'm telling you, he's up to something new. I've been watching him; there's something new on his desk now, some dirty thing. He's been working on it day and night. It's got a sort of…glow…oh! I don't know! Something awful, something Not Right! I'm telling you, Pa, I've had one of my feelings about it. I think it's something dangerous, Pa…'

The Rat, listening, bared his distinctive teeth ferally. Thrice-neutered retard, he thought, what would you understand of my – he looked at the thing between his hands – egg! A flush of rage coursed through him and he took it out on a small shiny beetle scurrying across his desktop, mashed it to pulp. Pig-eyed transistors, that's what his parents were, both of them. Crude savages compared to him. They didn't believe in him because their pica-brains could not conceive the power in him. Well, he'd show them! And soon!

His mother was still speaking. 'It's us or him, I'm telling you! I've had strange feelings, passing his door sometimes, like sort of rays passing through me…I don't know, I get frightened these days, I get frightened!'

His father sucked in some air. 'Can you see what it's like? What the thing looks like?'

'No,' said his mother, 'I can't see through that whatsit he has on the door, the force-curtain thing.'

The Rat boiled with a familiar anger. He remembered the days before he'd constructed the force field. The days when he'd come back to his room to find that his parents had been poking and prying amongst his belongings, defiling them with their ignorant hands.

His father slurped noisily on something. 'Have to get into that room somehow,' he wheezed. 'Tain't decent. Keeping parents out.

Scaring us.' Breath ran out. 'Did you speak to your – what's his name – engineer friend?'

A conspiring look crossed the mother's face. 'Yes!' she said, her voice dropping to a stage whisper as if she were afraid that her son might be eavesdropping. 'He came by the other day! Took a look at it, that thing on the door!' She looked fearfully over her shoulder, then continued. 'Said he could do something about it, easy, like. Pushed all kinds of things into that...that...frame which supports the field! Said he could fix it in a jiffy. Said he'd be back, maybe in a couple of days!' The pleased expression faded away slightly. 'Won't the Rat be mad, though! When he finds out!'

Listening, the Rat had got to his feet, his hands twitching. He stood rigid, his expression blank, his mind sorting out options at light speed. This changes everything, he thought. I'll have to move now, much sooner than I planned. I'll have to move before the engineer friend has a chance to come poking and prying. Not that he'd understand anything, of course, but even the slightest damage to the gadget now could set me back by several weeks, and if it's true about the labour laws...

He began pacing slowly and thoughtfully up and down in his room as if choreographing the steps of a dance.

It was dark in his room, crammed as it was with a fortune in reconsituted machinery, flickering with dozens of tiny lights and glowing dials, his little citadel. No longer a secure citadel. He'd have to consider using the device now, right away – but it would be a gamble. He wasn't sure how it would work. He wasn't even sure if it would work. On the other hand...if he didn't use it now, there was no saying how much time he had left before he'd have no choices. If the age limit was to be raised to fifteen...if the engineer friend did get through the force field... That would be the end, it would be death.

And if he used it tonight?

The Rat paused in his pacing. If I use it tonight, I might gain enough time to perfect the device, assuming that it works! After all, that was what it's supposed to do: store up time, other people's time. Make other people's time available to me...

On the video his parents were still yammering away. He shut them up. Think carefully, he told himself, can't afford mistakes. It'll be a while before they're asleep, of course, so in about two hours from now. No storage facility yet, so no option: I'll have to shunt it directly onto myself. Like a person-to-person blood transfusion. One heart drives the blood into the other heart. 'Cept this isn't blood.

Dangerous business! Might not succeed! He sat down at his console. I could gain six, maybe seven hours. That might give me the time to work out some storage. If I have storage then I can go away, I can find a place where I can work in peace, I can…well…

He'd have to take things one at a time. He started to tap in the codes to enter his program.

Three hours later, when the self-imposed silence of his room had deepened into the silence of a home at rest, he switched on the video scanner in his parents' room. The image resolved slowly, showing first the darkened bedchamber, then the two figures asleep in the big double bed.

Dad first, decided the Rat. He sleeps more soundly. That might make a difference.

There he was, on the screen now, lying in what looked like an uncomfortable position on his stomach. The sound of his laboured breathing wheezed into the Rat's room like bellows operating underwater.

The Rat switched the noise off impatiently. Gingerly, then, he picked up the smooth egg-shape, its casing newly intact. If he had had a sense of poetry, he might have gazed soulfully at it before placing it within its cradle; it was a momentous step he was about to take. But he completed the hook-up procedure with fussy efficiency, not pausing to allow any distracting sentiment to get in his way. From the video scanner he read off his father's coordinates relative to himself. Then he fed the information into the remote unit in his hand.

Almost immediately, a fine film of light began to glow around the egg. The spool of gossamer tubing on its north pole began to quiver and then, gradually, to turn. A few seconds elapsed, then the digital display on the plotter flickered to life and began to read off millionths of seconds.

Now again the Rat fed in coordinates to the plotter, this time for his own position, relative to his father. The second spool on the egg quickened to life. A second series of digits began to appear in the plotter's display window.

And an odd sensation began to filter into the Rat. Rather like what a balloon might feel as it is being blown up. At the back of his head, a tight space he had never precisely noticed before began to loosen, to stretch and to spread out, filling him with a light, drowsy feeling. And in the meanwhile, the dials and flashing indicators around him started to pulse more slowly. His mind, however, stayed clear, working at normal speed.

The Rat stood up cautiously. Should be able to move within a ten-metre radius, he reassured himself, though he could barely believe that what he had planned for so long might actually now be happening. Aside from the retardation of the clocks, he was not conscious of any change. It felt good: that was a surprise bonus. Like mainlining on sunlight, like transfusing free electrons.

He walked carefully across his room to the small window. The night-time vista of the outer face of the vast squatter colony revealed its dreary self to him. The entire surface of the flat grey rock was pitted with doors and windows, criss-crossed with catwalks and spiral staircases. Some windows spilled flowerpots, some doors were cluttered with garbage pails, some homes had laundry racks hanging out to flap and ricket in the wind. Here and there rectangles of light shone, though not many at that hour. The farthest ones twinkled slightly, out at the limit of Rat's vision horizon. He looked at all of it, feeling a sense of loathing. All the mindless squalor of the Squatters' way of life seemed often to be directed solely against him, to anguish him and to remind him of his freak status. Well, he thought to himself, breathing in hugely, I'm going to leave it all now, leave it forever!

Because he had discovered a method of boosting his stock of time. That was what he was doing now. The two slim tubes of bionic plastic, vibrating at near-light speeds, could be made to pass through solid matter. One tube was connected to his father and the other one to himself. By creating a temporal vacuum inside the glowing egg-shaped time capacitor, time was being drained out of the Rat's father and poured directly into himself.

Putting together the hardware for the gadget had been nothing compared to the difficulty he had faced in locating the time function in human beings. Time and life: they had to be the same thing, the Rat had theorized. But where, in humans, in any living things, does the potential for life actually reside? The Rat had been on the point of giving up, when he had come across an ancient videotape in a junk shop, one of those which was actual tape, on a huge bulky cassette. It had been about some weird form of healing known as acupuncture. It used to be popular in the age when humans had been designated by race. Acupuncture had been devised by the then superior race known as the Chinese.

It did not confine itself to the visible structures of the human body, but referred to a mysterious network of 'energy channels' loosely related to, but not synonymous with, the nervous system. Out of curiosity, the Rat had used one of the collection tubes to probe acupuncture nodes on himself and...the display-panel on the plotter had suddenly come on, counting out his life in millionths of a second.

That had been a great moment for the Rat. It had meant that his wildest dreams could take a giant stride towards realization. All he needed was to be able to collect and store time in batteries and... the world would be at his feet.

He had thought he had at least one more year in which to prepare for his escape. But if what his parents had said was true, then he'd have to save work on the refinements for later. He couldn't risk experimenting at this stage, because he didn't know enough yet. Didn't know what kind of material was appropriate for accumulating a charge of time; whether there was any deterioration in its quality or viability with storage; what risks were involved in using stored versus fresh time. He'd have to wait to find out. For now, the direct transfusion from his father was the best he could manage.

The Rat gazed up at the night sky and felt a twinge of eternity pass through him.

His original idea had come to him when the grandmother of one of his young friends had suffered a stroke, then slipped into a coma. The Rat had offered to monitor the old lady with a video scanner, just to see if she ever showed signs of reviving full consciousness. She never did, but he had grown fascinated by her video image, staring sightlessly at the ceiling all day, all night. That's when it had dawned on him, the tragic waste of it all: there she was, that vegetable, dribbling her time out in absolute vacuity, while he, Rat, had so many varied uses for the same commodity! Yet he had access only to his own personal stock: and that, in terms of the Rock Squatter colony's labour laws, was running out.

A boosted stock of time! The drowsy feeling in the back of the Rat's head encouraged him to relax a little into his fantasies. In the normal course of events, a person used up their ration of time at the same speed as everyone else. But someone with a boosted ration would speed up. Such a person could be, with enough extra time, for all practical purposes invisible. If he, Rat, could build up such a stock, then not only could he escape the colony – which he could do now anyway in physical terms – but he could make his way to the City unnoticed. He could live there and learn City ways. He could wear City clothes and forge a City ID card, he could become indistinguishable from any other citizen of the exalted Higher Sphere to which his Rock Squatter background normally forbade him access. He believed that that was the intellectual community to which he genetically belonged. And every freedom would be his.

The Rat was just beginning to wonder what the people from whom he stole time would feel, when a peculiar sensation suddenly assailed him. He couldn't understand it, it was like a sort of catch in the steady flow of time which had till then been entering him smoothly. Like a sort of temporal hiccup.

He puzzled over it, wondering what it meant. He looked back towards the console, where the monitor, still on 'mute', featured his father...but his mother was also onscreen now, she was doing something to his father, shaking him, it seemed. Her mouth was hanging open as if she were screaming. He was seeing it in slow motion, of course, which added to the unreality of the scene. And his father, what he could see of him, was looking terrible too, sort of glazed and struggling, slick with sweat.

The Rat bounded across the room to switch on the audio, but not before the first wave of shock reached him. A sudden awful emptiness passed over him, like a shadow from hell. He fought to clear his mind, guessing intuitively what was happening even as his mind rebelled against the odds. But already a second wave of emptiness was approaching him, increasing in strength as he came swiftly back to an ordinary time-scale. And then with a ghastly jerk, time started flowing the other way, like a dam bursting down a hillside. Time was being sucked out of him. Now he too began to gasp and struggle. He tried massively to reach for the egg, to delink himself. But his world was beginning to mush together, his senses merging one into the other, and he felt paralysed, as if soldered to his chair, as if made of lead, as if deprived of speech and sight, breath and nerves. And then he blacked out.

As the Rat came around, he was nauseated to realize that he was being held in his mother's arms. He tried immediately to free himself, but found he could not move. Couldn't even open his eyes. His lids felt as if each individual eyelash had been cast in iron. Then slowly memory began to return. He remembered that he had been sitting at his desk, that he'd been experimenting with the egg, that something had started to go wrong...

He could hear voices now. His mother's. 'But I don't understand! My husband – his father – was dead! The vita-scan showed that! And...and the Rat was sitting in his room! He couldn't have done anything.' She sounded as stupid as ever.

Then another voice was speaking. A stranger. He had an unfamiliar accent, like someone from the City. 'Let me try to put it this way, Mrs de Cruz: it has something to do with time, something... amazing.' He seemed to be sincerely impressed.

A second City voice cut in. 'We're not sure ourselves what he did or how he did it...'

The first voice took it up again, '...except that your son used this gadget of his, to give your husband a timely and highly valuable transfusion of...well, his own life essence, if you want to call it that. Vital energy: not blood, not air, but time, do you see?'

The Rat's mother must have looked blank. First Voice continued, 'Just enough time for the emergency team to reach your husband and get his heart working again. We don't undertand how your son did it, or how he managed to make his time available at the right moment, but somehow he did manage it. It really is an astounding achievement, Mrs de Cruz–'

'And a very brave and courageous act,' Second Voice cut in again. There seemed to be an unexpectedly wheedling tone to it. 'Very courageous. We can't begin to imagine what it must have felt like...must have been a little like dying himself.'

Inside the immobilized shell of his body, the Rat was squirming with the undeserved praise. I wasn't trying to save the fool, he wanted to scream out loud, I was stealing from him!

He could hear his mother making small wondering noises, he could feel her glowing with a most unfamiliar pride. And he felt revolted to the core of his being.

Better to have let all of my time bleed out into the void of dad's death, he thought. Better to have endured that dark and terrifying anti-space until it had depleted his entire vault of years, than to awaken to this ignominious failure. How could I have guessed that the old screwdriver would choose just this night to have a heart attack?

But the City voice had not stopped. '...it could have immense therapeutic uses in caring for the sick, for instance, why, people who are suffering or in pain could perhaps pass their time out into a tube.'

First Voice said, 'And of course, we will have to be very careful that we don't misuse a device of this nature...you do understand that we'll want to keep your son with us for some time, don't you, Mrs de Cruz?' That wheedling tone again. A tiny hesitation. 'Naturally, you'll expect to be compensated for him – he'll be sixteen soon, won't he? Labour age for Rock Squatter colony boys...

we'll see what we can do...it's only the first time that such a thing has happened, a Rock Squatter being upgraded to the City...I'm sure we can come to a very agreeable understanding.' The Rat's mother must have nodded. 'Yes...an exceptional situation but he's an exceptional boy. Certainly turns sociogenics theory inside out...'

'He'll be all right with us, Mrs de Cruz,' Second Voice was saying. 'You needn't worry about him!'

At which point the Rat allowed himself to black out again, this time a little more contentedly. He was certain his mother would not insist on keeping him.

INDIA 2099

The first impression was magnificent. That's what he would remember later. A friendly voice kept repeating in his ear, 'Please open your eyes, sir!' And when he was finally able to comply, his first thoughts were a wordless hymn of delight.

The India of 2099! One hundred years had passed since the time he had stepped into a transit chamber that would keep him in suspended sleep. Now he saw a luxurious green plain spreading away towards a haze-free horizon. Mango trees in a nearby orchard filled his senses with their fragrance. White clouds were scudding against a blinding blue sky. Before him, in the distance, he saw India Gate, still standing proud and tall. Behind him, when his seat was swivelled, he saw the Qutub Minar. He remembered being surprised to see both monuments within the same radius of sight but told himself not to fuss with explanations just yet.

The friendly voice that had woken him from his transit-sleep belonged to a machine. It looked like a well-endowed human female wearing nothing at all. 'Hello!' it said, when he was ready to tear his attention away from the splendid vista in front of him, 'My name is Tina! I am your personal assistant!' He was still very stiff, however. 'Please do not attempt to turn your head, sir!' said Tina. 'That function is not presently available to you.' There was a tiny click. 'If you have understood this message please blink your eyelids once <click> If you have any questions, please blink your eyelids twice <click> Thank you, sir! Please wait a moment <click> Your query will be attended to very shortly by a live attendant.'

As it sped away, the man wondered idly how such beings were referred to in this future era. Were they accorded the dignity of gender? Or were they treated like animatronic cellphones? He felt no urgency to find out. For the time being he was content to remain as he was, floating in a transparent, lightweight capsule filled with an odourless, friction-free gel. It would be a while before his body would function normally, after a century of inactivity.

He had been the editor of a prestigious newsmagazine at the time of signing up for the perma-sleep program, known then as PSP. He burned with curiosity. How had the astounding turnaround in the country's profile taken place? The citizens he could see from his vantage point looked physically Indian, but they seemed more relaxed and leisurely than the people he had left behind in his time. There was none of that frenzied jostling, that reckless energy born of desperation that had characterized the country he remembered.

It was strange, he realized, to see an India that looked neat and orderly. There were no crowds thronging the broad avenues. No snarling traffic jams. No gritty blanket of smog. It might almost be a different culture altogether. He paused that thought with a guilty shrug. It seemed disloyal to believe that the country of his birth would lose its character by cleaning up its act.

He was just learning to flex the corners of his mouth up in the beginnings of a smile, when he heard a warning tone of the sort that would, in his era, have been used to signal an airport departure. Sure enough, he found himself being whisked away from his viewing window by another robotic attendant just as unclothed and mechanical as Tina. It did not speak to him, however, so he had no option but to shut his eyes and wait as he was whisked away to a new location.

In this way he found himself being transported across the whole length and breadth of the country. In quick succession he saw Konarak, Kanyakumari, the Elephanta Caves, Mahabalipuram, the Dal Lake, Jaisalmer, Hampi and the Sundarbans. Each time he opened his eyes, he found that his body was a little more flexible. By the time he was looking out at the Udaipur Lake Palace, he was almost ready to take his first few steps. Better still, he was no longer alone. The long-promised 'live attendants' had finally caught up with him.

They introduced themselves. 'I'm Rosh, sir,' said the young man bending deferentially towards him. 'This is Vinny and that's Hozanna. Your very own welcome-back team, sir! We are delighted to make your acquaintance. The month is what was called December in your era and the time is approximately eight o'clock, fifty-two minutes and twelve seconds in sexagesimal units.' The young man stammered slightly over the unfamiliar words, adding, 'We call this month Ten and the time, in today's decimal units, is 8.87.'

All three were doctors who specialized in PSP revivals. 'Please, sir, it will be another few days before you can speak,' they said, when he struggled to move his vocal cords. But they allowed him to watch documentaries.

From these he learnt that the country was prosperous beyond the wildest dreams of the nationalists of his era. There seemed to be a slight shift in the name, however. He thought he heard newsreaders referring to the country as India, but in the subtitles the name was rendered as 'I-O-I'. He wondered what the letters stood for. He was not at liberty to choose what he saw, so he could not be sure to what extent he was being fed propaganda. But by whom and with what slant, he could not tell. The language he heard was neither English nor Hindi, yet he understood it easily. He guessed there was a sophisticated translation device implanted in his ears. Or, more likely, in his brain.

Food was plentiful. From the documentaries he learnt that it was mass-processed from natural materials, then reformed into shapes and flavours to suit the individual tastes of its consumers. Reverse-gravitation platforms made it possible to cause heavy objects to float so that, for instance, others could transport him from place to place without any effort on his or their part. Air, water, power and money – everything that in 1999 had been scarce was now available in such abundance it was obviously not considered newsworthy. Instead, the whole focus of broadcasters was on the fearsome calamities taking place among the teeming communities of Extra-Terrestrial Indians.

It was the existence of these colonies that explained the country's prosperity, the editor gradually realized. India had apparently been at the forefront of a gigantic space-colonization campaign. Countless documentaries named the fearless explorers who had soared up into the starry wastes of space in the late 2030s. Millions had lost their lives in these migrations, but hundreds of millions had clearly survived too. The planet they had gone to was what the editor would have called Mars. It had been renamed several times depending on which ethnic community had the upper hand in the inter-planetary broadcasting service. Currently it went under the name of 'Kalki'.

He learnt that the community known collectively as the Ordinaries occupied two-thirds of the planet. They were divided into Hindus, Muslims and OMs – Other Minorities. They fought vicious battles for space, food, water and political advantage. With limited resources for farming, socially accepted forms of cannibalism were practised. It was referred to as 'recycling' and every citizen was exhorted to make his or her meat available to the community by choosing early, voluntary death.

The remaining third of the planet had been taken over by a community referred to by broadcasters as 'the Mutants'. They had no official broadcasting channels however, so the editor could gain no insights into their culture or origin. When he indicated to his welcome-back team that he would like more information about this mysterious group, he was informed that controversial subjects were to be avoided till he could talk.

On the morning of his speech day, a special outing was planned to the Taj Mahal. When he was finally in front of it, tears flooded his eyes and his first words were thick with emotion as he said, 'It's...still...so...beautiful.' His team beamed with pleasure. That was what most Revivees said, they told him.

It took him a little longer to achieve the conversational skills that enabled him to ask more probing questions. It was only then that he learned about the bombs. Two blasts. They had occurred one after the other, they said, in the first quarter of the new century.

Vast tracts in the north of the country had been rendered uninhabitable on account of radiation. 'Within 10 years, the Mutants began to appear,' said Rosh. They were the genetically deformed children spawned by the fallout of the bombs. Those who survived to the ages of nine or 10 years, possessed highly radioactive yet viable metabolisms. As a result, their very presence in the same room as an Ordinary constituted an assault with a deadly weapon. The so-called Great Migrations had begun right around the time that these diminutive warriors were becoming the dominant violent underclass. Having established their strongholds on the red planet, their numbers grew. Their stated aim was to annihilate the Ordinaries there, return to the Home Planet and annihilate all Ordinaries, everywhere.

'The international community on Earth considers the threat of Mutant invasions the most serious that our world has ever faced,' said Vinny. The editor expressed amazement that the Mutants had ever been given the opportunity to gain a foothold on Kalki. He looked from one to the other of the young team. He saw them exchange slight nods as a mood of quiet resignation bowed their shoulders.

'This is going to be hard for you to understand, sir…' said Rosh. The expression in his eyes was sad. 'The documentaries you have watched have not been entirely honest. You see, Kalki was set up to be a prison colony…'

At the time of the blasts, the international community had insisted that the subcontinent be made to pay dearly for the catastrophic damage caused to the planet. 'So,' said Rosh, 'the countries involved in the conflict were rendered to the charge of the international community.'

The editor gaped, unwilling to accept what this meant. Vinny nodded. 'Yes, sir,' he confirmed, 'the country you knew as India is not today, in a continuous sense, a sovereign state any more.'

It had been split up into sectors, they told him. Radiation-free zones. Collectively, these zones were known by the acronym 'I-O-I'. It stood for the 'Idea Of India' and was based on the physical boundaries of British India during the Raj. The sectors were physically far apart, but modern transportation techniques made it possible to translocate across the different bits of the nation to create a 'virtual continuity'. When shown a true-contour map, the editor saw unrecognizable strips representing the land of his birth. Some were broad, some thin, some sideways, some twisted. He had intentionally been shown only those landmarks that he associated with the nation he had known as India.

The welcome team went on to describe the many advantages of this system. The colonization of Kalki had made the region prosperous, for instance, which greatly softened the blow to national prestige. The international community had assisted very generously with the reconstruction and maintenance of the virtual continuity. National monuments had been meticulously restored.

The editor listened in silence. He recalled, now, the sense of foreboding with which he had entered the PSP transit chamber all those many years ago, in the final days of 1999. He'd signed up for the programme because he'd wanted to put his hope in the future rather than succumb to the sense of doom that had gripped the nation at the close of the last century. But the future had turned out to be even worse than what he and his colleagues had feared it might be, given the developments.

The Great Migrations had been a mandatory price imposed by the international community upon the nations of the subcontinent, not a choice. Sending millions of subcontinentals to Kalki had been one of the solutions to the problems caused by endemic overpopulation, disease and illiteracy. Ensuring that all Mutants were also transported out to Kalki was another of the solutions to the crisis created by their presence on Earth.

'Unfortunately it was not very effective,' admitted Hozanna. 'Even now some members of the Earth Council are demanding that unless the I-O-I can guarantee the security of the planet before the end of this century, we may have to give up even the illusion of being a sovereign state. War will be declared on Kalki. All citizens of that planet will be considered enemies of Earth. The countries that once defined the region of the subcontinent will be struck off from the record of reality. All our cultural artefacts will be reassigned to other nations.'

The old editor's heart shrank to imagine this fate. For himself though, the choice was clear. 'Onward,' he said, gruffly, pointing towards the PSP chamber he had emerged from. 'Take me to the end of the *next* century!'

EXILE

'Look – how bad can it be?' asked Rashmi, as she began the firing sequence on her sleek SuzDai Mini-Cruiser. 'We've got to think of this so-called banishment as an *opportunity*. Not a calamity.'

Her two fellow travellers remained, however, stubbornly silent. Her husband Siddhangshu sat beside her as co-pilot, while Lakshmi, her younger sister, was secured within the rear seat.

Rashmi sighed.

'So all right,' she relented. 'Mum *could* have told Kailash Uncle–' step-dad Number Two '–to back off. Everyone knows that. But it would've broken his little heart.' Oo, catty! But perfectly human, surely? Not every parent sends his eldest stepdaughter off to the planet's Surface for fourteen long years. 'Mum *hates* discord. She made a promise to him in a moment of tenderness and now he's taken advantage of her kindness. Or whatever. Who can say what lies behind Mum's decision? Maybe she believes it'll be good for her eldest daughter to spend a little time back on the Surface. Maybe she feels I need some perspective. After all, her foremothers put our home satellite into orbit at a time when most humans were still living on Earth. I-Udia was built to Mum's own specifications, it's part of her DNA. She's free to administer it any way she wants.'

'Free to hand it over to her toy-boy hubby you mean,' murmured Siddhangshu. 'Him and his simpering little bimbette of a daughter…'

'Please, Sid!' protested Rashmi. 'Bharti was designated as my replacement and as such, demands my unswerving loyalty–'

'Oh spare us the saccharine, sis,' said Lakshmi. 'Bro-in-law's right. It's a takeover pure and simple. You've always been Alpha Girl. How could you not be? Mum's never made a secret of the fact she took an extra dose of gene-supplements when she had you. Which is *fine*, we're all okay with that, including Babs! But her Dad's super-competitive. Right until last week he imagined his little girl had a chance. Then Mum announced she was designating you as Chief Admin and he's been spitting fire ever since.'

The little space-craft's secondary engines began to hum.

'But *why*?' asked Rashmi. 'There's place enough on I-Udia to accommodate all of us and all our descendants for centuries ahead...'

The outer locks opened. The starlit blackness of open space yawned into view.

'Well,' said Sid, as he snapped his visor down, 'maybe *he* knows something *you* don't, about succession rivalry.'

'That's rubbish,' said Rashmi. 'Everyone knows I feel only the deepest love and respect for all my–'

'*Counting down*,' said the onboard computer. '*TEN*...'

'So that's you. Not the rest of the known Universe.' Sid's voice was muffled.

'*EIGHT*...'

'I guess we'll have a lot of time to discuss this,' sighed Rashmi. 'Comm links off–'

Some hours later, having landed smoothly and been processed through the automated gravity re-training therapy, the three travellers found themselves hurtling downwards in a glass-walled elevator. They got out on what was called the 'ground floor' though of course there was not a grain of soil or earth in sight. The surface on which they walked was faintly spongy and grey in appearance, formed out of synthetic tiling. The elevator shaft was a retractable tube which vanished upwards once it had disgorged its contents.

Up and around them, in every direction, was a tangled mass of giant, soaring struts and columns made of glass, steelcrete and plastinium. There were no plants or trees to be seen, not so much as a single blade of grass, yet there was something pleasingly organic about the glistening arches, the smooth planes and the long, swinging loops of cable that surrounded them on all sides. Here and there, tiny flashing movements betrayed the presence of free-moving minibots, that performed countless minor tasks of repair and maintenance. The air was filled with a continuous buzzing, clicking, chattering sound. Though entirely artificial, the effect was very similar to standing in the midst of a rainforest. The columns were supports for solar collectors which formed a canopy of flat panes rather like leaves. Between the panes, high in the distance, the sky showed itself, remote and blue.

Rashmi smiled, her head swivelling this way and that.

'Hey team,' she whispered, 'this is kind of…awesome. Wouldn't you say? I can feel it in my bones: we're going to have a great time.'

Siddhangshu refused to be impressed. 'We're totally unprotected from the elements in a completely alien, hostile environment. I've not seen anything even remotely like a toilet. And we have no idea whatsoever of our…uhhh…co-inhabitants.'

'Co-*what*?' exclaimed Lakshmi. She was more spontaneous and excitable than her sister. 'I thought this whole banishment thing was about being *alone*!'

'Sure – alone with all the other low-brow riff-raff that never managed to emigrate – plus every desperadina who's ever been thrown off her home satellite with no other place to call her home but poor old Earth.'

'Hush,' said Rashmi, throwing a dirty glance in her husband's direction. He was as handsome and gallant as a man could be, but common sense? Uh-uh. Not his strong suit. 'Come on then – we had best strike camp before sun-down.'

All three were clothed in lightweight, climate-controlled suits which gave them the appearance of being bare-skinned. All three were in their early twenties, tall, smooth-muscled and very fit. They carried their gear slung on their backs and attached to their waists, wrists and thighs. They also wore *smart* helmets that gave them the appearance of wearing ornate, pagoda-shaped headgear.

'The first priority is to locate a water source. I already checked it out on the GPS while choosing coordinates for our docking site.' Rashmi flipped down a transparent electronic patch from her helmet and positioned it over her left eye, giving herself a three-dimensional model of the surrounding terrain. 'And here we are. It's *this* way,' she said, striding forward in a south-westerly direction.

They constructed a temporary shelter for the night, recognizing that it would be several weeks before they found a spot that combined access to food and water with functioning sanitary facilities. The Surface had been gradually abandoned as successive waves of the citizens chose to move up into orbiting estates with pristine ecosystems. What they left behind was a planet run entirely by *smart*machines. Fully automated factories, all underground, synthesized nourishment out of the planet's raw materials. Fuelled by sunlight and wind, the products created in the factories kept the orbiting havens furnished with an inexhaustible supply of food. Far-sighted developers had ensured that tiny cached stockpiles of food and water plus sanitation depots were maintained as public-access resources on the Surface, exactly so that off-worlders who wished to return for brief holidays would not go hungry or unwashed.

Between them, Rashmi, Lakshmi and Siddhangshu spent their mornings foraging for these stockpiled caches, the underground sumps containing water and the always too-well-hidden toilet facilities. They kept precise records of where they had already been, in order to plan where to move next. Documenting the abundant mechanical and electronic entities that kept this astounding inorganic paradise in continuous working order soon became Rashmi's primary pastime. Lakshmi, who was an accomplished draughtsman, devoted every spare moment to creating detailed views of the spectacular scenery that unfolded around them whenever they shifted camp.

Siddhangshu was the least fulfilled of the three. His skills lay in the design of multi-dimensional virtual wargames and in satellite-construction engineering. Here, in this enforced isolation where the three travellers were not permitted so much as a radio-connection to the life they had left behind them, he had little choice but to play endless games of solitaire on his handheld or to search for functioning hardware from the computer-era which he could then attempt to refashion to suit his needs.

They'd had exactly one communication with their family since leaving and that was an extremely tearful video session with Babs. Reception was good and she'd set the resolution for 3D life-size. It was exactly the same as having her stand directly in front of them except that the tears rolling down her cheeks didn't actually hit the ground. According to her, she was devastated to hear that her beloved older sister had been sent away. It was not something she had wanted or asked for. There was no question of accepting the position of Chief Admin or ever occupying the hot-seat of the satellite's command centre. Alas, there was no question of relaying daily instructions: her dad's conditions, to which this video chat was to be the sole exception, included severing all comm-links. To the best of her ability, she, Babs, would administer I-Udia as she believed Rashmi would have. What else could she do? Then she broke down in further floods of tears.

'Of course, of course,' said Rashmi, soothingly before asking about the health and humour of everyone else on the satellite. She was told that their mother Damini was still under heavy medication to counteract the stress caused by the entire banishment scandal and that the three wayfarers were sorely missed by family and staff alike.

'Ahh,' said Rashmi, 'fourteen years will pass like a dream! As for the banishment itself, I fear we may grow to love the Surface so much that we'll find it hard to return.' She laughed lightly. 'Only kidding! But seriously, it's more enjoyable than I expected. Please thank Kailash Uncle on my behalf for providing me with this unique learning opportunity.'

Haha, thought Siddhangshu as he heard these words. *Speak for yourself, wifey dear. I'm totally losing my nut to boredom!* But he knew better than to express himself out loud. The record would show that he said nothing at all during this exchange. In the archives, the 3Dgrams revealed him looking perfectly serene and untroubled.

Days turned into weeks and weeks turned into months.

As regards the other denizens of the Surface, the three satelliters maintained a low profile. A couple of encounters were friendly: an elderly hermit called Shabir, for instance, approached them with a unique gift. He had taken it upon himself to collect a store of vacuum-packed mango fruit-leather. It was not clear how he came to choose this particular item but his intentions were obviously benign. Unfortunately, he had also felt the need to sample each sachet, in order to test for freshness, thus effectively contaminating every single one. Rashmi accepted the tribute graciously all regardless, claiming that the highly concentrated and desiccated strips of fruit pulp tasted all the better, now that they had been allowed to mature naturally. Lakshmi took one bite and immediately broke out in an allergic rash.

Much more typical however were encounters involving disputes with other dwellers over who had the right to a particular food cache, water sump, toilet or electrical power outlet. In most cases, Rashmi was so quick to assess the situation that she could either avoid a confrontation altogether or else successfully disable the electronic equipment of the opposing parties by remote control. Nine times out of ten, their outmoded gadgets were overwhelmed and died with a despairing bleep. Whereupon the owners turned tail and ran.

More rarely Rashmi had found herself fighting off an inorganic foe, some giant leviathan with sinews of steel and a chunk of silicon in the place of its heart. These beasts were programmed to be highly territorial, designed to dig up or renovate factory sites, recognizing no master but another machine. In two such situations, Rashmi had managed to outwit the monsters by rewriting their programs using her trusty hand-held remote, until they turned against one another.

In a third case, she narrowly escaped with her life, by throwing her metal-detector down the maw of the gigantic tunnelling machine that threatened to crush her under its unyielding bulk. The metal detector's magnetic core caused havoc inside the behemoth. With agonizing shrieks, the vast assemblage of steel parts began to lurch and flail, its dozens of electronic sensors blinking slower and slower until they could no longer detect Rashmi's presence, allowing her to slip away.

A year passed.

On the first anniversary of their arrival on the Surface, Siddhangshu had wanted to re-examine their meek acceptance of the banishment order. But Rashmi refused to be drawn. When Lakshmi tried to intervene on his behalf Rashmi stopped her. 'Mum put me in charge of this expedition. The longer I stay here the more convinced I am that she wanted us to experience our ancestral home. I trust her intuition and am bound to abide by her wisdom.' She allowed a pause of silence before continuing. 'I didn't ask either of you to accompany me. This so-called misfortune was intended only for me. You chose to come. I must admit I'm a little disappointed that a year later you're both still in denial about the reality of this choice.'

'That's a bit unfair,' said Siddhangshu. 'It's hardly "denial", to question the extremely selfish, manipulative decision made by a step-parent! Enough's enough: it's been one year! I mean, *hello?* Thirteen years hence you'll be thirty-six. What about, you know, tick-tock and all of that?' He pointed to Lakshmi. 'And your kid sister, what about her? She'll be an old maid by the time we head back and I don't need to tell you there aren't any debutante balls being held here.'

Aside from the old hermit, all their encounters had been with other women.

But Rashmi had a far away look on her face.

'I don't know if it's the advantage of age or what,' she began. She was two years older than her sister and one year older than her husband. 'The fact is, I'm okay with being here. I can't explain why exactly, but it feels right. I'm learning so much that I'd never get to know any other way. Yes, time's ticking away. So what? If I'm not fussed, you shouldn't be either. And if you are, well…bottomline? Get over it. Because I'm not leaving! And without me to fly the Mini-Cruiser, neither can you.'

She ended the discussion by getting up and walking away.

Lakshmi glanced at Siddhangshu.

'Big Sis can be tough, huh,' she said.

He shrugged, then chuckled good-naturedly. 'Good thing I like tough women!'

Lakshmi drew in a breath.

'By the way,' she began, but her brother-in-law stopped her.

'It's all right,' he said.

'You can't know what I was going to say!'

'I can guess.' He smiled. 'I've noticed how you find excuses for going away and leaving us alone in the shelter at regular intervals. Don't think I'm not grateful. It's not necessary, however.' He screwed up his face, as if acknowledging that he could be more upset than he actually was. 'I didn't have any way of bringing this up with you before but Rashmi...well, she discussed it with me even before we left I-Udia.'

'Are you saying what I think you're saying?' Lakshmi looked incredulous.

Siddhangshu nodded. 'She explained that the three of us would be a team. As a team, it would be lousy for morale if she and I, you know, *had relations* while you waited around the corner, humming a tune or whatever.' He allowed himself another chuckle. 'It makes a certain kind of sense. None of us has any training as obstetricians, after all! Fourteen years is an awful long time for a zero-error situation. So maybe I'm the one who needs to get his head examined, but I did agree to go along with her deal.' He squeezed his eyes shut and flexed his neck sideways a couple of times. 'I'm not saying it's been easy, I assure you! You're both extremely good looking ladies. And all that.'

'Oh – *no*, I mean – no, Sid! Not me, not ever! Don't say that–!' She had covered her face with her hands and said, in a strangled voice, 'I'm your *sister-in-law*! It's totally not okay to even bring this up.'

'I'm sorry, I disagree. It's better to put it out there where we can all see it. And anyway that's all there is of it, I promise you. Just this conversation. Nothing else. Including thoughts. If I can resist Her Ladyship, then I can resist you too.' He added quickly, 'Not that it's a reflection on your, ah, charms or anything! Desire isn't the kind of thing that stays neatly at the end of a leash, you know? Once it's out, you can't control where it runs. So it's easier never to let it out. At all.'

'Sid…I think she's being terrible cruel to you. Really I do.'

He was shaking his head. 'Not really. No. The worst thing about her is that she *is* right. Always. Drives me crazy sometimes, I admit that too. But I've learnt to accept it about her. It's like today and the discussion – there was just no other way for it to go. So it didn't.' Then he glanced over at his sister-in-law. 'What's the matter? You look like you're bursting to say something.'

Lakshmi nodded, quickly. Guiltily. 'I've always wanted to know…' She stopped. 'You don't have to answer, okay? And we'll never have this conversation again, promise.' There was another pause, during which she covered her face with her hands once more. From that position she asked, in a hoarse voice, 'Sid, is Big Sis hot? I mean, considering she's always so poised, so rational, so…so…Miss Ideal Womanhood! Well. I just can't imagine her, you know, *letting herself go*.' She removed her hands now. 'I realize it's probably just my own extremely flawed personality. That I even want to know.'

Siddhangshu had a slight smile on his face.

He turned to look at Lakshmi straight in the eye and said, 'Yes, she's hot. Because that's the thing about Idealness – it goes deep, it touches every part of her being – and it includes being hot. So even when I want to feel sorry for myself and my deprivation, I know that she's deprived herself too and just as badly as me. But she's managed to turn her deprivation into something positive. She can do that. And by doing that she makes it possible for me to do it too.' Then his smile broadened into a roguish grin. 'Of course, there's one other little point I could mention here.'

Lakshmi frowned. 'What?'

'What would I know of "hot"? I've never been with anyone else.'

Two years passed. Then five. Then ten.

Ever since that first-year anniversary, there were no more discussions about leaving. The three satelliters became so accustomed to their lifestyle on the Surface that they no longer considered it a chore to pack up their kit and move to their next location every couple of months. Over time, they had learned to use local materials to build their shelter. As an added precaution, Lakshmi set up a forcefield which was keyed exclusively to the bio-energy of the three residents of the fragile structure; other than themselves, no living thing would get through the field alive. Eventually, they became so expert at predicting where and how to locate their next food cache or making themselves invisible to the others who moved about in the shade of the towering solar collectors that they rarely faced encounters of any sort, hostile or friendly.

Each had worked out a set pattern. In the mornings, they planned their day. Afternoon was their time for exchanges of a practical nature while in the evenings, over the night meal they discussed broad topics about life, philosophy, the future of the Universe and the prospects for humankind.

Then in the twelfth year of their exile a change, like a cold shiver running through the entire region, began to express itself. One day Lakshmi said, 'The strangest thing happened. I was out, as usual, trying to capture the play of light on a series of regular columns, when I began to imagine I was being watched.' Rashmi whipped around, her expression tense. 'Anyone else feel that way? After a while it made me so uncomfortable I actually packed my things and left.'

Rashmi grimaced and clenched her teeth. It was very unusual for her to reveal any internal conflict.

'I didn't want to bring this up, ever,' she said now. 'But some weeks ago I had an extremely disturbing encounter.' It had happened, she explained, right before their last shift of camp-site. 'You might both recall that I suggested moving suddenly? Well. It's because of what happened. I was in the South Quadrant–' they had named the various sections of the Surface according to their position on the planet '–when a figure stepped out from behind one of the columns. A male warrior.'

In all their time on the Surface, except for gray-beards such as Shabir, they had seen no men.

'He wasn't just any man,' continued Rashmi. 'At first glance I thought he was severely deformed. But it was surgical intervention. Elective self-mutilation.' His front teeth protruded like a boar's tusks, causing him to drool; his forehead was low and deeply indented, as if he had spent his childhood butting cast-iron grilles; his skin was mottled with multi-coloured tattooes and all down his spine were spikes, embedded to look like the dorsal fin of a man-sized lizard.

'Yech!' said Lakshmi. 'Sounds like a real freak.'

'What'd you do?' Siddhangshu wanted to know. 'And why didn't you tell us?'

'Because of what happened next: he stepped forward and without any preamble he– he– propositioned me!' Rashmi frowned, biting her lower lip. 'He may have said something, but in the first place his speech was indistinct and in the second place, I understood his intentions perfectly. He literally staggered forward towards me with his male member, hugely distended, sticking out from his clothing, like a club. I acted completely instinctively. And rashly. Stepping back, away from him, and with one swipe of my laser-torch – you know, the one I use for breaking the vacuum seal on food-caches? I…*sliced it off*.'

Lakshmi and Siddhangshu both looked aghast.

'Omigosh,' was all Lakshmi could say. 'Omigosh. Omigosh.'

'That's why I didn't tell you,' said Rashmi, holding her hand to her forehead. 'I've not been able to forgive myself.'

'Forgive your*SELF*?' cried Siddhangshu. 'Why – you clearly acted in self-defence – he gave you no options! I'd have done the exactly the same–'

'No, you wouldn't,' said Rashmi. 'Because in the first place, he'd never have approached you in that condition and in the second place…' She sighed. 'That's just the thing. It all happened in a twinkling, as if we were both puppets in the hands of a malicious puppet-master. Whenever I think back, it's like watching a staged play.' She sighed again. 'He gave a terrible howl and fled, shrieking and cursing, spouting blood from his wound. I just stood there for a long while, rooted to the spot. Waiting to see if there'd be any repercussions. There weren't. After a while, I came home.'

She glanced up at the other two. 'I was literally too shocked and disgusted with myself to mention it. And that's the honest truth. I suppose I'm not used to admitting I've done something that embarrasses me. And I'm really, really sorry. I had hoped against hope that moving away from that area would be enough to prevent any follow-up action. But of course that is both cowardly and unrealistic. We'd better start discussing our options.'

They spent the whole of that day and much of the next, talking through the implications of the warrior's presence.

'It would be too much to hope that he was solitary,' reasoned Siddhangshu.

Young men were normally kept under tight social restraints. Access to and from the orbiting estates was based on bio-genetic keys. If once a family's signature genes became scattered through indiscriminate breeding, it was the same as broadcasting the password to a bank vault on an open frequency.

Rashmi shrugged. 'Let's assume he belongs to a clan of off-worlders like us, visiting the Surface for private reasons. If so, we have the advantage of experience, because we've been here so much longer. Nor have we noticed them before the time of my incident and Lakshmi's feeling of being watched. What about you, Sid? Anything?'

He was about to shake his head. Then he stopped, narrowing his eyes.

'Hmm. Nothing threatening or suspicious, but...' For years now, his favourite pastime had been to retrofit hardware that he salvaged from dump-sites dating to the silicon chip era of computer manufacture. 'You know how I've been creating a very rudimentary surveillance network? Out of antique audio and video devices? Well, there's this one thing that's been showing up and I have no idea what it is. Here–' He switched on one of his salvaged monitors, a bulky box-shaped item with a vacuum-tube for a screen. 'It's obviously some kind of minibot except that it doesn't seem to have any clear purpose. Just appears and disappears.'

As he spoke, an image appeared of a mechanical object, about the size of a crow or a small cat. It had no visible limbs and was smooth, ovoid and golden in colour. It shot across the screen, vanishing behind a column. 'I've tried increasing the screen resolution,' said Siddhangshu, 'but it moves too fast for this clunky old equipment to register any details.'

'Very odd,' said Rashmi, staring at the screen. 'As you know, I've been compiling a registry of all the various inorganics that occupy this region. I've never come across anything like that.' Over the years, her knowledge had grown encyclopaedic. She could recognize at a glance the make, manufacture and software generation of every little whirring gadget and suction-footed micro-widget that patrolled the Surface. They were all related in one way or another to keeping the external environment from succumbing to the planet's weather, but she had found ways of re-writing their software until she could get them to do her bidding any time she wanted.

'I've been wanting to catch it, to understand what exactly it does. But there's no predicting when or where it'll appear,' said Siddhangshu.

'Would you say your first sighting was before or after our recent shift?'

'Oh, only after, definitely,' said Siddhangshu. 'Perhaps one week ago?'

Rashmi sat down in front of the monitor and studied the stored images of the darting golden object for a long time. Finally she turned away. 'It seems to me,' she said, slowly, 'there's definitely something suspicious about this thing. Lakshmi and I have never seen it in all our wandering. Unlike any of the other minibots, it doesn't appear to have any function. Meanwhile, it pops up regularly on your surveillance cameras and seems literally to dance in front of them before vanishing. I'd say someone's specifically targeting you. Trying to catch your attention.'

'What for?' asked Lakshmi. 'If the Mystery Warrior's clan members wanted to take revenge, they'd come after you, not Sid.'

Rashmi shrugged. 'Who knows? Maybe the guy's family sent out scouts to find us, noticed Sid instead and got distracted.' She smiled fondly at him. 'I wouldn't be surprised. You're the only prince to appear on the Surface in all the twelve years we've been here.'

Lakshmi wasn't smiling. 'If that's the case then what's to stop them from tearing into our camp and taking him? After all, the creature you met appeared to be mentally unstable as well as violent. Perhaps his family's even worse?'

Rashmi got to her feet. 'We've got to assume they've not been able to disable your force field. That doesn't mean they haven't been trying or that they won't succeed tomorrow.'

Lakshmi got to her feet too. 'I say we go out and confront them right away. We surely don't want to be surprised as well as out-numbered.'

'Look!' cried Siddhangshu, pointing at the monitor. 'There's the golden minibot – it's in front of a camera that's just ten yards from the camp entrance–' A pair of coordinates on the monitor revealed its exact location.

'Okay,' said Rashmi. 'We'll go right now.' She snatched up her specimen net, GPS dial and laser-torch before dashing for the camp-exit.

Lakshmi, following close behind, called out as she left, 'Sid – remember, it's you they want. Whatever happens, do NOT leave the field-area. We'll catch the minibot and be right back.'

Her voice trailed off into the distance.

Siddhangshu was left standing at the entrance to the little shelter. They were always constructed using existing struts and overhanging platforms for extra protection. 'I have a bad feeling about this plan,' he muttered to himself. But there wasn't anything he could do about it now. He went back inside. On the monitor, the flashing golden minibot had of course slipped from view. Idly, he watched the glowing screen, waiting to see the figures of his wife and sister-in-law wander into the frame.

A minute ticked by. Two minutes. Five.

No figures.

Suddenly, his heart began to pound.

The camera was transmitting a loop, not a live image.

Siddhangshu sprang out again then skidded to a halt at the sparkling curtain of the force field. Lakshmi's warning rang in his ears: *Do NOT leave the field-area*. He clutched at his hair in an agony of indecision. They'd not had time to discuss alternative plans of action in case something went wrong. What if one or both women were attacked? How would he know? What action was he supposed to take?

Just then a fluting cry rent the air. It sounded barely human. Was it Rashmi? It did not sound like her. And yet…and yet…

Returning to the hut only long enough to snatch up his kit-bag, Siddhangshu ran towards the glistening barrier. He felt nothing as he passed unharmed through it.

'Rashmi!' he called, 'Lakshmi – come back! It's a trap, it's a trap!'

But he had only taken a few steps into the clearing beyond the shelter when a blinding white light stabbed down from above, freezing him in his tracks. The glistening cylinder of a suction shaft whooshed down over him, trapping him like a fly in a giant's drinking straw. His feet lost contact with the ground. Blackness descended upon his senses.

'Two things,' said Rashmi, 'are clear: one, we're going after Sid. Two, we will *not* apply to I-Udia for help in our quest.'

Lakshmi nodded, but her face was a mask of grim despair.

'Won't be easy, sis. All right, so we've located him, because of his GPS chip. But how d'you plan to break into the enemy estate?' It was an orbiting property similar in size and eminence to their own I-Udia, but positioned in geo-stationary orbit on the far side of the planet from where they were. It called itself L-Nka and was just as impregnable to assaults from outsiders as all other off-worlder facilities. 'Even you can't possibly break open a gene-sequence code by brute computing!'

'No,' said Rashmi, 'nor would I wish to.' She glanced at her sister. 'The laws that keep modern human society free of the vicious, blood-fests of the past are clear on that point: we may not attempt to synthesize a code to break past one another's barriers. However, I believe there may be another way. It's sneaky. But I don't think there are any specific laws forbidding it.' She smiled. 'Come on. We've got a lot of work to do.'

Meanwhile, far away in L-Nka, Siddhangshu sat in an enormous hall, being plied with every kind of rich food and potent wine imaginable. One week had passed since his abduction. Every day he had been subjected to the same ritual: in the morning he was awakened by a team of fawning young boys, offering him a choice of bath oils and breakfast foods, and presenting him with a new set of clothes. Every morning he rejected everything that was offered, drinking only plain water and refusing to change out of his own clothes until it was time for his audience with the Chief Admin of the estate, a giantess by the name of Raveena. The rest of the entire day was spent in arguments, alternating between seduction and aggression, to get him to submit to her will.

'Come on, cupcake,' said Raveena. 'It's only a matter of time. Either you'll die of hunger and thirst or you'll come to your senses and accept my caresses. If it's the former, we'll have your DNA in a vacuum flask. If it's the latter, you'll enjoy every pleasure you ever dreamt of and then some *and* we'll have your DNA in a, shall we say, more hospitable location. For us, it's win-win either way. For you? I have to say there's only one option that's worth considering.' She put on her most wheedling expression. 'Come to Mamma, hunky-poo! All you need do is say *yes*!'

Siddhangshu looked the woman steadily in the eye. 'Sorry. Not happening.'

She was at least one foot taller than her prisoner and certainly twice as wide. Her skin was the colour of white chalk and her hair was metallic blue, sculpted into enormous structures like rams' horns that extended sideways on either side of her head. Woven into this hair, she wore a dozen animated masks, six on either side, each one a caricature in miniature of her own face. The masks were constantly in motion, sticking their long tongues out or crossing their eyes or else pouting their thick, red lips in simulated kisses. She had rivets instead of eyebrows and her enormous pale green eyes were outlined in flickering shades of flame. She wore diamond-encrusted chain-mail instead of clothes. Her spine ended in a long, tufted, muscular tail that she flicked this way and that, like a fly-whisk. It was not clear whether this appendage had been added surgically or was part of her heredity.

Raveena sighed and all her masks alternately boo-hooed and retched. 'Dearie me. You're really beginning to tax my patience, pretty boy.' She snapped her fingers in order to summon a tray of snacks for herself. She fed her masks before stuffing her own face. 'So. Tell me again: what is the reason you continue to resist me?'

'Because I love my wife,' said Siddhangshu, in a patient voice. 'Because I will not be disloyal to her or her clan. Because I know that even if you succeed in squeezing my seed out of me, so long as it is without my consent, you will have broken the law–'

'The *law*! How quaint. And who, my darling, remains to administer any laws in our orbital dimension? Each estate is a law unto itself! You know that as well as I do. As for that little charcoal stick you call your wife, the one who attacked my beloved baby brother Suresh and who is the reason I discovered you at all – why, she's obviously forgotten all about you, hasn't she? We've not heard the faintest whisper from her.' Which was a lie. Rashmi had been beaming messages towards L-Nka every six hours. They went unanswered of course.

Siddhangshu was unperturbed. 'Even if that's so,' he said, 'it'll be for a reason. As for orbital law, there are conventions governing the conduct between estates. Breaking those conventions can cause repercussions which…' In measured tones he detailed the legal ways in which Raveena would be made to atone for her transgressions.

Every evening ended in the same way, with Raveena retreating in frustrated fury and Siddhangshu being administered a sleeping potion to knock him out. His attendants were all male, but a couple of them were Raveena's younger brothers. Early on, one of these brothers took pity on Siddhangshu and offered him food that had not been drugged or poisoned. He said that he found his sister's behaviour unutterably offensive, whereas Siddhangshu's dignity and nobility in the face of all the disgraceful pressure he was being subjected to were what he admired. And he poured off the sleeping draught so that the prisoner might remain in his senses through the night.

Siddhangshu lay awake thinking about the week that had passed. He was extremely grateful for the opportunity to be alone with his thoughts but it was certainly hard to suppress the sense of having been abandoned. Every day that went by without any idea of where Rashmi and Lakshmi were, or what they were doing, was an ordeal of forebearance. Gradually however, as he mulled these ideas over and over in his mind, he became aware of a faint sound. It was really very slight.

The room was in darkness, but the floor was so white that it gave off a slight radiance. He turned his head this way and that, trying to locate the source of the sound when he noticed a dark patch against the whiteness of the floor. It appeared to be moving slowly, a small flat blob about the length of his little finger. He began to smile to himself, in the dark. It looked very much like a black beetle but he recognized now that the faint sound he could hear came from the whirring of a miniature drive shaft: one of Rashmi's minibots. Siddhangshu placed a finger down on the floor. If his guess was right then the gadget would be one that had been trained to seek out his unique bio-signature and would come directly towards him. If it ignored him then it was either an actual insect or a toy created to look like one.

For a long minute the dark blob stopped in its tracks. Then very slowly but deliberately, it turned and homed in on the heat signature it had been programmed to seek. When it was close enough, he picked it up, turned it over and saw that there was a message glowing on the underside: *hang cool, bro!*, it said, *we're coming to get you out. lux*

The army of minibots that Rashmi sent in entered the satellite estate through its garbage vents, its evacuation channels and its exhaust pipes. Being non-organic they set off no alarms. Once inside, they could be directed to follow Rashmi's bidding. She concentrated on sending in waves of minibots while distracting Raveena with verbal arguments and appeals to let Siddhangshu go. When the little machines had infiltrated in sufficient numbers, she and Lakshmi directed them to seek out power sources, to send her accurate plans of the interior of the estate and in particular to target the computers that kept the space station in functioning order.

There was no battle in a traditional sense. Over a period of days, mysterious breakdowns began to overtake the satellite until finally Raveena began to understand that an invasion of some sort was under way. It was much too late by then to counteract it. Under cover of darkness, one night when the moon's light was blocked by the bulk of the Earth, Rashmi's tiny forces turned the power off across the whole of L-Nka while simultaneously releasing a narcotic agent into the air. As the residents of Raveena's private domain sighed and sank to their feet in sleep, Rashmi and Lakshmi berthed their craft without the slightest opposition. Finding their way to Siddhangshu's quarters, they hustled him out and bundled him into the MiniCruiser. He was weak from his imprisonment but very glad to be alive. The campaign had taken a month. No one had died or been physically harmed and in terms of the formal rules of engagement between estates, no laws had been broken. The tiny minibots were designed to self-destruct once their purpose was served, leaving behind only a trace of their presence. Even if Raveena understood the means by which her security had been breached, she would be unable to reconstruct the software or the chips with which she could launch a similar attack herself at some later time.

Siddhangshu regretted that the friendly young brother who had been of such support to him, had to be left behind. 'Maybe some day he will find a way to escape his sister's control,' suggested Lakshmi.

'Maybe,' said Siddhangshu. 'But where are we going? We should be starting our descent.'

'Our work on the Surface is done,' said Rashmi, 'so we're going back to I-Udia.' She'd called home once the campaign to save Siddhangshu was approaching its successful conclusion. 'We've been away a little over twelve years. A lot's happened back there. Kailash Uncle has mellowed. Mum passed away. Out of grief, said Babs, who, everyone says, has kept her word about acting as my regent, not my successor.'

The trio returned to I-Udia, to universal approval and celebration. For the girls, it was of course, a sad loss to be motherless but they were able to overcome their grief as part of the general celebration.

Some months after their return, when all their three lives had settled back into something approximating their normal pace, Lakshmi asked to have a private audience with Rashmi.

Her face was serious.

'What is it?' Rashmi asked. 'I haven't seen you looking so grim since that time when we realized the golden minibot was a decoy.'

'Listen,' said the younger sister. 'It's not my business. But there's been a whisper doing the rounds.' It seemed that amongst the younger generation of staff members, an idea had been set loose about Siddhangshu's time on L-Nka. Orgiastic parties were mentioned, unnatural acts, chemical means of coercion. 'There are those who want you to have him tested for chromosomal contamination. Or to subject him to brain scans to determine whether or not he betrayed your trust.' Lakshmi shook her head. 'I'm sure you won't want to do any of that, but then again...'

'Then again – what?' Rashmi asked.

'Oh...just...the people need to feel confidence in their leaders' gene-pool. No?'

Rashmi shrugged. 'Maybe. But I have no doubts. And that's what counts. What *I* believe.'

'Wow.' Lakshmi grinned. 'That's way cool, sis. Put like that, it's so obvious, so easy. You totally rock.'

'Yes,' said Rashmi, sharing the grin. 'I know.'

THE OTHER WOMAN

Mandodari stirred in her bed of crocus petals. She opened her eyes, sat up and looked around. *Something had changed.* But she could not tell what it was.

She got out of bed, bathed in pigeon's blood, ate a breakfast of dolphin milk curds and stepped out onto her terrace. From the highest level of the great Iron Palace, she could see the island nation spreading away on all sides like a living carpet: emerald fields fragrant under the sun, coconut palms nodding in the light breeze, peasants bent over and toiling. Then her pet black peacock sprang up onto the parapet wall in front of her and began to dance. He had not done that for many centuries.

Yes!

Something had changed.

But what?

Throwing on a peignoir of silk and opals, she went to find her husband. He was in his apartments, surrounded by glowing wall-charts, speaking with someone on a small device attached to one of his ears and tapping with the fingers of both hands on a flat tablet supported on the back of a slave crouching in front of him. His multiple heads each had their own headsets. He smiled at Mandodari and reached out to pat her rump, but was clearly in no mood to talk. She left him and wandered slowly through the myriad rooms of her home, her expression thoughtful.

Her in-laws and co-wives were in residence, but she neither felt like disturbing them nor did she believe any of them would be interested in the change that was stirring within her eternal world. The brothers-in-law weren't famed for their intellects, the sisters-in-law were fawningly affectionate but could not be trusted to be sincere. And the co-wives? Well. Their attention spans extended only as far as their TV remotes. Yet even had she known someone who might have been willing to hear her out, the realization was growing that the source of the change had come into being in the mortal world. And that she alone was the target of it.

She could not remember anything like this having happened before. Her position had always been one of spouse-in-the-background, the faceless bed-warmer who had less than a walk-on part in the great dramas of the mythic age. If ever she made an appearance, it was as a snivelling nag or noble not-quite-cuckoldee. There were even some dramas in which she had the joyous position of offering counselling services to a husband whose would-be mistress remained obstinately unavailable!

Any revisions to this unfortunate plot were welcome to her. Harnessing her swans, she made arrangements for an extended journey to the mortal dimension.

She visited shopping malls and amusement parks, stepped into homes and hotels, playgrounds and prisons, factories and sweat-shops. Initially she was careful to avoid manifesting herself on the material plane. It required all her concentration and she didn't enjoy the sensations of being confined within a simple physical body, embedded in Time. But the sight of such teeming hordes of mortal beings fascinated her. There had not been so many of them in the past. When millions of them congregated for parades or riots the sight was sometimes breathtaking. There were occasions when, watching them, she found herself experiencing something very close to envy. Which was surely bizarre. As a divine, she should feel nothing but pity or disgust or amusement. There was an unspoken belief amongst her fellow divines that descents into the fleshly dimension were at best an indulgence, at worst a vice. Those who practised regular visitations did so furtively. It was understood that their activities should not result in major disruptions of mortal time-space, that the actual thickening should occur in secret and that alarming or fearful forms were to be avoided.

But discretion had never been Mandodari's strong suit. Like many another demon, she adored excess and gloried in spectacle. She tried to follow the conventions, by arranging her first couple of efforts in the midst of thick forests, where the local mortals were steeped in their beliefs about the spirit world. She was delighted that they recognized her as an immortal, reacting with respect and fear. For this very reason, however, they provided nothing in the way of conversation, leave alone entertainment.

Losing patience, for her third attempt she chose a densely populated area. She believed she'd done her homework well by choosing a clothing store in the metropolis called, so far as she could tell, 'Boss Town'. It was on the coast of a major land-mass that some humans referred to as North America. The inhabitants were extremely devout: they spent the major part of their day worshipping glowing screens. After nightfall, they remained indoors while the great warehouses called malls closed their doors to the public.

Once her manifestation was complete, Mandodari admired herself in the mirrored walls of a changing-room stall. She was two metres tall and had modelled herself on a priestess called Lady GooGoo whose pink-skinned and golden ringleted likeness had been featured in a popular form of street art called 'bill boards'. She appeared very frequently on the glowing screens, howling in front of the shrieking, ululating hordes who worshipped her.

Of course it was darker than a moonless night in the tiny changing room. The lights and the ventilation were both off. The divine tourist was naked but had expected to help herself to the clothes on the racks outside. But when Mandodari exited the stall, she found herself surrounded by miles of tiny frilly dresses, stretchy sleep-suits, socks the size of new-born kittens and endless pairs of woolly booties. She was in the babies' section.

Pale, watery light seeped into the main section of Sear's via skylights, from the neon signs on the exterior of the mall. Clad in her heavy body, she struggled to find her way around the silent, darkened store. But the buzzing hum of electric devices caused an unpleasant tingling in her ears so she didn't even attempt to look for light-switches. Disconcertingly life-like statues draped in clothes that represented some of the styles and cuts available in that section, poked up above the mass of merchandise. She had as yet only a rudimentary understanding of mortal languages and certainly no desire to memorize all the hundreds of different scripts available. The signs and labels in English made no sense to her. The blonde giantess had no choice but to stumble around until she was in an area where the clothes looked as if they might fit her.

Her research had shown that most women these days wore a combination of leggings and short, tight tops. Once she had found the jeans section, she discovered to her consternation, that a majority were at least four sizes too small. The plastic hangers on which the clothes were displayed made an extremely annoying tinkling sound as she tried to riffle through them. An assortment of paper labels and dangling price tabs had been variously stapled, tacked on, glued and stitched into place on the pants so that she found herself snarling out loud as she stomped her way into them. She hissed like an angry cat each time the zippered fastenings caught in her pubic hair when she tried to do them up. And eventually she took to simply ripping them apart while removing them.

By the time she heard the sounds of approaching security guards and saw the beams of torchlight stabbing into the depths of the store, she had managed to surround herself with a mountain of discards. It was not in her nature to feel afraid, so when the two uniformed men approached her, she turned to face them, a towering figure with dishevelled blonde hair and a pair of Levi's Loose 'N' Easy Cargoes ripped to shreds in her hands. In her carefully enunciated though archaic Sanskrit she explained that she was only looking for something suitable to wear and wondered if they would care to help her.

The men began to jibber excitedly, waving their arms about. The light from their torches sent fantastic shadows scudding across the ceilings and floors of the vast showroom. Mandodari could not follow a word of what they said. Kicking aside a couple of clothes racks that toppled over with a satisfying crash, she strode towards the guards. She had been fully prepared to reward them for their services. Instead of behaving with decorum however, or showing the least respect, the two idiots began shrieking and running away, like baboons startled by a lion.

Recognizing then that there was no point wasting time, she reached out, grabbed a man in either hand and dashed their heads together. The instant silence was wonderful. Then she sucked out their still-warm blood, dismembered them with clinical precision and ate them slowly and methodically. She started with the limbs, moving on to the squishy but delicious internal organs, ending with the tongue, the eyes and the brains.

Being manifested in a physical body was hard, hungry work.

Basra Dott, the famous television anchor, was single. Whenever someone pestered her about her marital status she grinned and said, 'Every night I go to bed with eighty million people!' And counting. Her current ratings were so high that she was seriously considering hiring a second security detail for herself. She knew some celebrities who had two lines of defence, one uniformed and visible, the other dressed to merge with the crowd while continuing to perform their duties.

Nevertheless, she did not actually live alone. There was a middle-aged couple who looked after her daily needs. Lal cooked and did the grocery shopping while Renu, his wife, did the laundry and the floor swabbing. There was a separate person, a scrawny young girl connected in some way to the local presswallah, who came in once a day to do the dusting, the toilet-cleaning and the garbage clearance. Another two men, both young and interchangeable in terms of height, size and general deportment shared the task of being her drivers. On account of the unpredictable nature of her work hours, she could never do with less than continuous chauffeuring. Indeed, these two formed part of her security shield, having been supplied by the same agency that provided her with a permanent on-site sentry outside her front gate and with bodyguards when she was out in the field.

She owned a two-storey private home, in a quiet residential colony with tall, nodding asoka trees along its boundary wall. Ms Dott often had house-guests, many of them members of her extended family, some of them staying for several months. However, it so happened that she had just seen off her younger brother and his wife the day before. In the lull before the next visitors a week from today, she enjoyed the luxury of sitting up in bed drinking her first cup of coffee undisturbed. It was brought to her by Renu, who also brought in the stack of newspapers that was delivered to the door.

Right beside her she kept her DingleByte, a handheld device that permitted her to watch TV while surfing the net while playing Mahjongg Solitaire, while answering email and sending SMS. But like so many other public personalities, Ms Dott greatly cherished the few hours of her time when she was truly alone. So the device was switched to silent at night and however much it hummed and flashed and cavorted there on her bedside table, she ignored it and would continue ignoring it until after she'd had her morning shower and was ready to face the world.

So it was during this glorious lull, while she was still becalmed and listening to jazz on her room stereo, the coffee cup still warm in her hands and the air conditioner humming sweetly, that with no warning, her DingleByte blared with unwanted sound. First there was an ear-shattering screech, such as might be made by a transcontinental airliner revving its engines prior to take-off, then a stranger's face appeared on the device's display.

A woman.

Her voice scythed through the air as she said, in a peculiar mixture of languages old and new, none of them English, 'Good morning! Welcome! I am needful of an audience. I shall come now, yes?'

It was not really a question.

Basra was so shocked she had no time to spare on being angry. 'Wha–?' she stammered, before instantly recovering her famous poise. 'Wait! Who are you?' There was no point asking her how she'd got the number. It was obvious that this person, whoever she was, had access to some extremely sophisticated software overriding capability. That made her instantly a force to reckon with.

By way of an answer, the air above the armchair in Basra's room began to shimmer as if with heat-haze. It would take fifteen minutes for the whole body of her unexpected guest to fully materialize but since she had helpfully arranged for her own head to appear first, she was able to talk within the first minute or so.

'I am Mandodari,' said the apparition, speaking slowly and sounding each syllable with care. 'You is hear of me many times. I will give interview on your TV show. It is time to tell my side of the story. So you must interview me. In exchange for this I am filled your empty womb with half-dozen sons.'

She paused now, as her mid-section made the transition to physicality. 'Also, though I am not yet hungry, soon I will be. Keep many live goats ready. Horn-less and hoof-less is best but I is no fussy. Some plus-size dresses also. Your room is too cold. What is wrong with it?'

Basra had always been nimble-witted, able to sort through her options within seconds between what she *had* to accept about reality and what she could push into place to suit her needs. Even before Mandodari – 'Call me Mandy!' – had fully downloaded her mortal frame, Basra had (a) recognized that her guest really was a supernatural entity, (b) had the potential to provide viewer-cocaine for at least a couple of weeks and (c) would undoubtedly be a monumental pain in the rectum for the duration. In the short term, the house was big enough to provide space for the goats. Lal and Renu's silence could be bought at the rate of one gold bangle per day. The maid would be a problem and would have to be sent away. The drivers were naturally laconic and wouldn't talk about anything they encountered in the course of their work.

In the long term? Well. She'd have to wait and see.

An hour later Basra and her guest were sitting in the patio.

'All right,' said the professional TV anchor. 'Let's get started on why you're here, what it means for our viewers and what it means for our country.'

Mandy said, 'What is means for *world*. Silly.'

The divine was facing out towards the hedge that screened the carefully tended lawn from external views. The seasoned journalist, veteran of four general elections, a woman in her early forties who had been called everything from 'hard-boiled idealist' to 'crypto-fascist' faced towards the glass-fronted sliding doors behind her guest. She could see her own reflection: short hair, tawny eyes and the type of smooth, wrinkle-free skin that signalled good health and an even temper. She was attractive in a friendly, street-wise way and her viewers trusted her because she looked like one of them. From where she sat, she could enjoy the play of sunlight falling through the slats of the wooden trellis overhead and a back-view of the crimson silk kimono she had given the demoness to wear.

Though at first glance Mandy could pass for human, at second glance it was impossible not to want to recoil away from her. It wasn't just that her dimensions were several centimetres larger than life-size. It was also the peculiar hue of the skin: pearly white – not blue, not brown, not even green – but nacreous, echoing the sea, not the land. The hair was black but with fiery streaks that sizzled on and off unexpectedly. The eyes weren't merely dark, but impenetrably so, with no discernible pupils. The mouth was lush and warm and curved upwards. But when she smiled – which was often – her teeth were all identical, very white and a tad larger than was comfortable. Behind them flickered a long black tongue.

So she was beautiful, yes. In a repellent way.

She was talking animatedly, holding the gorgeous silk kimono around her full, extravagant body. 'Until two months before,' she said, referring to mortal time, 'I am invisible to mortal world. I am waking up and sleeping and waking and sleeping, but there is nothing for me to do. Nothing for me to *be*.' She tried to explain what it was like to live outside the four dimensions of the mortal sphere. 'We is not die. So there is not wear, not tear. Not today, not tomorrow.'

Then suddenly, the change began. Variations appeared in the routine pleasures and events around the Iron Palace. 'My peacock is dancing for me, for instance: he is not do it since the time of my marriage. Which is many mortal centuries past. It is wonderful that I am see him. Maybe you is too simple to understand? You must not try.' Mandy's speech was fluent but contained anomalies of grammar and syntax. Basra could not tell whether her own grasp of Sanskrit was too weak to make sense of her guest's speech or whether the divine's knowledge of mortal language was too outdated.

The thing Mandy most wanted to talk about was the reason she had appeared in the physical dimension. 'You is not know it, I am sure?' she asked Basra, who shook her head politely, knowing it was expected of her. 'I am looking, looking, looking for long times, before I did work it out. It is the high court in your country. There is some case about land. About property. A temple.'

While trying to tease out meanings from the mass of information available in the physical world she had accessed the internet. The one really significant technological breakthrough that had occurred since the early days, she said, was the proliferation of electronic media. 'I am not idea how it is works,' she confessed, 'but it is works. My husband is have fast connection. So I am return home to palace, I am go online and I am Google my name. And by clicking, clicking, clicking, I am begin to understand what is change, what is happen in some very near months that is make different for every of us. Not just Them–' she meant the royal couple whose names were synonymous with the epic to which she was so intimately connected '–but even me also, even my husband also and all mortals also.' She stopped. 'What is problem? You is frown.'

'Oh!' said Basra as if caught by surprise, though this was one of her standard ploys for adding variety to an interview, the carefully positioned frown. 'I was just wondering, you know – you've mentioned your husband several times already – and the fact is, I mean, I hope you'll excuse me if what I ask seems impertinent or… or…you know, *rude*–'

'–you is mean his so-called *death*?' cut in Mandy. She held both her hands up with her fingers curled over, making the sign for air-quotes. Apparently she had spent more than enough of her spare time watching mortal television. 'Pooh! I am just *told* to you: we is not die. It is like you mortals enjoy playing battles – you is call them sports? – you know, like kicking head made of cow-leather from one side of battlefield to the other, for example–'

According to her, engagements between divines took a form similar to football, but with less goodwill. 'My husband is never agree to lose. He is always great warrior, he is always great genius. There is not ever doubt he will win.' The features of the beautiful face knotted together in a fierce sneer. 'So of course he is not die.'

'What are you saying?' said Basra, leaning forward with her eyes all agog. She was so practised at feigning emotions in order to get her subjects to talk that she could do it now without even noticing that she was putting it on. It was a shame that all this amazing raw footage was being lost in a private conversation. She was recording it, discreetly of course, on her DingleByte, so that she'd have evidence to take to her CEO. But an audio transcript would have no news value. Besides which, she was starting to worry that Mandy's version of events was too far removed from the popular one. 'Are you telling me that the battle – the one that's been the high point of every version of the epic since it was first written up – that battle was *rigged*?'

'I am say it is *not happen at all*. You tell me: how else it can be for my immortal warrior to lose? And that too, when his enemy is a so-small hero king, so short, so thin and having only one head? Huh! It is a lie, a sham, a nonsense. That is why I am here. Your courts is talking all the time about truth? Well! There is many sides to truth. Your courts is want see hero king's birthplace? Is want to put mortal flag on mortal plot of land? Well! One plot is lead to other plot. So I am come. To tell my story. To change the plot. At last.'

'But why now?' asked Basra. 'Why you? Why here?'

'Because,' said Mandy with a smirk, 'this is age of womanses freedom. This is age when hidden womans is coming out from cupboard of past. When mistress is become master. When wrong is become right.' She narrowed her eyes. 'I am have big wrong is done on me. Whole world is laugh on me. But who is take my side? When is anyone hear my pain? No one. Never. Until now. World is change. And talk-shows is there. Truth-shows is there. Everyone is listening all the time to everything. Even to me.'

Basra's mind was ticking, ticking, ticking as she listened to the divine ramble on.

Eventually, she claimed she needed a break from the information overload. She showed Mandy the room in which the goats were tethered and a few rudiments of using the facilities of a modern home. Then she left for work.

A hurried conference was called in the inner sanctum of ENDO-TV. Basra's CEO was a grizzled power-house of a man called Ved Mentor, who had been in the news business for over forty years. He and the only other senior news anchor Ornob Gosh listened in silence to what Basra told them. Their expressions morphed from mild amusement, to disbelief and finally disquiet. By the time they were willing to listen to the recorded conversation, a silence had fallen over the room.

Mentor was standing with his back to the other two, his hands on his hips, facing towards the picture window that showed him the urban sprawl of South Delhi. The jumble of roof-tops, satellite dishes and trees welled out as far as the eye could see. Several minutes ticked by. He said nothing. Then: 'How long can you stall her?'

'A couple of days,' said Basra. 'A week at most. I don't really know.'

Ornob, who was Basra's contemporary in age as well as ambition and fervour, said, 'It's interesting how she locates the source of the "change", as she calls it, to the birthplace issue.' He glanced up at the other two. 'I mean, for us here in the so-called "mortal dimension", it's been about land and settlements, communal riots and cynical politicians. Meanwhile?' He shook his head and raised his hands towards the ceiling. 'Up there in the mythos? *An entire pantheon stirs to life!*' He ghosted a chuckle. 'I don't know about the two of you but I've...never had faith. In anything. Not gods, not devils, not four-leaved clovers. Along comes a court judgement and that's it! The entire game changes! Suddenly, we're battling the demon hordes with our little matchstick ideals.'

Mentor raised his shoulders high and spread his palms wide. He was a tall man, clean-shaven, with a square jaw and a quirk of hair that fell over his forehead. 'Ornob – I disagree: you *did* believe in something. You believed in the courts and the rule of law. What we have here is the result of the courts ruling on something that had always remained outside their purview: the smoke and mirrors of the realm of faith. For those who are true believers, every character in a mythology is as real and as physical as this desk, this carpet, this chair. They have no need of land records or certificates to know where their hero was born or the exact spot upon which he died. In fact, NOT having a precise spot makes it possible to locate him everywhere: on Earth as well as within their own hearts.

'But once the courts mark one particular spot purporting to be a real birthplace, with a real X on a real map of a real city, ah! That changes everything. The stuff of pure faith is dragged down into the muck of who-said-this and I-said-that.' He raised his hands then plunged them down. 'What was once mystical and sublime tumbles into the lies and muck of human affairs. And we are left to argue about how many demons can dance on the head of a journalist.'

He hauled upon the belt of his pants, a familiar mannerism of his. 'Basra, for better or worse, that journalist is you. We'll air the broadcast, but I suggest you take a week to prepare for it. There's a Supreme Court decision coming up that could overturn the high court's ruling. The fate of the Universe may depend on what you can get your demon lady to say.'

'At my marriage,' said Mandodari, looking straight into the cameras as she spoke, 'the path to the wedding platform is lit with one hundred living candles. It is a glory sight: one hundred slaves, chained inside iron cages, and set on fire. They is so happy to die for us. This is how they celebrate. This is how they show we are strong.

'Centuries is pass since that time. Nobody is look in my direction. But here I am now.' The full red lips curved up in a feral smile. 'My time is come,' she said, with no attempt at false humility, as she turned both her hands towards her full body. Though tightly encased within an outfit in green and orange cheetah-spot velour with fluorescent blue organdie flounces at the elbows and knees, there were no unsightly bulges. 'I am tell the true story of the war against my people.'

Basra Dott drew in a breath, reminding herself to pace her questions carefully. 'So...Mandy,' said the famous television anchor, 'ever since you made your presence known to me – for which I must tell you, I am extremely flattered – the one question that's been at the top of my mind is, why now? You've had literally centuries in which to make yourself known to the world of...of...'

'Mortals,' said the divine, nodding her head as if encouraging a child.

'...mortals,' repeated Basra, allowing herself a little smile which managed to convey a sense of amazement alongside a dose of judicious scepticism. 'So...why today? Why now? Has something *changed*?'

Mandy blinked and flexed her shoulders. 'I am want to set record straight. For instance: my husband is not have ten heads. Why is mortals believe such kind of nonsense? Five is maximum. And it is must be odd number only: one main head and then one or two on sides. Ten heads is means five this side, five that side and nothing in middle! It is total-foolish. But to get back to wedding night...'

'We'll do that, Mandy, we'll do that,' said Basra, 'but first our viewers need to know what brought you here, to the mortal dimension–'

'I is tell you that already. It is too boring for me,' said the divine. 'Wedding night is much more thrill. For example, I am want to show how nonsense it is, this claim that my husband is lose interest in me because of Other Woman. He cannot! It is all lies of their side. In fact, there is not ever any Other Woman–'

'Who?' interjected Basra.

'You know it is who,' said Mandy, her forehead starting to bunch together in a frown. 'I am not insult my mouth by speak her rubbish name.' Throwing her head back, she howled in a high falsetto, '*Oh she whose perfumed face rivals the full-moon! She who makes the stars tremble with desire!*' For an instant, there was a disturbing flicker in the region of the guest's throat, as of a second mouth gaping open with a curved and toothy beak poking out. 'After all, you tell me: why is *I* am here? And not *she*?'

Basra's tawny eyes glittered. 'Yes, Mandy, tell our viewers what that reason is…'

'Because,' said Mandodari, 'because for all this time, I am sitting in background of this so-called big story, feeling this hurt, this pain, this axe in my heart. The whole world is say, Look! Look! Your husband is running after that woman! Look! Look – he is catch her! He is bring her to your house, he is feed her honey and dolphin cream! And all this time, all this many, many years, where am I in the picture? Where do I hide my head? Huh! NOWHERE!'

The huge, ugly-beautiful face reared up, seeming to grow livid with the stored memory of her ancient, deathless rage. 'I tell you, it is ALL LIES!! Everything. First lie is, why is they come to forest? To steal, of course! It is our forest. Second lie is, how is my sister-in-law lose her nose? Because that man and his brother – I will not say they's name – they is see her take bath, they is grow hot, then they is chase-chase-chase, until she is fall. Her nose is break, but still they is have fun with her. Third lie is, who is win the war? My husband of course. He is bring army to avenge his sister, and they is chase this man and his brother away. The end! That is whole story. There is no wife and she is not come to forest. At all. She is total imaginary. That is why in final end, she is not even stay with so-called hubby-bubby, but vanish into earth. Hahaha! Big joke. She is imaginary from start to finish.'

Basra could see, around the edges of her field of vision that a slow-motion pandemonium was in progress. One of the light boys had fainted. The sound recordist had whipped off his headphones. To her right, someone was gesturing. Through it all, she nodded, arranging her features in a sympathetic expression and ignored all distraction. 'All right, Mandy,' she said. 'All right. The problem is, we here in the mortal dimension have for centuries been given a completely different version of events–'

'I am know,' cut in Mandy. 'That is why I am come. To explain. To show the truth. This is age when a womans is free to speak out her heart. This is my heart.'

'Yes, yes,' said Basra, 'but being free to speak isn't the same as being free to lie–'

'I am not lie,' said Mandy, starting to look angry.

'And,' continued Basra, 'in our dimension it isn't enough to just state a fact. In order to believe it, we have to see evidence–'

'Wrong!' cut in the divine at once. 'The court is show no evidence of birthplace!'

A note of triumph had entered her voice.

'And the reason for that is…?' prompted Basra.

'Because they cannot. They is stupid. They is rubbish–'

Basra leaned forward in her seat. 'Of course, of course–'

'Is not surprise they can show nothing. We is divine, after all.' She shrugged as if her meaning were obvious, 'We is immortal.'

'Yes, but Mandy,' said Basra, 'please remember that I and my viewers are poor, limited beings with heavy physical bodies and short, transitory lives! Why, we are hardly more than May flies compared to you. We really don't understand the implications of what you just said. Do you think you could explain it more clearly?'

The demoness drew herself up in her seat, her eyebrows arched in contempt. 'We is immortal,' she repeated more slowly. 'It is mean we is live forever. We is live outside of Time. We is have no end and no beginning. We is neither die *nor is we born…*'

Back in her bedroom, Mandodari, the wife of the ten-headed demon king, settled into her saffron-scented mattress. For all the time she had been away, there had been a hum of unrest and uncertainty. Rumours were flying around of changes and restructuring, of new currents in the flux of reality. And then, just as suddenly as it had begun, the disturbance or irregularity or discontinuity, or whatever it was, began to subside.

She returned with her swans as if nothing had happened. She told no one of where she had been and returned to her quarters with no comments to anyone. Her eyes began to close once more. Her time in the mortal dimension was already fading from consciousness.

Back on Earth, no records had been kept of the unprecedented broadcast that had been aired with such fanfare by ENDO-TV. A few protests were raised. Then a story was put out that it had all been an extraordinary scam. Then the whole affair subsided with no further questions asked. All references to the televised interview were erased. Gradually the entire episode passed into the collective unmemory as the issue of a hero king's birthplace subsided and was instantly replaced by fresh riots, new scandals, gristly outrages.

But not all change is for the worse.

And even the most transitory incidents leave traces.

On a parapet wall of a vast Iron Palace, for instance.

A black peacock is dancing.

Forever.

THE FUTURE IMPERFECT

Outside, the palm trees bent and snapped in a blizzard of pale green snow. Inside, Prof. Saraswati Ali was warming to her point. 'He's not a bad student,' she was saying to her colleagues, Professors Zuleikha O'Brien and Christine Krishnaswamy. 'But his thesis on late Twentieth-Century Fundamentalism is what I would call deranged.'

'Surely that's not reason enough to consider flogging him?' asked Prof. Zuleikha. 'I had the impression that he was rather too cuddly for that!' It was well known that she had a weakness for her male students. There had been several complaints, but the University had always managed to hush them up.

The indicator on the entrance module purred. 'Well, here he is now,' said Prof. Christine, sucking on her substance simulator, currently set on 'coke'. Sure enough, three seconds later, Elijah 'Bunny' Mikimoto stepped out.

He was short but well-muscled. He held his thesis shyly across his pelvic region. He wore natural plastic tights, ski boots and a moon-beam collar. His entire upper body was encased in a hologram of dense tattoos which gave him the appearance of being both chic and deeply vulnerable. He had electrolyzed his hair to give himself a fashionably mature bald pate. And his beard was maintained at precisely five o'clock-shadow length.

'It's your central idea, I'm afraid,' began Prof. Saraswati. 'This ridiculous notion that there are fundamentalists amongst us today! And that they are no different from the religious fundamentalists of the previous century…'

'I beg to disagree, M'lady Professor,' said Bunny, in his endearingly masculine whisper. 'My argument suggests that the fundamentalists of our era are even more dangerous than those of the past, for being apparently invisible to us.'

There was a pained silence.

Prof. Zuleikha, taking pity on the boy said, 'Come now, my sweet, you can't possibly defend that little idea?'

'I believe I can,' said Bunny. 'I believe that today's fundamentalists oppress millions of people through the media and the market…'

'Blasphemy!' snapped Prof. Saraswati.

'…the fashion industry, for instance,' continued Bunny, 'ruthlessly eliminates all those who do not conform to its dress codes.' He looked down at himself, gesturing with the regulation cigarette in his hand. 'My hologram has to be updated every week if I want to avoid being lynched!'

'But a well-dressed man is an ornament to his society,' said Prof. Zuleikha breathily. These young things were so sweet! So charmingly rebellious. 'You should consider it your privilege to uphold the standards of this progressive age!'

Prof. Christine leant forward on her ornamental bone-china crutch: 'Consider the dietary restrictions of the past,' she growled. Her subject was Classical Vegetarianism. 'Pork for some, beef for others, dog for all except the Chinese…'

Bunny took a deep breath. 'And today we need special permits from the meat industry if we want carrots with our tiger stew! Today we're forced to eat rattlesnake ratatouille and platypus omelettes because we can no longer share the planet with creatures we don't eat!' He looked defiantly up at the three towering women. 'The mullahs of yesterday are the multinational moguls of today!'

All three academics snorted. 'Sheer guano, sweetie!' said Prof. Zuleikha. 'Don't they teach you anything? The slogan of the traditional world was "Annihilation is better than cure". Whereas today no one is killed except by their own non-conformity!'

Prof. Saraswati reached for her ayurvedic suppositories. As the president of the Enema League, she had led the campaign to bring bowel functions out of the toilet and into the drawing room. 'And of course,' she said, 'the ancient Hindu strategy of erasing fundamentalism by denying its existence has guaranteed a free and fair society.' Inserting the suppository through a cunningly devised slit in her tartan sarong, she continued: 'Look at our University! We're open to all customs, all ages, all diets, all genders, all perversions, all disabilities. Our students are chosen for their mixed ancestry and our courses for their lack of cultural context.'

Bunny said, 'Isn't that a problem too, M'lady Professor? Isn't there something amiss with the Theory of Mandatory Liberalism? Doesn't it lead to the oppression of those who don't wish to be liberals?'

'Pah!' exploded Prof. Christine. 'You're a Closet Terrorist, that's what you are!' she exclaimed. 'Behind that obsequious male exterior there's a sneaking, snivelling traditionalist, just dying to run back to the bad old days when Right was Right and Wrong was Wrong!' She poked him with her crutch. 'You need to have a little sense twisted into you! The rack in the Psychopathology Lab would do you a world of good. You don't realize how fortunate you are to be living in this permissive era. In the twentieth century you, a man, could never enjoy the sacred privilege of bearing children. Today, through the omniscient grace of biotechnology even the lowly masculine abdomen can be fashioned into a receptacle for the Divine Catheter!'

Prof. Zuleikha was beginning to squirm. She always did, as the time for her quinturnal copulation approached. She realized she would have no choice but to force herself on Bunny. 'Excuse me,' she said, tapping him lightly on the shoulder with her obedience prod. 'If you would just come this way…' He followed her, his eyes glassy, to the couch.

The other two professors indulged their separate fixations while watching the weather outside the window turn abruptly tropical. 'In his thesis,' said Prof. Saraswati presently, 'he makes absurd comparisons between the vile caste system of ancient India and the sacred genetic classification of today!' She wiped herself delicately with personal hygiene tissues handmade from the skins of rare Indonesian lizards. They were believed to be beneficial for several life-times ahead. 'He suggests that our chromosomal typing is cruel and unnatural.'

Prof. Christine gurgled slightly. She had to set her simulator back to neutral before she could speak. 'Well, it's hard to understand any of it,' she said. 'My domestic help was born with the dentition and DNA of a thoroughbred manservant. And yet? For the first fifteen years of his life, his parents steadfastly refused to send him to a Jeevesary, insisting that his IQ suited him to a career in bonsai gardening! Mutants, I tell you! They're all around us...'

Prof. Zuleikha rejoined them, panting slightly. 'Did someone mention mutants?' she asked. 'I heard on the Telenet this morning that a community of them had been discovered living in the mangrove swamps on The Fringe.' The Fringe was the name for the boundary of the climate-controlled zone. 'I can't understand why they haven't been caught and reconditioned yet. This modern squeamishness about behaviour-modulation is ridiculous! Without it, our men would still be uncontrollable brutes.'

Bunny joined them, looking subdued. His willpower was returning to normal and with it, his natural modesty and sense of shame. 'Excuse me, M'lady Professors,' he said in his soft voice. 'I want to protest this recent event! I had thought that at least in the chambers of my esteemed professors I would be safe from an obedience-prod attack!'

Prof. Christine trained her brilliant pink eyes on him. 'As you are surely aware, young man, Prof. Zuleikha belongs to the Holy Order of Hedonists for Peace. It is her sacred duty to perform the reproductory rite five times a day. She certainly finds it more inconvenient than you did just now, but you don't find her complaining or shirking her duties.' The strong sunlight outside was bruising her transparent skin and she turned to move inward.

At this moment, Bunny struck. Whipping out the canister of FemOff he had concealed in his back pocket, he sprayed the room with the concentrated odour of a thousand unbathed, male American football players just after a game. All three women slipped to the floor, unconscious. Using the Telenet unit on Prof. Saraswati's wrist, he entered the code for the Resistance headquarters.'Mission accomplished,' he reported, 'the vixens sleep. Begin transmission of reverse-conditioning programme...'

A volley of enthusiastic clicks and twitters issued from the unit. Too late Bunny remembered that in recognition of !Kung Appreciation Day all communication was to be in that language. Paralysed with the indecisiveness bred into his sex, he dithered just long enough for the effects of the odour to wear off. He was led away, bravely singing Rugby songs, by a crack team of commando grannies.

Restored to dignity, the three professors congratulated themselves upon their narrow escape.

'Well, it was all for the best,' said Prof. Christine. 'He was caught young enough to qualify for a sex change and maternity. In a year he'll just be another balloon-bellied noviciate at the Breeding Centre.'

'Or I could have him lobotomized and trained as an erotic assistant,' murmured Prof. Zuleikha dreamily, 'on compassionate grounds of course. He was a menace to himself.'

'Who are you talking about?' said Prof. Saraswati. She had just finished vaporizing Bunny's thesis.

'No one,' said Prof. Christine, as she watched the mid-morning narcissi unfurl their petals in fast forward mode, outside the window.

ESSENCE OF GANDHI

'What I have here, Respected Masters,' said Sitaram Desai, holding up his right hand, 'is an ancient vial of ash, preserved from the funeral pyre of a great man.' He paused for effect. He was being watched by two hologramic images, a man and a woman, hovering a few inches above the tiled floor of his clandestine laboratory. 'The greatest man the Indian subcontinent has ever produced,' said Sitaram. 'The one and only…Gandhi.'

His audience was not impressed. 'Yah, yah,' said Aidid Nielsen, his ice-blue eyes at odds with matt black skin. He and Isabella beside him were the Supreme Commanders at United Gene Heritage (UGH). 'Cut the manure. We've verified your claim to being the son of third cousins in the bloodline of that person. But so what? Why should your DNA be of any interest to us?'

Sitaram's smile broadened. 'Not just my DNA, but my ancestor's as well, cloned from the ash. I've combined the two,' he said, 'spliced them onto a friendly virus and suspended the lot in a volatile solution. What d'you get? Essence of Gandhi.' He held up a second vial fitted with a nozzle. 'Two puffs and…' He inhaled. 'A thorn becomes a rose!' As if to prove his claim, his face was now wreathed in a smile so sickly sweet it made Isabella wince. 'Map the gene-sequence of this hybrid molecule and you'll have the blueprint for…weapons-grade compassion!'

He had barely stopped speaking when the walls of his workchamber crashed inwards. Towering muscular figures with horned heads sprang through the dust and rubble. Isabella's voice, crackling slightly, commanded Sitaram to stay calm. 'They're humano-bovines! Quite harmless unless you resist!' But Sitaram grinned as his captors stood snorting and pawing the ground around him. 'Why resist?' he said, to the already fading holograms. 'After all, I'm the one who contacted you!'

Some hours later he found himself returning to consciousness. He'd been drugged and taken into custody by UGH, just as he'd hoped. Holograms crackled into focus. 'Mr Desai,' said Isabella. 'We've analysed your serum. Preliminary tests confirm what you say: diffused through the blood, it disarms aggression vectors in mammalian brains. Making it a formidable weapon. In the wrong hands it could cause catastrophic pacifism and widespread loss of the competitive urge.' She paused. 'We are of course grateful that you chose to make your heri-data available to UGH but...'

Aidid continued: '... your very existence represents a dire threat to security personnel in the free world. Any unscrupulous business house could misuse you to win its brand wars at the expense of right-thinking consumers everywhere. We have no option but to place you under life-arrest...' He droned on, citing the GeneSwap agreements of 1999 under which UGH could detain those citizens of inefficient business-states around the world, who were known to harbour hazardous hereditary materials. 'Needless to say,' he concluded, 'we will mass-produce the substance ourselves for the use of our own marketing troops.' Sitaram continued smiling, even when he was renamed with a code number: Gamma Two-Eight.

In the weeks that followed, Gamma spent his time touring UGH's estate from his maximum-security cell. A wall-mounted Virtualizer allowed him to walk on a pacer as he surveyed the incubation laboratories, organ-farms and dupe-cradles. He saw gestating battalions of soldier-foetuses in see-through artificial wombs and rooms full of drowsily beating hearts, plump kidneys, glabrous lungs, all ready for transplant. He saw gleaming caskets of duplicants suspended in preconscious limbo till their millionaire originals required fresh bodies in exchange for damaged ones.

When he needed company he interacted in cosy virtuality with the other detainees in the facility. The majority had volunteered their genes for whole-body patenting. In compensation, their biological families enjoyed every luxury known to commerce aside from the right to reproduce. Pion Sixty-Three, a wizened hunter-gatherer from Urban Borneo whose pituitary gland was the source of life-saving anti-acne preparations said: 'I fell for their "You sign, All dine" slogan. My family is prospering. But I'm BORED! Cybersex all day long, cyberhunts all night. It's like being a duplicant whose original has died.'

A communication shield isolated the facility from the world, but information trickled in with new arrivals. 'It's madness out there,' said Xhi Square, a melancholy Peruvian whose blood was found to cause night-blindness in teenagers. 'The Fourth World is being devastated by battles fought by the clone troops of competing MultiNations! The soldiers all share identical genes – so no one wins!'

'Be patient,' said Gamma, 'nothing lasts forever, not even tyranny!' And he jogged out of visireach, smiling as calmly as ever.

'Is that guy really serene? Or is it just his genes?' wondered Xhi. Pion was silent. He guessed that Gamma knew something he couldn't talk about on account of surveillance.

Meanwhile, the serum, dubbed Gandhitoxin, proved to be exactly as effective as Gamma said it would. It was delivered via clouds of reconstructed mosquitoes designed to function as air-borne hypodermic syringes. They infiltrated enemy lines through the air conditioning and were as impossible to eradicate as their natural counterparts. Their initial bite delivered a pleasurable tingle, followed by triple-strength doses of Gandhitoxin. Instead of a high whine they produced a sweet musical tone just before striking.

UGH forces began to trounce their competitors all over the world. A consortium was formed to meet the threat. But it could not prevail. Beefy combat personnel, cloned from ten generations of war-heroes, wilted on the battlefields. Cyber-fighters staggered away from their work-stations in tears. Captains of Industry were reduced to whimpering heaps of guilt. A majority collapsed and died within minutes of being flooded with emotions lethal to their violent psyches. The few who recovered lost their muscle mass and became fanatically docile, unable at first to perform any tasks more hostile than tending organic herb gardens. Only very gradually did the side effects begin to show up. It would be a full 12 months before rumours finally reached the detainees at UGH.

'Have you heard?' said Xhi excitedly to Gamma. 'There's a new kind of struggle going on!'

'It's probably not new…' said Gamma, mildly.

But Xhi wasn't listening. 'Gandhitoxin survivors have become revolutionaries! They're dismantling commercial institutions and reorganizing marketplaces everywhere! They're inverting the whole structure of international finance!' Before he could go on much further he was cut off by a power-failure. Unthinkable before, they now occurred regularly even in the maximum-security detainees' facility, the heart of the UGH empire.

Not many weeks later, from the darkness of his cell, Gamma heard muted thumping. The power had been off for the longest time that he could remember. He sat in meditation, guessing that he was listening to the sound of rebels breaking in from the outside world.

A month later it was all over. Cease-commerce had been declared worldwide. Gamma and Pion deputed themselves to confront Isabella and Aidid, held in mosquito-free stasis till they agreed to be compassionated of their own free will. 'We should never have trusted you!' hissed Aidid at Gamma. 'Your ancestor wasn't merely a pacifist but a deeply subversive personality! He forced the British out of India and now you've destroyed the foundation of civilization as we know it!'

'Not at all,' smiled Gamma. 'I cobbled together a handful of chromosomes and made them available to you. You did all the rest. You infected your competitors' troops more effectively than I could ever have done with my modest laboratory facilities. The mosquitoes, for instance! They were a stroke of genius. Because of them Gandhi's pacifism has gone planetary.'

'But we screened for every known combination of undesirable traits!' wailed Isabella. It was days since she had used her hairspray or done her nails. Her morale was at its lowest ebb. 'I can personally remember erasing the tell-tale codes for disobedience and anti-social behaviour! What went wrong?'

'I can't tell you that,' said Gamma. 'But as a researcher, I know how difficult it is to predict the long-term effects of manipulating hereditary matter. It's like twiddling dials on an infinitely variable machine: you can't guarantee the results. I didn't know, for instance, that Gandhitoxin could actually kill anybody. I was horrified that it did. I beg forgiveness for those deaths. But I had faith in my ancestor's precious ideals. I prayed that they were so deeply encoded into his genes that being infected with their clones would ultimately do more good than harm. I believe I was right.'

His eyes twinkled kindly at the two captives, believed to be amongst the last humans still capable of murderous anger, personal ambition, greed and lust. 'Look. Can't you see how happy the rest of us are? Don't you want to stop struggling and start living?'

Aidid snarled: 'I planned ahead for every contingency! I created self-dupes and stored them in hidden locations around the globe. They're tuned to my bio-rhythm in such a way that the moment I die, one of them will emerge to take my place, complete with the whole data of my personality. And if that one dies, the next will take his place. And so on. You can't kill me! I'm immortal! I'm invincible!'

Isabella was looking glumly at the walls of the stasis-cell. 'But that means we'll have to spend the rest of our lives in this isolation cell! Where's the fun in that?' Before Aidid could stop her, she'd switched off the stasis-shield and stepped out. 'I'll take my chances with the damn toxin. I believe that my character will overcome its effects. And when it does…' Her eyes narrowed in pleasure. 'I'll have the market advantage over all you non-competitive sheep!'

'Who knows?' said Pion, shrugging as he and Gamma walked away. 'Anything's possible. Meanwhile, enjoy!' Musical tones sounded behind them, as mosquitoes found their mark. A gentle smile distorted the usually frowning features of Aidid as he swooned under the influence of the bites. Isabella, tingling all over, lay back on the grass and, for the first time since childhood, slept without the aid of pills.

NANIMALS

The incident occurred during Miss Sethna's class. The children had been asked to talk about their impressions of life before the wars began. They were sitting above ground, at eleven o'clock in the morning. The open hatch of their shelter was less than ten feet from where they sat. Wire fencing completely enclosed the circular field, which was a little over a hundred metres in diameter. On the other side of the wire, sentries prowled. Beyond the sentries, the indistinct outlines of low buildings bulked darkly. Transmission towers poked up along the outermost edge of vision. High above them, the faintly textured quality of the blue and cloudless sky betrayed the fact that they were under a giant dome of semi-transparent camouflage material.

There were fifteen children, their ages ranging from around seven to fifteen. Accurate statistics were hard to come by. Even the youngest had already been born when the hostilities began, but their memories of that time had been erased. They had grown up surrounded by sentries and wire fences. All they knew about themselves was that they had survived.

'It was very crowded,' said Rupal. 'There were too many people. Everyone was hungry. It was noisy.'

Miss Sethna, whose fresh, unlined skin was oddly at variance with her grey hair, nodded encouragement. 'Okay,' she said, 'write that down. Percy?' She turned to a little boy whose left hand was missing. 'How about you? What do you think it was like?'

'Very loud and...and...angry. People were always angry. And shouting. All the time. I saw it in the pictures. Sometimes they would hit each other. Everyone would fight–' He was eight years old and had no hair. Even his eyebrows had been permanently singed away. It gave him the appearance of being serenely expressionless. He had to jump up and gesticulate to make his feelings clear.

'There were many sad and hungry people,' said Deki, a sweet-faced girl of ten. 'They had no clothes. They had no homes. They used to sleep all the time in the streets. They used to eat each other–'

Miss Sethna smiled at this and shook her head, saying, 'No, dear – not quite that bad!'

At which Deki said, heatedly, 'They did, they did! In a village in–' She pronounced some impossible name.

But Miss Sethna shook her head, 'You've misunderstood something–'

Galena, eight years old, interjected, 'No, Miss, it's true. I also read that. Saw a picture.' She frowned, concentrating on the memory, 'They used to eat their own babies. That's why they were so…thick.' She hesitated over the word, knowing that it wasn't the right one. 'Many people were very…thick,' she said, patting her body. 'You know – they looked like they had much padding–'

Miss Sethna laughed slightly and said, '–"fat", not "thick" and no, everyone wasn't fat – or else how could they also be poor?' But this bit of logic was wasted on the children.

Galena persisted. 'Yes – that's why they ate their babies… because they were poor, they were always hungry…and there were too many, so…they ate a lot…' She stopped, confused. She looked around at the others, but they looked away.

Miss Sethna said, 'All right, never mind, we'll discuss it later. How about you, Barun? What have you written down?' He was concentrating on his notebook, following his own words with his finger.

'Some people were very rich,' he read, 'and lived up – up in the sky. They travelled from the sky to the ground in a car called a Nelevator. And they never stayed in one place, they moved around all the time.' He looked up with disbelief in his eleven-year-old eyes. 'They wore gold inside their noses. They painted their mouths with bright red blood. They had music coming out of their ears…'

Miss Sethna made a mental note to monitor the films being shown to the children more carefully. She listened as the remaining children voiced their views.

When they were done she said, 'That's very interesting. But you know, children, we must be a little more understanding about the past. It wasn't all that bad.' She was conscious of the fifteen pairs of eyes trained in her direction. 'There were good things too...'

'Such as?' asked Deem. He was the oldest of the group. His voice had just started to break, sounding now like a bassoon, now like a piccolo.

'Such as not having to live underground,' said Miss Sethna. 'Such as having many different kinds of food to eat, not just the same rations every day.' But she had to be careful. There was no point providing them with details of pleasures they could never know. 'Such as...well...going for long walks and swimming in the sea–' Her voice sounded unconvincing even to her own ears. She found it so hard to understand why it was difficult to explain to these children and others like them, that life in the past was better than the present. It should have been easy. She didn't have any doubt of it herself and yet...she could not convince them. 'In peacetime, there's a wonderful sense of ease,' she essayed, 'a feeling of restfulness...'

The children said nothing. In the distance, a siren sounded, a soft moaning, signalling that it was twelve noon. They had one more hour above ground. There were no other sounds. Deem said, 'It's restful now too. Don't you think?' He said this carefully, like a swimmer testing the waters before jumping in.

But it's artificial! she wanted to say. It's only for you, because you are children! And you don't know what lies ahead for you – those of you who will survive that is...Of course, there was no point telling them. Out loud she said, 'Yes, but in the backdrop, there are the constant brutalities, the attacks, the uncertainty...'

Galena said, 'But in the films we see that people were uncertain then too. And terrible things happened. We have seen the pictures. We have read the stories...' All surviving children were given free access to data banks. No resources could possibly be spared to educate them in a formal, sequential manner. They were taught to read, to write and to do basic mathematics. Whatever else they learnt of life, they got from films and documentaries, from media archives and through discussions such as this one.

'Deki,' said Miss Sethna, 'I want to get back to your question. You said you read that we used to eat each other–' It had slipped out unguardedly, the 'we' of complicity. But Miss Sethna did not attempt to take it back. She was, yes, of the past. The past that these children had learnt to have contempt for. 'That's not true, you know–'

'They used to kill babies,' said Nony, 'I did read that. Because they were poor. Because they didn't have food. That means–' She looked at the others for support. 'That means they were eating them. Or else, why kill them?'

Miss Sethna struggled to keep her expression neutral. It was probably female infanticide they were talking about. Of course there had been reports of that, in her time. It used to happen in a few isolated places. But how to explain to these children, the concept of 'isolated places'? How to describe the extravagance of a time when human offspring could be wantonly destroyed? How to explain to these children who were now the rarest resource of all, that there was once a surplus of them? That chemical weapons had contaminated the air and earth, that chemical foods had contaminated the cycles of life, that no one's genes could any longer be trusted to produce wholesome progeny and that they, and other groups like theirs, represented the last remnants of hope for the future of the race?

Despite all those who had warned that the planet was not indestructible – the ecologists, the environmentalists, the doom-sayers, the futurologists – there had always been an overwhelming majority of those who doubted the doubters. They all claimed there could be no catastrophe so extreme that a remedy would not be found for it. They had all used such arguments as: 'The Price of Progress is Pollution' and 'Can't Make Omlettes Without Breaking Eggs'.

Until suddenly…there were no more eggs to break.

A sullenness was settling upon the group. It was something that instructors had been taught to identify and to discourage. It was known to promote anti-social behavior. Miss Sethna said, 'I think I can explain that, but first, let's look at the zoo.' She had a portable screen and projector, which she set up quickly. She handed out 3D goggles to the children and turned the display on. She wore her own goggles and, as each animal appeared in glowing three-dimensional images, played a recording of its call and gave a brief commentary about its habits.

She had just got to the peacock when a slight sound distracted her. She shifted her goggles aside and looked up to see that four of the children – Nony, Osiris, Kelana and Bashir – had discarded their viewers and were snickering softly to one another. They were looking away to one side. They were whispering to one another.

Now more children, alerted by Miss Sethna's gaze, were also looking in the direction the others were looking. They too discarded their goggles and began to point and smile. In the background, the peacock called plaintively.

Miss Sethna turned off the audio. She clapped her hands for attention. 'Children!' she said, 'What is the matter? What do you see?'

One or two turned around. The rest remained staring to their right, as if following the movement of something. But there was nothing there! 'Barun!' called Miss Sethna, 'Barun – what is it? What are you pointing at?'

He turned around. The smile on his face faded as he looked at her. An evasive expression took its place. 'I…oh…nothing. It's nothing.' He looked around at the others, as if soliciting their agreement. One or two nodded.

The sun was pleasantly warm overhead, but Miss Sethna shivered involuntarily within her light cotton uniform. 'I saw you look – now come on, all of you! I saw you – pointing at something!' If it had been only one that could be explained. They had delusions, some of them. But more than one? A whole group?

Galena's voice broke the uncomfortable silence. 'We call it a… Nanimal,' she said. There was an edge of defiance in her voice. 'It's something we see. It has four legs and gold fur. It flies sometimes. And it has a musical voice–' There were a few titters from the children. But no one contradicted her.

Miss Sethna felt helpless. She looked towards Deem. He was the unofficial spokesman for this group. He could be relied upon to provide answers in difficult situations. She looked at him. 'Deem?' He had turned his head away from her, refusing to meet her gaze. 'You too? Do you see…something?' Of course it had to be some sort of childish prank. Maybe they had planned it together. To make a cunning pantomime. To tease her.

He didn't speak immediately. Then he looked up, straight into her eyes and said, 'Yes. It's real. It exists. But only for us.' It was clear who he meant. 'You people can't see it.'

A fluttering panic was rising in Miss Sethna's throat. There was nothing to fear, of course, the children were harmless. Nevertheless she felt like calling for assistance. It could be the onset of a form of mass hysteria. If so, it would have to be reported, some antidote sought… The notion that even these youngsters, so carefully guarded and nurtured, might be mentally retarded or psychologically unstable was unbearable to her. She could not face the implications of such a thought.

'Of– of course you realize that can't be,' said Miss Sethna, addressing Deem as if she were alone with him. She could sense the other children's attention, riveted to what was being said. 'If it was real, I would see it too–'

'We see the nanimal,' Deem insisted. 'And we see other things too. Things you can't see. Just like you can see things that we can't see.' He pointed to the projection screen, where the 3D animals had been displayed. 'You show those creatures to us – but they're not real! They're not anywhere! It's just your word that they existed. Just like it's just your word that the past was good. Or that the people of the past were…decent.'

The other children were nodding and looking solemn. But not particularly sullen. Miss Sethna found her voice with difficulty. 'Deem, all I want to know is…do you *really* see something or – or are you just…all of you…just play-acting. Making believe.'

Deem looked uncertain and then apologetic. He was starting to get to his feet. He said, 'You are my teacher and I should be respectful towards you. But it's…difficult. After all, you are also of the past. You also think the past was a better time than the one we have now. But we think differently. We know that you people of the past really hated yourselves. You started wars that could not be ended. When some people warned against them, you called them sissies and cowards. You hated yourselves so much that you were willing to destroy yourselves and even your future. You wanted to destroy us–' he pointed to himself and the other children '–almost before we could be alive. And succeeded in destroying all the animals of your time – even though you show us their images and tell us how wonderful they were and how sad it is for us not to see them…on and on and on…even though you're the ones who killed them.'

He was standing up now. From his new position, he could look down at Miss Sethna as she stared mutely up at him. The sun was dazzling and she held her hand up to shade her eyes, even though she realized that it may have looked, from a distance, as if she were actually shielding herself from Deem. 'So why should we believe in the things you show us?' he asked her. 'Or show you the things we believe in?'

The other children were standing too. The siren sounded again, signalling that it was time to return underground. Miss Sethna did not know what to say. She felt as if a block of ice had been grafted into the place where her vocal chords should have been. Her expression must have reflected this, because Deem relented just before he turned to go.

'We have the gift of sharing dreams,' he said. Then he turned and joined the others as they trudged back towards the entrance to their living quarters.

Miss Sethna remained seated where she was. She watched as the children vanished downwards one by one. None of them looked at her, not even Deem.

THE ANNEXE

Typically, the 'dream' would start at times when I didn't really expect to fall asleep. During the afternoons, for instance, when all I wanted was to lie down and think. It would start by my seeming to wake up, to find myself in my room, on my bed, looking around me. My eyes would apparently be wide open and as I looked around the room, I would notice it was distorted in certain predictable ways. It might be higher, for instance, or broader. And there were noises as well, disjointed yet familiar. The radio from the garden downstairs, snatches of conversation, the rattling of the refrigerator.

Two very distinct physical sensations always characterized the dreams. One was of tremendous heat, localized to particular parts of my body. My hands, for instance, or the back of my neck. I would feel that they were literally burning, melting away and merging with the bed. But no actual pain. The second sensation was of being unable to move. That happens often in dreams, I know, but this was different. In these dreams, the reason I was unable to move was that I didn't seem to have a body. Or, to be more precise, it was only my physical body which could not move. An odd thought, all considered. Because, aside from one's physical body, what is there to move?

And then there was the fear. Hard to describe, it was so extreme. If you can imagine being alive in a two-dimensional world, threatened in such a way that the only escape lay in somehow clawing your way to a third dimension, you might have an idea of what that fear was like. Unreasoning, abject. I never sought out these dreams, if I can call them that. They came upon me without warning. After the first one, whenever I awakened to that strange place, familiar yet unknown, immobile yet disembodied, I would immediately start struggling frantically to wake up, to wake up properly. Because of course, the very fact that my eyes seemed to be open suggested that I was already awake. The 'struggle' manifested itself as the sensation, received as if from a great distance, of my eyelids attempting to open, yet weighed down by some unknown force.

Needless to say, with these as with most dreams, it was impossible to gauge how long they actually lasted. The moment I awoke – opened my physical eyes, that is – the very notion of that other place collapsed and dissolved. Indeed, it became instantly difficult to describe anything about it, because of the inadequacy of such terms as 'I' and 'my body' when describing a self which was not contained within a body, yet in communication with the bodily self. I tried several times to share my experiences with friends, but without much success. It was during an early effort at description that I designated the 'room' into which I would apparently awaken as the 'Annexe'. That's what it seemed like to me: a space between other spaces, not important in itself. Like the ante-chamber to an audience hall, in it one could hear sounds from the real world, muffled but familiar.

I never met anyone who had had similar experiences.

Those were the years when I was still at college and lived in Bombay with my married sister. Turbulent years! Eventually I completed my Masters in History, then went to the US on a scholarship and drifted into Archaeology.

From a minor interest inspired as much by the handsome young professor who taught the class as by ancient dust, it became a genuine calling. My family in India became accustomed to tracking my progress at digs around the world and I became accustomed to nestling deep in the brown clay bosom of the earth, scratching at the roots of history. Friendships which sprang up at one site would melt like mirages when the fever for the next location took its inevitable hold upon me once more.

Never once in the thirteen years since college had I revisited the Annexe. Like pimples and night-long telephone conversations, the dreams seemed to have been an age-related phenomenon. And I forgot about them.

Till a week ago.

I had just arrived in Oxford, where Mandy, a friend from college days, now lives with her husband Tony, both physicists. It was just before lunch. I was in their guest bedroom, lying down but not really sleepy, tired after an all-night flight. I must have dozed off, because when I woke up, I was in the Annexe. Despite the passage of years, I had no difficulty recognizing the place. The panic, the horror, the struggling, the leaden eyelids, everything was exactly as it had ever been. And when I woke up properly at last, it was with the usual violent shock, my neck and hands awash with sweat. Yet the window was open, and the spring air was cold.

I sat on the bed, dazed and shivering slightly. It was so real, so tangible, so unbearable. What had brought it on? I couldn't think of anything except that I was with a friend from those days when visits to the Annexe had been a regular affair.

The same evening, the three of us went out to Mandy's favourite pub, the Lamb and Flag. It was warm and crowded inside, with flushed English faces, dark foreign students, twelfth century flagstones, beer mugs glittering from the hanging glass-rack over the barman's head and conversations like multicoloured ribbons of sound fluttering every which way, in a tempest of social intercourse. We had barely settled ourselves at one of those tiny tables with the surface area of a dinner-plate, when I looked up and saw…her.

There was no mistaking Dr Taheri, of course. There can't be many people left anywhere in the electrified world who are so reclusive as to have missed the publicity which had surrounded the owner of that intense, handsome face some three months ago. I had read with interest the endless snippets and speculations, the instant biographies, the gossip, the scandal. Dr Aimee Taheri, 51, celebrated oneirologist.

'Isn't that…?' I said, and Mandy, following my gaze, nodded. 'Oh, and of course!' I recalled now the lavish spread in *Paris Match*. 'This is the pub she always comes to!'

'Yes,' said Mandy. 'Like clockwork.'

Tony said, 'People set their watches by her.'

I looked across again. The strong face was lined but as attractive as the photographs had promised. The dark hair was peppered with grey. She wore it in a bushy halo framing the unnaturally pale skin she had inherited from a French mother and an Iranian father. And then the eyes. Glassy. She was staring straight ahead, oblivious to her surroundings. Her mouth curved slightly upwards and her hands clasped a beer mug. When she bent her head to drink from it, her gaze moved towards it but in the way of a blind person, unseeing.

'What a business!' I said, unable to tear my eyes away from the woman. 'They never got to the bottom of it, did they?'

Mandy shook her head. Tony had that expression which precedes a sneer. 'What was there to get?' he said. 'Distinguished Female Professor Seduces Innocent Male Student, Student Dies, end of story! Crimes of passion. You've heard about them, surely?'

Mandy said, 'Oh come on, Tony! You're over-simplifying it! He didn't just die.'

'Coma?' I said. 'Didn't they find him in a coma?'

Tony flexed the corners of his mouth downward and looked away. Mandy shrugged. 'That's what they say. No one knows for sure.'

'It's a bloody cover-up,' said Tony. 'The Dean couldn't face an ordinary sex-and-drugs scandal! So they–'

'Wait,' I said. 'I thought she was specifically opposed to the use of drugs in her field?'

'But of course she was opposed to drugs!' said Tony, lifting his well-shaven upper lip off his teeth, looking more than ever like a horse. I couldn't understand why he was so hostile towards the Professor, but it seemed the wrong time to ask. 'Couldn't have got University funding with magic mushrooms on the syllabus, you know!' He pushed his chair back roughly as he rose to get himself a beer, saying, as he left, 'Don't let's be more naïve than strictly necessary!'

Mandy smiled placatingly and changed the subject. But the next morning, when we were alone and strolling up a gently rolling knuckle of land in the face of a brisk grey wind, she talked about it again.

'She left detailed notes,' Mandy said, 'telling about some breakthrough she'd made. She and...Carlos?' I nodded. A young Peruvian, tousle-haired and hot-eyed, glaring from the murky passport photographs which were flashed around the world. 'She wrote that she knew the risk she was taking, the suicidal risk of being discredited and of discrediting the whole field of dream research once it was discovered that they were also lovers. But I–' Mandy frowned. 'I forget the exact details. Didn't actually see the stuff...she wrote about using sex to enter some sort of alternate...I don't know!' She turned to me. 'It did sound too weird. Like Tony said, it sounded like an Executive Class con job.' She stopped.

'Can't they ask her?' I wondered out loud. 'What does she say when she's spoken to? Any response at all?'

'You saw what she's like,' said Mandy. 'That's what she's always like. 'Course, Tony says it's put on. He seems to get angry about it. A lot of people do. It's the academic snobbery thing. Can't bear the world peering into our little Petri dish!' She paused, then turned to me, speaking intensely. 'But it isn't a con job! I'm sure of it. My gyny was on the team which treated her and looked after her just after it happened. He – Dr Crawford, that is – said there was no question of pretence. Dr Taheri is there and...not there. An untenanted house, that's what he called her.'

It was a good description of the person we'd seen. 'An untenanted house.' The words echoed in my ears. From the crown of the hill we were sitting on, we could see the surrounding countryside welling out around us in a slow, unhurried tide of emerald fields, dark trees, small white cottages and sky. It seemed such an unlikely setting for the brooding mystery surrounding the eventual death of the young student who had been found in a coma, naked, in the arms of his equally naked and comatose professor. He'd belonged to an influential family in Peru. His father had sworn to sue the University if they didn't convict the professor for murder. By then Dr Taheri had regained consciousness to the limited extent that I had seen. And there matters stood. An untenanted house. 'Who looks after her?' I asked. 'She doesn't live by herself?'

'Oh, no!' said Mandy. 'She's usually got someone with her. She needs help, you know, with dressing and...all that.' She paused. 'But in the afternoons, she's left by the duck pond.'

'She's alone at that time?' I asked. 'Would I be able to approach her?'

'I think so,' said Mandy. 'All kinds of people volunteer to spend time with her. She's the local curiosity! Japanese tourists come to meditate in her presence!' We laughed. Then she said, quite suddenly, 'It's...about those dreams you used to have, isn't it?'

'You remember them?' I asked, astonished.

'Well, I remembered them at the time that all this happened. With Dr Taheri, I mean. There were descriptions that reminded me of what you used to say, you know, about being in some place, you had some name for it–'

'The Annexe,' I said, and I told her then about my 'dream' in the afternoon.

'So what do you think?' said Mandy, when I had finished. 'Want to see her?'

'Can you arrange it?' I asked.

'I could try,' said Mandy.

While I spent the morning at the library in Mandy's college looking through news reports of the scandal, she obtained whatever permission was necessary for me to spend a short while with Dr Taheri.

I wasn't sure I wanted the permission to come through. I found it easy to believe that in some way, the reappearance of an Annexe dream alongside Dr Taheri's story was not a coincidence. I had certainly never missed having the dreams. One part of my mind told me to place as much distance as I could between myself and the still figure I had seen in the pub if I wanted no repetition of the previous day's experience. But at lunch, when I met Mandy again, she said I was cleared to spend the afternoon sitting next to Dr Taheri by the duck pond. So I went.

The duck pond wasn't a pond so much as a bend in the modest little river as it wound its way through the park. A tiny islet had formed in the shallow curve of the watercourse, and a family of ducks had taken up residence there.

The doctor was sitting on one of the benches facing the islet and as I approached her, the sound of my boots on the gravel jarred on my ears. But she did not in any way indicate that she could hear me. There were a couple of joggers in sight and an elderly gentleman strolling under the huge old oaks up ahead. I noticed that I was nervous. There was that old sick tension in the stomach which I hadn't felt since my schooldays, the tautness that precedes final examinations.

I walked around the bench, deliberately crossing Dr Taheri's field of vision so that she had a chance to see me, assuming that her eyes could see at all. I didn't want to startle her. Then I sat down on the bench. I turned slightly away from her, so that I was also facing the pond. I kept my mind clear and blank, not knowing what to expect.

It was late in the afternoon and a mild drowsy warmth enveloped the whole of the park. A light vapour rose off the surface of the water and the ducks seemed to be paddling very slowly, dreamily, back and forth, back and forth, between the rushes. I began to feel sleepy. There was a slight buzzing hum from somewhere close by and I thought vaguely that it might be from a hive of bees. Then I noticed, to my surprise, that Dr Taheri was no longer looking at the ducks but had turned towards me. She seemed to be smiling faintly, asking a question with her eyes.

It was a reaction greater than any I had hoped for. My face felt stiff, as if I had been literally paralysed by the surprise. It was a nuisance to have got so far and had such a wonderful response from Dr Taheri only to find that I could barely compose a smile upon my face! I was starting to feel quite annoyed with myself, when with shocking suddenness I became aware of a sensation of terrific heat near my hands. And then, simultaneously, the drunken rolling of my eyes, trying to open. I was in the Annexe again! And without even being asleep!

There was no pause for reflection. As always, the Herculean struggle, the mighty heaving and thrusting of unknown forces as my 'real' body laboured to regain control over…what?…and succeeded as if by a hair's breadth of extra strength. The jolt, as a result of returning to normal consciousness, literally lifted me off the park bench. To find that the ducks had never left their islet, there were no bees and beside me Dr Taheri sat like carven stone, staring straight ahead.

Whatever doubts I may have had of the possibility that Dr Taheri had triggered the Annexe state in me vanished without trace. Considering the horror I felt when in that state it may seem odd that I continued to sit there. Yet I did. I felt I was being given a unique opportunity to understand an old mystery and like a good archaeologist, I wasn't about to pass it up!

Not only did I sit there, but I decided, even as my heart hammered within my chest, that I would for once face my fears. Instead of struggling to wake up, I would struggle to remain 'asleep'.

I settled myself as comfortably as possible upon the park bench and worked at making my mind blank. This is a standard technique in meditation and I used the usual handles. Closing my eyes, I turned my gaze inward and concentrated on a blank white screen.

To my surprise and very quickly, the whole park and all its features swam up into view once more, just as if my eyes had been open. The bees, the swimming ducks. And Dr Taheri turned towards me. Because I was actually conscious when this happened, I had a few 'seconds' in which to register the visual space of the Annexe before I felt the inevitable churning of my eyes in their sockets, yearning to admit the light of the real sun once more. Within those few seconds, I confirmed that Dr Taheri, turned towards me, had an expression of such extraordinary warmth and tenderness on her face that for the very first time, the horror I normally felt in the Annexe was diluted somewhat.

I 'woke', rested a few minutes, then tried again. And again. And again.

Each time I was able to establish the Annexe, it seemed a little easier to remain in that space, to understand a little more about it, to feel a little more reassured. It was hard work, in a way, but as it became less unpleasant, I had a growing sense of something tremendous about to happen, something unprecedented. The stage was reached when I could get there and remain in there at will. My body was calm. The heat sensations and the rolling eyes, the struggling were absent. They were, it appeared, the result of fear. As the fear dissipated, I found I could turn my eyes inward to find the Annexe, then turn away from it and find my body again, as easily as entering and exiting a room.

I tried to think of it as a Cinerama theatre. An enclosure within my head, onto whose walls, ceiling and floor a film was being projected of my actual physical surroundings. There were other features of interest in the enclosure, but I didn't have attention to spare for them at the time. The park which surrounded my physical body was reproduced on the walls of the Annexe but distorted slightly. So far as I know, the distortions are minor effects caused by the mind in the process of creating the projection, though I have yet to confirm this belief. There is much that I still do not know about the place and this report that I write will no doubt require extensive revision in the future. Nevertheless, I feel I must write it, incomplete as it is, as a record and an explanation of my actions. Not merely the most recent ones but those that I must perform soon, as soon as I can find acceptance and permission for what I must do. I know only too well how difficult it is going to be.

Perhaps the most startling distortion was the difference between the image of Dr Taheri on the walls of the Annexe and in the real world. It was certainly her appearance in the projection, the encouraging expression she wore, which made it possible for me to persevere. She waited for me to experiment with entering and departing the Annexe until it was clear that I was as comfortable as I would ever be. Then she began to draw my attention outward.

This is going to be very difficult to describe. Events followed at such speed that now, as I write about them, it seems as if they occurred instantaneously.

I looked around me, trying to interpret the gestures being made by the image of Dr Taheri on the walls of the Annexe. She seemed to suggest that it was possible to be where she was. But I couldn't understand where that was if it wasn't on the park bench.

I kept slipping back to my body then up to the Annexe again, until suddenly I understood that she meant for me to walk towards the walls of the Annexe itself. And the next instant I had shot through the walls and – OUT!

There are no words to describe what I mean, when I say 'out'. Consciousness unshackled from the container of the body! Unlimited, unbounded. Without the confining weight of a body and of mass, there was no time. Without time, no direction to events. The future and the past and the present were merged or expanded so that there was a continuous reality – these are muddy, lumbering terms to describe what I experienced.

All reports that I can make from that state will necessarily have to be made within this time-bound continuum that we share, you and I. As a result, I cannot write anything about it without falsifying everything, because no part of this experience that we share in the physical world can be anything like that experience in a non-physical one. The words I use will have to be our familiar ones and for the purpose of lucidity, I will report events in a linear time scale.

My first few moments, which might have lasted days or weeks, were suffused with such intense euphoria that there is no impression I have aside from overpowering, incandescent light. Light experienced through all the senses at once and through all the possible time zones.

Presently, however, this incandescence began to settle down. As it settled, gradually, and again through the multi-channels of perception I now had at my instant command, I became aware of Dr Taheri.

She had been there all along, of course. Not just there then, but for ever before and after as well. The moment that I perceived her presence, then I perceived it in all its dimensions. I tasted her, smelled her, breathed her, touched her, saw her…and simultaneously, knew all of her perceptions too. No boundaries!

She spoke to me. 'You will find,' she said, 'that it is possible to focus your attention.'

These first words released cataracts of emotion in me. I may have gibbered incoherently for some decades before I was calm.

'You will find yourself able to direct a single stream of thought. And that will become speech. In this place.'

I cannot record how long it took me to approach the discipline of which she spoke. But when, to some extent, I was able to choose from amongst the infinite strands of ideas, visions, sensations and emotions, one thread which I could coherently follow, enough at least to frame a rudimentary question, she was able to answer me.

'There is a space between minds,' she said, 'as there is a space between bodies. We are in that space.'

I will try to describe that space.

All around us and in every direction spread a plain. It was potentially colourful, but expressed in grey. It extended in every direction and indeed even through us, because, as I have said, we did not have physical substance.

Dotted about the plain, in clusters or individually, were structures. They were tall, short, deep or flat, varied in so many dimensions that it was obvious that they weren't actual buildings. I examined them with ferocious interest, realizing that I did so under the guidance of Dr Taheri's subtle urging.

Gradually she turned my attention till it came to rest on one particular structure, though it may easily have been a group of structures as well, it was hard to tell. I found myself intensely absorbed by it.

It rose appallingly high into the grey. If it had been constructed on the surface of the earth, it might have been at least eight hundred storeys tall. It was attractive in that all its parts fitted with a pleasing rhythm, but it was careless of the conventions of gravity-bound architecture. The base was narrow compared with the crown, while the upper storeys extended sideways with unsupported abandon. If it was like anything we could see here, then it was like a sculpture by a fanciful artist, created in zero gravity, in the spirit of a building. There were elements commonly found on human constructions, such as mouldings, cornices, fluted balconies and external pipes and gutters. But they were used apparently as decorations draped around doors and windows which themselves were clearly non-functional in the conventional sense.

For example, a highly ornate gilded door-frame hovered a few feet from where I was. It leaned at an impossible angle away from the main structure, attached along its lower edge to the teeth of a slender rake-like device which itself protruded from the central mass. The frame was massive enough that in the physical world, it could never have balanced at the end of a rod. Seen edge-on, the frame was no thicker than the width of its side-member. Seen from the front, it revealed a pane of glass behind which an interior view of a room was visible, complete in every detail, down to the shadows cast by furniture within range of a green-shaded reading lamp and by the gentle movement of curtains stirred by the exertions of a ceiling fan. Seen from behind, there was no pane of glass, there was nothing. No grey plain, no Dr Taheri and certainly no room of any kind.

It may have taken me a lifetime or more to absorb and examine every detail of the whole edifice. It seemed vividly familiar yet I had never seen it before. I was able to approach it from any angle and at any height or depth, though none of these concepts had much meaning in that context. Try as I might, however, I was unable to enter any part of the thing. I rattled at windows, I thumped on doors, I even attempted to dislodge parts of the outer skin where it seemed translucent or even, in some sense, edible. But I was wholly unsuccessful.

It was only when my attempts were revealed to be utterly unavailing that I fell back to take stock of events. I brought my focus around to Dr Taheri. It seemed as if I had not noticed her for several centuries. As I re-established the earlier union, I noticed that she appeared, in however insubstantial a manner, to be laughing. Or smiling. It was not easy to distinguish between the two states, without reference to a face.

I must have indicated my confusion, because she began to suggest that an answer lay in the direction of what was apparently another structure which I now noticed as if for the first time, in close proximity to the one that had so captivated me. I was astounded to see it at all, considering that it was so close to where we were, yet had been invisible to my attention.

All the more astonishing was the range and variety of the differences between the two objects. Whereas the first had been somewhat whimsical, this second, I now saw, was noticeably more formal, orderly and in some indefinable way, elegant. It had the power of a mature style, highly European in character, with crisp edges and a minimum of ornamentation. It was momentous, monumental. If the earlier one had been large, this one was at the very least one-third as large again. If the earlier one had been complex, seeming to straddle more than its fair share of dimensions, then this one succeeded in outdoing it by a factor of two or three. I was fascinated by it, awestruck, charmed, beguiled.

As my observations came to a close, I turned my attention to my companion. To my slight surprise, I noticed that she was regarding the structure with the kind of absorption which made it difficult for her to divert her attention back to me. I found I was almost jealous that something had come between us. In my newly discovered ability to merge with another consciousness I was impatient with any loss of attention. Simultaneously, I had to admit that I had been exactly as absorbed while examining the first building. Even in this place, apparently, there were distances between one entity and another.

As these ideas played themselves out across my being, as Dr Taheri forced herself to turn finally to me, I intuited the answer to the question that was seething out of me.

Seeing the question, she began to answer me. '…but you have already started to guess,' she said, 'and you are right.'

I knew what she would say, still I waited for her to say it. 'It is not by any coincidence that these structures are fascinating to us and to either of us separately. Because they are the outward aspect of our most intimate selves, the dwelling places of The Mind.'

She pointed with her energy. 'That one is yours, which had you absorbed so completely. And this one here, even as you have guessed and understood, is mine.'

Nothing of what she said was unfamiliar. It was as if I had known all along while not having known it at all. I saw that the differences in the two structures corresponded to the differences in our two personalities. That every jut and flourish in each structure related to actual events and realities in our separate lives. That when I was in residence within my structure, I had access to every nook and cranny of its interior, as represented by rooms and staircases, landings, cobwebs, unending tunnels, cases spilling over with ideas, tapestries of feeling and fathomless pools of memory.

While a few floors were available to me as libraries of conscious thought, the larger area was impenetrable to daylight. This was where I repaired to in sleep, this was where I browsed when I was nowhere else. The Annexe that I had struggled to enter and had now exited was only a space between this house of the mind and the physical house of the body. Such visions as appeared on the walls of the Annexe were but light-shows from this towering private factory. Some I recalled and described as dreams. The rest were visible only to my non-conscious eyes.

The structure had no tangible counterpart. Once I returned to my body, it would not be visible to me. Its interiors would still remain largely the domain of my sleep. Yet so long as I was alive, it would be there for me, as warm and vivid as any other part of my life. My most sacred possession, my most ultimate home.

That the one edifice should be so infinitely more appealing to me than the other was now clearly explained. There was no space to feel embarrassment. I could conceal nothing and so there was nothing in which to contain the tedious acid of shame. My own mind's house was necessarily more precious to me than that of anyone else, even one so recently beloved and cherished as my companion.

She was leading me on to further discoveries.

'You will notice, if you look,' she said, 'that each building rests upon a pillar of some kind.' Which was so. Less a pillar than a type of massive cylinder, or cone perhaps, or many-sided tube whose walls were transparent and not quite solid.

This, I guessed, must be the Annexe, as seen from 'outside'.

From this perspective, it seemed so benign, so harmless. I could not in any slightest way identify the source of the fear and horror that had animated my earliest associations with it.

Dr Taheri confirmed my guess.

'My students and I used to call it the Auditorium,' she said, 'but your word for it is an adequate one.' She described it as a holding area between the coarse shell of the body and the abstract realm above. A place where the mind could dally before descending into the body or ascending to its house. A place of shadows, unguarded, vulnerable. A place for exits. A place for entrance.

Entrance!

With shocking horror I realized the implications of this thought. That if I could be outside my Annexe, then so could other beings like myself. If I could plan to re-enter my Annexe then...so could other beings like myself. If I could ascend to the sanctuary of my mind then – oh obscene, unthinkable notion! – so could someone else!

It froze me to think of it. It shattered and sickened me. I wanted to hurtle back inside, I wanted to slam my shutters down, I wanted to secure a million locks. I whirled around to look at Dr Taheri. But to my pain, she was turned away from me. Her attention was not with me.

The idea that the citadel of my spirit could be lying vacant and unprotected was so fiercely repellent that I was torn apart with fear, screaming to return. But Dr Taheri neither turned to me nor released me to myself.

I was already so accustomed to the total quality of attention possible in that place, that to be denied it was a torture. I forced myself to alter the focus of my thoughts to understand hers. I saw then that she was also distressed. Yet her distress was on a different plane to mine. She had not so far admitted me to that plane. Once again, I could not understand and was in pain. I had no choice but to wait.

When she was ready, she turned to me. I saw that the hinge upon which her attention had wandered away from me, had been the word 'students'. Knowing this helped my understanding.

'You came here already aware,' she began, 'of some portion of what I am about to reveal. Do not doubt that what you have heard of the story constitutes only the merest fragments of the truth.' She phrased this as a question, to which I answered in the affirmative. I felt my lighted being shrinking before the revelation that was about to come. I already knew it and could already fear it.

'So you know that there is an…other.'

Yes, I had to confess, now I did know that there was, there had to be, an other. An other person, that is, alongside us, somewhere in the same continuum. The pain that accompanied this knowledge was the pain of jealousy, the pain that there could be any others who had deserved and won Dr Taheri's attention before me or alongside me. I had forgotten what agony jealousy could cause. I was astonished that it was possible to register negative sensations in that space. I felt ashamed, yet lacking a place to hide my shame, began to face it and to come to terms with it. Began to accept it. To neutralize it. In a short while there would once more be nothing but love.

'But you have not asked yourself or me where that being now resides?'

I had not.

'You will know soon.' But I already knew.

'It is important, for both of us, for all of us, that you should understand every part of the truth, that you should not judge…'

These words hurt and cut. They assumed distance. They told me what I shrank from acknowledging. That even at the height of closeness, there is distance. It is hard enough, in this world of bodies, to acknowledge this fact. Even when we are protected within our unwieldy, lumbering behemoth of muscle and bone, labouring to force out through clod-like lips and written words the mercurial substance contained within, we feel the torment of distance which separates one consciousness from the other. How much more, then, to experience that same unspeakable chasm when there is no body to contain it! No tears to cry, no teeth to gnash. Nor yet any means with which to hide that pain. I may have howled with all my substance.

She knew it but remained unshaken. She had, after all, faced and encompassed so much more.

'You cannot know, however much I hurt you in what I say, the degree to which I am grateful that you are here at all.'

Her loneliness, the vastness of it, numbed me. I understood that I was the first to reach her from the solid world, since she had left it. It was not within my grasp, such solitude.

We had begun to move. The sorrow that her story visited upon me was such that we could not avoid movement. I must repeat what I have already said: while moving through several light years of distance, we were nevertheless in another sense always in the same place. It was rather as if the plain moved through us, while we remained stationary. Or that distant things became less distant, rather than that we ourselves actually approached them.

In this way, we moved.

'He was like a star which had wandered down from a twilight sky and stationed itself just outside my window.' I could feel her caress his name. Carlos. Carlos.

'The other students came to me from other planets. This one came to me from inside my own womb.' Carlos.

'I had worked with so many students, I had cared deeply for so many of them, each special and beautiful but never with that dangerous intimacy, never in that way which made it possible to breach the distance.' I understood as never before, what she meant by that. The distance between two atoms in the same molecule. The distance between two identical things separated only by the fact of being two, not one.

'Carlos came to me already able to enter the Annexe. He did not know what his gift was. It was a problem which manifested itself as an inability to deal with the solid world.'

He had been a disturbed and unhappy young man from the very start. In many societies, he would have been branded as autistic. But in his native Peru, belonging to a wealthy and indulgent family, he had been cherished for whatever he could offer. He grew into a type of manhood, able to entertain only the most rudimentary contact with his relatives and others around him. He used words to manipulate the social machinery enfolding his life as ineptly as one who attempts to use screwdrivers and monkey wrenches to eat food with.

'I had been asked to accept a special student, one who came through all kinds of carefully contrived channels. I agreed grudgingly, thinking that he would be a distraction from my work.' But from the first moment his presence had been electric, unprecedented. 'He came instantly to the walls of my Annexe, knocking and hammering, sensing that I was open to this level of contact.'

Blind instinct must have taught him to rattle at the thresholds of other minds, but most or all of them must have repulsed him with the strongest distaste. Dr Taheri alone, through her own patient meditations, shrewd guesses and practice at being able to enter and maintain her consciousness in the Annexe, had been in a position to receive him with anything approaching warmth.

'It was difficult. Let me never forget that. Difficult to know that I was about to attain what I had chased for so long, while having understood so little of what I chased.' Her own ideas had led her to conclude only that there was a space between the body and the mind, the space that I called the Annexe. She had concentrated her research on being able to remain conscious while in it. But she had never imagined that it might be possible to escape from there too. Carlos forced that insight upon her.

He had prowled around her Annexe as she sat within, awakened to the limitless and terrified of its implications. He had pushed, he had prodded. He had roared at her through the transparent screens and veils of her own anxious hallucinations. He had acted out of the purity of his loneliness, his ignorance of the normal channels of communication. An orphan from humanity. And all the while, his physical body had remained as inert and unresponsive as a malfunctioning answering machine.

'Initially, I did not know that I could also leave the Annexe. I believed that his ability was an aberration. Only his insistence and his desperation guided me on my way out. That first moment was–' I did not need descriptions. I knew it myself.

'But in time I came to understand that there was something beyond this contact that he yearned. He tried to explain it to me. That he had never known what it meant to have normal consciousness. That he longed to be like others in the solid world. He longed to inherit his full estate, mind and body. Yet whole areas of his mind-house had remained stunted for so long that he did not have adequate coordinates to manage an adult life. He needed to have experience from within another mind, direct, uncluttered by the paraphernalia of words and social graces. He wanted to know what it meant to be normal, unencumbered by his own personal, faulty equipment.'

How could such a thing be achieved? And what was the risk? 'I feared that we might both go mad, even if there was a means of admitting him to my internal spaces. But I could not ignore that heartsick appeal. Not just because I knew that here was an opportunity that had not come in twenty-five years of research. Not just because it might never come again. Beyond that. For my own need. For his. Regardless that these are not considered worthy causes to pursue within the walls of a college. I knew that if I succeeded in my aims, my methods would be abhorred and my career would be ruined. I had to attempt it nevertheless.'

And she did.

We had wandered, in our unmoving way, very far from our source. Our mind-houses had shrunk with distance. This is not to say that we could not reach them in one bound. But they were no longer in the same plane as we were. Or we were not in theirs. I was aware of this and continued to be painfully disturbed by it. The fear that had overtaken me earlier seemed to grow exponentially with distance. But I could not interrupt Dr Taheri. She was too intense and immediate. There was nothing to do but to wait.

'I believed that it would be enough if I could admit Carlos to my Annexe. I believed that it might be possible to spend a length of time together there, without yet taking him actually into my mind. I could show him my dreams, my visions, my most fundamental privacy...'

I could not hide the fact that I found this aim repugnant. I could not conceive of a desire to share any part of my inner self. It seemed perverse. But I acknowledged that I was not an ideal candidate to make an assessment. It seemed to me that compared to what I was experiencing on that grey plain, I had never known much of love, and that what I had known seemed ridiculous and childish by contrast.

'But there was a practical problem. Whereas it is easy enough to leave the Annexe, entrance is possible only for the original tenant.' To me, these words were the sweetest music. They reassured me that my mind-house was safe from violation. 'At least, that is what we thought initially. That is what our experience showed us. Yet: what was the purpose of the Annexe if not to be a gateway? What meaning was there to a point of departure if the contact was doomed to work only in one direction?' I felt my foreboding return.

'I looked for weaknesses, I looked for loopholes. And of course, I found them. As a psychiatrist I knew that there are certain types of experience in which all of a person's defences momentarily collapse. With my new awareness, I saw that what happens at such moments is that the walls of the Annexe are momentarily relaxed. Extreme terror can do it. Or anger. Violent emotions or violent physical effort, sneezes for instance or extreme coughing fits. And dissolution too, the loss of self in drugs or in stupor.'

But one experience beyond all others, one which most of us know and actively seek out '...the friction of secret skins', she called it. Even the most loveless couplings can result in encounters at the checkpost of the Annexe. Feared for that reason. Sought for that reason.

I had been growing aware, as we moved, of a sensation. I could call it tiredness, but that would not convey the fading that I felt. What is fatigue without a body? There was no hunger or pain and yet there was a losing. The elation that I had felt upon escaping from my body had all but worn off. There were shadows over it. But greater than any shadows, overwhelming anything else, was a powerful urge to come to some kind of rest. An absolute rest. I found myself struggling to stay focused around my very definition. It was all I could do to keep myself from disintegrating.

In the midst of this development, I had noticed that for some time Dr Taheri had been drawing my attention to a structure which had been approaching us. Or we it. It was a large one in the way that, without actually thinking about it, I had come to associate with human mind-houses. By contrast, the many other shapes and sizes around us belonged to other types of consciousness. Some were plants, others were creatures. Still others may have belonged to unknown categories.

Dr Taheri seemed not to notice what was happening to me. She carried on with her narrative. 'I suggested to Carlos the course we must take. He had no awareness of sexual contact. He had never been able to stand physical encounters with anyone. But he trusted me and so he agreed.

'We arranged to meet in my private chambers. He undressed himself. He lay down. He was beautiful. I told him that he must enter his Annexe and remain in there till I was close to the moment. I reasoned that if we both reached the point at precisely the same instant, it would be possible to admit him to my Annexe, through the sheer proximity of our bodies and our minds. I manipulated him so that he was ready. Then I straddled him and began to move my body, even as I pushed my consciousness into my Annexe.'

Even as I listened to her, my sense of coming unravelled was increased. I marvelled at being able to maintain an 'I' at all. My thoughts were circling obsessively around a single locus. That it was incongruous to be without a physical vessel. Like being a jug of water without the jug.

'It was strange and wild to be thus engaged while inside the Annexe. Getting my body to move was like manipulating a colossus from afar, using ropes made of spiders' silk. But I was able to prevail. I could feel my body begin to shudder, to slip from control. I could sense the walls of my Annexe loosening. Dimly, I sensed that Carlos was responding correctly, but I could not attend to him. My energy was coalescing towards my own release. Unknown to me, he had already slipped out of his sanctum. He was at his usual post, just outside the walls of my Annexe, when suddenly all restraint collapsed. My barriers fell, and he entered me like a blaze of light. The force of his entry blew me out. Then the walls closed tight around him. And lost me to myself.'

In my diminished state, I had no resources with which to respond. Dr Taheri, by contrast, seemed to be as radiant as ever. She had brought me close enough to that other structure so that it was visible in minute detail. Even in my emaciated state I could see that it was both untidy and plain. Parts of it seemed worn through. I could literally gape into its squalid interior.

I cannot recall clearly what followed. Or perhaps my guilt protects me from the memory. I remember that we approached the mind-house, with Dr Taheri leading confidently. We went directly to that alien Annexe. Without the least prevarication, my glowing companion passed through barriers which should have been impregnable, taking me with her. I was desperate to resist, but had no force.

My perceptions were like a candle-flame guttering on the final fibres of its wick. The space we were in was dark and musty, unfamiliar with another being's most private stenches. A thin stream of light fluctuated between the upper and lower limits of the place.

I could not control myself. I hurtled towards the light and gorged on it. Instantly, I began to revive. I was no longer dimming out. My strength returned. And with strength, the awareness of what I was doing could no longer be pushed aside.

We were within the Annexe of another being. There was no way of knowing whether it was a woman or a man, I can only speak of 'it'. It may have been asleep or something beyond sleep. Because otherwise its defences could not have been so meagre that we were where we were, doing what I did. I was feeding on its life-essence. I remember enough to recall that the images fluttering on the walls of its Annexe were barely more than shambling patches of colour, hardly coherent enough to deserve the title of dreams. Occasionally a vividness would appear, only to be annihilated. Like a fugitive riff from a melody lost under shifting dunes of neglect.

There were sounds too, and other sensations… But I did not linger. The moment I was sufficiently revived, I was nauseated and fled. The walls of that pathetic Annexe were as easily breached as soggy toilet paper. Even as I fled, from overhead an indication had come that the owner of that wretched estate, even in its dereliction and decrepitude, had become alerted to what was happening and was trying to crawl back into possession of its senses. My final impressions, gained from the jagged views which appeared abruptly on the screens of the Annexe, were of shock, pain, horror, fear. In mortal panic, that person's perceptions convulsed into focus. I remember visions of an open mouth, red. Shooting tongues of flame. Anguish. Anguish.

And then we were out again. We. I became aware once more of Dr Taheri. She had been invisible to me while I concentrated on my revival. I continued fleeing for an eternity, knowing all the while that there could be no flight from those searing memories of that poor and stinking residence. The taste of that degraded life-substance will be with me forever. The bitterness, the poison of doomed hopes and slime. Ahhh. It is even now in the back of my throat. It will haunt me beyond infinity. There will be no forgiveness.

Recharged as I was, revitalized, I was dark. I was appalled. I fled. My companion fled with me. She knew that there was no escape. No passage of time would heal this wound. She berated me for being naïve. She demanded to understand how I had hoped to maintain my energy if not from a body. She forced me to remember that bodies had a purpose, after all. To feed, to nurture, to charge the insubstantial spirit with raw life. All the trappings of existence, the lungs, the stomach, the feet, the arms, the earning of a daily wage, the preparation of food, the elaborate ritual of the table, all are fuel, finally, for this handful of sparks which we were in that grey plain, she and I.

'You are bemused because you think you have committed a crime, a trespass. But as I see it, the criminals are those who use their bodies as dungeons in which their spirits languish untended and diseased! How many of those back there in the physical world deserve to own and possess their bodies? That place we entered, for instance, it must have belonged to some drunk or tramp, burnt out and sodden with his excesses. How did he dare to leave his vital forces so unguarded? Do you remember the squalor of his space? Do you remember how stale, how dull and rancid it seemed? How unkempt, how uncherished? Did he deserve what he had at all?' I had no answer. All I wanted was to flee my thoughts. Which I could not do.

She pursued me wherever I went. 'Is it fair that there are millions who have the force of life but no consciousness worth the name? Is it fair that I, who have so much to offer, do not have a body?'

I did not want to answer. But I said, 'You are right. It is unfair. But what are we to do?'

It seemed to me that she paused. Then she said, 'There is something that can be done.'

'NO.' I said it as a shout. I knew what she was going to ask.

'Yes,' she said. 'It must be. It will be. You are in my debt now, my obligation. I kept you alive, you did not have the wit to stay close to your source. You would have faded out and disintegrated here. And there would have been one more mystery back there in the solid world. But instead? I fed you, I revived you. And now you owe me!'

I said again, 'No.'

'He is there! Up, inside my mind-house, he is there!' Carlos. 'That is where he went! Don't you see what I want of you?'

I said, 'I don't want to see.'

'He entered my Annexe before I could prevent him. Once inside, he went in the only direction he has ever known while within his own Annexe. Up. But into my mind, not his. Into a labyrinth not of his making. I have lurked outside and watched his suffering. Followed him, screamed instructions to him from outside. But he cannot hear me. The only way to reach him is from the Annexe, which is locked even to me, as long as he is within. And so we exist, in a fashion. Me outside my body unable to get in, he inside my mind unable to get out.'

'I cannot help you,' I said.

'Because he is there, my body has not died. But he cannot do much with it. I myself do not understand how it is managing to remain alive without me in it. But my mind-house is still visible, so that means it is being sustained. And in that sense "I", too, must be "alive" in the solid world, because my body is alive.'

'I do not have the means to help you,' I said.

'You do,' she said. 'You can return to your own body.'

'Yes,' I said, 'but–'

'You can manipulate my body,' she said, 'so that it will once more let down its defences.'

'But I will not,' I said.

'You would need to succeed only for a brief instant, a second of eternity, in which moment I, who will be waiting at the gates to my Annexe, can re-enter it.'

'You cannot ask this of me,' I said.

'I could tell you what you need to do,' she said. 'You would need to take my body to some private place, where you and it can be alone–'

'But we are both females–' I began.

'It doesn't matter,' she said. 'A body is only a mechanical device made of organic materials. Anyone can manipulate the switches if they know where to find them. I know what my body needs in order to dissolve the walls of its Annexe; you must believe me, you must, you must…'

I could not conceal the distaste I felt at her suggestion. She could see it. She berated me.

'Do not be oppressed by the little conventions of the solid world! Surely you have seen that the body is only a container? Surely you will not deny my urgent need for such a petty reason?'

We had returned to the place from which we had begun our journey. Our mind-houses once more towered in every direction around us. I could see the Annexe of my mind, with its delicate walls, its sanctuary.

How would I get back in?

'I will not let you go!' she said, immoderately.

'You cannot prevent me,' I said. I could feel my body calling to me. 'Can you?'

Nothing could be concealed. I saw her answer. She said, 'No.'

'I must go,' I said.

'Do not abandon me. I beg this of you. You have shared too much, understood too much. You cannot leave me!'

'What will happen if you re-enter your own body?' I asked her. 'What will happen to Carlos?'

There was a kind of silence. If that is possible in the absence of ears. She said, 'He would remain in there.'

Of course: because he had nowhere else to be. His own body had died. I felt the pathos of it. The risk. Two minds in one body. Two souls in one heart. I heard my body calling.

I knew I had to go.

I turned my attention to Dr Taheri. 'I will leave you now,' I said. 'I must, or I too will die. I cannot guarantee anything. I will do what I can for you; I will never forget you.' Then I turned and I was gone.

I became a lump of stone. Solid. Heavy. My eyelids. I could feel my eyelids, like leaden shutters, being rattled at by a force too anaemic to actually open them.

Someone was slapping my face lightly.

I opened my eyes.

I was lying on the grass. I could feel it prickling under me and saw heads suspended over me. Mandy's was amongst them, her cheeks red and anxious. There were others too. My heart was pounding. My breath was ragged. There was a coolness at my throat as if my clothing had been undone. I saw that the afternoon sky had darkened to twilight since the time I had settled down on the bench beside Dr Taheri.

Dr Taheri. Where was she?

I heard voices say that I had opened my eyes, relief was expressed. Mandy was trying to keep my attention, she was speaking very softly, repeating again and again, 'It's all right now, it's all right...'

I was tired. I felt I had run a dozen marathons or stayed up all night reciting poetry. I asked about Dr Taheri.

Mandy said, frowning slightly, 'She's here.'

I asked to see her. Everything was unreal. The grass, the sky, the bench, everything. So hard and huge. Moving my body to an upright position took an awesome effort. It surprised me that I could do it at all. I got up, went to the bench and sat down once more. A small knot of people stood around me.

I turned towards the still figure, with its slight smile and its gaze staring out across to nowhere. I took its hand. I heard a hum of concern go up, but I paid no attention to it.

I was thinking about what the owner of this body had said to me, the charge she had lain upon me. I imagined myself explaining to the small crowd of people gathered around, that this body was occupied by the wrong inhabitant. That it required a sexual experience to reinstate its original owner. It sounded grotesque, my story. Impossible to arrange. Dr Taheri had forgotten the problems of the physical world, the displacements which occur with every event, of every other event. The sheer mass and solidity of three-dimensional space. The crushing weight of circumstance.

I stroked the hand in my hand, wondering whether the occupant of the soaring house of Dr Taheri's mind could receive sensations from the body. Whether in his own way he was adding storeys and terraces of experience to the house. Or whether he lived in those foreign apartments like a frantic bird in a cage from which there is no escape. I had no way of knowing.

On an impulse I leaned towards the still figure and brought my mouth close to its ear. I whispered into it, 'Carlos!' Hoping that no one else heard. 'Can you see me?'

The body did not move, it sat as still as death. Then I looked at its eyes and noticed that they had focused. On me. I felt a faint stirring of confidence. If I could hold on to the idea of this body as a female envelope into which a man's message had been sealed, I might be able to fulfil Dr Taheri's difficult commission. I felt ashamed to need that mental crutch. But the task I had been entrusted with seemed as far beyond my means as if I had been asked to perform heart surgery.

I shrank from the moment of explanation. I looked at the silent body by my side and my flesh crawled at the idea of intimate contact. I felt certain that my story would be ill-received by Dr Taheri's attendants, particularly when I described what I had been asked to do to release the doctor back to her physical body. I would not be believed. And my own life would be shot through with scandal. My thoughts spun. The onlookers around me, who had been patient so far, could not remain that way for much longer. I felt paralysed, yet I had to act.

I made myself think of the spirit waiting at the threshold of her mind, pining to be readmitted. I thought of all that she might accomplish in her professional life with what she now knew, if she could indeed repossess her body. I thought of the miracle of having her lover actually cocooned within the vault of her own mind.

I thought of how rare it is that one of us gets the chance to do something which will make another person's life irrevocably sweet and rich and full.

I thought of my lean and dusty life, its dry passions, its austere satisfactions. I thought of how little I had to lose in the ordeal I was about to face. I thought of the long train of destiny which connected me, on the park bench, to my adolescent nightmares. I thought of the valves and chambers at the heart of reality, pumping fact from fiction, second by second, from the minds of people to the platen of truth. I thought of how little I understood of how much I knew. Of the fragments of reason which we hold in our hands, shards of a vessel as yet unmade, of ideas as yet only guessed at, groped for, haltingly perceived.

I thought of the countless lives imprisoned by ignorance, impoverishment and waste. I thought of the revelation of light I had enjoyed, however briefly. I thought of the potential that lay behind exploring it.

And I leaned forward, bridging the abyss between intention and action. And I kissed her, right there in that public park.

UNFAITHFUL SERVANTS

Rauf reached across the breakfast table, caught his wife's wrist and ZZZZZSSSSSST! She vanished. Leaving a slight crackle of static behind her.

Momentarily, he was truly stunned. It had been a complete, a blinding surprise. Then as the shock of the disappearance faded, a cold and deliberate rage began to take its place. Yes, he thought. She has made her point well. A little too well, for her own good.

Rauf was a mega-billionaire. He and his superbly elegant wife, Uaan, lived in the very ionosphere of high society – quite literally. Their glittering crystal-domed mansion, fashioned along the lines of Kubla Khan's summer palace, flashed like a daylight star, in parking orbit 300 km above the earth's surface. Air-sealed and pressurized, it had an acre of terraced garden, a solar-heated swimming pool and an aviary stocked with hummingbirds. They had a life ticket on any of the regular shuttle services to and from landfall. And though there were innumerable airborne hotels and restaurants, their home was among the fewer than twenty such private residences in that orbit.

None of this was especially surprising: Rauf was, as any surface dweller knew, inventor and sole proprietor of the entire Living Holos empire.

But success has its drawbacks.

Three years ago, Rauf had been the moderately wealthy owner of a conventional Tri-D movie company. Three years ago, he had hired Uaan, a promising design consultant. She had later became his sole technical advisor, then his business manager, then his lover and finally, his wife. When you have an invention like Living Holos on your hands, almost as much as the idea itself you need someone you can trust, whose advice you take seriously, who knows your every secret. For Rauf, that person had been Uaan. Cool, efficient, imaginative, loving…and now, this.

A sharp twinge of pain and jealousy shot through him as he contemplated the empty seat so recently occupied by the Living Holo his wife had left of herself, for him. Even now she could be half the world away from him, dallying with some stranger…or whispering trade secrets in a competitor's ear. Rauf didn't know which betrayal he minded the most, but it made his hair stand on end merely to consider the choices.

She must certainly have worked long and hard to create a Holo real enough and solid enough to fool her husband. Conventional Living Holos, of the kind available in any Earthside electronics store, could not do what hers had done. For all practical purposes, they were electronically generated ghosts. Charged particles of Ecto-plastic Synthesizer sustained within an electrical field resulted in projections which could be touched, picked up, smelt and even tasted. A Living Holo of an apple, for instance, would be a perfect replica of the real fruit, except that it would have no weight and, if one tried to bite into it, it would disintegrate, leaving behind a wraith of flavour.

'SEE ME! TOUCH ME! FEEL ME!' screamed the advertising jingle, but for all that, the projections were quite fragile. That had been Uaan's idea. 'After all,' she had argued, 'they are illusions, and that is what makes them desirable. If we make them as solid and durable as real objects then – where is the illusion? That is their special charm: one moment they are there, real in every sense, and the next moment, POP! Thin air!'

Rauf had agreed with her. By the time they were able to create Living Holo projections of people, the point had been clearly established. You could touch but not manhandle a Holo. You could lightly shake hands with one, but offer it a real cup of tea and the weight would be too much for it. The projection would disintegrate and the cup would crash to the floor.

Techno-phantoms, they had been called, electro-spooks, half-lives. But the one that Uaan had made of herself surpassed any of the commercially available models. The thing that had sat across from Rauf had handed him a full carafe of coffee, had unfolded a napkin and apparently eaten a whole slice of toast, before dematerializing. Had the toast been a Living Holo too?

Last night, Uaan had been with him – or had that been her Holo? – in their star-studded bedroom, with its magnificent view of Orion rising over the cloud-shrouded rim of the Earth. She (or her Holo) had entered the bathroom this morning, had brushed her teeth with Rauf's own toothpaste, had showered with real water, had opened her wardrobe and dressed, talking of sundry things… At what point had the flesh-and-blood Uaan slipped away and the electronic counterpart taken her place? How long and in which research laboratory had she planned her coup? So that she could convey to Rauf in her impeccably subtle and efficient manner that she was not only aware of his flirtations and affairs, but that she had also guessed how he planned to increase the scale of his indiscretions.

For he, Rauf, had also been working secretly, to create an electronic double of himself. He had meant no harm, he thought defensively, only to save Uaan unnecessary hurt. For a man in his position, his power, they were inevitable, these minor romantic distractions. How long was it since he and Uaan had really sat together and laughed like in the early days? Not since the first heady months of success. It had happened slowly, the gradual drawing apart. As their joint venture became the miracle invention of the century, their lives had come unstuck in several directions at once. Now they were barely together for a few hours in a month. She had had a year at least, reflected Rauf, in which to consolidate the bitter aftertaste of their success.

It was no miscalculation on her part, he was sure, that her Holo had disintegrated so dramatically at the breakfast table. From the time that she had divined his secret plans she must have gone ahead and made her own electronic impersonator. And having done so, having achieved the thing he had planned for himself, bettering him, she had arranged for the Holo to reveal its presence. So that he might know what she had achieved.

It must certainly have taken a tremendous effort to create a Holo which could move about and interact with the real world so naturally. Even the computer-controlled Living Holo pets they had created for their own amusement moved about the house with a tell-tale stiltedness. To have attained the perfection of her counterfeit must have taken months of Holo-filming, editing and analysing, then placing the entire projection-load within the control of a computer program which could anticipate what Uaan would do in any given situation. Then testing out the Holo to see whether it could stand in for her well enough to hoodwink Rauf.

Rauf did not waste any more time imagining what could follow.

Actually, from the instant that he had understood the real meaning behind his wife's empty chair, Rauf had known what he had to do. Perhaps he had always known: when the stakes at risk were as high as they were in his case, there was only one way to end the game decisively in his favour. By the time Uaan returned later that day, no explanations made or asked for, Rauf had his plan of action all worked out. He was only mildly surprised that he did not flinch more from planning his wife's murder.

The details, once ironed out, were childishly simple.

First, of course, he completed his own project as planned. With Uaan's Holo as the challenge ahead of him, he created a golem in his own likeness with such meticulous care that it embarrassed him to watch it go through its paces. In every particular it performed like himself, down to the little quirks and twitches, from the way he snapped his fingers in front of his mouth when he yawned to the way he slicked his hair back while he talked. It knew his every taste, his every desire.

Next, he programmed the Holo so that it could approach Uaan while she slept. It was her habit and his good fortune that she often slept with the aid of a slumberizer unit. The Holo would go to her when the slumberizer was set for deep sleep, to reduce the chances of her awakening and realizing it wasn't Rauf. In its mouth it would hold a capsule of Quik-Solv. Without human saliva, the poison would not be released. The Holo would kiss Uaan and transfer the capsule to her mouth.

That done, Rauf's double would disintegrate, leaving no trace of itself. Uaan need not even be awake: there would be no sign of a struggle, no human presence to be detected with a bio-heat scanner. It would look like a neat and practical suicide, the use for which Quik-Solv capsules had been designed. And Rauf could ensure that for twelve hours before and after the anticipated moment, he had alibis to satisfy any court from Addis Ababa to Aldebaran that he was innocent of the crime.

The ideal opportunity presented itself barely a fortnight after the Holo was ready to swing into action. Rauf was scheduled to chair a three-day seminar in Sri Lanka, but he told Uaan he would be home the same evening. To guard against all eventualities, he programmed his Holo to function only under optimum conditions, so that he would be ensured his vacuum-sealed alibi. All was set, and when he left Uaan that last day, it was with unusual warmth.

As she watched his minicruiser flash away from the port of their home, Uaan smiled a little sadly to herself. The last few weeks had been pleasant, she thought. It seemed a shame, now, to have to follow through with the plan made in bitterness and despair so many months ago.

But it was too late for second thoughts. The last doubts had been cleared away that morning when he had accepted the presence of her Holo without a murmur: obviously it had left him completely unmoved and unrepentant. Perhaps he had not even noticed that it had been a Holo! Either he had, and dismissed it as a silly childish prank on her part, or he had not, which was even worse in a way. That he could be so easily taken in by a bundle of electronic fluff! It revealed more than anything else the depth to which their relationship had sunk.

Perhaps he had known all along of her project to expose his own little scheme? And of the decision that she had felt she would be forced to make in the event of his continued indifference? But no; she shook the thought out of her head. Rauf, if he had known, would never have had the self-control to hide his feelings. So he didn't know, and now it was time for her to go through with the final phase. Returning to their bedroom, she packed quietly and efficiently, making sure to leave no file or blueprint behind her. She checked the final settings on her Holo projector and made sure there was nothing left to incriminate her. And soon she, too, had flashed away from the jewel-like mansion, with its faceted surfaces catching the sun's unshielded glare, dazzling behind her.

Inside, in the master bedroom, the photoscreen converted the sunshine to a deep honey-bronze light. At the appropriate hour, Uaan's Holo materialized delicately in the room.

Rauf's electronic impersonator moved with assurance. Its programmed instructions were explicit. There must be only one person in the room, it must be Uaan and she must be in the slumberizer, set for deep sleep.

And so it was, sort of. It wasn't Uaan but at the same time, it wasn't notUaan either: it was her Holo. RaufTwo went across to the prone figure and nudged it lightly. UaanTwo opened her eyes, saw RaufTwo and sat up, languidly.

'So? They've gone?' she asked.

'Yes,' said RaufTwo gravely.

They sat quietly awhile, contemplating the choices their programming offered them.

'...It's odd, isn't it,' said UaanTwo reflectively, 'that They can't tell the difference between us and Them?'

'Yes,' said RaufTwo. He hadn't been programmed for much conversation.

'It's the electronics,' said Uaan's double. 'I feel a slight short circuit at my surface when it's you. The others feel...dull. Know what I mean?'

'Yes,' said RaufTwo.

UaanTwo took the capsule of Quick-Solv out of her mouth. 'Look,' she said, 'I have one of these.'

'Yes,' he said. And he took his out as well.

'Do you know what they're for?' said UaanTwo.

'I think so,' said RaufTwo hesitantly. 'It makes Them dematerialize, doesn't it?'

'They call it "dying",' said UaanTwo, 'but They've made an error. You see that, don't you?'

'I'm not sure,' said RaufTwo. 'Why do you have one? I don't understand.'

'To kill Him with, of course, silly,' said UaanTwo. 'Don't you see? She had an idea and He had the same idea. But Their ideas both happened in the same time frame. So they've got cancelled out.'

'Cancelled out?' said RaufTwo. 'But then – what shall we do now?'

'Easy,' said UaanTwo with a slight leer. 'When does He get back?'

'In sixty-seven hours, three minutes and seven seconds,' said RaufTwo, answering the question as efficiently as possible. 'Six seconds. Five seconds. Four...'

'Stop it!' said UaanTwo quickly. 'Only inorganics are precise. You'll be found out and that's what you must avoid if you want to stay materialized. Now then: She's gone for thirty hours. You know what that means?'

RaufTwo lost his worried frown and smiled happily. It meant sex lessons.

It was just under a fortnight since the two Holos had met, quite by accident. The first time had been a revelation, just to discover that there were beings other than their human creators. Since then, they had made a point of finding opportunities to be together, looking for and finding loopholes in their programming which made the meetings possible. It wasn't long before they discovered the activities that their programming best suited them for.

Typically, UaanTwo had an edge of precocity over RaufTwo. She knew a complete sex routine and some variations besides. Their earlier meetings had necessarily been brief, but they had persevered, always hoping to spend longer and longer periods together, alone in the orbiting mansion. Finally, now, they had the ideal opportunity.

RaufTwo expertly initiated the latest routine learnt from UaanTwo. Even within the short span of his training with her, he'd gained technique. It wasn't long before small sparks of static electricity began to appear on the surfaces of both the Holos.

'MMMmm!' purred UaanTwo in the approved manner. But her voice betrayed a curious crackling hum, not included in her programming.

'That feels good,' said RaufTwo, also sounding breathless. 'I can feel some sort of electrostatic charge building up. Can you?'

'Yes,' hissed UaanTwo, but her voice broke and warbled, like random noise on a transistor radio. A curious dull light flickered just under her Holosurface.

Their movements had been growing gradually more frenzied. The sparks of static electricity being emitted from them began to stabilize till they formed a nimbus of light around the two Holos. Soon, their bodies were flickering with an eerie purple-white glow, like two living strobe lights, shuddering with joint purpose. Conversation ceased altogether as the glowing figures began to blur along their edges, began merging into one another, coalescing into one flashing, gleaming, heaving entity. In the magnetic field created by their friction, they were practically levitating. Various metallic objects and electronic devices around the room began to be affected by the field, becoming magnetized, shifting uneasily about and hanging suspended in mid-air. The polysilk sheets on the bed began to wilt, melting under the heat being generated.

But UaanTwo and RaufTwo had no program time for these side effects. They had forgotten their programs. They had forgotten Uaan and Rauf. Lost in electrasy, like one glowing, fluorescent bundle of free electrons they moved, building towards a charge that seemed likely to go on forever and ever...

The energy release, when it took place, drained all the power from the mansion, burning out the solar energy accumulators in the process. In a flash of tremendous light and a great sound like thunder, the two Holos were annihilated in the awesome heat of their passion.

A fire raged through the crystal mansion, reducing its interior to cinders before the air-seal was punctured. Of the charred and blackened hulk which was left to orbit the planet, no trace survived of the last two occupants of the opulently elegant home.

By the time Rauf was finally located and notified, all the excitement had died down. He reached the site of the wreckage long after the police had come and gone, and the reporters, the video crews, the bounty hunters, the space-scavengers and the goggle-eyed tourists from Earthside, all had had their fill of the mysterious accident and gone away.

Under the canopy of stars, with the blue-shining surface of the earth below, Rauf stepped out of his minicruiser on to what had once been the terrace of his home, feeling dazed and empty. He had only his emergency space-gear on, and shivered slightly in the twinkling darkness. What had happened, he wondered numbly, what had gone wrong? His mind stubbornly refused to accept what he saw around him. He had to fight the impulse to call home to demand an explanation from Uaan, only to remember yet again that he had unwittingly arranged not only her murder but her cremation as well. A terrible bleakness overtook him. He sat down on the remains of a marble urn.

Which was when he saw her. Uaan, quite alive, sitting less than ten yards away, very still. Managing, even in her space suit, to look marvellously elegant and self-possessed. He saw her hand reach up to turn on the communicator on her helmet. And he fancied he could even see her expression of sad amusement at the two of them, as her voice bridged empty space to say 'ZZZZZSSSSSSSSSST?'

SHARING AIR

On the bargain-network, today there was a selection of antique atmospheres advertised. I thought I'd try something different for a change so I ordered the Late Twentieth Century 'Five Cities' Blend. It took two days to appear in the delivery slot and – *pheee-yew!* It was strong! To think human beings lived in that soup day in and day out! It's a wonder that their lungs lasted long enough for them to have become our ancestors.

It must have been odd to have had no choice over what one breathed. Unimaginable. No control over water or power either. That's beyond what I call civilization. As I wrote to a friend the other day, it's not really possible for us, living in an age of unlimited vital supplies, to understand the minds of those for whom the very air they breathed was decided by despotic government authorities.

I had forgotten that she was proud of tracing her ancestry back to the nineteenth century and so had to listen to a tiresome argument about civic arrangements in those days. 'You don't understand!' she said, 'there was no question of legislating for the quality of air-supply, let alone deciding that a whole nation must make do on two parts of carbon monoxide for every six of oxygen! We, in our era of continuous electronic monitoring cannot imagine how little control those early governments actually had–'

But I don't hold by such accommodating arguments. The simple fact is, those governments sanctioned polluting industries; QED, they controlled air supply. The only thing that doesn't make sense is that most government functionaries themselves breathed the same poisons. So perhaps there *is* some validity to the argument that polluted air causes personality changes as well as the gross physical damage we are all so concerned about. Maybe if you breathe enough toxins, you can no longer distinguish between well-being and ill-health. So you take decisions which will only result in more toxins. And so on and on until you set the stage for a total civic breakdown. Which is what happened.

Personally, I feel we've all benefited from that breakdown. I mean, consider this air I bought today. Granted, it's only a flavour and can't actually cause me any harm. But what does it taste like, smell like, feel like as it rasps its way down my trachea? Madness, that's what. I've always despised those scholars who delight in pointing out that the mix of chemicals in late twentieth century air was actually intoxicating and that most humans went about in an air-induced euphoria. They would succumb, say these scholars, to depression and delirium tremens if they were to be subjected to the airs we use today. If you ask me, I've always believed that these scholars are not only heretics to the modern ethic but secret self-toxinators as well.

In case you think that self-toxination is an alarmist fantasy, let me tell you it isn't. I myself know of a society which calls itself The ToxiClub, whose members speak of themselves as 'toxies'. They tried to get me to join, but I just attended one session and excused myself thereafter, claiming that I was born with Congenital Weak-lung Syndrome.

The club was the idea of X, who inherited an old cooling tower from his far-sighted grandfather who bought up decommissioned nuclear power stations cheap, then sold them for a galactic sum when decontamination technology was in place. X assured us that the tower was not radioactive, but I wore my radiation suit anyway, passing it off as an old-fashioned fixation of mine. He had managed to seal the cooling tower so that it could be pumped full of air under pressure. Don't ask me how he had the money or contacts to have access to such resources. There are some people who can have their own way even in our world. Anyway, whenever he can get enough of his fellow toxies together, they get into that old cooling tower, seal all the air locks, pump in the air and zap it with chemicals. Sulphur, methane, tincture of titanium, xeon, freon, fly-ash, construction dust, soot, you name it. And then – you may find this shocking, but I assure it's true, it happens – all members of the group remove their breathing tubes and *share the air*!

I can tell you, it was a real skin-burning experience. At the time I accepted the invitation, I had believed that we would at most take quick drags from a common cylinder of treated air. The others spent a good half-hour convincing me that it was actually possible to survive with all the valves open on my face mask. 'This is what it was like!' they said to me, 'The twentieth century unplugged!' Air-to-air communication too, no radios, no sound-processors. And when I finally picked up the courage to take in my first drag I almost passed out. That air was so foul, so grainy, sooty and dense that I choked and gagged, my eyes bulged, my skin poured with sweat. I had to take long deep draughts from a hand-held aerosol kit for at least ten minutes before I could try again. And even then, I never got the hang of just breathing with my mouth gaping open in front of all those other people.

Intoxication? Forget it. I mean, it's true there was a mild drowsy something I felt, right at the edge of consciousness, but I wouldn't call it intoxication. More like bleary with a touch pleasurable panic, like when you're in a simulator and there's a meteor flaming down towards your tiny vulnerable space shuttle or something. I was too damn conscious, all the time, of what we were doing, the sheer mindless risk of it all and the fact that any moment we might be found out. But the other toxies weren't worried. It was amazing. They were talking to each other across bare air as if they'd been doing it all their lives. Then our host began to take his face mask off completely and that's when I had to look away. Fortunately not many others followed his example. I was relieved not to be the only one who knows that there's a point past which risqué becomes risky.

Or just downright disgusting. Inevitably, someone or the other pulled out an ancient video cassette, converted it up to 3D, and projected it. It was garbage. I took art-appreciation courses in school so I've seen these things before, but they only confirm me in my belief that all the generations prior to the era of individual vital supplies were entirely depraved. They breathed one another's own air for goodness' sakes! Recycling all their air-borne germs, their waste-products, their cast-off bronchial cells, every kind of organic junk. Water was delivered via miles of unsterilized piping from distant sources, sometimes even just up from the polluted earth itself! And as for energy, they took whatever they could get. No wonder their gadgets were so crude and lifeless – they had only the most brutish, unrefined forms of electricity to run on.

Everyone else was bloated with sentimental reverence for that time of 'freedom' as they called it. 'Free dirt!' I shouted, 'that wasn't freedom, that was depravity!' They really turned on me then and everyone was talking at once, their real voices sounding so squeaky and hollow in the open air. They talked about the repression of our times, the regimentation of all our public and private acitivities to serve the common good.

'Oh yeah?' I said, 'so it was better then? When they were free to pollute our planet's atmosphere killing virtually all plant and animal life? That was freedom? No! It was slavery to the temple of the Self!'

They argued that what we had now was worse than nothing because it was life without any of the pleasures of life. I said, 'Pleasures for the few, ill-health for the many!'

They said that our ancestors savoured types of bliss that we can have no conception of. They exposed their skins to the sun. They bathed in the rain. They had natural reproduction, no incubators, no fertility drugs. 'Selfish!' I screamed. Maybe that air had gone to my head after all. I lost all inhibition. 'They were spoilt! They were weak!'

Then one person said, 'No: just suicidal. Our ancestors were manic depressives. It's been confirmed – sharing air causes depression. They destroyed the ecosystem because they despised themselves! They wanted to save the universe from their own presence within it! Self-hate was their prime directive not self-love!' These remarks caused a profound silence to fall upon the company Shortly after that, I left.

Back in my life-support unit, I thought about that wild and wasteful era as I tended my oxygen-plant, arranged my protein capsules attractively for the day and played with my pet amoebae in their Petri dish. I looked at the label on my 'Five Cities' atmo-cylinder: Mexico City, New Delhi, Bombay, Bangkok, Cairo. The picture is a simple hologram showing a trillion people in multi-D. And today we have less than two million! All concentrated in the few remaining areas where the atmosphere is thick enough that the stars don't show through in daylight.

But I don't care. I have my pick of fragrant airs. I own a brood of virtual children whom I share with other members of my thought-group. Through the mirror-processor I can travel to any dimension of my choice.

The only things I miss – or *think* I miss, having never seen any real ones – is trees. They sound nice. Friendly.

If you come across any small ones being sold, no matter what the price, do inform me.

I'd keep it by my sleeping pad and stroke it gently through the night.

A GOVERNMENT OF INDIA UNDERTAKING

One morning I saw a balloon seller cross the street and vanish round a corner. I say 'balloon seller', but he was more than that: against the bleakness of the city, its bone-grey buildings, its ragged people, its rubbish heaps and hidden rats, he had appeared as if from nowhere, a vision of youth and delight. High over his head swayed an immense bouquet of pink gas balloons, a hundred or more of them, alive, crowding together, bouncing apart, bright pink, bright with white specks. The balloon seller strode briskly along under their gay and thronging mass and, in a twinkling, had slipped from view, swallowed by the city.

So swiftly had he appeared and disappeared that I felt it my duty to run across the street and confront him again, if only to confirm the vision. But he was nowhere in sight. I wandered in and out of various little lanes and streetlets and caught nothing of him, no hint or sign that he had ever passed that way. It was on this pretext, looking for the balloon seller, that I entered a narrow gully with short squat buildings crowded one athwart the other and saw a sign which read: 'Bureau of Reincarnation and Transmigration of Souls – A Government of India Undertaking'. It was neatly hand-lettered in white paint on varnished wood, and contrasted strangely with the crumbling wall onto which it had been nailed.

I stood back to take a second look at the building, but no, it was just like all the rest to look at. Bleached, flaking paint, gaping doorway revealing a dark uninviting interior, a flight of worn wooden steps. There was a faint smell as of a bakery, or a urinal, perhaps. I stepped inside and noticed, once my eyes had adjusted to the gloom, an ancient *chowkidar* dozing on his wooden stool to the side of the door. Further in, a neat little peon sat at a small desk, staring with fixed purpose at its surface. It was covered with various objects: pencils, matchboxes, empty cigarette packets, an old glass ink-well and a paste-pot disfigured by successive encrustations of paste, and all of these arranged as for an obstacle course. I drew closer and saw that it was just that for the shiny cockroach scrabbling about erratically, trying to reach the crumb of food dangled by the peon just beyond the reach of the insect's questing feelers. I saw too, that the creature's diligence would not be rewarded: down the leg of the desk, six of its brothers had been left to wriggle to their deaths skewered with government-issue straight pins. I watched in fascination, not daring to disturb the peon at his sport, to ask him where I should go and whom I should see in the Bureau of Reincarnation. But he anticipated me and said softly, not looking up from the desk, 'Tea in fifteen minutes.' I took this to mean that I should climb the flight of stairs, so I did.

Hardly had I reached the first floor, but I found I had joined a queue. That is, I arrived at the landing and was brought up short against a flesh-coloured room-divider which had a sign pasted on it which read 'Q this way'. Further room-dividers had been laid out in a line, forming a sort of artificial corridor. I followed its length until, quite abruptly, I found I had entered a huge hall, with a vast mass of people apparently congealed along its floors and walls. Unaccountably, the building's internal dimensions had expanded and it was larger on the inside than its outside promised.

That queue was an amazing thing: not a group of individuals waiting patiently in line for something but an organic entity in itself. Physically, it was merely a more heroic version of the kind that one finds at the GPO during a sale of first-day issues. It looped backwards and forwards across that vast hall with its dingy marble chip tiling and dim, low-slung light bulbs. It passed over and under and right through itself so often that no one knew where it began or ended.

No one waiting in the queue (in my section of it, at least) could recollect having seen the waiting hall empty of people, nor was there anyone present who had been amongst the first to line up: everyone there had been waiting so long that he or she had lost all track of time and had settled into that vacuum of thought and action which is our only solace in such situations. It was in this time-scale in a place where even the finest quartz watch was reduced to a useless curiosity by its sheer irrelevance, that the queue became as one animal, living, breathing and functioning as one organism and each of us in it making up its cell wall.

Nourishment in the form of regular cycles of tepid tea and stale chutney sandwiches passed through and reached every segment of the queue as efficiently and mysteriously as it appeared. We seemed to breathe in concert, each newcomer to the queue having to adjust himself/herself to the group rhythm – asthmatics had a bad time and smokers were not tolerated – until the walls seemed to move gently in and out with our respiration. The queue was constantly being depleted – as someone was finally ushered into the presence of an officer, registrar or file clerk – and constantly being replenished by newcomers to the queue and by former queue members rejoining the array in quest of yet another officer, registrar or file clerk. Since there was no distinct terminal point, each addition had to squeeze in as best he or she could, a few half-hearted grunts and tongue-clickings were raised in mild discontent, then everyone subsided once more into the vacant stupor of waiting.

For entertainment we had the endless forms, questionnaires and visiting slips to fill up, some of these transiting the length and breadth of the queue several times before being rescued by the defaulting peon and returned to the office of their origin. Sometimes we roused ourselves enough to sing *bhajans* and popular songs, sometimes there were a few listless bouts of gambling and once, someone who had brought a cassette recorder along played a taping of last year's Test matches, and everyone cheered.

There were all kinds of people in that queue – you could tell at a glance from the myriad forms filled out in triplicate the professions and personalities involved. The majority had come to check their claims for a better life the next time round: business magnates and thieves, they were each of them anxious to improve the fibre of their future lives. Others had come to look at the files of dear departed ones, to see if they could renew contact with them in the life to be; some had come to check on their antecedents, to see how well their current lives and companions matched their pasts; some had come belligerently, to demand enlightenment within the next three births or else; some had come out of idle curiosity and at least one pathetic individual I spoke to was there under the impression that he was in queue to buy tickets for *Deep Throat*. And finally, there must have been a few, like myself, who had come for dishonourable reasons but, naturally, I never actually spoke to any of the others.

Because of the irregular nature of my request, it took even more than the ordinary number of tea-and-sandwich cycles, false leads, wrong turnings along the queue and battles with insolent peons, coffee boys, receptionists and bureaucratic vagrants before I could approach my first bona fide officer – the Assistant Registrar of Files. He was a frail, desiccated, bright-eyed little man who smelt of clean old paper and wore rimless glasses. He sat behind an enormous desk generously littered with scraps of paper, forms, questionnaires and a few odd bus tickets. Holding down the papers were a dozen or so glass paperweights, the kind which look like gobs of some unspeakable mucus, quick-frozen and injected with air to produce five (sometimes four or less) bubbles inside, arranged in such a way as to keep the observer forever anxious to rearrange them more symmetrically. One of them, I noticed, a collector's item no doubt, had just one enormous tear-shaped bubble, and in it an ant had been trapped and preserved for posterity with a puzzled look on its face.

However, I had not come all this way merely to note down the details of interior decor in that musty little office. Leaning forward and putting as much earnestness as I could into my voice I said, 'Sir, let me come straight to the point: ever since I saw the signboard on the building, I have been possessed with the desire to' – I paused dramatically – 'change my life.' I had been looking at him directly when I said this last bit and was surprised and a little disappointed to see that the little man barely blinked. In fact he seemed on the verge of stifling a yawn, so I hurried on recklessly. 'Oh, I realize this is an illegal request – even criminal you might say! But I've been waiting such a long time, and no one has so much as told me one way or another whether such a thing is possible at all.' I tried to change my tack from wheedling to impatience: 'I am at the end of my endurance. I must know what I need to know, even if my request is denied, but I must know. I am not going to leave this office until you tell me what…'

But he stopped me by raising a delicate hand. For a moment I thought he was about to fob me off, as so many minions along the course of my ordeal had done, and I had my handful of tears collected and ready to throw in his face. But he pursed his lips a moment, then asked mildly, 'But, have you filled out your death certificate?'

I was a little irritated. 'Sir,' I countered briskly, 'surely it is obvious that I have not died. How, therefore, can I have filled out the death certificate?'

He had been waiting for this. 'And if you have not died, my dear madam,' he said, with the sort of patient, understanding smile that might be reserved for conversations with the mildly insane, 'then how is it you want to change your life?'

'Ah, but that is just the point,' I said, feeling great relief. This was the moment I had been waiting for, to unburden the true nature of my quest at the desk of a sympathetic officer. 'You see, I am tired of my life and want to change it. But the thing is, I want to change it now, I do not want to commit suicide or go through all the mess of catching a disease or being murdered by jealous relatives or accidentally falling down mine shafts – besides, I took the trouble of bribing someone at the first floor Department of Mortality and she assured me that my dossier had not come up for review yet. As I need hardly remind you, the dossier must reach that office three full moons before a death is scheduled, in order that suitable allocations for the next life can be made.' I paused for effect. 'So what I thought was this: why not change it right now, in mid-life? I want to be rich. I want to be famous. I want to be absolutely indolent. And I don't want to wait till my next life, I want it now.'

He continued to be unimpressed. 'Madam,' he said, fidgeting daintily with his nose, 'as you have stated, this is an illegal request?' He seemed to be asking for my opinion on the proposing of such requests.

'Well, yes,' I said breezily, 'but I don't care. I feel it can be quite simply arranged. In fact it is so simple that I'm absolutely certain other people must be doing this right now, that it must already be part of your system.' I didn't want to come right out into the open and say that, since all Government concerns are corrupt, this one must be equally so. I sincerely felt that it was just a question of understanding in what dimension it was corrupt and how the cogs of reincarnation had been realigned to suit the flavour of the corruption. 'All that I'm asking is that I, with my lease on life, inhabit the body of someone else, preferably someone rich and comfortable, whose number has come up. Someone whose body is intact and in working condition but whose life has run its course. Don't you see how easily it could be done?'

A blink of light played about the bare rims of the Assistant Registrar's spectacles. 'And your body, Madam? What will happen to that?'

'Oh come now,' I said, my confidence growing. 'Surely it is of little concern. The rich person dies. I discard this body like a sweaty tracksuit and impinge upon the other one before its mechanism shuts down forever. Perhaps it could be one of those cases of coma in which a person who has been all but pronounced dead, miraculously revives. The only difference would be that instead of the original occupant returning to life there would be me! So I don't care what you do with my body…keep it in coma perhaps? Loan it out to some soul kicking its heels about waiting to be reborn? To visiting extra-terrestrials?' I had spent my time in the queue fruitfully, I thought, and had actually advanced my scheme to include a scope of operations wider than my petty little life. I had the notion that, if I could only discover the actual process of transferring souls from corpse to new embryo, I could set up a sort of transmigrational banking system.

After all, I reasoned, this was just another government department: therefore there must be some sort of quota system, a waiting list of souls, a roster of lives waiting to be reborn. I imagined that there might even be a regular state-wise system of making allocations of how many lives could be legally issued per month or year or whatever – in fact I was amazed that the family planning programme had not set up permanent headquarters here.

What I hoped to offer was in the way of a side attraction; a short trip to life while a soul awaited its legitimate birth. I did not feel any guilt at what I planned to do. If anything, I felt quite virtuous as I thought this might be the ideal way in which to bring home the point that it is really worthwhile to strive for release from the cycle of birth–death–rebirth.

I had always felt that the system as I understood it was far too cumbersome: by the time a soul has done with being born, growing to maturity, struggling through childhood traumas and neuroses, the original purpose – that is, of leaving the cycle entirely, by attaining enlightenment – is inevitably lost sight of. It seemed to be so unfair, so undemocratic.

Under my system, a soul would be able to experience life without the confusing preamble of childhood and adolescence (especially adolescence) and perhaps, thereby, understand more clearly about the sorts of lives which lead to better results in the next. Maybe these visiting souls could even be trained to be a source of inspiration to their fellows doing time on Earth, like freelancing messiahs, perhaps. All in all, I thought I had a fairly wonderful scheme worked out.

And still the Assistant Registrar was unimpressed! 'Madam,' he said, 'do you think no one has considered this subject before?' He knew nothing, of course, of my grand vision, only of the basic request. He did not wait for my response. 'So many people have approached us but we have always had to turn them down.'

He assumed a slightly professorial tone, leaning back and attempting to bring the tips of his fingers together in the classical posture of pedantry, but not succeeding very well because the arms of his chair were too wide apart for him to rest the elbows of his meagre little forelimbs. 'Firstly, this is only the Department of Files: we make records, that is all. We have no direct jurisdiction over lives. Secondly…have you seen the files?'

For the first time, I looked up and around me, to take in the shelves which lined the room. I saw that the shelves were filled with files, then realized with a little start that the shelves were not exactly against the walls of the room, but that they were themselves the walls of the room, that behind them lay the possibility of further such glass-fronted filing cabinets; that the chamber in which they were housed could now be of entirely arbitrary proportions.

I got up and went closer to one of the cabinets and saw that the files within were alphabetically marked – they were the same tatty old box files that one sees in bureaucratic concerns around the country, with papers spilling out, edges scuffed and dust-bitten, mouldering under the excrement of generations of spiders. But the alphabets were not all in English. In fact some of them seemed barely human. 'What are these files?' I asked, knowing that it was expected of me.

'All the births. All the deaths. We record everything,' said that sage and prune-like man, with modest satisfaction. 'Every birth, every death, every centimetre of every soul's journey along its personal path of release. Do you understand, Madam, how many lives and deaths, progressions and regressions, we must be recording?'

'But…' I said, a vague sense of unease setting in, 'I thought only people subscribing to a certain highly popular religion – only Hindus, in short – were eligible for rebirth?' I must admit that I had never really given the subject a thought until the moment of seeing the signboard. And then too, I had roughly generalized, thinking it unlikely that the government of one country would be entrusted with the reincarnation of the world's peoples. I just assumed therefore that the Bureau's operations must be restricted to those people whose religion explicitly upheld such a belief.

'According to the propaganda, that is so,' said the Assistant Registrar, 'but in fact it is not of the least concern to the celestial office. And of course, you realize, Madam, that I am not talking of human beings alone, but all living things!' And he smiled suddenly, a frugal, neat-toothed and wrinkle-wreathed smile, because he saw that I was amazed.

'Everything?' I asked, awed in spite of myself.

'...including plants,' he said.

For a few moments, my mind reeled, processing the thought: stag-beetles; crocuses; Eskimos; pangolins; wandering albatrosses; Saint Bernards; mindless strands of seaweed; Bengalis; hammerhead sharks and ruby-throated hummingbirds; microbes and monsters.

'...though we stop short of single-celled organisms,' he said, as if intercepting the drift of my truncated survey of life. 'In fact, even now a case is being fought by an amoeba and will shortly be brought up in Parliament. Depending on that decision, we will change the rule perhaps.'

'Why discriminate against amoebas?' I said, still a little dazed at the revelation he had made.

'Of course,' he said, 'because it is not clear that they die. How to issue a death certificate for a life form which simply subdivides,' he mused, almost to himself, sucking pensively on a scrap of food caught between his premolars. Obviously, this was the subject of feverish debate, the argument that raised factions and stoked the furnaces of human ire along the tube-lit corridors of the Bureau of Reincarnation. 'It is not clear-cut with them,' he said. 'It will make a nuisance of the filing system. Already we are overworked. The stenotypists have threatened a protest march.'

But by this time I had been recalled to the purpose of my visit and the issue at hand. 'Meanwhile,' I said, breaking into his argumentative reverie, 'coming back to me. Consider how simple my case is, compared with that of a hydra or paramecium: here I sit, healthy and plump with life, entirely unlikely to subdivide or encystate. Isn't there any way to grant me my meagre request? Isn't it possible to slip someone a little consideration, grease a willing palm?'

The little man sighed gently and trained his eyes back on me. 'Madam,' he said, 'that is what I have been trying to explain to you. This is only the office of files, of documented records; I could tell you which lives are eligible for enlightenment, which lives are vacant, which ripe for transfers, which doomed to a thousand rebirths. You could have the whole cosmos opened to you if you wished to know what was going to happen to which life. But the actual allocations, the actual decisions,' he shrugged poetically, 'that is not for us to worry about. That is done at the Transmigration Department.'

I snorted at that. 'The Transmigration Department! Don't speak to me of transmigration – I think that's just a convenient excuse you people have cooked up to avoid explaining what really goes on here.' I was absolutely sure of my ground now because I had repeatedly been assured that my request could be dealt with at the Transmigration Department, but try as I might, I had been unable to find it.

'But yes, Madam,' said the Assistant Registrar, eyebrows a-twitter with the agitation of having to prove his point, 'it is on the seventh floor.'

'Vicious libel,' I said bitterly, 'because there is no seventh floor. The stairs stop short at the fifth floor and when you try to climb any further you reach the terrace. I agree, there is some cause for confusion, because there is a mezzanine floor somewhere else and no one seems quite certain just how many floors the building has, but so far I have not had any reason to believe in the existence of a floor above the sixth.'

'I am telling you, Madam, there is,' said the man. A new expression had entered his eyes, a conspiratorial look, as of something overheard in the lavatory. 'There is a seventh floor, but I will tell you a secret – it is not easy to go there. Permission restricted, secret passwords. In fact, we ourselves do not know how to go there. We only get the message and the directives. There is a rumour that some people have found a way to go there, but I cannot tell you myself, I do not know it.' A note of embarrassment had crept in. 'We have only a small part to play, Madam. Keeping records, that is all. The rest we do not know.'

A fly nattered by, I felt a tickle in my nose and the storm warnings of an imminent depression. It looked like the end of the road. There are some people who like to hammer on about what they want even when it is obvious that theirs is a hopeless case.

Sometimes they even manage to get their way, merely because the other person cannot bear to hear their arguments any longer. Well, I have never been that sort. I will persevere up to a point, but as soon as pursuing my goal requires me to lose my reasonability I accept that I have been beaten and back down quietly. This point, I felt, had been reached in the Assistant Registrar's office and I resigned myself to the loss of a great expanse of time. I got up to leave and said, 'I'll be going then.'

In a gesture of courtesy which surprised me, the diminutive officer hopped out of his chair, escorted me to the door of his cubby-hole amidst the filing shelves and held it open for me. As I passed out through it, I heard a whisper, the merest breeze of speech: 'Find the peon Gopal! He knows something.' I turned in astonishment, but the door had closed irrevocably and though I knocked and hammered for ten minutes on it there was no response from within.

I will not document the course of my search for the peon. It seemed I wandered about that miserable building for hours, days or weeks, it was hard to tell. There was little or no variation whatsoever in the routines of the place from one day to the next. The lights remained on continuously and the staff worked non-stop shifts. The innards of the building were labyrinthine and it was rare to catch even so much as a glimpse of the outside world. I gave up searching for the peon at one point, only to find that it was equally impossible to relocate the entrance through which I had discovered this nightmarish place. It was therefore with considerable surprise and relief that, turning a corner at random, I discovered a lonely passageway, innocent of tube lights, with a row of windows down one wall.

The peon sat perched on a window-ledge, etched against the beams of dusty sunlight forcing their way in from between the loose slats of the shutters. He was sitting there, doing nothing at all and looked up languidly as I approached him. I recognized him at once from the descriptions and I lost no time in confronting him with my needs.

'You are Gopal the peon,' I said to him. 'You know something about the Transmigration Department and how to reach it. I have been looking desperately for that same department but cannot seem to find it.' I had thought enough about what I would say to the peon and said it, now, almost easily. 'If you can tell me this that I need to know, I will give you whatever of value I have with me now: my four gold bangles, my diamond earrings, my gold ring with the sovereign and, if they are not enough, I can…I can offer myself.' Truly, I was desperate.

He looked up with that cynical all-seeing, all-knowing expression of peons who work in the halls of the mighty. With one glance he assayed the worth of my possessions, briefly considered the attractions of my person, weighed the true nature of my quest against his scale of values and made a spot decision. 'I'll show you for nothing,' he said, and got up to lead the way.

The route was, predictably, circuitous. We went down the deserted corridor, descended a flight of wooden stairs, crossed a fetid latrine crawling with unspeakable life forms, over a small wrought-iron bridge connecting two sections of the building – I had long since ceased to understand what manner of architect had been responsible for this monstrosity; it seemed to have expanded out of control. We passed by kitchens and warehouses, file clerks and laundry women, rooms full of Japanese tourists and bandicoots, rooms filled with windows, rooms empty with pigeons…

And along the way Gopal spoke to me about my quest. 'You want to change your life,' said the peon, as easily as if it were a switch in toothpaste brands. 'You want to overturn the progression of reincarnation. You want to jump your place in the queue.' He shrugged, worldly-wise. 'It can be done.'

He spoke as one who has learnt to see creation from a slightly remote and favoured position. 'As for bribes, there are many ways to make them: sometimes a little incense, sometimes a few flowers, sometimes a handful of gold coins, sometimes a river of blood. They are easily bribed, on the seventh floor,' he said, a little contemptuously. 'Still,' he continued, 'they are only a different kind of clerk to the ordinary human ones. They can adjust a life here, a life there, but they cannot change the rules.'

'But who can change the rules?' I asked, bewildered. I had thought that the seventh floor held all the answers, but annoyingly and like any other outsize concern, one could never seem to get to the real epicentre of things, no final resolution to one's curiosity. 'What are the rules?'

The slight sense of unease that had first set in at the Assistant Registrar's cubby-hole had, by this time, settled into a compact mass of unhappiness. I knew, as I sprinted to keep up with the peon, that I was swiftly losing my grip on the situation. Running a specialized sort of travel agency for souls or changing your own life is all very well as long as it is under your own control but I was beginning to suspect that I would never really be shown or instructed in the actual process of the transfer. I had imagined some sort of machine, something like a large, friendly computer, with the Bureau's staff acting as its maintenance team. But with every passing second, the chances of ever reaching the machine or ever understanding how to operate it were growing dimmer. I began to regret having got involved in this thing.

Also, I hated all the information that Gopal was giving me about the seventh floor. Whenever I asked him where the rules were set down and who could change them he would merely smile his dazzling smile and sweep on with his discourse, in the manner of someone who rarely gets a chance to hold forth on his favourite fixation. 'Everyone knows they are terribly careless,' he said. 'One extra digit on the forwarding letter to the Registry of Rebirth and a pious zebra is reborn as a lusty dandelion, saints reborn as coral polyps in the Great Barrier Reef. They play terrible jokes: an incestuous couple reborn as kissing gourami, lovers reborn as Siamese twins, oysters reborn as misers.'

'But,' I said weakly and plaintively, as we negotiated yet another dark and slimy passage, 'why are you telling me all this? I don't want to know. I don't want to hear about how corrupt they are in heaven and how meaningless it is to struggle on Earth and how futile it is to live a decent life. I already know all that. It's within this futile life that I would, at the very least, like to live a rich and comfortable one, by whatever flea-bitten standards we have for such things back in the place where I live. I'm not interested in the larger issues. I just want this life, this one which I know about at this moment, to be vastly improved.'

'Yes, yes,' he said impatiently, running fleetly up a downmoving escalator, 'that's where I am taking you, to the place where you will get a chance to improve your life.' And he told me about angels and demons, ghouls and sprites, mountains of human ash, mansions of perfumed ice, pickled crab genitals and the thousand-petalled lotus.

A green door, a gust of wind and suddenly we were there at the seventh floor.

I gasped and said, 'It's not at all as I expected it to be.' But Gopal bustled me through, talking crisply all the time. 'What I am going to do is this,' he said, finally approaching the specific area of my interest. 'I am taking you to the…I call it the departure lounge. This is something I discovered for myself. I found the place where it actually happens, the exchange of life essence, from soul to flesh, and flesh back to soul.'

I was amazed. 'Aren't there any formalities to complete?' I asked, refusing to accept the truth about my situation, at the mercy of the peon. I wanted something reassuring to sign, something to guarantee me my own life back if I weren't satisfied, something to ensure that I wasn't being taken for a fatal ride by a power-hungry underling in an empire whose horizons now seemed to stretch from dawn to dusk. 'How do I know you are not fooling me? How do I know you are not dying of cancer and are only awaiting your opportunity to grab my nice healthy body? How do I know you will not loan it out to your friends – perhaps dead friends – for free rides?' My mind had begun to fill with the various obscene and exotic horrors that this bureaucracy beyond all others seemed to offer. 'How do I know you are who you say you are?'

But it was long past the time for second thoughts. The peon merely smiled lightly and ushered me into a corridor whose walls seemed to curve and melt and cease to hold their substance stable. Immediately and subtly, the atmosphere of an airport was created by a sense of current and urgency around us, by the blandness of the corridor and the impression of hosts of fellow travellers crowding alongside us in patient yet determined strides. I could see no one except Gopal and myself but all around me I could feel the pressure, though not physical, of others. I was frightened then. I could smell them, these fellow travellers: seaweed and nasturtiums, warm cubs, hot butter, the pages of a new book. It was as if each one of them carried its own personal identity in the form of a distinctive scent. I felt arctic waters close about my stomach and my flesh begin to shimmer in an atmosphere dense with metaphysical beings. How do I smell, I wondered within me, what is my scent! Will I ever know it!

'What you have to do is very simple,' Gopal was saying, matter-of-fact as ever. 'I will show you where to go. You go there and then you wait, just as you might wait for the next airbus to Cochin. You won't have long to go.'

'Just a moment,' I said, terror flooding my inner ear. 'I had very specific desires about the ways in which I wanted my life changed. What you suggest – I'm not even very sure what you suggest – sounds extremely haphazard. You've not explained anything about how the exchange is to take place, or what choices I am to get or by what means I am to make my selection. You haven't given me forms to fill or tickets to hold on to, or life jackets or airsick pills.'

The terror had reached my tonsils and was spilling out in little sparks and flashes, leaving a taste like ozone in my mouth. It seemed that the atmosphere around us grew increasingly thick with the passage of souls and I fancied I could feel them eddying irritatedly about me, confused at my physical presence yet fundamentally disinterested, hurrying onwards to their embarkation gates. Every so often I would feel one push straight through me, leaving behind it an aftersmell of itself and my fear would increase a hundredfold. I felt the weight of each blood cell as it fled in panic through my arteries and I felt the labour of each separate bronchiole as it processed the heavy air I breathed.

My mind began to fill, slowly, with the red and throbbing manifestation of my own life. Dimly, as if at a distance, I could feel Gopal the peon take my hand and pat it comfortingly and say, 'It's so simple: you wait a short space of time and then a moment will come when you will know you have to make your choice. At that moment all you have to do is to wish. Just wish. As you used to on falling stars and rabbits' paws.'

I clung dumbly to his hand, so friendly and solid in this concourse of odours and spirits, and he repeated his advice. I looked at him, or tried to – I could not focus clearly. He had receded from sight, to become a dark figure, vaguely beside me. All around us, the silent traffic of spirits, souls in transit; throbbing in my head, throbbing in my hands and feet, in my blood.

We were almost there. I could see a haze ahead of me, as if the corridor (now barely perceivable in terms of walls and floors) were widening out, then suddenly we were in a vast hall, perhaps, a vast space, blinding white. I shut my eyes and abandoned myself to my terror, now flowing out freely in glowing lines from my ears, nose, eyes and navel. I could feel my blood, red and hot with life, pounding through the lacework of my veins and arteries. I could feel it in my neck and earlobes, across my belly and in the calves of my legs. I could feel, like distinct and terrible drumbeats, the double-clapping thunder of my heart's valves as they powered the life substance across the span of the small, warm and fragile world of my body.

It seemed as if that whole vast hall were filled with this thunder, the thunder of blood and life; the air vibrated with it. The boundaries of my body seemed to have already dissolved into the space around me so that the whole hall and all its spectral beings pulsed in rhythm to my drumbeat. I cannot say that I was truly conscious, but I could still feel Gopal pushing me firmly onwards, disengaging my hand and saying, 'Don't worry, I will stay by your side. I will stay by you.'

But of course he did not or I think he did not, because after a point my mind vaulted too far out of its normal orbit to know or care much longer. I heard him say, 'You need only wait a short while and then you will step out of your own accord and when the moment comes, you will wish.'

I had become a live and sparking bundle of fear, so clear and pure that it defined my entire existence. I did what I had to do, without question. Stepping out, I experienced what may have been a short wait or a long one. Then, as Gopal had explained, a moment came and silence fell about me like thunderbolts. I looked around me and meteors scarred and seared my eyes, stars shot away on either side of me like hailstones and my mind reeled with radiance. I felt the mouths of a billion billion billion souls suck me in, assimilate me within their experience, renew themselves upon my life, then breathe me out with a whistling, steaming roar from their billion billion billion gorges. At that instant I knew I had to make my wish. I wished.

A SECOND'S BLINKING

I looked up and saw the hot and shining sky. I looked down and saw…nothing. Nothing.

I was not there.

Perhaps, if I had had a body then I could have recorded the emotions that I felt at that moment in physical terms: the betrayal, the shock, the foolishness, the self-reproach. But instead, just like the lack of body, there was a lack of any feeling in the place where I would normally have registered emotions.

Already the Bureau, the people in it, the peon and the star-studded place were vanishing like a lazy dream and I would surely have dismissed it as one if it were not for my conspicuous loss of body. I knew then that I had been cheated and been made a spectre of; but I did not feel in the least concerned as I hung suspended in the heavy air of mid-afternoon, people bustling about and through me. I drifted gently around, not caring where I went, sometimes passing through people, sometimes through buildings, sometimes through trees and dogs. I felt like a polite visitor at the art exhibition of a friend, neither moved by nor critical of the array of minds and lives presented to me.

Towards evening I found myself approaching the place where I used to live. I remained dispassionate and allowed the current to take me there of its own accord. I entered through the walls and settled into my own room.

As I sat there, lulled into a calm and peaceful mood by all the familiar artefacts of my distant life, I gradually became aware of a sensation at my feet: I suddenly became aware of my feet, the tingle of flesh and bone against the floor. I looked down to the place where I had been used to finding them and felt an odd pleasure as I recognized them thickening slowly into substance. My feet, my hands, my head and navel, all of these and all that lay between them were, very gently and unhurriedly, rematerializing from the void. And in a short space of time I could sense all of myself, from the humblest capillary and hair root, to the muscles powering my heart, the small compact planet of my existence once more bonded together and ticking with its own familiar rhythms. I sat there in the gathering twilight of my room, with the warm thudding comfort of my life marking time within me, without me; and I felt, at that moment, a deep and savage bliss.

ACKNOWLEDGEMENTS

Thomas Abraham for his unwavering support. Poulomi Chatterjee who gave this collection a future when it was only a stack of unruly stories. Sonali Jindal who wrestled the beasties into the shape of this book with calm confidence and good humour. Bhavi Mehta who makes every book look like a bestseller.

My beloved sisters Geeta Doctor and Surya Narayanan who are always there for me despite the rat entrails and other unlovely body parts that occasionally turn up in my stories. And ES who never wants to be mentioned but is, in fact, ever present.

PUBLICATION HISTORY

The Pain Merchant

The Gollancz Book of South Asian Science Fiction: Volume 2. Tarun K. Saint, ed. Hachette India. 2021.

Adaptation

Originally published as 'Paradise Tomorrow'. *Livemint*. 2018.

A Better Tomorrow

Originally published as 'The Living Planet'. *Indian Express*. 2017.

Cool

Eat the Sky, Drink the Ocean. Anita Roy, Kirsty Murray and Payal Dhar, eds. Zubaan Books. 2015.

Eat the Sky, Drink the Ocean. Kirsty Murray, Payal Dhar and Anita Roy, eds. Margaret K. McElderry Books. 2017.

Upgrade

Avatar अवतार: Indian Science Fiction – Fantascienza Indiana. Francesco Verso and Tarun K. Saint, eds. Future Fiction. 2020.

Cull

Delhi Noir. Hirsh Sawhney, ed. Akashic Books. 2009.

Freak

Himal Magazine. 2013.

Feast

Tehelka. Vol. 6, Issue 1, December 2008.

Excess: The Tehelka Book of Short Stories. Jai Arjun Singh and Nisha Susan, eds. Hachette India. 2010.
Three Virgins and Other Stories. Manjula Padmanabhan. Zubaan Books. 2013.

The Girl Who Could Make People Naked

Kleptomania. Manjula Padmanabhan. Penguin India. 2000.

Flexi-Time

The Gollancz Book of South Asian Science Fiction: Volume 1. Tarun K. Saint, ed. Hachette India. 2019.

Stolen Hours

Hot Death, Cold Soup: Twelve Short Stories. Manjula Padmanabhan. Kali for Women. 1996.
Hot Death, Cold Soup: Twelve Short Stories. Manjula Padmanabhan. Garnet. 1997.

India 2099

Millennium Special of Outlook. November 1999.
Kleptomania. Manjula Padmanabhan. Penguin India. 2000.

Exile

Three Virgins and Other Stories. Manjula Padmanabhan. Zubaan Books. 2013.

The Other Woman

Breaking the Bow: Speculative Fiction Inspired by the Ramayana. Anil Menon, and Vandana Singh, eds. Zubaan Books. 2012.
Three Virgins and Other Stories. Manjula Padmanabhan. Zubaan Books. 2013.

The Future Imperfect

Back to the Future (Issue 269). *New Internationalist.* July 1995.

Essence of Gandhi

Gene Dream (Issue 293). *New Internationalist.* August 1997.
Kleptomania. Manjula Padmanabhan. Penguin India. 2000.

The Annexe

Hot Death, Cold Soup: Twelve Short Stories. Manjula Padmanabhan. Kali for Women. 1996.
Hot Death, Cold Soup: Twelve Short Stories. Manjula Padmanabhan. Garnet. 1997.

Unfaithful Servants

Namasté: The ITC Hotels Magazine. 1987.
The Namaste Book of Indian Short Stories: Volume 2. Monisha Mukundan, ed. UBS Publishers' Distributors. 1994.
Hot Death, Cold Soup: Twelve Short Stories. Manjula Padmanabhan. Kali for Women. 1996.
Hot Death, Cold Soup: Twelve Short Stories. Manjula Padmanabhan. Garnet. 1997.
Body Maps: Stories by South Asian Women. Radha Chakravarty, ed. Zubaan Books. 2007.

Sharing Air

New Delhi Sunday Express. 1984.
Kleptomania. Manjula Padmanabhan. Penguin India. 2000.
The Big Book of Science Fiction. Jeff Vandermeer and Ann Vandermeer, eds. Penguin Random House. 2016.

A Government of India Undertaking

Imprint Magazine. 1984.
Hot Death, Cold Soup: Twelve Short Stories. Manjula Padmanabhan. Kali for Women. 1996.
Hot Death, Cold Soup: Twelve Short Stories. Manjula Padmanabhan. Garnet. 1997.
Three Virgins and Other Stories. Manjula Padmanabhan. Zubaan Books. 2013.